The
NUTSHELL
LEGACY

Inspired by True Events

LORRIE P. GROSFIELD

TO NELL AND ALL HER FAMILY EVERYWHERE

"Even if the world is going to pieces, still plant your trees."

OTHER BOOKS BY LORRIE P. GROSFIELD

Library of Congress Control Number: 2023918728

ISBN: 9798988836230
ISBN: 9798988836230

Acknowledgements

True events have inspired The Nutshell Legacy.
Without my Uncle Jack I wouldn't have known all of the story, and without my brother I wouldn't have had the enthusiasm to finish.

I would like to acknowledge a quote from the Bible, that I read when I drove to the Glisson homestead for the first time in 2014: Psalm 33:11 "The counsel of the Lord standeth forever, the thoughts of his heart to all generations."

I've been blessed by many people to help me write this story: my daughter Anysse and son, Parker, my parents, my grandchildren, my family, and my extended family. Fellow writers: Denise Walnofer, Mary George, Lee Porter, Shirley Rushing, Sierra Zemke, Bev Hopwood, Esther Phillips, Kristine Parenteau, Janie Brooks, Lenore Puhek, Carol Vincent, and Lynne Redding. To my dear friends: Denise Schenk, Jan Roberson, Jeanete Habetts, JoAnn Cobb, Danni Parcell, Annita Benedict, Karen Chadwick, Gail Neuman, Linda Brierly, and the Aasheims.

Special thanks to members of TWG Canada. There are many I won't name but you know who you are, and I thank you for the help.

My husband, Brin Grosfield, has stood beside me through many years of writing and has been a vast storehouse of knowledge. Most of all I would like to acknowledge the Good Lord for all of His inspiration.

To my Uncle Jack for sharing the story, and to my brother Gary, three sisters, and all of my family for their love and support.

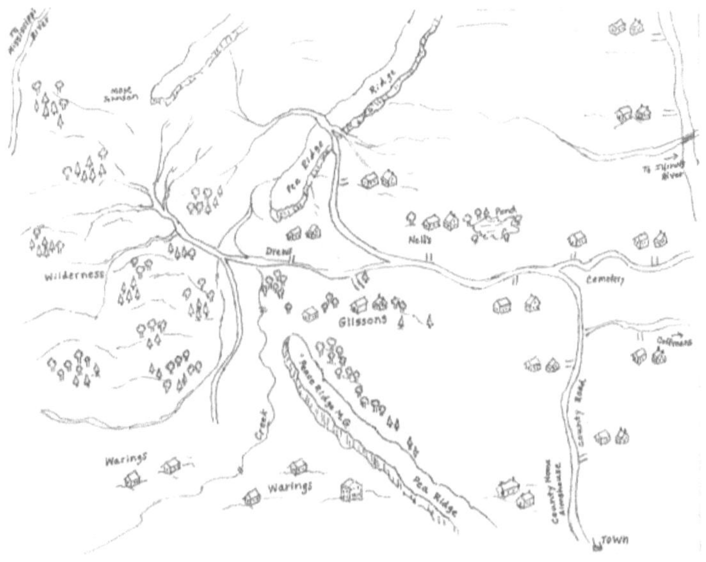

TABLE OF CONTENTS

CHAPTER 1
The Nutshell Legacy

September 1875 A Difficult Birth

The sun hung low over Illinois's forgotten land between the Illinois and Mississippi Rivers. A shout came from the direction of the hitching post. It shattered Doc Simpkins's quiet evening of reading a worn medical journal. Then he heard a strong pounding on the door.

"May I help you?" Doc ushered the man in his early twenties in.
"My Ma," he panted, "had an accident."
"Take your time. Catch your breath," said Doc.
"I'm Michael Patrick Glisson's second oldest," he said with heavy breathing. "Edmond."
"What happened to your Ma?" asked Doc, putting on his overcoat.

"My father, Michael, everyone calls him Da." Edmond gasped for air. "He and my sister Honora heard a scream. They ran to the thicket and found Ma dizzy and wobbling on the ladder. Ma may be expecting her ninth child. She wasn't aware she was pregnant, or she wouldn't have been picking plums." Edmond drew in his breath. "She fell."

~~**~~**~~**~~

I've sure gotten my money's worth out of these buggy bells. Doc chuckled to himself as he followed Edmond riding far ahead. He jounced over potholes, the bells jingle-jangling on the "wash-boardy" road.

Hmm … I figure the Glisson's must be three more miles further north from town. I've never delivered the baby of an older woman injured the way Edmond described his Ma.

Doc Simpkin's mind raced with memories. He kept up a brisk pace. He could see through the dust Edmond's bouncing back in the distance. He pressed on toward the backwoods of the county. I've heard some Irish families out in the sticks struggle, to clear the land.

Don't know what to expect. Can't be much worse than what I saw in the goldfields—enough to raise the hair on my head. Few docs to be found in the goldmining, all of us went for the gold!

"Pick it up there, boy." Doc flicked the reins and caught another glimpse of Edmond's distant filly. Doc gave a crack of the stiff whip and his mare picked up speed. *There've been few babying calls since I've returned to Brownsville County.*

"Whoa there!" Doc called to his horse. "This is a difficult stretch. The road's rutted."

Hard to hear myself think over the jangle of chains and squeaking of the buggy box down through one gravelly creek bottom and back up another. For a minute, the racket took me back to the greed of the goldfields.

Edmond made a long practiced turn up a steep drive that curled up and around to the southeast off the

county road. With another flick of his reins, Doc tried to keep from losing Edmond. As he gained the top of the steep incline through all the trees he saw a cabin. The windows held a yellow glow.
Looks like folks are gathered on the sagging front porch.

Doc sprinted toward the porch and one of them threw open the door of the old log cabin. Doc rushed inside. A young lady opened an interior door for him, and he carried his bag past a large stone fireplace with a few glowing coals into a room lit by a single kerosene lamp. An atmosphere of an untold future seemed to hover over the quiet home.

~~**~~**~~**~~

The delivery was difficult, not due to the size of the child. "On the contrary," said Doc Simpkins, "it's the tiniest baby I've ever delivered. Your wife, Sadie's, lost a great quantity of blood. Her age complicates things. She's fractured a few ribs and hurt her back and right hip. Bad shock to the neck and head. And her arm's broken at a strange angle. Some paralysis."

Noticing Da's drooping posture, Doc allocated a chair for the older man.
He appears worn from a long day in the fields.
Many of the farmers were beginning their harvests. And yet Da brushed the chair out of his way. His attentiveness to his wife, his precious Sadie Jane, didn't waver. Doc sighed.
Perhaps not having an extra mouth to feed would ease the man's load.

3

Doc squeezed his hands to keep them from shaking. He wrapped the undersized baby in a blanket. Then as soft as if cradling a baby hummingbird, he laid her on a folded quilt, which was placed at a safe distance from the table's edge.

Hearing Sadie's moan, Doc Simpkins reached for her wrist. Her pale color and grimaces told him she was fighting terrible pain. She gripped Doc's hand.
He peered down at her, his face set. "You need rest."
He gave Da a grief-filled shake of his head. Da's eyes filled with tears. He brushed off his face and thanked Doc. "Sadie shouldn't have been on that ladder. Too shaky to climb with all that pain before she fell. She grasped her belly and her back. Said it felt like labor pains."

Doc nodded, as the poor man's voice continued to break, worn ragged but still eager to help.
"It's a thicket in the wild plum orchard. I forced my way into her, but I was too late. She crashed to the ground. My daughter, Honora, threw down her basket of plums and they went everywhere. Red, green, and soft ripe purple ones. I knew Sadie'd been overdoing it. But we thought we were well past the expecting years. She asked for you, Doc. 'Doc Simpkins home from the goldfields.' Her breathing was ragged. Then she grew still. I had Honora run for help while I had a look at the situation. I did what Sadie wanted. I kept brushing her hair with my fingers, swatting away all the bees in the sun's low light. I told her how much we had to be

thankful for. The rich black soil, enough to feed all of us." Da turned quiet.

Doc asked, "Did you jar her much by bringing her out?"
"No, Doc, I asked the children to hold back the thorny branches so as they didn't scratch at her. We carried her in here on a board. Her arm was bent funny underneath her, and I ...." Da paused. "I was fretting about broken ribs, her back, and her neck."
"Yes," added Doc, "it's hard to know where to begin. She's in so much pain. Her hip is very bad."
"I recognize that look on your face, Doc. I'm sixty-three, Sadie's forty-six. We thought our four-year-old, Jack, was our last surprise."

Sadie tossed and turned. Moaned.
"Lie still, Sadie. You're hurt," pleaded Doc.
Sadie awoke, her voice hoarse. Exhausted. She made some croaking sounds and then, "Your folks were good neighbors, Doc. You've been gone," she panted, "a long time." As she rolled on her sore hip, Sadie let out a scream. "Obliged if you'd consider my other eight." Sadie's raspy voice was racked with coughs and choking sounds. "What's wrong with my legs? I can't feel them."

Da stepped in for her. "She wants you to know about her eight births. She delivered one herself. She doctored them through all kinds of sicknesses. Nary lost a one."
Doc soothed, "There, there, please, lie still, Sadie."
"Honora's fever was so high," Sadie continued to gasp in pain.

Da continued, "Sadie knows healing. She can bring the worst fevers down. Honora lived, is what she's trying to tell you."

Doc's shoulders slumped under his mighty sigh. His head bobbed to his chest. "It's an honor you called for me, with all the doctoring you've done, Sadie. Your midwifing background, and although I doctored some of the worst tragedies in the minefields," he faltered, and dabbed her forehead with his handkerchief, "there's not much I can do."

I remember how my face can look like an old map lined with roads of heartbreak.
Doc sighed and attempted an encouraging nod. "Mrs. Glisson, you've sustained serious injuries. You need rest. This injury and the birth have weakened you." He squeezed the bridge of his nose, with his eyes on the floor.
I'm unable to hide my worry that is thicker than this still air.
"We've got to attend to your wounds and let your spine set again, so no more numbness sets in. You mustn't get out of that bed."

She cried, "But what about my baby?"
Doc uncovered his face and noticed Da's hands folded in prayer. Dropping his hands to his sides, he looked away and busied himself over his medical bag. Sadie fell into an exhausted sleep.
Doc muffled his voice and Da leaned closer to hear, "This infant won't live an hour. She's certain to be

underdeveloped. Look at the size of her. Too small to cry. Mr. Glisson, she'd have a lifetime of health problems."

The infant made a feeble bleat.
Doc shook his head. "So weak." Doc noticed Da staring into his little newborn's eyes as if willing another cry from the thin line of her mouth. She was alive. Her breathing labored.
Da pleaded with Doc. "Our neighbor, Reverend Webber, lost his wife and infant in childbirth. He's a good friend and appreciates that I didn't clear-cut all my trees. Sadie's known him since childhood."

Doc's mouth gaped open with Da's next action as he called out to his daughter, "Mary-Jane, send Edmond inside to me. I'd like him to ride for the Reverend. I want your newborn sister christened."
Mary-Jane nodded. Soon Edmond entered. "I'll be right back," he acknowledged, and slipping his jacket on, disappeared out the door.
They waited. Hadn't been an hour and they heard the Reverend's light rap at the door. Bible in hand, the Reverend entered the room.

Da's face broke into a weak smile. "I want this baby christened. Sadie's injured and sleeping now. I know she'd approve of naming her Bridgett Ella. I've a sister, in Australia, with the name."
"These are difficult times." Reverend Webber put his arm around Da's shoulders. "It's been several years since I lost my wife and son. I'm thankful I've Bertha to

raise. Sadie's as tough as nails, although an older mother. Da, you've requested a christening. Difficult to deny since life remains."

Da bit his lip and bowed his head. The Reverend knelt over Sadie with a tender smile. He placed his fingertips on her forehead and bent down close. "Thank you, Father, for being with these dear friends tonight. Heal our dear Sadie." He returned to the table. He stood, his lips motionless, eyes full of love over the sleeping baby on the table. Tracing the sign of the cross with water and letting a few drops fall on the baby's head, he prayed, "We christen this tiny infant Bridgett Ella Glisson. We ask that your will be done. In the name of the Father, the Son, and the Holy Ghost. Lord, strengthen this family for what lies ahead."

Donning his hat, the Reverend gave a slight nod to Doc Simpkins, and tiptoed from the room. Da followed and ushered Reverend Webber out. He thanked him in a hushed tone. Doc joined Da in the parlor.
Doc's voice was soft. "Mr. Glisson?"
"'Tis Da," replied Da.
"I'm sorry, but your newborn has no chance of living. A weakling. Zero chance. She will die in a few hours, unable to keep herself warm," murmured Doc.

"A bold one ye are. Ma thought ye were different. She said, 'All docs have a beard, a pipe, and no church.' But I saw your face before the Reverend prayed. We've got a chance." Da's jaw set with determination. "We haven't lost a child. But Sadie's never been injured like this, sir."

Doc nodded and tipped his hat to the family members. *I've done all I can for them. I wish there was something more. Now for another hasty exit.*

"Six children?"

"Aye, eight," said Da. "We've one son, Martin, and one daughter, Kate, in Kansas. He tapped Edmond on the arm. "This is my son Edmond. He's as strong as a horse. He's twenty-three. My oldest girl, Mary-Jane, is twenty-two. All of 'em born right here." Da cocked his head to the side. He gestured the younger children out of the shadows. "This is Honora, and she's ten. Mortimer, er, Morty, he's nine. Michael Junior's six."

"No. I'm near seven," offered Junior.

"This is our youngest, Jack. He's about four but looks a lot bigger. We have three girls. Och, aye. That's *four* daughters now and five sons."

Doc took a long breath. "Your wife is strong, but I'm concerned about her injuries. The lack of feeling. The newborn is too small. Mrs. Glisson cannot take care of her. She must keep her back still or suffer paralysis. I wonder if I could join you by the fire tonight. Keep an eye on both of them."

Doc patted Da's shoulder. "If the child must be set down, let's keep her warm in a small box by the stove. That walnut cradle is too big for her. Would you mind if I stayed?"

"Aye, Doc, take a chair to rest upon. Aye to no cradle for her." Da put his hands deep in his pockets. He mumbled, "Show me what to do, Lord. I can't argue with this learned man, he's here to help, and as the Reverend said, let your will be done."

"Edmond, Mary-Jane, all of you. Don't sit there gawking. We need your prayers for this little one. As God be my witness, it be grand for her to grow into the cradle like one of pap's walnut seeds that grew into a mighty tree. Someday when things are easier, I'll plant mine." Da swiped at the dust on his jacket and laid it aside before he lifted the tiny weight from the table.

"No walnut cradle. Poor little thing. We all slept in it." Morty wiped tears away.

Da took the reins of the floundering situation. "Jack, retrieve Mother's basket of wool by the spinning wheel. Mary-Jane, carry out your duties. Take the raw wool and wrap the little girl all over her with care. Each leg and arm since skin and bones are so tender. Honora, find the warmest infant clothes. Take any unmatched socks. Fill them with salt. Tie them up tight. Put them by the hearth. They'll warm. We'll put them under Ma's blanket. The salt will draw."

"Ed, Morty, are ye' a listening to me? She's too small to suckle. You boys check each of the nannies. What milk ye find, we'll dabble on her lips. Morty, we'll need enough kindling for the night. Junior, stop your gob about Doc being a goldminer and help your brother."

The children, although wrought from the day, stayed alert for whatever their Da would think of next. Da unbuttoned his handspun shirt and placed the infant under his chin and against his bare chest. His calloused hands stroked her. "Lift that wool blanket all around both of us. Jack and Junior lend a hand."

I don't know what I've gotten myself into here, but I feel a longing to be with this family.
Doc scribbled a few notes in his journal.
I feel a comfort here in the midst of death. In my medical training it looks like death, but not to this man, Da. I admire his ingenuity to fight for his tiny daughter's life.

CHAPTER 2
Castles and Clouds

The children stood wide-eyed in the cabin shadows. The coals in the fireplace popped and hissed down into ashes. *I'll keep my hand over my mouth. I don't want to get in the way of the older man. I'm amazed at his care of the infant.*
Da's firm voice stuttered with exhaustion as he clutched the tiny, fragile baby close.
The child's weight is nothing to the towering rows of logs behind him. I'm sure Da lifted these logs into place himself to build this cabin. Doc's eyes widened.

The fire cast an amber glow on them beside the hearth. "There, there, Bridgett, Bridgett, Ella," hummed Da. He rocked forward and back. "Aye, now about your ancestry."
I'll be danged, but the man has a sense about him.
Doc's eyes widened as he peered again at the baby girl, Bridgett. She had the look of the dying, caught in the struggle to survive. She pulled her little knees to her chest and made a grimacing sound. Da continued to find a way to soothe her.

The man's determined she won't slip away. Perhaps he's right. It's not her time, yet.
Doc felt helpless and watched spellbound.
Why, I might be the most educated person in miles, but I'd be a fool to not see the baby's in excellent hands.
Drifting off for a minute, Da sat up straight with a jerk. "Poor baby, aye, aye, aye. And poor Mother, she didn't

realize her condition and fell from a tree. Someday she'll be able to care for you proper."

Doc twisted in his seat to cast a better look at Ma, and then at Da's face.
Can Da will life into the wee infant?
"Aye, Bridgett." Da's voice rose and fell at the end of each sentence. An inquiry of her. "*Sláinte, Sláinte,* the Irish toast to your health. Drink up. That's a girl." He dabbled more drops of warm milk on her lips. "That be what ye need." She remained soundless, but he kept patting on her back. He gave her limbs a massage. His voice soothed and calmed.

With Da's rich accent and mollifying tone, I feel the tension ease.
Every little while, Da tipped her back away from his bare chest to check on her breathing. "If only this wee one of mine gleaned a way to breathe easy." His rhythmic voice comforted and added warmth like the fire.
Doc's mouth, a long thin line, blinked his eyes in wonder. "Aye, little one, your grandparents were poor, but your home's here, in central Illinois, where there's an abundance." Da patted Bridgett and dribbled more milk. "Your Grandpap gardened in a landowner's orchard, he did. He passed his ancestor's castles on his way home. 'No one should sleep past dawn,' he'd say. Grandpap's vision was unclouded when he discovered a legacy for his sons to take to America."

With a hearty cackle, Da continued, "I've an idea that the gift of the world fits in a nutshell, not in tall castles.

Pap told us, 'I bequeath thee, lads, three gunnysacks of walnuts from good Irish soil, the gift of the world if you're willing.' Aye, Bridgett, but your uncles had no common decency. I saved their bags from the high seas."

Da nuzzled Bridgett's ear. "Aye, me brothers thought it was malarkey. Trees? But this land I bought is perfect for trees. At the hearth, we listened to stories of our ancestors, descendants of the clan Colla. They sat alongside King Orgiall instead of at the length of his sword. One day, when you see Pea Ridge, you'll say, 'Look at these beautiful rows of walnut trees.'"

~~**~~**~~**~~

Morning after morning Doc stopped by the somber household as those first few days turned into the early, cloudy weeks of December 1875.

Is it my eagerness for more of Da's stories of Tipperary and the walnuts? I hope my need for a friend isn't starting to show. Old family doctors checked on their patient's progress without being called.

Doc checked on Ma's lack of feeling and if he'd find the infant still alive.

I'm humbled that Sadie Jane and Da value my advice.

Mary-Jane worked hard, so that Ma could rest. She resorted to carrying the tiny girl while she worked. Doc said, "I'm tickled with all the fussing over her and trying everything to get some goat's milk in her. I realize it's a full-time chore, you, packing her everywhere."

The pale thin body's still alive, though.

After the meal, Ed and Honora helped their sister catch up on her chores while Morty kept his two younger brothers out of harm's way.

I'm surprised how these subsistence farmers use everything they have to survive. I'm touched by their hope. Doc noticed the scant supplies, but they made do and insisted on a warm meal for him.

How attached I've grown to this family.

Several days went by as Doc's services were required further north of the Glissons. But on his way home, he found himself driving his buggy up to the Glisson cabin. *Strange I feel a kinship to these folks. I know it's time to move on. Must keep a roof over my head.*

The younger boys peppered him with questions about goldmining, even though Doc discouraged them. Every time they asked, he said, "Next time." But he enjoyed their enthusiasm. "It can change a man. Forget about the goldfields. Help your father." With a tip of his hat, he left them to their games and rapped on the cabin door. *I'd like to put that part of my history behind me.*

"Come in," called Da from a chair by the fireplace. "When you're done with your visits of Sadie and Bridgett, pull up a chair. I've seen your weary nag. Poor brute, over those muddy, frozen roads. Mary-Jane, if you've a mind to, would ye get a bowl of potato soup and bread for Doc? Warm him on the inside." Da waited while Doc finished his soup.

I'd like to avoid any discussion about myself.

Doc asked, "I've got a question for you. Did you leave during the potato blight?

"About 1847, Doc. It was called the Black '47. So much suffering my folks hustled us out of there. Don't like to talk about it much."

"Some of the miners told a little about their hardships. Many died, and many moved away." Doc grinned.

I don't believe I've ever seen such genuineness as Da's.

"It makes a man thankful," confided Da. Then Da repeated what he had done that first night. "Aye," he told Doc, "my seven children's deep yawns and snores rise and fall with me tales. We all murmur prayers for Bridgett to live through another night and for Ma to regain the use of her legs. Our warm regards to your care, Doc. Ma was right. You're the one we needed to call. She's made it this far. We'll maintain from here on unless things get plum frightful."

"Not at all." Doc placed his hands in the air in protest. "No, Michael, it's you that insisted the infant would live. For some reason folks in these parts don't want or need my services as much as I hoped since my return from the goldfields. I thought this was still my home and they'd welcome me back." Doc pursed his lips. "I'll see myself out. May the little girl continue to grow. If I'm in the area, could I make a friendly visit?"

"Aye, you'd be most welcome. As far as the country business it might take them a while to get to know ye again. Have ye considered turning your doctoring south toward town? It's growing." Da's attention was drawn away by a soft cry. He placed the wee little girl on his shoulder.

Da's right. I need to go where I can drum up business. I'll miss their charm.

Doc watched Da patting Bridgett's back.

If the Glissons call for me, I'll be quick to return.

"Bridgett, have I told you about my pap's gift to the world?"

A tiny bleat, and her eyes fluttered open.

"Doc, we're glad to have ye join us. This child needs to know about my pap's gift to the world and how my brothers wanted me to buy the flatland. 'Buy the flatland,' they said. 'Who wants to wait sixty years for lumber.' But no," Da sputtered. His voice rose. "I told them it's not for me! I'm going to plant nuts."

Bridgett stared back.

"My brothers left me as I drove my old shaggy horses onto my land of forest and unbroken prairie. My inheritance."

Again, she fussed.

"Agree with your old Da, eh? Such waste."

Bridgett grew quiet.

"You'll meet the ridge, little princess. You'll rumble over roots, taste bubbling springs cutting through banks of good stone, and chuckle at the bounty of local walnuts on the ground." Da laughed.

Bridgett's eyes crinkled at this new sound. She peered into the long narrow face outlined with white hair.

"Blimey, Doc, I knew I'd seen a glower like hers before. Aye, the look of the immigration inspector when I arrived to this country. With mother down, it's a good thing she's got my smiling gob to know how much she's wanted."

I relish Da's buoyant ways.

As the time crawled by, family routines went to the wayside. The hectic days for Mary-Jane, the oldest girl, kept her away from enjoying time with beaux. Unread newspapers piled up and turned yellow. Even with the oldest boys' help, Da struggled to make a large enough harvest to last through the year. Over time Doc heard Ma's sighs over numbness and that she must keep her back still.

I worry a depression isn't setting in. Sadie's been so used to being strong out foraging.

"I see folks are interested in bartering with you for your walnuts," observed Doc.

Ma moaned in pain.

"Not any longer. The neighbors stop now to make sure Bridgett and I are improving."

The feedings are a challenge.

Will Bridgett grow into a more normal size for her age? Will her breathing problems go away? Will poor Ma recover the feeling in her legs? Arm? Hold her youngest?

Doc's head spun.

I hope my stopping by doesn't make them feel obliged to pay me.

He heard Ma balk now and then at the goat milk. "Smells like n-n-nanny's too close to the buck."

"Bridgett's frail and bone thin. I'd like to see you hold off on any offer of crackers or pickles to suck on. She'll get better with the goat milk. Keep her inside to observe her breathing."

I've spent enormous amounts of time in this primitive cabin. But I wouldn't change places with any doc in the country.

Doc's eyes roved over the rustic room.

On the dreariest day, I'd steal away from my duties. I look forward to these visits. I need these folks more than they need me. I sense they've financial restraints and as a doctor I feel I must wait for them to call.

~~**~~**~~**~~

Doc's appreciative look included the whole family as he hesitated near the door. He'd been so busy he hadn't stopped by for what felt like a year. It was now mid-March with the ground frozen since harvest. The infant must be two years old now. "A belated Happy New Years. I'm stopping by for a friendly chat, no calls for doctoring. Michael, I take it you had time to celebrate somewhat of a Christmas?"

"The children played in that bit of snow we had. Ma called for them to come in. Honora asked if she could take Bridgett out for a minute wrapped in thick blankets. Bridgett caught the snowflakes on her tiny warm tongue with the rest of them. They all cheered. When I helped Ma to the door her cheeks flushed rosy. Aye, it was grand to see them moving around bit by bit. Sadie took

19

it a little hard to think that she's not seen much of the outside. Mary- Jane does everything for the baby."

Junior piped up. "Ma loved the smell of the fresh outdoors on each of us."
"Ma surprised us. She had a gift for all of us she'd sewn or knitted over many weeks," said Honora. "She's gone back to sleeping more."
"No candy rained down on the children through the floorboards of the loft. The older children were accustomed to this in past holiday seasons." Da took a deep breath. "I can't even think about dates or celebrations. Another poor harvest yet we've got our bills paid."

Da told the others to go outside. Doc sat close to Ma. *Sadie and Da look a little bedraggled. I'm worried about Sadie. I don't want that after birthing depression to set in.* Doc glanced around the cabin. He cleared his throat. "Sadie, I've been thinking about you and Bridgett. I'm stopping by out of friendship."
"We're always pleased to see you Doc," said Sadie.
"I want you to get well," said Doc. "Michael, you're tuckered out from staggering through each day between farm chores and making sure Bridgett's breathing's easy. We don't want her feeling pushed away by her busy family."

"With all Bridgett's neediness, I still believe that she was born for a mighty purpose." Da grinned at Bridgett's inspecting stare. "Watch this, Doc," he mumbled. "She'll fuss when I slip me jacket on. Wants us all together."

Doc chewed on the grumblings of the older children on his way out.

They're overwhelmed with their home duties. The hand-braided rugs need a good sweeping, and the haphazard row of pumpkins the children jammed on shelves above the windows is an additional sign that Ma's not getting up on her feet. Ma doesn't realize how much she's got left to offer. If I could think of a way ...

CHAPTER 3
Bill Drew's Good Sense

It's been a couple of years without any word from the Glissons.

Doc's business had grown with his office in town.

The little one must be at least four years old. Time for a visit.

With the lovely fall weather, Doc stopped unannounced. The sprigs of dried herbs swaying from the rafters were drained of their pungent scents after hanging there for four years. Lopsided gunnysacks of beans had been left near the door in trade for a bucket of walnuts. Everywhere Doc looked were signs of Ma's dwindling.

Of what service can I be?

It must be almost four years that have slipped by since Bridgett's birth? I'm certain Da's done his best with his concerns for his wife and daughter's health.

Doc relaxed his hunched shoulders from the damp and stepped onto the Glissons' porch.

I feel for these poor folks. Hard enough to make ends meet, without worrying about doctor bills. I miss old Michael Patrick and the love of family that keeps this meager place going. Perhaps the little girl, Bridgett, has made great strides?

"Aye, we're still following your advice, and managing." Da lowered his voice while ushering Doc in. "Bridgett's growing by and by. But Ma, I wish you had a cure for her in your bag, Doc. Seems to have gone to her mind that she's old and done for."

I notice a shroud over poor Da's sparkle.

"I still sleep in fits and starts beside the hearth. Bridgett's breathing is a little worse in the close cabin. The fireplace smoke doesn't help. It's been a long winter," said Da with a dismal frown.

"I'm trying to assist Ma up on her feet little by little. We're working on Bridgett's short temper and fitful sleeping. She's little enough that Mary-Jane carries her on her hip, through most chores which is easier than hearing her whine. She kicks up such a ruckus if she isn't held most of the night. Days too. The wheezing breaths grow more labored after her piercing howls. I've resigned myself to wait to plant the walnut seeds I've collected. Still got me a map of where I'd like other trees to go once I plant my inherited walnuts and the local black walnuts into a sound orchard grove. With my four sons, it could happen."

"Aye," Doc's forehead wrinkled as he found himself saying, 'aye.' "Although this is not a medical call, we can do better than this behavior from a four-year-old needing to be held. And Ma still abed." Doc cleared his throat. "Some changes are important. This clinging will hold Bridgett back. We don't want a chronic condition. Even if she stays diminutive, it won't serve her well in school."

"Oh, no, don't bring wet wood. How it will smoke," fretted Ma, throwing the covers back.
The younger children had learned to creep into the dark and shadowy cabin. They inched around, anticipating

Ma's scolding. "Children, mind the breeze. Doc said no drafts. Must you come in and out so?"

Doc drummed his fingertips on his chin. "Yes, we must keep Bridgette's lungs clear. Steam baths will help and afterward greasing her chest with pine tar."

"We're still putting pine tar on her chest to open her airways." Ma's voice shook. "Bridgett, sit up on the edge of the bed like a big girl. Let Doc have a look."

"Let me listen to your lungs. Breathe in and out. Slow. Through your nose. Ah, I remember the night you were born." Doc sat back. "Her lungs sound constricted. Again, breathe in. Let the air out again. That's the way. Ah, my! You're not warm. No fever. The little lass shows improvement."

"No *little* lass," she said with a fierce scowl and sharp fingernails.

Doc sat back.

I wasn't prepared for a sharp tongue from someone sucking her thumb and still being carted around like an infant. She's not an invalid anymore. There's a mountain of feistiness there. No wonder she lived.

"Don't be so temperamental, child." Ma sunk back on the bed and turned her head to the wall. Da and Doc crept outside.

"Aye," said Da, stepping onto the porch with Doc. "It's good of you to stop."

Jack jumped off the porch after them, shouting at Junior, "Doc's done. Maybe he'll tell some yarns of the goldfields?"

Doc kept his word to answer the boys' questions. A neighbor boy, Bill Drew, joined them, playing a sad discord on his harmonica.

"I remember how far out of harmony the goldmining got in those days long ago." With a vigorous wag of his head, Doc followed the word *gold* with a dramatic whistle that sounded like *rrush*. "Mark my words, boys. When you put those two words together, it creates a fever. Men cherish the glitter of gold." With a flash of his fingers, Doc reached into his vest pocket, removing a blue-velvet bag. Out rolled a gold nugget into the palm of his hand. The boys gasped. Junior's eyes sparkled. They'd never seen a gold nugget.

"That's about the size of a blackberry," squealed Jack.
Doc tucked the blue-velvet bag away with a warning. "Once it's discovered, thousands of men abandon all reason and head to the hills. They put their health in jeopardy with such a focus on their mining. Being so far from proper care, death and illness are always looming." Bill stopped playing his harmonica. "Illness looms here too. Especially in winter. My pap says sunshine and fresh air's medicine." Bill Drew shook his head. "My pap's not much better. He wonders about Ma and Bridgett always inside."

Doc cupped his fingers around his chin and gave Bill a curious look. "Hmm. Good point. The indoor air might not be a cure-all for Bridgett's breathing, or Sadie's recovery? By Jove, yes," exclaimed Doc.
"I haven't been sick for years," said Junior.

Doc's brows knit into deep furrows. "There's no law and order in the goldfields. If you're accused of a crime, they'll hang you off the second story of a building."
Junior's eyes opened wide. "It must be plumb wild."
"You've let those far-gone gold rush days go. That's what Da told us," said Jack, "they made a lot of men penniless."

"Some miners didn't use good judgement. Some were dishonest. I'd like to add that most leave each other's gold alone." Doc smiled, "They trust one another when it's sitting in pans and out to dry. But when they find missing possessions, there's no mercy. They hang you if things are stolen. Any more questions?"
Wide eyes answered Doc.
"Not everyone strikes it rich. Listen to your Da. You only hear the miners' splendid accounts, but not the awful stories. If you make it to the mines and want to make your fortune, I know you'll be used to hard work."

Hard workers. I've got them pegged right. The only gold their Da hopes they'll ever need is from the husked corn.
Doc flicked the reins.
I don't know how he'd make it without these sons. I don't know how I thought their backwoods know-how wasn't important. But with all the progress in medicine, I'd best have another look at the medical journals.

~~**~~**~~**~~

Months went by until Doc's next visit. He found the younger boys grouped beside the drive. As soon as Doc stepped from his buggy, Jack couldn't wait another moment to ask, "What's a prospector?"

Doc stretched out his hands. "Hold your horses, young man. There's something important young Bill Drew said. Bill, you mentioned your pap thought Bridgett and Ma needed to get outside. Has Bridgett's waxen color improved?"

The boys all shook their heads no.

"It's time for the Drews' new prescription with spring coming." Doc grinned. "By the way, Jack, a prospector's a man who searches an area for mineral deposits in the soil."

Junior fretted, "That's what I do out back on our coal vein—prospect."

"That works here in Shawnee Township. But ...." Doc wagged his head with an unsearchable look in his eyes.

"I'd love to hike those western mountains. I bet they go on forever, don't they?" Bill wiped his harmonica off on his trousers and stuffed it in his pocket. "Jeew, Jeew, Chir-ee, Chir-ee! Look at that little fledgling on that limb."

Doc squinted into the brush. "Why, I remember that call. Well done. The bluebirds' morning song when they're out foraging for food."

"Poor Ma. She misses the bluebird's song. Her favorite memory of when she was young collecting herbs, she'd call them, and once one lit on her shoulder," said Jack. "She hasn't heard it since Bridgett was born."

Doc's forehead wrinkled in thought. He gathered the boys around him. "Boys, do you think you could wait by my buggy while I go inside and visit Ma? When I come out, I'd like Bill's help. His good sense and talent might mean Ma's healing."

Bill nodded. "I hope you'll share more yarns about the West?"

"I want to be a goldminer!" sighed Junior. With enough gold, I could build us a castle." Doc rapped on the cabin door.

~~**~~**~~**~~

"How are we going to pay the bill for more doctoring?" Mary-Jane grimaced as she peered over the cloud of flour from her baking and saw Doc already in the door. "Hello, Doc," she said sheepishly.

Doc greeted each of them, inquiring how they'd been since last time.

It breaks my heart to see Ma still in bed.

"Now, Bridgett, let me have a look."

Bridgett let out a piercing screech and clawed at Doc. Doc stammered, and his words dried mid-speech. Mary-Jane locked her arms around Bridgett and plopped her back in front of him.

Another modest problem needs curing.

Doc laughed. "My heavens, she and her vocal cords have grown! Can't miss the growth."

"My dear Sadie, I've been over and over my medical journals on complications from ague-like infections that creep in and cause rheumatism, or chilly evenings in plum orchards, or over-exertion in labor pains, or insect bites causing complications with paralysis. Not to mention the danger of blood clots after falling, with no answers."

Doc's eyes squinted, and he slapped his thighs. "Ma, I'll be right back. Must run out to my buggy. I've come to a surefired cure, so you can resume more of your former habits."
Da ran to the door to make sure Doc was okay. "Well, I'll be," Da muttered.
Doc rushed back inside. "Now, Sadie, I've been thinking on your neighbors, the Drews. Their idea is fresh air and sunshine. Use this cane. No overexertion. Before spring ends, you'll be running this homestead again."

"We're going to have to go with small baby steps at first. No foraging around in the woods for the time being. But I acquired this diamond willow cane on my Western excursions. Why don't you increase your walks around the cabin a couple times a day no further? A little more each day, stop, and rest. Fresh herbs will be here soon for your capable hands to collect. I'll be tickled if you start these short walks and build up strength. You'll be able to manage with your poor right side."

"At some point, my patients must return to life's joys …, why, what's that?" Doc's face filled with a curious expression. "Jeew, Jeew, Chir-ee, Chir-ee!"
Bless Bill Drew's heart. He mimics the bird's call beautifully from the porch.

The family exchanged curious looks.

Doc's sparkling eyes swept the room from Ma to Da at Ma's squeals of happiness. "That sounds like the bluebird that used to land on my shoulder," said Ma, placing her pale feet on the floor. "Doc, I'd be obliged to take a go at that cane."

"A taste of the real world, for Bridgett too."

Time for her to be removed from all of this coddling.

"Only an hour outside per day," warned Doc. "Evening time's not good for her lungs. Too cool and damp. She needs sunlight, fresh air, and exercise. She must pursue long naps in the afternoon. She should be sent to bed, trained to remain there alone, not toted around, and rocked to sleep."

Da's face split with his big laugh. Mary-Jane's feet tapped a gleeful rhythm on the plank floor. Everyone was cheered by Doc's declarations of vigor.

"But." Ma stood with the cane; her face lined with worry. "What about Bridgett's breathing?"

"Och, aye, not a 'tall," interrupted Da, taking Ma's elbow. "'Tis right, Doc, you've more than earned your fee. Ma will once again be able to forage outside and care for her children and household. She'll let go of her youngest. Bridgett will grow stronger outside."

Spinning around, Mary-Jane's joy filled her face.

"What will you do Mary-Jane with your afternoons free while we nap?" asked Ma.

"Sorry for the clawing, Doc. Bridgett's cantankerous without sleep. She isn't going to soften overnight to all these changes," said Mary-Jane, dabbing her eyes with her apron.

Hearing the latch, Mary-Jane yanked it open. "Why, hello, Bill Drew." She almost lifted him off his feet with her big hug. "How's your pap faring?" She clapped the young man on the back. "Doc Simpkins can't say enough good about you Drews."
"Pap enjoyed my retelling of Doc's stories from the goldfields." Bill chuckled.
"William Drew Sr. suggested we add in some walnut milk for Bridgett," offered Da. "Oh, a grand man he is. But you, Bill," Da clapped him on the back. "Doc said you suggested getting our patients outside. We all pull together when times are rugged."

Bill smiled at their compliments. "Doc Simpkins. I, er, wish I could ask you for some ideas for how to help *my* pap. It's hard to see him failing."
Doc's mouth opened wide.
"I've me a remedy," interrupted Da. "You see, Doc, William Drew was my overseas traveling companion, and closest friend. He contracted pleurisy and has been bedridden ever since. Since William can't visit, Bill stops by. Bill's an unusual farmer's son. If anyone asked him farming questions, such as the yield from their fields, he shrugs, 'no idea.'"

"You heard Doc. Time for a taste of the real world." Because she was still the size of a four-year-old, Mary-Jane set Bridgett down. "My chores will get done now. Bill, you kept 'Miss Cantankerous' mesmerized with your owl feathers, whittling, and your stories about the thickness of the muskrat dens. I can't thank you enough."

"Now that she's near six, her skin's not so blue anymore," said ten-year-old Jack. "Her legs are still sticks. Her head's a lot bigger than an apple now. Not ready for school, though."

"Outside." Ma's voice softening. "Honora, take Bridgett outside before Doc leaves. Never mind, not ready. She's ready for an hour outdoors. We all need to hear positive words like strong and healthy." Ma's voice broke at the sight of Bridgett's clenched fists gleaming ghost-like against her ashen-colored dress. "With her congested lungs we'll keep it short. Don't want her catching every contagious bug."

"Yet, you're both going to make it through now." Da patted Ma's back. "We'll pray for William's healing. There's something that will speak to William Drew's old croi, er, heart. You'd enjoy being part of this, Doc. An evening off to hear some good music. Why don't you stop by, and we'll make an evening of it now that fall's upon us. Lord, help us." Da sprang toward the door, waving the others out. "Even better. Join us in the forest for gathering firewood from the native black walnut trees. Those thick hardwoods hold in that deep earthy scent William loves. The burning walnut and our little ditties will rise into the air like a prayer for him."

"The black walnut has a nice scent when burning?"

"Yes, and when it's being cut. Why don't you come with us, Doc? I'll show you some of the native trees in the woods. We'll gather some firewood for William's campfire celebration, and you can hear some of the music from the old country."

"I'd like that," replied Doc.

I don't remember a greater joy in my doctoring. To see Ma hobbling around in the sunshine and that little rascal beside her. I haven't been logging in years. I wonder what kind of a hillbilly ball Da has in mind?

CHAPTER 4
Logging

Late one crisp, Friday morning in November, the sun was about to burst from behind the clouds as the logging group neared the ridge. From this ridge, they could see all the way to Missouri. Doc strolled along beside Da. Two axes, some saws, and burlap bags rattled in the wobbly cart. They heard the boys halloo to Bill Drew on a deer path. The morning warmed with Da's cheery whistle, the boys' raucous whoops, and good-natured wrestling. Doc followed Da onto a rocky path that cut northwest into the forest.

Doc turned back and watched the four boys playing on the ridge in some downed logs left behind after clearing. Doc remembered their tale of how they'd spent long days playing on the sloping sides of the ridge. Groups of four logs were rolled end-to-end in a square on the ground, touching one another to form each room, with openings for doors. Each room's walls were only one log high but wide enough for the children to stand and play.

Leaves glided down from trees above. Doc saw Da waiting. *I'm glad he decided not to hurry the boys along.* "Aye," said Da, the wind whipping his white hair around his leathery face. "Once these boys receive a break from fieldwork, they'll skip and soar. They'll catch up."
Seeing the boys' antics and eagerness to begin logging, Doc smiled.
A day away from traveling the dusty roads from one sickness to another.

"This forest land doesn't belong to anyone?" inquired Doc.

"It's part of the forgotten land the pioneers left behind. Difficult farming. It'll be here years from now," responded Da.

The boys joined Doc and Da as the path skirted by downed timber, rocks, and swampy places on into thicker forest. *It's a good day to be here in the tree shadows. Perhaps my decision to move back to this part of Illinois and continue doctoring will prove most providential.*

"If it's a warm evening," Da blew on his hands, "we'll have ourselves a campfire with fresh-cut walnut wood and play tunes for Bill's pap. He'll enjoy that. I'm glad it's time for our logging day."

"We haven't done many fun things, since, oh, ..." Junior shook his head. "But now Ma's on her feet most every day."

A familiar smile split Morty's face. "Bridgett's six years old. Imagine that. Never expected to make it a day. And now Bridgett takes short trips outside if the weather's sunny. Doc says they're improving. Da says the puny, runt of a girl was born for a purpose."

"Once, I took care of a baby opossum that my pap said would never live. Bridgett will be strong. Have a family. Your Ma will manage." Bill clapped Junior on the back.

Morty slid onto his back on some colorful, wet leaves. Junior heaped more handfuls on him. They both wrestled around while laughing in the leaf pile.

"Keeping food on the table's always kept Da busy. But that Bridgett." Morty shook his head. "Yet, she's lived, but she makes things harder."

Jack voiced his longing for the upcoming campfire at the Drews.

Something whizzed by as Bill ambled ahead through the shadowy trees. Bill bent over double in agony, gasping from an unexpected pain. He dropped to the forest floor, gripping his bloody leg, and fell to the ground. "Oh, ow. Someone hit me with a rock."

Doc hurried to his side. "Are you all right? That must've hurt. Oh, mercy, bruised your shinbone. Let me stop the bleeding." Doc rinsed it with clean water and made a compress. He wrapped Bill's shin. "Da, can we rest a minute?"

A young stranger, a few years older, emerged from the brush, laughing at Bill. "Say, I didn't think that would hurt you that bad. I'm Sam Waring's son, Bud. But why are you trespassing on our land?"

"I've heard the neighbors tell of you," said Junior. "Everybody in the township crosses each other's land. You can credit that. *We* don't have high airs."

"You're all Irish moved in here," said Bud with a snort.

Da offered his hand. "Say, we'd like to become better acquainted. I've been here since '49. We're having a campfire. Do you like boxdees, er, um, potato pancakes?

This will be at the Drew place. Why don't you join us? Aye, we can all shake hands."

"No," replied Bud. "My father wants me to warn Bill Drew, the sly fox, or any others. No more cutting across our fields. Dad told Stephen, our hired man, to fire a warning shot over his head if he keeps trespassing." Bud decided to run off in the opposite way.

"Och, aye, Lord help us." With a yank, Da pulled his cap down over his ears.

"His father's taught him to think he's better than us, Da," said Junior. "He even pushed Jack, a ten-year-old."

"Feisty Bridgett's another one he better not tangle with." Jack stood with bared fists.

"Sam Waring's president of the bank, not a farmer," explained Morty. "He calls us substance farmers or something like that. Folks who live off of their day-to-day work. They're never in the lobby of his bank because they don't deal in money. If they have any crop left, they barter with it." Morty rolled his eyes.

"No wonder Bud called us ignorant, and me meek," said Junior, brandishing his fists. "He doesn't know that if our Uncle Willie comes by, he'll get more'n he bargained for. We've got boxing in our blood."

"Let's present them with a chance to know us. No fighting. It's new to you that a neighbor child has city clothes, shoes, and socks," remarked Da. "Aye, the lad hasn't learned what true strength is. But a neighbor's a neighbor. Aim to keep it that way."

As they moved through a pure grove of hickories, the group became quiet, eyes wide with admiration. They trekked on. As the underbrush thickened, the boys started to grumble. Doc sensed their impatience.
They're right. These woods seem endless.

Da remarked how they'd find the best trees with twelve-inch-diameter logs. "They're in here. When we cut them, we'll know if they hold enough scent to please William. The good wood has a sweetness when it burns. I'll know it when the axe hits it. Ground's turning cold, but weather's still balmy. Sap's running some, deep inside there."

They found their way through the thick wilderness. Da led them past a pure grove of white oaks. Several yards ahead, he pointed out a mature black walnut. "The trees are so overcrowded, it's hard to approach. We'll leave behind the large trunk and take only what we can pack onto the sled. Wouldn't want to return next spring. We'd be covered with ticks chest-deep in this grass."
A flurry of wiggling and scratching came over Junior and Jack.

"I'd like to fell that tree. Split it up. There's straight lengths of lumber on her," shouted Morty.
"Aye," agreed Da. "In parts of this country, men fell trees, certain the trees would never run out. But they passed over this wilderness."
"Will it be here a hundred years from now, Da?" called Junior, further ahead.

"It'll be here more than that. Impossible to clear by hand. There are too many cliffs, backwaters, and ravines all the way from here to the Mississippi River."

"Teacher said all the wilderness is gone here. Now it's mostly known as all prairie." Junior moved back closer to Da.

"Och, aye, all row crops. Watch what you're learning, son." Da patted Junior's head. "That woman needs to take a ride out our direction a couple of miles."

If that isn't wise. Doc's eyes twinkled. *The man's a teacher in his own right.*

"Teacher also told us that one of our first governors built his whole mansion out of black walnut," added Junior.

"Tie that white cloth to the lowest branch of this one. We'll leave the sleigh here, hike in further, and tag a few others."

I'll keep it to myself, but the new neighbor, Bud Waring, is following us, ducking behind tree trunks. I remember that feeling. Friendless when I came here. Not now.

Doc peered overhead. "It's pertnir' dark in here. Any chance of getting lost?"

"Och, aye, wait for the ringing of the axe off the stones. We'll hear where we are. Let's work our way back to the first tree we marked." Da turned back. "Proud of you men. You've covered some country. Let's start felling. I'd like each of you to do your bit and learn which way a tree is leaning. Go ahead and tie a cloth to that one. We'll be able to find it. Always keep an eye for the tree's leaning side.

"Follow my directions to the letter. Ye shan't be hurt. If I say right here on the trunk, mark the spot." Then Da circled his finger for them to go around to the backside. "Right there. Go straight through, behind my mark on the other side. One moment." Da held up his hand and cleared his throat. "Bud, come on out from behind that tree."

No answer. The boys raised their eyebrows.
"I'd like to have you help if you have a mind. You might as well be hung for a sheep as for a lamb with all this sneaking." Da rocked on his heels.
"We'd hate for you to learn which way a tree falls the hard way," said Doc with a welcoming wave.
The intruding youngster didn't move.
Da asked Morty for his axe. "A gentleman's always glad to take a hand from his neighbor. So, Bud, here. Take Morty's axe. Please, we could use your help."

Bud came out from behind the tree, frowning. "My dad will teach me."
"Is that so, son? You're here, and it's good you've done. But, since you've got to go back, I'd like you to avoid any falling trees. Come over here. Hand him the axe, Morty."
"Okay, Bud, I want you to swing it right at this spot."
Bud did.
"Take a few more swings."
Da chuckled. "That's it, son.
Doc crowed, "You've got a good arm."
"Morty." Da sounded excited. "Help Bud out. We need to cut into that trunk about one-third of the way in. Och, aye, the tree bark's on there right tight. He's about

through. Focus right there. Hip height. Give her some chops, Bud. Let her have it."
"Junior and Jack, remain right beside me," Doc warned.

Da noticed Bud's interest. "One more good tap. Remember, only one-third in. Not another tap. That'll do. Now, Morty, you make a forty-five-degree cut upward right there on Bud's last cut. I'll meet Morty's cut on the end. That's the ticket, boys. Let's push her. Over she goes."
"My, that was easy. Look at the rings." Doc whistled. "Been here long before any of us."

Wood chips flew. The axe made a resounding ring off the hardwood. Instead of the sun in the cornfields during harvest, they had the canopy of the trees shielding them from dirt and dust. A rat-a-tat-tat of a red-bellied woodpecker protested the boys' hacking at branches.
Pointing at an older tree, Da said, "Next, we're going to go around to the backside of this oak. The side it's not going to fall on."

About two inches above their first cut's height, Morty and Bud made a cut on the back where they'd all be safe. Da pointed, "On this smaller trunk, we're only going to go in about one-tenth of the way. Give it a good nick in there. Now, Jack, you drive the wedge into this last spot right into Morty and Bud's cuts."
"Spa—lit!" With a satisfying crack, down it came! Da caught Jack in a bear hug. "Aye, that's enough for today. Let's load a few lengths for the sleigh and head home."

Doc helped load.

This man has a true gift for cheerfulness. What I wouldn't give to know all he understands about trees, and his bedside mannerisms with people.

Bud tilted his head back, peering to the treetops. "How long does a walnut tree live?"

"Some of them grow for two hundred years. If they have room, they'll grow from a foot to almost three feet a year," replied Da.

With a resigned look, Bud said, "I'd like to make me something that flies."

"Aye, that flies?"

"What's the best wood for wings?" asked Bud.

"Not the walnut. Humph." Da thought long and hard. "Claim ye some straight grain spruce. Maybe white spruce. No knots in it, mind ye."

"You're not ignorant, Mr. Glisson. My father said the church felt sorry for you, buying that poor land, and they let you graze your livestock on the ridge."

"Even if I used it, I wouldn't have accepted charity. I traded with them for what was due." Da gave Bud a piercing stare. "Aye, where I came from, only the rich landowners had estates lined with trees."

"I've seen pictures," concurred Doc.

"My pap gave me three sacks of English walnuts when I left County Tipperary. That was my inheritance. I worked and saved my earnings from farmwork, knowing I'd have to have my own land to plant a landscaped grove. No, Bud, don't look down on a puny walnut. It's not what you have. It's what you can do with what you have that counts."

"That's something to remember," declared Doc.

All of the helpers finished Da's directions. "Let's store this green wood in the stable. Now we'll use the last of the dry walnut for William's bonfire," said Da. "I've got me an idea. It might help Bridgett's lungs too. Bud, why don't you join us?"

"My father won't allow that." Bud bit his lip.

"But I thought Doc didn't want Bridgett out in night air?" questioned Junior.

Doc put his head down, deep in thought.

"Aye, there's memories to be made. For William, Doc, Bridgett, for all of us. Some of the best ones take place outside," said Da. "I like to think of this as for the good of the community. Yes, 'tis history taking place. This wood has a memory in it, so we'll burn the twisted limbs and save the straight lumber. Doc, you approve of Bridgett attending the campfire?"

"I think it'll be an important evening," confirmed Doc.

He knows my answers before I do.

~~**~~**~~**~~

Honora and the younger boys waited. At last, Da stepped off the porch and handed Edmond the bundled Bridgett, wrapped in mufflers.

"Not Bridgett." Ma stood on the porch. "Not for my water pitcher full of gold."

The children's eyes widened.

Doc cleared his throat. "Sadie, she'll be warm enough. If we remain close by the fire."

On their way to the Drews, the children skipped around to the beat of the lumbering cart and Da's cheery whistle.

Over the months, Bill Drew's father, William Drew Sr., had wasted away. With ease, Da carried him out beside the campfire he'd built from the hardwoods. The dense walnut wood burned slow and hot as if its flame would endure forever. The Drews' place contained fewer trees than the Glissons did. The men helped each other clear the prairie grass and trees from their crop fields. They'd supported one another building their cabins.

Da's idea of a campfire looked like a party with music and food. Fiddle, harmonica, and ballad singing embraced William as much as the ambrosia of wood smoke in the still air did around the farm's woodlot.

I learned something tonight. Sometimes people can treat me as a neighbor—not their doctor.

Surrounded by simple, good people around the campfire, Doc accepted cups of hot cider and enjoyed his first taste of boxdees.

I don't always have to be on call. William Drew appreciates my friendship at being here more than any doctoring I could do in these late stages. I fit in.

When the music stopped and everyone was enjoying the campfire, Da asked William to tell a tale of their beloved homeland or of one when they settled their homesteads in Illinois. Silhouetted against the sunset, William drank in the walnut wood's unmistakable sweet earthy scent. The fire crackled and popped.

William's voice, in a jagged whisper, broke the silence. "Here's ye a short tale for both times. Your Da took all of us under his wing. One day while clearing trees, we took a break. Da had his old cart with some burlap bags in the back. It was late fall, but warm. An old Indian man and his wife came through the Brook Hollow down on Crooked Creek. We'd gone down there for water, and a strong breeze silenced our coming. Otherwise, we might not have seen them. They looked mighty hungry and weary. We all surprised one another.

"None of us had much. We had tools. Da rummaged in his bags and found a sack of salt. They placed a high value on salt. Common salt. They headed west along the creek bottom, where the cliff with the shiny rock juts out before Mose Johnson's place." William paused to catch his breath. "They looked back and waved at us before they slipped out of view. I told Da they must've come back for something. Your Da said maybe they buried a loved one in the caves. We heard tales of the earlier pioneers about caves staying good and dry, winding their way west to the Mississippi."

William swallowed, unable to speak. He rested for a bit before he told his second yarn.
"When I think back on Ireland, I remember how we tried to manage. Same as here, except here we own our land and grow our food. It occurred to me in those dark days that one of my cousins in County Tipperary bore a weak,

undersized child. Grandmother soaked walnut meats for a few days. She ground them fine and mixed them with sugar and water to make a creamy, nutty gruel for the child. It filled an empty belly with sweet warmth and a milky fiber to live on." He smiled at Da, who was dandling Bridgett on his knee.

"Oh my," said Da, setting his fiddle down. Ma was limping out of the dark trees on her new cane to join the party. "You reminded me of those Indian people William told us about."
"Yes, William Drew," said Ma, stretching out her hand. "I wanted to thank you in person."
Doc's eyebrows arched high on his forehead, and his face broke into a big smile for Sadie.

I've learned a lot about these people and their local wisdom and cures. As much as in the goldfields, there's hope all around for the future. That tiny scrap of a human being fought for her life. Life's a bit easier spent with friends, and Old Mike's cheerfulness is good medicine.
I'm so glad I didn't miss this celebration. There's much to learn about these country bumpkins. Two things are friendship and doctoring. The poorest ones to work with aren't all that simple. The Warings act superior, but they're wrong.

I'll always treasure the time I had with the Glissons these first six years back in Illinois. Most important to me, I learned about how close families can be with their wit and their determination. Doc cleared his throat. *What amazes me is the simplicity of their lives. They work as hard as any miners, if not harder. They may not have any big gold nuggets to show, but they have their land and their dream. How they treasure that. I'll keep an ear cocked for how that tiny Bridgett fares. She's old enough to tell her story* now. What a knockout that'll be.

CHAPTER 5
Bridgett's Story

Doc hadn't stopped by since the Drews' campfire. Sun high overhead as winter neared, Bridgett turned seven years old, but far from ready for school. Bill Drew's days of roving around the forest, playing his harmonica, and visiting the Glissons ended. Months had passed since Bill Drew's father, William, died.

Bridgett's snarl revealed sharp teeth, tiny bony limbs that elbowed their way, and hair spiked like a much-maligned badger. Da flung his arms out as if he could calm the storm of grumbling over Bridgett's behavior and how far behind she was. He joined Ma on the porch, singing Bill's tune, "If it's all bad we're to have, what's the use of living a' tall, a' tall."

Bridgett's gruff voice punctuated the older children's comments. "Why are you talking about me? I'm the youngest. Ma'll tell you."
"You abide right there. It's time Ma has a break from all your babying," muttered Edmond.
Bridgett glared at Edmond before he could reach to ruffle her hair. "Don't touch me," she snapped.

"Doc says you're better and can go outside." Mary-Jane frowned. "We won't be seeing that much of Doc anymore. He's doctoring closer to town now. Ma has her cane to get around. Besides, the rest of us spent our days outside."

"What are we waiting for? If she can be this big of a tyrant inside, she's ready to be treated like someone her age outside," ranted Edmond.

Doesn't Edmond love me? He gives me piggyback rides? I'm his baby sister, his tiny Bridgett.
Bridgett threw her spoon and walloped the heels of her feet on the floor.
I'll fix them. I'll cling to Mary-Jane. She'll scoop me up. Edmond'll wish he treated me better.
"I for one am ready for her to be outside," yelped Mary-Jane.
I can out-scream her.
Bridgett put her head back and screamed.
Don't they love me?

The Glissons were undergoing many changes. Da, stoop-shouldered and careworn, slumped beside Ma on the porch, trying to help him resolve his land struggles. "I want land for each of their inheritances."
The warm winds at autumn's end made the cabin muggy with the hearth aglow, and Bridgett was even ornerier. Ma had managed to limp further each day on her walks around the cabin. Inside, Mary-Jane groaned, "How long of a wait until Bridgett can spend the entire day outside?"

To shut out their complaints, Bridgett cupped her hands over her ears.
I'm not whining. I want to be with them, that's all.
Bridgett bashed her corncob doll on the floor.

I'm the baby. They need to hold me. I feel safe inside with Ma and Janey.

"Mary-Jane, we've never seen any family member act with such disagreeableness as Bridgett? Have we?" Edmond listed how different things had been before Martin and Kate had moved to Kansas. "No one around here listens to my orders."

"Feels like you're outgrowing the place," muttered Morty. Then he and Edmond arm wrestled at the table. "This isn't a barn." Mary-Jane slapped dinner down. "Our poor sister Kate, losing her husband. She's coming home soon." Mary-Jane sighed. "It'll be good to have her back. Make plans for her wedding."

Arguing over the bigger portions, Edmond pushed Morty into a bench. Morty's shoulders drooped now that he was working with Edmond full time. Junior scuffled with Jack. He was with the men now too.
Nobody wanted to force Bridgett to eat. At seven years old, she whined for crackers and ignored Honora's impatient words. "You're big enough to help out and eat what you're fed. Scrape your bowl."

"No chores. I don't want to. I won't do my chores."
"I'll hold my breath, you hear?"
It's enough about how teensy I am, clinging to their skirts. Don't they know I'm scared of their coming and going every day?
Bridgett squeezed her eyes shut and hunched her shoulders.

I want to be with them. When Kate meets me, her baby sister, she won't leave me or let anyone call me Bridgett Midget. At least I've outgrown Doc.

"Oh, we hear you, all right, Brid-gette. Even Doc couldn't help *your* behavior," said Honora.
"No Doc. I don't like Doc." Her bowl crashed to the floor. Honora's face crumpled. A hiss escaped from her clenched teeth like a tea kettle ready to explode. She wanted to holler, but she only glared like a bull. "One more wasted meal or word of this tiny rascal's feistiness, and I'm going to scream." Breathless, Honora towered over Bridgett. "You're turning into a real little *ty-runt.* Won't give a body a chance to let go of you. You don't help with anything."

What's a ty-runt? What does Honora expect from me? Her baby sister? Does she know how it feels to be Bridgett Ella?
Bridgett clenched her teeth together.
Never met my sister Kate, or brother Martin. Kate's coming! She'd never call me a ty-runt. She won't leave me.
"Well, well, we've all let her rule the day." Da stalked inside from the porch. "Come and sit with me. Do I see a bit of the meat on your arms? Yes! I think Doc would agree you're ready for long days of playing outside. No more being cooped up inside. Except for your nap? She's ready. Right, Ma?"

Ma stood in the doorway behind Da.

"We can see that Bridgett's fine without Doc," interrupted Junior, searching for crackers to add to his soup. "I've still got questions about the goldfields?"
"We're out of crackers." Mary-Jane wielded the large kettle of potato soup with a scowl. "Da'll purchase a case of them when he pays Doc's bill."

Bridgett rushed over and wrapped her arms around Mary-Jane's waist. The soup sloshed. Spilled. Mary-Jane dropped it onto the table with a bang. She stomped off. "I vow I'll never have nine children."
"You love me, though, don't you, Mary-Jane?" *I'm your little Bridgett. The other kids get what they want.* She started to follow Mary-Jane. Da held her back. Bridgett swung her fists and kicked at his shins. *The others don't behave. Mary-Jane'll always stay close to me.* "Let me go! Let me go!"

"You're all correct. If she's this ornery, she's ready to be out from underfoot all day. Right, Mother?" puffed Da.
"Out you go!" Edmond flung his arm at the door, exasperated. "Time for you to be a big kid even though you look like a four-year-old. Feisty isn't all. Mean, gruff, and pocket-sized."
Jack joined in. "The rest of us were about four when we spent the day outside."
The wooden planks vibrated with Bridgett's pounding heels. Da waited for Ma.
After a long pause, Ma stepped forward. "Bridgett, you'll be fine. Outside."

~~**~~**~~**~~

The outrage on Honora's face couldn't be topped with the demands of her youngest charge.

Bridgett's rage at being left to spend the day outside with chores for most of the day didn't make it any better. "I want to stay inside with Ma and Mary-Jane."

"You already receive plenty of their attention," replied Honora.

Rocks zinged by. Sticks flew. Bridgett screamed and kicked up a cloud of dust, waiting to get what she wanted. Da told Honora, "Don't console her. She needs to learn how to fare with others."

Burying her face in the long grass, Bridgett sobbed.

Honora told Jack that if he even so much as went near Bridgett, she would flatten him.

Flatten?

He was shocked to hear such talk from his darling Honora. "Da said no one is to go to her aid," shared Honora. "Good thing Junior's with the older boys now."

"Where are you, Janey?" wailed Bridgett, incredulous at her new situation. "Ma?" No one responded. She wept. "Who will come for me?"

"You earned that name 'tyrant.' You also don't help. You'll always be behind, needy, and we'll have to care for you," spluttered Honora, crossing her arms over her chest.

Jack's comments didn't help. "Bridgett's hair is like straw. The little tufts stand straight up. Her eyes are red from crying. The corners of her lips turn down."

Honora's voice was gentle but stern. "Let her be."

Leaping to his feet, Jack said, "Can I run for her bottle?"
Honora shook her head.
"What'll we do if Bud bothers her?"
"Listen, I'd be more worried about Bud. The more bitter
the medicine, the stronger the cure." Honora stood with
her arms crossed over her chest. "Do you follow me?"

Jack nodded.
"Stop!" Honora's sharp cries made Bridgett jump.
Honora, capable and good, appeared empty of all her
empathy and patience with Bridgett's pouting and
kicking.
Morty came to Honora's rescue. "Ma wants us here for
the Proverb tunnels. Ma said, 'Watch the ant, observe
how it works and stores food, and become wise.'"
"Ma also says you'll catch more bees with syrup," added
Junior.

Honora stood her ground. "Flies, Junior. Not this time."
She turned her back on Bridgett. "Mary-Jane's at her
breaking point. What will Kate think of a tyrant?
Enough's enough. Ma and Da don't know what type of
cyclone has hit. Bridgett might be small, but she's
stubborner than a donkey colt.
"We've got a big job to do," reminded Honora. "Let's do
our part with the cabbage, potato, and apple mounds.
It's supposed to be a hard winter. Whoever gets in line
first receives the job they want." They'd spent months
under Honora's good but serious discipline. "We need
to bury all the apples, cabbages, and potatoes."

She repeated Ma's words about the vegetable and apple mounds she called Proverb tunnels. "Without them, we'll never make it through the winter. There's been no delicious jams to go with the corn muffins. Now I'll have time to pick a basket of wild plums."
Honora spent time disciplining Bridgett. When Bud came by to cause trouble, things got worse.
"Take a gander at those log mansions on the slope."
"Mansions? My dad said that's a joke. Those aren't houses, or impressive. Suppose you think that walnut wood's valuable. He said the big timber doesn't matter. Ha! Saving junk trees isn't an accomplishment. Money's in the field crops."

Honora held Bridgett.
"Your farm hasn't much land for good fields," Bud scoffed. "No wonder it doesn't thrive. My dad says it's no wonder you're all poor. Who's the little midget?"
"We don't want to fight," stammered Junior. It was too late. Bridgett had clawed her way away from Honora. Bridgett bent over Bud's arm. She bit him. Bud screamed.

Jack pulled Bridgett off. "She's only broken the skin a little."
"Da's right," said Honora. "No fighting. Bridgett, you are never to sink your teeth in anyone again. Bud, everyone has some good in him. But some are so bad, it's hard to see."
"Did you know this might not even be your land?" Bud hollered from the trees. "Squatters. My father lists a reason on every finger that I am not to linger." He ran.

"Let's check with Ma and make sure we got the tunnels the way she wants them." Honora's face was red as she rounded up the younger children.

Shoulders dropping in relief, Ma said, "I'm so glad this is getting done." She repeated the directions step-by-step. "The Gallatins are a good apple. They'll last us all winter."

"That name, Gallatin." Morty bit his lip. "We learned something about a man named that."

"Morty, I'm hoping you'll be our first son to complete your eighth-grade education. You've got an excellent ability to influence the younger children," said Ma.

"I remember," shouted Morty. "They're named after the Secretary of the Treasury, Albert Gallatin."

The shovel split open the black soil as Morty dug the trenches. The three youngest helped make a great row of the apples on the ground inside the trench. Then they assisted in helping place forked sticks that stood up over the Gallatins. They covered the apples with heavy layers of straw. They scooped dry dirt over the whole thing. It took all of them to dig a trench around the long row of apples. Next, they shoveled fermented horse manure onto the dry dirt. The long mound would smoke in the winter, but the apples never froze. The family knew that this method of storage always guaranteed them the best-tasting apples.

In other years, Ma had counted on sixty bushels of potatoes to survive the year. Bill helped them install the potatoes, and cabbages, like the apples. They buried the cabbage heads with their roots up about a foot and placed the forked sticks over the cabbages and potatoes like a tent. They loaded brush and straw piles over the sticks and repeated, as the apples.

"Bridgett, crawl into the cabbages and retrieve Morty's knife. Your size keeps us behind. He's misplaced his knife, and we need it." Honora's face looked stern. "Do it now."

"No, you can't make me go in there." Bridgett crossed her arms over her chest. *They wouldn't dare.*

Honora gritted her teeth. "Oh, but I can." She unclenched her balled fists. She swept Bridgett up as if she was a bag of vegetables. Along with flying straw, Bridgett's bare feet soon stuck out one end while headfirst inside the tunnel she crawled along for the knife. Then the pile collapsed. *What's happening? I want out of here!*

Bill snatched out the kicking and screaming Bridgett. He brushed away the dirt, straw, and manure and sat her down.

"That's enough fresh air for Bridgett," suggested Da. "She's growing, but still time for a short nap. Every week through the winter, Honora, you, and your sister haul out more manure and spread it over the mounds. Next spring, we'll tear down the apple, cabbage, and potato piles. The boys and I'll spread it over the garden and fields."

~~**~~**~~**~~

The log walls were steeped in the aroma of the morning's cornbread. It was late November, and the school remained closed. Kate was never expected to return from Kansas until the death of her young husband. Now she was seated beside her brothers, reading a Bible story. The cheery fire's ambiance could not out-gleam Ma. She hadn't done anything extraordinary but, since she'd worn a dress the family hadn't seen in years with her red scarf around her neck and radiant smile, she lit up the room. Morty set the Bible aside, and thumbed through the newspaper, searching for any more information about former President Lincoln.

The Glisson family outdid one another, trying to show how well things were at home. "I'm so glad I got to see you while you were still little," Kate told Bridgett. "Eight years old." Kate would be leaving for Kansas again soon. The older children shared memories with Kate. Jack had been so little when she left. Frustrated with the attention that Bridgett received, Jack asked Kate if she remembered him as a baby. "You said you'd never seen such an easygoing baby like me. Right, Kate?"

"The easiest disposition in this township. You got along with everyone and anything. We all have to make adaptations as things change," reminded Kate. "I lost my first husband in Kansas. I've been helping Martin's wife, Bridgett, with his twins. An old friend from Shawnee Township, Henry Webber, asked for my hand in marriage."
Bridgett whined, "Will you live right here with him?"

"No, sweetheart." Kate smiled. "We'll be leaving for Kansas soon. We're going to clear more land."

"Then you'll come back? Martin and his twins too," pouted Bridgett, kicking her feet on the hardwood planks.
"Listen to this newspaper story." Morty cleared his throat. "After last year's amazing and clandestine events when Lincoln's body was reburied in a shallow grave, it was exhumed. Kate, does that mean dug back up?"
"Yes, Morty. The poor man," Kate tutted.
"It was exhumed to make certain it was still there. Now it's reburied."
"All must be quiet now in Oakridge Cemetery in Springfield. Thanks for reading that, Morty. I don't hear much in Kansas about Lincoln, being so far from Illinois. Ma taught us so much about him."

Da enjoyed his cornbread with blackberry jam beside the stone fireplace. He smiled at Kate with the rich velvety jam filling in between his teeth. "Oh, Kate, your Ma's but a rosy finch perched in her prettiest dress with that red scarf on."
Everyone seemed relaxed with Bridgett not misbehaving in front of Kate. She was entertaining *herself* with her corncob dolls. She frowned at Ma's words of praise for the others' reading skills. "Jack, you worked so hard last year. I'm afraid we're going to hold Bridgett back until we're sure she's ready."

Bridgett's lips turned down. Kate found Bridgett's hand. "I want to stay home with Ma," whined Bridgett.

Kate'll understand. I'm the baby.
"I like the way you're sitting like a big girl and listening."
Kate patted her hand. "That'll help you be ready."
"Aye." Da reached for his pipe. "In the old country, my
pap believed that if a child went straight to walking and
missed crawling, it created poor reading. But, with those
sharp eyes and ears, she'll catch up."
"Bridgett didn't crawl?" asked Kate.
"Once she started walking, she was always underfoot.
Into everything. Clamoring to be held," said Mary-Jane.

"Och, aye, Morty. Anything else of interest about former
President Lincoln?"
"Yes, I found this clipping in the Bible dated the year
Mary-Jane was born." Morty read the late President's
words. "He will not fail to provide us his continual care."
"Who's He?" asked Bridgett.
"Why, Bridgett, it's the Lord," crooned Kate.
*I'm so happy we're all together. My family. I don't mind
if I don't know how to read. I've been too ill for school.*
Bridgett put her chin on her chest.
*If only Martin was here. Kate'll understand. I'll show her
how smart I am. We'll all stay together.*

"Did President Lincoln say anything when Kate was
born?" asked Bridgett, wedging her way between Jack
and Kate.
"Yes, I wrote down a Lincoln quote for the year that all
of my children were born before Lincoln's death,"
replied Ma.
"What about my quote, Ma?" asked Bridgett.

"No." Ma sighed. "You youngest three were born after he was assassinated."

"'A-sass-in-a-ted?'" repeated Bridgett.

"What was mine?" asked Kate.

"And mine?" repeated Honora.

"Here it is," said Morty. "In Peoria, Illinois, 1854, Mr. Lincoln referred to the fact that all men are created equal. Slavery and sacred rights can't stand together. They're opposites as God and mammon are. When Honora was born, he went on to say, "Nothing stamped with the divine image and likeness was sent into the world to be trodden on, degraded, and imbruted by its fellows."

"Imbruted?" said Junior. "I'll inquire of the new teacher what imbruted means."

"Oh, Da! Here's mention of that sailing vessel." Morty held the paper up close. "A few years back, there was an article about the sailing ship from Maine. 'Twas wrecked in a hurricane, the *Ellen Southard,* at Liverpool, England. You enjoyed the story, Da."

"Aye, I recall the men on the lifeboats after the shipwreck, who went out in the storm to rescue others." He nestled the bowl of his pipe in his hands.

"Yes, they were awarded over thirty gold lifesaving medals."

"I wonder how many ounces of pure gold were in those medals?" asked Junior.

"It brings back the memories of my months at sea," reminisced Da. "I'm thankful for your reading of the news. It's good to not hear complain, complain—

'There's not a spot of sugar in the house,' or 'What have you done now, young lady?' I think with Kate's visit, Ma being up and around, and Bridgett's days outside, we're living like a family again."

"I'd dare say we're having a drop of glee," added Ma, squeezing Kate's hand.
"Did your sailing ship have lifeboats? Steered with oars?" Junior's eyes got big with excitement.
"Yes, son. 'Tis good to show an interest in more than farm equipment. How many times have you inquired of this? Out of Liverpool, I recall the lifeboats." Da paused deep in thought. "With rudders of elm."
"Why elm?"
"Let's make a raft. With an elm rudder." Junior clapped his hands together.

With a quick bob of his head, Da said, "If I could get that bockety wheel to yield on the handcart, I'd show you where the slippery elms grow along the creek."
"You sure know your wood, Da," said Morty.
"I'd like all my sons to learn joinery."
Jack stopped sucking his thumb. "Me too?"
Junior squinted at the drawing of the three-masted sailing ships. "Is the ocean scary?"

"Time to eat." Mary-Jane's pleasant tone surprised them so much that Jack jerked his head and tripped on a coal chunk spilled from the cast-iron spider. Mary-Jane poured the gravy with care over Ma's bubbling baked beans. Kate scooped the errant coal back into the fire. She smiled, with her bright red cheeks highlighting her beauty. Bridgett pressed against Kate's side but stopped her clinging. Mary-Jane gnawed her bottom lip, peering around to see if there was anything she could help Ma with. She stacked the dirty pots and pans. Honora toted in more water.

Da put his arm around Mary-Jane's shoulders. "There's no denying Ma's running her household again. We'd have been lost without you."
"Here are your muffins and beans," crooned Mary-Jane.
"That's my girl, off with a wink. It's of an immense value to the eyes," declared Da. "My dear Kate, you're an example to all. You've handled the loss of your husband. And you're ready to remarry."

Letting out a long sigh, Mary-Jane held her arms out to Bridgett. "Say, you little pixie, let's brush your fluffy hair away from those snappity eyes of yours."
"Best be my arms," said Kate. "I want to hold her close. I'll smooth her hair pretty."
Everyone laughed at Bridgett's uncontrollable, downy white hair.
Honora, strong and tough, shoved the chairs under the heavy walnut table. "I bet the ocean's grand."
"Yes, Honora," said Da. "The ocean is one of the loveliest sights in all of nature. Let's go for a family walk. It's been a long time."

Ma can walk now. I can go outside. Breathe. I'm stronger. Kate's here.
Bridgett noticed her legs like sticks.

Kate's strong. We'll all be together. I want Kate to stay. What does that old Kansas have that we don't? Wild Indians? I'll show her a wild Indian that'll make her scalp fly up

Oh, for a sight of the male bluebirds! The whistles, chatters, and warbles," rejoiced Ma, hobbling along on her cane. "We've got our Kate here visiting and about to marry. I hear love songs in the air."
Dancing a jig, Da placed one arm under Ma's elbow and the other around her back. With his love for Ma, he trilled like a songbird. "It must mean so much, Ma, to have the soft ground beneath your feet, leaves and twigs budding, and all but one of your children at your side again."

The smell of the land and warm March soil made everyone probe for the henbit, dandelion, and chickweed. Birds gathered pine needles and straw for their nests. The children picked supple stems, soft leaves, and tender flowers for Ma's stews and salads. Ma probed for red root and sycamore leaves for tea in the fall. Ma's face lit up with the warm sunshine.
"Yesterday's beautiful, early spring morning caused us to sow the first of the corn," said Da. The relief was obvious in his lightness and jaunty stride.

There were plenty of fierce growls, but Bridgett's hysterics had lessened. "Don't look at me." She didn't drown out the arriving songbirds. "Don't look at me," she repeated.
"Oh, your walnut mansions." Ma caught her breath. "They're splendid in this light."

The pleasure on Ma's face grew. Honora beamed. "You taught us that in Jesus's home, there are mansions. We rolled the big logs on Pea Ridge end to end, which made the outline for our walls. These logs provided us with play mansions."

"How wonderful that each of you has your own," exclaimed Ma.
"Bill even has one. Honora's is the biggest!" shouted Jack. "The dollhouse one's Bridgett's."
Bridgett pushed the hair out of her face with a rough swipe. "No, it isn't."
"You're crosser than a nesting crossbill." Ma shook her head at her youngest.
"This one's mine," croaked Bridgett. "Mine."
"With her frailness, we've allowed her whatever she demands," sighed Da. "Now she's putting on a show for Kate, acting like a cranky wildcat. Even after long days in the walnut mansions." He put his arm around Ma. "More of this good air will help her improve. If Doc said it'll make her easier to abide, it will."

"Bridgett Ella," called Jack. *Thump*. Jack landed on his back from her fierce, unexpected push.
Through clenched teeth, Bridgett panted. "'Member, don't call me Bridgett Ella. Call me Nell."
Leaning on her cane, Ma swatted Bridgett on her bottom. "Don't act so frightful, child. We'll have none of your shenanigans. No one will have anything to do with you."

"What's all this with Nell? Your name's Bridgett." Da's stern tone made her burst into tears. "Do you want to have a tongue like a hoop snake?"

"She's always telling me to call her Nell," explained Jack. "She kicked Bud's shins. Said her name was Nell. Bud called her Bridget Midget. He bothers all of us. Bud swung Morty's rope hard. The iron ring grazed right close to Morty's eye. Don't worry. I've run Bud off plenty."
"Bud complains about our logs littering the ridge," said Morty. "Sam Waring wants to pull them out of here."
"The mansions are only part of his problem," said Honora. "He said Ma was a member of a church group from Kentucky that wanted social equality. He called them a bunch of Lincoln-ites."

"Women aren't allowed to vote." Morty's mouth bent to one side. "But, if they could, why Ma'd a voted for Abraham Lincoln."
Jack said, "Bud's father worked in Jacksonville, Illinois. He met Stephen Douglas. His father thought Stephen Douglas would've made a better president than the old log splitter, Abe."
"But the 'worstest' thing," interrupted Bridgett. "In an old cabin, Ma helped doctor slaves. That's what Bud said."

"Quiet!" Honora glared at Bridgett. "Bud said he can tick off ten reasons he doesn't like us. So what if we weren't fans of Stephen Douglas? Ma, you told us kids that Abraham Lincoln compared Stephen Douglas to the lost sheep that went astray. And the crowds cheered. That may be a long time ago, but people around here still quote old Lincoln, not Douglas.”

“Oh, children.” Ma’s face filled with concern. “I’m sorry I haven’t been strong enough to teach you much these last years. There’s still folks angry with me for being in a group that left Kentucky because we were against slavery. But I’m not sorry that several years back, I helped a slave girl deliver her baby with Mary-Jane. Bless Kate’s heart, she watched all the rest of you.”

“Bud may not be mean or dangerous, but he’s unkind to the youngsters when one of us older ones isn’t around,” added Honora.

With a fierce scowl at Honora, Mary-Jane changed the subject. “Ma, Henry Webber’s friend, Dennis Dillon, has been inviting me to join Kate and Henry on their walks.”

“Has Dennis been discussing marriage again?” Ma kept her eyes on her two daughters. “We should have a chat. It’s time you talked to both of us. It’s Bridgett’s nap time.”

As the group turned back toward the cabin, Kate swung into step with Ma. “How did you know Da was the one for you?”

“When I told him I’d found the prettiest farm around, Da made up his mind.”

Da’s eyes twinkled.

“Oh, nuts to that!” said Mary-Jane. “He made up his mind because you were young and pretty.”

“You’re still pretty, Mother.” Kate looped her arm through Ma’s. “You and Da are still in love. That’s why you two used to celebrate the ninth of every month. Not only your May-ninth anniversary."

"We can start that again." Ma squeezed Da's hand. "Your Da loved the plaque on the church I attended. It contained a quote from Martin Luther: *'Even if I knew that tomorrow the world would break into a million pieces, I would still plant my apple tree.'* Da adopted this motto, and he continued saving trees and dreamed of planting a walnut grove. The walnut orchard holds his grandchildren's legacy. That motto applies to all of us. If you want to plant your apple tree, or whatever's your dream, you must plant it. Do it! No matter what's happening all around you."

Bridgett's voice was soft. "I like stories. I liked William's stories. Da told me lots of stories about the protected king's orchards inside the castle walls. That's why I want a strong name like Nell. Bridgett Ella sounds like a sissy. I'm not weak."
"How long have I been away?" Kate said with a chuckle. "Never heard any child choose their own name or have a reason like that."

Wiping happy tears away, Da walked beside them. "Mother, we misnamed her Bridgett Ella. Nell. Sounds American. Yes, Nell is a fitting name."
Kate and Mary-Jane's eyes popped wide-open as they glanced back and forth at one another.
"It's good to hear your kindness." Ma hugged her. "Nell will do. Would that make you happy? *'Nell*?' It's time for

your nap, '*Nell*.' Tuck yourself in. Da and I need to visit with the older girls."

~~**~~**~~**~~

From the porch, they could see far to the west, with the sky an ocean blue. They waited for Ma to put *Nell* down. Da said, "I've never known any family to let an eight-year-old order her name. You older girls' eyes pertnir' sprang open like hungry baby birds peering from their nests. I'd recommend we all forgo the name Bridgett Ella unless someone wants a bloody lip."

"The ridge has been good for you to grow up on," whispered Ma. She pressed a finger to her lips and pointed upstairs as they entered the cabin. "We've enjoyed you girls."
With a tip of his head, Da peered above. He'd heard something in the loft.
I better be quieter, or they'll make me sleep longer.
Nell pressed her ear to the floorboards.
Don't they realize my whole world's all tied up in knots over my brothers and sisters? Keeping the whole family together. That's a big part of Da and Ma's happiness too. Kate's here. Maybe she won't leave.

"Oh, my Sadie, your face isn't racked with tension and pain. I see you only want your children's happiness." Da honed in on Ma's reassuring look.
"Girls, pour out your hearts," said Ma.
The sun through the window cast a glow that lit Ma's cheeks, her graying, straw-colored hair, and her hands

enlarged from years of arduous work. Mary-Jane and Kate scooted their chairs closer to their parents.

Kate's voice was soft. "We have something we need to ask you both."
"Henry's a close friend of Dennis, who has asked for my hand in marriage." Mary-Jane cleared her throat. "We want to all travel together to Kansas."
I heard that. I can't breathe. I can't breathe with my mouth and nose stuffed tight into my apron.
Not batting an eye, Ma volunteered, "I've wondered, Mary-Jane."
With the sweetness of Ma's tender smile and frequent nods, I know they'll be leaving.

"God has a purpose for your midwifing skills in Kansas, Mary-Jane. They'll be important if you marry and move to the frontier."
"I remember about twenty-some years ago when Da and the older boys went to Beardstown to hear Abraham Lincoln speak." Mary-Jane's sharpness was gone. "It frightened me for you to deliver Mortimer alone in the cabin. I'm thankful to know midwifing."

"Bless your heart. What would I have done without your help? Mortimer arrived in a big hurry!" Ma stroked Mary-Jane's hair. "Your levelheadedness at Mortimer's birth. Caring for Br... I mean Nell."
"That night at the end of the 'War between the States,' when the Coffmans' hired hand took us to that cabin far back in the trees, I felt so sorry for that runaway slave," Mary-Jane tutted. "Da worried about us out in that

terrible blizzard. Ma, with all your experiences, me, a novice."

The sun streamed through the forks of a nearby tree, slicing the stripes on Ma's handmade dress. The two girls sat on the edge of their seats, their hands covering their mouths.
My sisters, my sisters.
"I wanted to help her so much, Ma. Remember the hogs frozen in the field?" Mary-Jane's voice broke. "I've been so impatient. I don't think I'll make a very good wife or mother. I'm so sorry. How'd you do it, Ma?"

"Praise the Lord. He provided for all of us that night." Da placed his arm around Ma.
"We're all born free to go after our dreams." Ma glanced at her framed portrait of President Lincoln.
With Kate's head nestled on one shoulder and Mary-Jane's on her other, Ma asked, "You're sure Mary-Jane will be right there on the same road with you and Martin?"
"Yes, Ma, Henry's been out there, and he knows the land. Dennis too. He needs a wife to come along beside him. His parents are also moving West."

~~**~~**~~**~~

The last days of May were approaching full of glorious sunshine. Beautiful warm weather spilled over all the excitement. The older girls' double wedding was an elaborate occasion for the community. Mary-Jane said she would not leave unless their wagon contained a framed photo of her parents. Photographers, trained in the "War between the States," circulated across the county, looking for work. A wagon with a darkroom in the wagon bed plied the Glissons' muddy road. The girls insisted on hiring the peddler-photographer to take their parents' portrait. "We'll need multiple copies."

"The wedding's like a walnut bee in the spring," said Morty. "There's wagons parked out on the ridge. But it's not fall. No one's collecting nuts."
"Reverend Webber said we're going to have a dessert table like they do at a quilting bee. Walnut bees are about like those boring quilting bees." Jack squirmed in his new hand-sewn shirt, rubbing his hands with glee. "I saw the cake."

"If Bud doesn't show up, we'll enjoy ourselves more," said Honora. "The whole neighborhood will come, the Drew brothers, and Bill with his harmonica."
"I'm glad Bill's coming," remarked Da. "Nell might need a friend. I've got an idea the two girls leaving'll be hard for Nell. Aye, I've a stabbing pain in my heart. Will they ever be back? I see Nell's little pointy face amongst all the jubilant guests. She's a sharp little thing. When it comes to someone leaving her, Lord help us."

The portrait was displayed for all to comment on. The cameraman caught a tear in the corner of Da's eye. All the oohing and aahing over the photo, followed by the nay-saying about the glistening eye, mattered nothing to the Glisson family.
"Otherwise, the portrait would have been perfect," one neighbor cooed.

"The portrait is perfect," insisted Kate with a fierce smile for Da. "Imagine, each of us will have one in our homes someday."

Across the lawn came both girls, one on each of Da's arms. Reverend Webber officiated from the wagon bed where he played the organ. He spoke comforting words of guidance for these four young people. "Trust in Him, who goes with us, and remains with us, and is everywhere for good."
I 'spec Kansas too.
He told the group how much the girls had helped their parents, and all Mary-Jane's work when Ma was injured.

Mary-Jane, a determined-looking bride, wore a store-bought brown plaid skirt and cream-colored blouse with a dark calico ruffle around the bottom. Kate, so graceful in her movements, wore ribbons and lace at her throat and on her bonnet, with a new traveling skirt and jacket. The tree branches behind them swooped upward, their arbors scalloping the sky while their sturdy roots anchored them to the farm. Like ship sails, the blossoming branches floated and bounced in the west wind while fragile leaves, buds, and blossoms glanced off the flapping white tablecloths. The women clapped their hands over the gifts being loaded into the wagons.

Da said, "Come on Bill, and Jack, grant us a tune. Doc Simpkins loves your harp. It'll help keep the water behind me eyes."

Each brother and sister took turns holding the reins on the elevated wagon seat. When Nell's turn came, her new brother-in-law, Dennis, handed her up high over his head. Honora stood behind. Da had nurtured all of them with his stories of the bittersweet sight of covered wagons forming a backdrop for years.

"Da, remember when I was so little, and I skipped down the drive as some of the lines of wagons went by here?" asked Mary-Jane.

"You'll never forget," said Da softly. "We broke the prairie across this major route for the gold seekers in 1849. Doc was one of them. They keep coming."

Nell's little bare feet didn't reach the floorboards as her long homespun dress covered her brown legs. Her eyebrows slanted over her sharp black eyes. Mary-Jane told a neighbor they'd be together. Mary-Jane meant her and Kate. She didn't mean the whole family.

Nell pleaded, "My Janey. Kate. We'll all stay together."

"No." Mary-Jane shook her head. "I meant Kate and I will be together. I didn't mean you."

Even the glad commotion couldn't drown out Nell's shrieks. "You can't leave me."

Mary-Jane said, "You'll always have Honora and your brothers around, Nell."

Grasping Nell under her arms, Honora took the uncontrollable girl upstairs. Da said he remembered the feeling when he left Tipperary, a dark abandonment. "Och, aye, 'tis hard not to feel that way too."

I'm sorry, Da. I can't hide, no matter how hard I kick and scream.

Nell scrunched her head down like a turtle.
I can't hide. My Janey. My Kate.

With Nell still pressed to the loft window above, the final wagon loading began. Da and the boys carried two walnut cradles, replicas of the one in which nearly all of the children had slept. With a nervous cough, Da said, "You don't need these now, daughters," his voice broke, "but, one day." Then he cleared his throat. "That's an extra seventy pounds. I hope they'll suit you out West?"

Big sister Mary-Jane sat up ramrod straight, holding her treasured copy of the framed photo of her parents. Kate and her husband sat likewise in their wagon. At the loft window, Nell held one hand out with a pleading gesture to stop them. The other hand motioned the girls to come back. Her eyes were hidden in pencil-thin lines, with her burning crimson face contorted in a full tantrum.
Homesteads were like the cycles and rhythms of trees, with leaves having to let go of their independent branches in time.
Which branch'll let go next?

Doc bent down beside Nell. "Ma said you're breathing's still poor after the wedding." He peered into the ten-year-old girl's frowning face.

"No need for that pout, even though I've recorded you in my journal as Bridgett Ella Glisson. Aye, I've got me wits about me. I know it's Nell." He winked at Da.

"Let me listen to your lungs. Breathe in and out. Slow. Through your nose. You're experiencing severe inflammation." Doc Simpkins sat back. "Your lungs sound constricted. Again, breathe in. Let the air out slow again. That's the way. Ah, my! You're not warm, no fever. This little lass has improved with time."

"Don't call me 'little' lass." She flashed a fierce scowl and sharp fingernails.

Doc apologized.

With a thrust of her chin, Nell cried, "Don't need no doc. The other kids don't."

"I can understand that, Nell." Doc patted her knee. "I understand this episode started when your older sisters moved away? We all have emotional responses to things. Life is difficult at times. But you must keep an even keel. Breathe. When you become overanxious and fraught, you have a tendency toward illness."

At least he knows not to call me Bridgett.

Nell squared her shoulders.

He said, "Nell." I'm moving my lips. I'm not sure if I'm making a smile or not?

Doc said, "Have you been crying yourself to sleep?"
Nell's little pointy chin bobbed.
Rummaging in his bag, Doc seized a tiny envelope. "Sadie, these peppermints might help her throat. Let her decide when she needs one. It's scary when you can't breathe. She's much better than a few years back." He patted Nell's shoulder. "Never relinquish hope that these conditions will improve as you're maturing. It's tough having two sisters move far away."
I'm glad someone knows it's not easy.

"You might not be a large person, but it's what's inside that counts. You need to remain away from things that constrict your breathing."
I don't care what's inside. I don't want to be puny.
"I'd recommend you remain indoors again for a short spell and take steam baths each day and not a great deal of physical exercise." Doc nodded at her little barrel-shaped chest. "Young lady, you'll be fine. You've made it through worse. Play indoors and remain quiet. Use this pine-tar salve on your chest. School is not out of the question. Reading would help with the quiet."
I'm glad Doc didn't treat me like a baby.

Nell scrunched her face up and then instead of making the crunching sound with her teeth, she said, "Thanks, Doc."
"I'll be back again. If you don't fret over your sisters too much, you'll be healthy for school. I dare say, the prolonged time indoors will end soon." Doc stepped outside with Da.

Doc thinks I'm growing up. He's not looking so worried about me staying inside like an invalid. Even though I am the baby.

Outside, Jack dropped his hoe at the jingle of Doc's buggy bells. He shouted to Junior, "He's still here," and sprinted up the drive.

"Doc's got other patients," scolded Da.

"I've got plenty of time for these boys. Ask away, whatever I can help you with."

At the faint chime of medicine bottles, Nell peeped around the door as Doc rested back on the buggy seat.

Some people that head West, you never see again.

Nell closed the latch softly.

Thanks, Doc. Thanks for coming back. Thanks for being our friend.

~~**~~**~~**~~

Everyone had heard enough of Edmond's grumblings about the cobbled-together homestead. Morty said his ears hurt from listening. They'd all heard Da's defense of the superior quality of a handcrafted building. "Although dilapidated, a cabin's fireplace with the natural stone arching over the flame is a comfort," said Da. "Aye, maybe the large walnut tree towers too close to the house, and the moss growing on the wall casts an abandoned look, but it's ours. We'll repair those split cedar shakes that are cockeyed on the roof. But the sprinkle of leaves and nuts everywhere adds some character."

79

Da continued, "What bothers ye boys most is autumn. When everything's all leafed out, all the layers and layers of trees must create an uncivilized feeling around the homestead for ye. But the cabin has served eleven family members. These last ten years, time became divided into before Nell's birth and after. We've let a few things go."
"Any one of us knows Ed has worked hard. He's a man. How could I manage without any of you boys?" rambled Da. "You're growing up. Morty's nineteen, Junior's seventeen, and Jack's fourteen."

Smelling breakfast, Ed hastened toward the cabin. "I'll work on a needed barn, not a stable with a lean-to."
"That's enough of this drizzle, greasing leather reins." Da turned toward the cabin. "Enough criticism and steering of every conversation back to what the farm needs." Sounds of hacking, retching, and crying filled the air under the loft window.
"Nell's breathing's not good. Ma's worried sick. Doc hoped she'd be okay now that she's older. He gave her those mints." Morty bit his thumb. "She's so puny."

Ed swiped a raindrop on his brow. "That girl's always been hard to hit it off with. Now that the girls have left, she's downright impossible. If I had more time, I'd find more ways to help Ma. Trick's to keep from upsetting Nell and, at the same time, not spoiling her like the girls did."
"With Martin, Mary-Jane, and Kate in Kansas, she feels deserted. None of Honora's good sense." Morty held the door for Da.

"If Nell doesn't improve, Ma'll have Doc out again. The two picture frames we built would brighten Ma's day. Nell will have to accept the family portrait hanging in the parlor. I've got the girls' letter." Edmond tapped his pocket. "Why, there's Nell sitting on the loft ladder."
Da looked at Edmond's face. He placed his arm around his shoulders. "Read us the girls' letter again, son? Maybe that'll bring them close."

Dear Family,
We arrived in Wichita on our thirty-third day, June 9. One of Ma and Da's anniversaries! I mailed this letter of our adventure. We crossed a few rivers on barges. One stream with no barge. Almost too wild for the wagon. A nearby river rose with the heavy rain, and we learned of folks a few days ahead of us who camped there and drowned in a flood. The team pulled us through, and the wagon bolts held. Good old Illinois ingenuity.

Heading further north from Wichita, I worried when only two wagons beelined to Sedgwick. I admit being scared in the open country. We drove cows with us. Edmond, we miss you. You've always been good help with the livestock. The land is fair. It's selling for about four hundred dollars for a quarter section. The soil is nothing to Illinois.

Nell let out a long, mournful wail from the ladder.
"It would be thrilling to drive those cows in that big country," continued Edmond.

We're living in the wagon for now. Dennis and Henry are looking into buying lumber to build a 10 x 14 ft. board house. Martin's a good help to us. His twin girls are darling. Da, we won't have log homes like you built that kept us warm for years. The country's much drier than Illinois. Scattered trees, and flat. The dust comes up, and the wind, but never like our memories of Brownsville County. I wash our clothes, and they're dry by the time I reach the end of the line! But full of dust.

It's been exciting with all the rush for the land, the railroad, and the cattle drives. There are plenty of Indians who camp on the outskirts of our land, traveling through like the buffalo roaming across our homestead. Kate and I shared our flour with an old woman and her youngsters. Starving. My! Do the buffalo chips make for good fire. We miss all of you!

Nell, be good and help Ma and Da. You're growing up. No need for spoiling. Tell Bill Drew he'd love the wildlife out here. Few trees, but lots of wildflowers and new critters.

Your daughters,

Morty read the buffalo and Indian line again. "Da, do you think there's still good land prices there? Honora, that smells good. Scones with cream? Like Ma's?"
"Cream's freezing early this fall." Da's mouth watered at the sight of the black walnuts piled on the table. "I love cornbread and biscuits, but scones! Honora, you've gone all out."
She twisted her neck to glance back at Da, with flour on her cheek. "You look so happy."
"Nothing competes with the black's unique taste, both fruity and nutty. I'll be proud if they'll always recall them if they're a Glisson," said Da.

Morty agreed. "I'm tickled that things are running smoother without the banging of pans. Honora's easygoing like Ma." He glanced up at the coughing from the ladder. "Sure took a toll on Nell."
"Da, can we discuss the need for a barn?" asked Ed. "I'd like to see you in a dry place to grease the reins."
"With all the expenses, isn't a new barn doubtful?" Honora's scoop went back and forth, sprinkling black walnuts on each scone.

A harsh cough came from the ladder.
"Poor Ma. She's never seen a child plagued by such anxiety and breathing problems," said Edmond. "Nell's spent half of her life fighting to stay alive. No wonder the folks have given her everything she wants."
"Uh, ahem! Edmond, Da's not the only one who spoils her." Honora slid the scones into the cast-iron skillet.

Junior's voice came from the loft. "I'll carry her, Ma."

"I'll do it myself. Put me down!" Nell kicked and fought. "I want to go to the stable. Ed! Morty!" She cried, "Why did the horses go to Kansas?" Nell loved visiting the new team of young draft horses in the stable.
If only they'd stay forever. At least Da's still got his dream of the walnut orchard. After losing so many of his older children, he's still got six of us.

"You're staying right in this cabin until your wheezing improves," said Ma.
Stopping to cough on each step, Nell came downstairs. Ed scooped her up at the bottom. "Are you feeling better, milady?"
"Morty told me to always stay in the horses' line of sight. They don't realize I'm in here!" wheezed Nell. A slight blue tinge formed around her small lips.
"I meant so they didn't kick you," explained Morty. "Remember how they galloped up the drive straining, squeaking, and passing gas? About like your lungs will if you don't rest and recover."

Nell stuck her backside out at Morty as he and Ed prepared to leave for the northern acres. She made a tacky sound. Morty swatted her with the envelope.
With a loud sip, Da drained his tea.
"Can I keep the girls' letter?" wheezed Nell.
"We better be off." With a flutter of make-believe wings, Ed cooed, "Jeew, Jeew, Chir-ee, Chir-ee! Nell, you know what that call is. Ma loves the bluebirds' cheery song

and blue feathers as they fly along the roadside. Soon the bluebirds will leave the area."

"No," Nell sobbed. "Don't leave."
"You're up bright and early, Ma. Let me." Morty grabbed the slop bucket and reminded her he'd do whatever she needed.
"What about me? I want to go before the bluebirds leave," rasped Nell. "Ma said the sight of them strengthens her on the inside. What about my lungs? Aren't they on the inside?"
"They're real family birds." Ma's voice chirred. "They come back year after year."

Ma and Da finished their scones while Ed and Morty prepared to leave. Honora threw her hands up in frustration. She used her foot to hold the door closed. "You can't have everything you want, Nell. You're supposed to remain out of the chilly morning air."
"Ed, Morty, look what you forgot." Coughing and hacking, the tiny ten-year-old ran to them. She stopped to catch her breath. "Here's your lunches. My Ed, my Morty." She hugged them both. "Take me with you. It'll help me not think of the girls."

"My, I hadn't noticed how strong she looks." Da winked at the big boys. "Let's bring her along. We could use her help. Maybe a different solution is in order."
Under Honora's disapproving stare, and with Ma untying her red scarf, and tying it beneath Nell's tiny chin, she marched out of the cabin with her own lunch. "Too bad we don't have Janey's cooking anymore. They

never forgot their lunches. Now, Honora, I trust you made sure to place a little dainty in there for me."

I don't know if I'm going to like leaving the homestead. Why do we need these northern acres

"Those infernal Warings! Going to get rough here," hollered Edmond. It was so hard to talk over the jingling of the chains, squeaking of the wagon box, and clomping of the teams' hooves as they went down into the gravel-filled creek bottom on their way home. "This road never had so many holes. With Warings' wagons going back and forth to town. They've shot out all the rabbits, squirrels, and even the drummers. No hunting left. Whoa, Nellie."

"My name's not Nellie," snapped Nell.
Da's mouth formed into a circle. "It's not the same as this morning. Now we've got a load on the roads with our logs. The team's a little green. No sense in pushing them. Keep 'em under control. The steep, winding grades are scary no matter how many times we've been down. Ease past the turn off to Mose Johnson's cave and keep heading home."
Caves sound dark and spooky.
Nell stayed face down on the floor of the wagon bed.
I like the team. I wish I could run so fast.
She looked up. "Does Mose live in a cave?"
"No, Nell. He mined coal out of it," said Da with eyes on the countryside.

Edmond's voice sounded as if he was holding his stomach in as he yanked back on the coarse leather reins. The chains on the tongue rattled. "Did you hear me, Da? Nell? Morty? Gonna' get rough here. Hold on.

Hold steady, Chester. Right down the middle of the road. Attaboy."
The wagon grew quieter on the flat straight road. They passed Mose's turnoff and then they were along the field where they'd seen the bluebirds. "You're right. Their perches are gone. As many loads of logs we've brought home from the northern acres," added Morty, "they're gone."

"Da, can you tell I greased the wheels like you asked?" Edmond squared his shoulders.
"Aye, I can tell the horses aren't huffing and puffing. Grant 'em a little rest halfway up the next hill. Wheels sound good." Head bobbing, Da closed his eyes under his cap to keep the sun out. "Let me rest my eyes. Did either of you tighten up those iron bolts on the frame?"

They descended into another steep, rocky gully. The wheels rumbled and groaned under the heavy load of logs. "Steer around that rock there. Don't need a broken axle." Bouncing up and down, Da snorted at Edmond's driving. Edmond's boots stretched out and pointed straight up on the floorboards. The jostling and squeaking of the wagon, the sounds of leather and chains, and the harness jingling made Chester keep glancing back. Dolly stayed straight, as her head bobbed up and down in the traces.

Chester, you better watch where you're going. Look at our pretty Dolly.
Nell blinked her long eyelashes.

She looks straight ahead and stays on course. I can't believe they let me swing the axe on the northern acres. Glaring over the backs of the team, Edmond yelped, "Yup, there's Warings' foreman, Stephen. He's trimming the brush along the roadside."
Morty lowered his voice. "Shh, Da's sleeping. I've been wondering about hunting west of here. No Warings out that way yet."

Da's only pretending to be asleep, Nell smirked. *He's like me—afraid to be hurt again. How do they think he'll make it if they go after their dreams? He's going to say his old croi's breaking.*
"But more than hunting," Morty continued, "I want a stove for Ma. Peaches growing nearby. Da working in a barn out of the weather."
What does Ma need a new stove for? Peaches? Yum. A barn?

"I want to run a respectable farm. Lots of acres." Edmond picked at the log's loose bark. "Grandpap didn't know how serious farming can be in America, or he wouldn't have chosen the ridiculous idea of having a walnut grove. None of us is going to go for that."
What? Don't they remember Da's castle stories? The lumber? The nuts?

"No kidding," Morty whistled. "You spent your earnings buying peach saplings? It's a suitable time to plant them. Tomorrow might be even warmer. There's improvements needed around the homestead more important than planting a peach orchard. A hearth, for one. I mean, after all, winter's coming, and this isn't the middle of the 1800s. I'd like to buy the folks a stove."

"Stove's a great idea," praised Edmond. "We've got to plant the peaches. Ma'll love them since the bluebirds are leaving."
With his knuckle rubbing his eyelids. Da sat up. "The draft horses are working hard pulling this load up out of the gully. Talk to 'em, son."
Edmond hollered, "Er, giddyup there. You don't have to bog down in every hole in the road."

Da's nodding head alerted Edmond of Da's slumber. "Imagine how much Ma and the girls will enjoy fresh peaches right beside the house. Don't aim to slight Da, but he doesn't notice things like he used to."
"He said we'd start clearing the land for the barn," interrupted Morty. "I'm all for anything to do with logging. There's plenty left on the northern fields."
It sounds like they're both interested in things other than farming. Nell frowned. *How can that be?*

They gazed at the early evening lighting, which was beautiful as they passed one of the Warings' roads.
"Is Bud's uncle coming here?" Morty's question jarred Da upright.
"Malcolm Waring?" grunted Edmond. "He teaches at a military school. Hasn't returned since heading East. Don't worry about Bud's threats of when his Uncle Malcolm comes home and how he'll teach the boys a lesson. Ha."

"I wouldn't want Bud's life. Dad's gone all the time. No mother."
I couldn't live without my folks. Or my brothers, and Honora. I guess.

Morty said, "What about Uncle Willie? He'd convince our other two uncles to help with the barn."
"Can't imagine seeing our uncles." Edmond pulled his shirt away from his chest and sniffed it. "Da, you awake. Would you mind if we stopped at the creek? Wash up? You okay, Da? You've been quiet."
Da winked at Nell. "Why don't you let Nell drive the team on the straightaway before we arrive?" She sat up as tall as she could with her little back so rigid.

~~**~~**~~**~~

The sun didn't struggle to warm the bright evening wading in Crooked Creek. The creek formed the border between the Warings and the Glissons.
"Do you think Uncle Willie will come? Uncle Pat? James? My hopes are high Uncle Willie can teach us boxing." Morty waded into the creek.
"Hush up. Let Da soak. Enjoy his pipe. Da needs peace, not thinking over an old argument. He wanted a place for trees. His brothers didn't. Ridiculous." Edmond pulled his shirt over his head and rolled up his trousers. "It's time they buried the hatchet. Hope they'll help with the new barn."
"They don't talk to their brother?" Nell ventured into the creek up to her ankles.

Da swallowed. "No. They don't listen to me."

Water swirling up to his chest, Morty charged in. "Where's the spring in your step? Jump, Nell. Maybe the chilly water isn't good for your lungs, but it feels warm. I'll show you how to kick and do your arms."

"It all started with those infernal walnuts. The others wanted to throw their sacks of walnuts away, but not Da." Edmond dived under the water.

"Da went his own way." Morty laughed, spitting out the water, and dived after Edmond.

Nell shivered in the delicious coolness. The water churned green but not deep.

Coughing and spluttering, Edmond resurfaced. "They haven't spoken in forever."

"Those the three gunnysacks from Tipperary Da's kept buried in that hole?" asked Nell.

"Yup. No time to plant them since your birth." Morty stroked across the pool of water. "You can't plant them any old way. The rich landowners in Tipperary had groves and trees. Planted with adequate spacing." Morty floated on his back.

Edmond splashed him.

"When the trees have room to fill out, the lumber's more valuable." Morty picked up Nell, tossing her high with a splash.

"Don't do that," screamed Nell.

The sunlight speckled the water drops on their shoulders.

"Morty, I don't want to leave thinking Sam Waring's high-handing this family. And I don't want our younger brothers to face his bullying forever." Edmond splashed

from the creek. "Nell, get back here. Scrub your dirty arms and legs. Where's Ma's soap?"
Morty fished the bobbing soap out of the stream. They tossed it back and forth like a hot potato.

Little Crooked Creek was thick with trees on their side. There were cleared banks on the Waring side. Da let himself drip-dry. They noticed the rustling bushes. They caught a glimpse of Bud Waring running across the cornfield. From the opposite direction, Bill Drew was rambling through the brush, headed toward the group.
"Bill, hello," called Edmond.
"Evening, Da, and family. Tired, I bet. You've been logging those northern acres? To think you and my dad cleared all this prairie."

"When I think of those long roots under prairie grass, I'm impressed," said Edmond.
Morty replied, "Their roots are taller than I am."
"Plenty of backbone." Edmond rubbed his arms to warm up. "Our farm can't make it with the eight of us now. Land prices are high. Forty acres cost as much as a quarter section out in Kansas. Our folks know the truth."
"My mother wonders if we'll be able to keep our land," shared Bill.

Nell squealed at the green leaves plastered on her arms and legs. Edmond slapped his thigh and the boys' laughter got louder. With all the silliness, the creek's slippery banks proved hard to scale. Morty slid down the muddy bank and went right back under the water like a river otter.

Perched on his rock, Da enjoyed his pipe. "It's good to hear you having fun."

The boys splashed, whooped, and dunked. Water fountained up in the warm evening air. Edmond yelled, "*Now* where did Ma's bar of soap go?"
Everyone studied the water.
Edmond bellowed, "What? Nell? Look at the bubbles! What in tarnation?"
"Don't you know how to pluck off those leaves?" asked Morty. "Dunk under a little ways and don't waste the soap."
"I won't."
"Let me splash them off of you, Nell," pleaded Morty.

Having fun, Edmond swung her up and sat her down on a branch growing over the creek. She screamed and screamed. Edmond snatched her right off. "Now, calm down. I used to put Jack up there."
Bill Drew shinnied up the branch. He sat down. "It's okay. I'll be right beside you. Keep your eyes on the pleasant view."
Panting for air, Nell pointed back up to the branch. Edmond, incredulous, set her up there again, next to Bill.

They all stared, dumbfounded. Bill wrapped an arm around her. "Yep, Nell, don't let your fears conquer you. That's what your Da told my dad on the three-masted sailing ship they came over on. A journey like that makes families of men."
"Jump to Edmond," shouted Morty. "He'll catch you. Don't be afraid. Jump, jump. You're brave. Spring!"

"Do it," the others crowed.
Chance after chance. But Nell wouldn't jump.
I wonder if I can touch the sky?

"Brave," gulped Nell. "But I'm not ready to jump. Can I drive the wagon home?" A rippling breeze sent more leaves falling. She accepted Edmond's piggyback ride up the creek bank to the wagon. As the sun was setting behind them, he asked her if she liked peaches. She smiled, with her eyes bright with earnestness.
On days like this, I know Ed won't leave me. Morty, never.

CHAPTER 9
Ten-Year-Old Ty-runt

The Glissons' place buzzed with activity one summer morning, with everything bursting into full bloom after the heavy dew. Neighbors arrived in their wagons and buggies. Ma started the reading for one or two neighbors. It expanded into several folks eager for news. Most didn't have an eighth-grade education. They struggled over some of the concepts and vocabulary in the newspaper. Ma enjoyed helping those she could. They enjoyed her sweet nature and got an earful of current events.

"Honora, why do these folks stare at me? Can't they get their own newspapers?" whined Nell. She glared at them. She stuck her tongue out as they climbed the porch steps. She stayed hidden behind the curtain as Ma read aloud to the group gathered on the porch.
Working his way through the group, Da greeted the neighbors as they voiced their concerns to him.

"Your youngest is the talk of the township. Ten years old and not in school?"
"A pixie face. But an ogre-like personality."
"What's next if a parent allows the child her own name?"
"With those piercing, inspecting eyes. Can you imagine that she'll be eleven years old soon?"
This was followed by the usual praise for sweet Honora and Sadie Jane Glisson.

"Why, hello, Da. Beautiful day? Your barn raising is coming up soon." With a tip of his cap, Robert Coffman looked for a seat.

Da nodded, scurrying through the front door, leaving their clucking behind him on the porch.

"Of all the luck, to have a hellion like that for a ninth child."

"How can the older ones put up with her? I've heard they're all leaving."

"So rude. Disrespectful."

"Pshaw! You heard the neighbors grumbling about the high price of land here? That's not the half of it."

"Stick her tongue out at me, will she?"

The latch closed behind Da. "Nell, your mother's well-known in these parts, although her parents came from Kentucky. Ma avoids giving her own advice by citing newspaper articles credited to Abraham Lincoln. 'Freedom lies in being bold.' I need a bit of that myself. You've had plenty of extra time to tame that wild thing inside, Nell."

"Stop squirming." Honora bit down on the hairpins. "Your hair's so flimsy, it feels like a young chick. I'm trying to come up with a newer style for your hair before the barn raising next week. Something becoming. It takes practice. Then'll come school."

"Shush, Honora, I don't want to go. They won't notice my hair," said Nell. She jabbed her sharp fingernails into Honora's arm, leaving little half-moon bruises.

"Nell, just when I thought you were maturing!"

Da's dry cough. "Have you been rude to the folks here for Ma's reading? They enjoy listening to Ma. They could buy their own subscriptions, but they appreciate Mother's touch. She's good at breaking the story into little parts and adding her own horse sense to help explain what's being said."

Nell couldn't wiggle away with Da's grip on her. "Ma's known around the county for her cordiality. She's one of the pioneers. Folks around here trust her."
"What's *core-jee-al-ity* 'bout sharing your newspaper?" asked Nell.
"Well, it helps you be like-minded with others. You need work on that."
"Your brothers and sisters go straight to the woodpile for being disrespectful to their elders. Mother's afraid of your health, with your breathing and such." Da sighed. "She doesn't want you spanked."

Nell glared at the neighbors and focused her evil eye on Gertrude Rein, a little girl about her age with thick curly black hair. Next to her sat another neighbor, Robert Coffman, and his daughter, Luella.
"I've a request from a young man starting work here in Shawnee Township, for living quarters." Robert's voice sailed through the window. "You know the place, Sadie Jane. It's the only rental. It's the cabin where you and your daughter delivered a young runaway slave. No one thinks too much of the history, but some remember."

Ma nodded.

"By the way, are there any rental ads in the newspaper? I'm after a notion of how much to charge. The rent's to be paid by the agricultural college."

"Remember when you read those book chapters several years ago?" cried Luella. "Are there any such articles? I enjoyed waiting each week."

With a pleased smile, Ma searched for an ad. She found one describing a small farmhouse for rent for fifty dollars a year, payable to an Adams County farmer.

Robert said, "Most folks in this township are some of the proudest in the state. We're mighty close to Lincoln's old route. We're proud to be from this area, part of the original stomping grounds of the traveling lawyer and former president, Abraham Lincoln."

"Perfect timing for a quote." Ma held her finger to the column on the page. "Here's one I've grown to love over these last difficult years. Perhaps it will speak to one of you now. 'Often more courage is required to dare to do right than to fear to do wrong.' Folks have teased me that I'd arrive in heaven and begin looking for Mr. Lincoln before searching for my Michael." The neighbors laughed and peppered Ma with questions about the oldest girls and Martin in Kansas. Ma reached into her apron pocket for a much-handled letter.

Dear Ma, Da, and family,

We appreciated the Christmas parcel you sent on the train—the jam everyone enjoyed. Da, we're obliged for sending the walnut seeds. I'm hoping to plant them along the drive. Mary-Jane and

Martin got their share. We followed your direction. By crackity, they are sprouting beside the greased paper windows. Da, did you ever think part of your legacy would wind up in Kansas?

We've all been wondering if you'd spare Junior to help us with breaking the land. We're pleased about Morty and his interest in continuing his schoolwork. Would Junior consider coming to Wichita on the train? We'd love to have him, and I'm sure he'd enjoy meeting some of his nieces and nephews. He'd be flummoxed at the weather, no doubt. It looks like it's gonna rain, but if a body don't look out, a twister comes. There's still good land here, and from what Dennis summed up, it appears four hundred acres sell for about the same amount as forty acres back home.

We love hearing about how well Nell is doing. The story about Ed and Morty helping Nell dig up the hillside where she'd planted her taters was a hoot. Picturing her put us in stitches. Nell just a digging and rolling her taters, down the hill to her big brothers, and to think they found the walnuts the squirrels planted. Ed and Morty, you sure did a right respectable job of playing along. Sounds like fun. Wonder if that'll remedy Nell of her fear of squirrels?

Love,

With Nell kicking and squirming on Da's lap the reading, came to an end. Da carried Nell piggyback outside. "I'm giving you fair warning. Next time you're rude to Mother's guests, we'll clean out the chicken coop together. Poor breathing or not."
After comparing a few last letters and jokes on the front porch, the neighbors departed. Ma promised Luella she'd keep an eye out for book chapters they'd all enjoy.

Reverend Webber stopped by to visit after most of the group disbanded. "Hello, Sadie, Da, and Nell. Sadie, the folks love your newspaper reading. I'm glad you've heard from the older girls."
"I'm grateful they survived their first Kansas winter," said Ma. "They've asked about Junior traveling out to Wichita to help with tearing up the sod."

Reverend Webber unfolded his arms and patted Ma's shoulder. "Is that all, Sadie Jane?"
"Yes. I mean, no."
"What is it, Sadie?" the Reverend frowned.
"Reverend." Ma took a deep breath as Nell scooted further away. Again she lowered her voice. "It's not the girls. Edmond's outgrowing the farm and finding faults with things on the property. It hurts us to hear this after years of hard labor. Da needs him. He worries he will never lay eyes on any of them if they go and he will never plant his walnut grove."

He sighed and put his hand under Ma's elbow.

"Nell took the girls leaving so hard, I don't know how she could handle Edmond going and Junior traveling with him."

Cupping his chin in his hand, the Reverend said, "This situation is becoming more common with young people today, leaving their families behind. Doesn't mean they weren't raised right. It's a sign we live in a time of opportunity."

"Remember when we were pioneers coming into this area?" His eyes roved across the fields. "The frontier spirit is inside them too. It's something God unfetters for the next generation. Why, I myself have an offer to preach in Missouri. I'm not happy to leave Bertha behind."

"I know she's going to make a good teacher here," confided Ma. "Ed and Mortimer are preparing a site and cutting timber for a barn. They've got an itch in their hearts that a barn would prepare us for the twentieth century."

"A big order," he agreed. The three of them laughed together. "I will let the congregation know. We'll be ready for a barn-raising project. The church members respect your family." The Reverend squeezed Ma's hand, sharing his ever-ready, gentle smile, and patted Da on the back.

A loud noise exploded nearby. The Reverend's eyes narrowed. Ma's hand went to her heart. "Nell was right here. Where is she?"

Da sprinted away. A white, fluffy blur darted into the long grass. Nell stopped in her tracks. Bud Waring, under cover of a hedge, snuck up on the small animal. A puff of a tail disappeared into a log.

"Nell, come back here," yelled Ma.

"A gunshot? That hurts my ears. Ow." Nell gasped for breath.

Da strode up between her and Bud. "Someone's hunting too close to the house."

Bent over, puffing from her run, Nell coughed, and clutched her throat. Then she stood up and crept closer to the log. The small, limp animal had an ugly red hole in its side. A dead rabbit, not a kitten. "I thought it was a little kitten," she whimpered. "Da, why'd he go and shoot a bunny?"

Not taking his eyes off Bud, Da frowned. Bud knelt down on one knee, gripping his rifle.

With her gruff and gravelly voice, Nell wheezed, "It's lonely without my oldest sisters."

Bud stood up. "I didn't mean to shoot your rabbit. I don't have any sisters. You're lucky you've got a big family. I'm always alone."

"Have you heard what people call me?" Nell's raspy breathing continued. "A tyrant. I wish my sisters would come home. I loved them."

"Are you all right? Please, calm down. I'm sorry I shot it. I didn't know you were chasing it." Bud glanced at Da. "There haven't been any rabbits around here. Had a good coat on it." Bud's eyes shifted back and forth from

Da to Nell. "I hope you meet my Uncle Malcolm. He's coming soon. He's an instructor at a military school. A great shot."

Nell met Bud's eyes. "I wanted to catch a kitty." Whimpering, she fell into Da's arms.

"Wait." Bud came closer. "I'll bring you a white kitty. Would you like one? He's a real gentle little thing, not a barn cat. Okay, Mr. Glisson?"

"Would it be all mine?" asked Nell in her gritty voice.

"I'll run and get him. He'll be all yours," promised Bud.

She and Da sat on the log and waited. Bud ran and got it for her. He presented the kitten wrapped in a cloth like a doll. Nell's thin face broke into a smile of delight. Bud bit his bottom lip and sighed.

As she tried to pet the kitten, it crawled up and down her cotton dress, onto her bare leg and foot. She caught him up and wrapped him in a hug.

Nell thanked Bud. He lit out for home.

"Don't squeeze him to death, Nell. Can't hold onto him forever. He's got to learn. Hard to believe Bud's in cahoots with you. The kitten's yours, and he's precious, as you are to us." Da combed his fingers through her white pixie hair.

"But Bud's behavior was wrong," barked Da. "He shouldn't have been hunting rabbits so close to our home. If the chicken coop bothers you, then don't put the cat right up to your face. You have enough breathing problems. Remember what happens when you put your face on the draft's mane? Ma won't let you have him inside."

"Da, what does cahoots mean?"
"When you work together with another person and help accomplish a plan."
"I'll name my kitty Cahoots. He and I'll stay together. Even inside."
Ruffling the hair on Nell's head, Da turned toward the fields. Honora came out with the little neighbor girl, Gertrude, searching for Nell.

Gertrude spotted the kitty in Nell's arms. Gertrude mewed to the fluffy animal, "Here, kitty, kitty, kitty."
"It would be good to share with Gertrude," offered Honora. "I bet Nell would let you pet her kitten. Nell will be glad to make a friend." Honora pushed Nell.
Honora turned away for a moment.
The neighbor girl howled, "Why'd you hit me so hard? You hurt me."

Standing with her hands on her hips and a ferocious glare, Honora asked, "What did you do, Nell?"
"It was Gertrude clutching the life out of my cat," insisted Nell.
Honora circled her arms around Gertrude, pulling her in close. "Oh, my, look at your arm."
Nell stood all alone.
"She slapped me hard," whimpered Gertrude. "Then Nell's kitty scratched me. Hasn't she learned to share?"

Nell stomped her foot. "You hit me first, when I pulled him away from you."

Honora didn't waste a minute to think before swatting Nell right on her bottom. "You don't hurt others, and you shouldn't have hurt Gertrude. You need to learn how to get along. Thought you were maturing. Come here, Gertrude, let me help you."

"Da," Nell balled. "Honora took Gertrude's side over mine, her own sister. How could she 'bandon me?" Nell kicked. Hollered. Da swatted Nell. Ma gathered her into her arms. Ma's soothing voice got Nell's breathing back under control. Nell wailed.
"Your hiccups could wake a bear in his den," said Da.
"Honora loves Guh, Ger, Gert-rude more than me. It's my kitty, Ma, Da."

Frowning at Da, Ma shook her head as she spoke to Nell. "Of course, Honora doesn't love Gertrude more. These lessons take time to learn."
"Now that her breathing's better," replied Da, "we'll start letting her see how much it takes everyone working together to keep the place going even with neighbors."

~~**~~**~~**~~

Another year passed by and with a smattering of walnuts rolling around on the forest floor signaling fall, Nell turned twelve. The Glissons were working in a grove of trees west of their property in what they called the wilderness land. Plenty of native black walnuts could still be found in the nearby forest. With overcrowding, they didn't produce good lumber, but plenty of nuts.

"Da never liked the ripe nuts to sit there for long. It feels like Da and I've been collecting black walnuts all of our lives. Gathering makes the family strong." Ma and Honora leaned against their baskets. "Our neighbors are eager to trade things with us for the black walnuts."
Da, the boys, and Bill rested in the shade beside them. The sun shone down in shimmering lines through the layers of branches.
"Our neighbors don't husk their own walnuts?" asked Nell.

"The nuts are difficult to smash. Your brothers'll show you how we do it. They're good at not breaking them to pieces. They remove the halves in one piece. The hulls don't let go without a fight." Da enjoyed his pipe in the shade. "Aye, it takes time to crack the shell and pick out the meat. Things are more enjoyable when you do a big job together with friends, like shearing sheep and quilting. To keep good relations with our neighbors, we work together and trade with one another."
Nell smiled at Da.

Bill thanked Ma for reading to his mother about Putney, the English village where Bill's Uncle Joseph settled. "We've all gotten to know our uncle through your reading. A gardener for a castle. Aye, a bit of a botanist. He uses the moon and an almanac for raising varieties of rain lilies. He wants to send some bulbs."
I bet Ma would love to have some of those bulbs. "I picked the most," boasted Nell. *How many castles are there in England?*

"You're closest to the ground." Rising from all fours, Honora grinned at Nell. "You're so calm out here, Nell. Cahoots makes you less anxious."

"She's overcoming many fears. School's only a few weeks away. Farm life, school, animals, heights. There's fear to be found everywhere. Got to learn to adjust to the tough times and make good memories every day," said Ma.

"Like Da?" asked Nell. "He 'members where the trees with large walnuts are. Those must be what squirrels 'member?"

"He still remembers the day he went to Quincy to file his land patents. A little worried. All alone, but he found some of the biggest and best nuts on Quincy's tree-lined avenues," replied Ma.

"When we went to Beardstown to hear Abraham Lincoln, he gathered," said Edmond.

Nell caught sight of a little streak of white scrambling up a tree. Nell froze as Cahoots capered from branch to branch. The kitten found refuge on the end of a limb about fifteen feet up. Honora gripped with her left hand, and with her right, she reached out. The terrified Cahoots clawed the back of her hand. Nell stood on tiptoes, peeking out behind her. She stroked his body like a baby bird. "It's hard being the runt."

"Look at you. You're so caring to Cahoots. Someday you'll be like Honora. Climb high!" praised Edmond. "It's tough being the oldest. If I don't look out for the others, the folks scold me. If I do, my brothers and sisters don't want me bossing them. The homestead's long overdue for a barn. There's plenty to do on the barn before school starts. We'd better measure the footings."

"No need for more grumbling. We'll leave the logs here to season. Then clear weeds and brush." Da narrowed his eyes at Edmond. "Let's remember we've plenty of time to dry the lumber for the footings."
"Morty, the boys didn't pick up the tools." Edmond kicked the dirt. "Let's cut those last few logs. I'm holding you 'countable for the wedges. Jack's always losing the steel wedges. We're down to two. Don't drop those in the brush. Leave 'em in the chopping block, where we can all find 'em."
"Thanks, Bill, for your help," said Morty. He set the last short pieces of wood on the stump with the narrower end up, so they didn't fall over. "We'll cut the last of these."

Wood chips flew into Edmond's hair. "Boys," his voice barked, "use the back of the maul, not the blade. Drive in the wedge between the heartwood and the sapwood. Nell, grab your kitty and get back."
With a smile for his two younger brothers, Morty said, "Notice how the wedge has four sides. Two wider and two narrower. If your wedge pops out, it'll fly in the direction the narrow edge is facing. Don't face the narrow edge. You risk the wedge flying out."

With the sounds of axes and handsaws, evening came on. Junior squinted to make a cut in the dusk. It was hard to split. Hungry and tired after several unsuccessful strokes, Junior kicked at the obstinate log.

Edmond was quick to advise. "That's too long, Junior. Da taught me that length has twice the strength to resist your axe."

Junior bellowed, "Enough lessons from you."

Edmond chopped the log in half.

Junior turned and walked away. Morty and Jack followed.

"Don't let yourself get on your ear, Edmond. Let the younger boys figure things out," said Da. "They're capable of the same work you learned to do. We'll all have to take things in smaller pieces like Ma recommends instead of all at once."

"Nobody'd be harping at me if I owned my own place in Kansas," Edmond griped.

Da took Nell's hand in one hand. He reached for Edmond's elbow with the other. "I don't know what I'd do without you. All of your work's appreciated. We'll start on the barn. We've got the winter to pace ourselves for the foundation. The barn's a tall order, but with everyone working together, I don't foresee any problems.

CHAPTER 10
A Million Pieces

One spring morning, the sun rose through a sky diffused with layers of reds and blues, then turned gray as the sun inched a bit higher. Shadows of cumulus clouds loomed over stubble fields that gave way to rolling hills and rocky outcrops with valleys below. To the northeast, the forest followed the creek. The forest widened out and appeared impassable.

The foundation stones were in place, glinting in the sparkling dew at the base of the new barn. Mist brushed the frosty plow, tree stump, and stubble in the distant grain fields, brushing them with a frozen gauze-like veil. A soft, cottony frost collected on the tree trunks, bordering the crops and in the valleys. Rich, black soil ran through the fallow like creased corduroy.

The men tapped their feet waiting for Reverend Webber. He promised to lead them in prayer, blessing the new barn. Nell flitted around.
Da's keeping the men waiting to build the barn. Where's the Reverend?
Da wasn't alone. His four sons, good neighbors, and his youngest daughter gathered close. His posture relaxed as he greeted more workers and thanked them for coming.

"My sons have waited for this day. We've made a good deal of progress on this homestead. Having five sons has been all the help any father needs. I can't take my eyes off the peaches they planted for their mother. They've added to the improvements on the old homestead."

Ma was in charge of the refreshments. Honora tended to the potatoes and meat inside. Nell would have to return to her cookie baking. She followed Ma to the spring to refill the crocks for cool water for the workers. Bill Drew carried the full containers to the work-site tables.

"Oh, this must be Reverend." Ma turned as a wagon drove up.

"That's not him." Da's voice had a catch in it. "No, it's my … brothers."

Da scurried around, discussing construction specifics as groups assembled around the sections of the frame walls.

Strange. Da seems nervous his brothers came. It's his land. There's no need to be nervous. Nell cocked her head to the side. *I wonder why Edmond didn't tell Da he'd invited them?*

Edmond and Morty greeted Uncle Willie, James, and Patrick. They looked around for Da.

Patrick and James hung back, shuffling their feet.

They're big and stronger looking than Da. They look nervous too. Nell stood on her tippy toes. *They've never even met me.*

Uncle Willie chased Da down. The other two uncles, dragging their feet, joined them.

"Hello, Michael," they mumbled without any eye contact.

"Glad to have you." Da stuttered, "We …. We've got a good turnout."

Uncle Willie's wide grin eased the awkwardness. "Yup, better pitch in."
Patrick and James peered around.
I wish Ma would greet them. She's so busy with refreshments. Nell tutted. *Better return to my cookies soon. Honora'll be mad.*
Patrick and James lagged behind, cinching their tool belts.
Morty welcomed them with a big smile. "Let me make introductions."
James and Patrick said no.
It's not hard to tell. James and Patrick haven't gotten over their argument with Da from years ago. Nell wiped her hands on her apron. *This is a big day for Da. I hope they don't start now.*

"Michael, quite a crew here." James sounded disappointed.
"Where do you want us?" Patrick grumbled.
Casting a scornful look at the church volunteers, James muttered, "It looks like you've got plenty without us. Isn't family enough without asking all these others for help?"
Uh-oh, they're looking to cause Da trouble.
Nell's hand went to her mouth.

The men from the Pea Ridge Church remained busy. Da let them know where he wanted things. One of the men from the church strolled over to talk to James and

Patrick, but the two brothers shrugged their shoulders and marched off. When Ma tried to approach then, they tightened up the circle they'd made with the boys. James joked about Da always having a bumper crop of wild plums and persimmons. "No barn. Ha, ha."
"And, after thirty years of farming." Patrick's guffaw rang off the new walls. "Imagine being a farmer with no barn." The boys' laughter lessened. Ma hurried to the cabin.

James added, "In Lee Township, there are few trees left. The farmers have broken their backs to clear all of their forests. What wife would want to live in the gloom of all these trees?"
Da's face reddened.
They didn't even say hello to Ma. They came only to hurt Da. Nell's mouth gaped open. *So what if we've got more trees on our property than other farms do? They think Da's a failure. Ma loves the trees and collecting native walnuts. This is our property. I know how to stand up for Da.*

Patrick shook his head. "Aye, and pap's walnuts! Brother Michael found the perfect place for them." He roared with laughter. With the hog pen close, the poor hogs squealed at all the ruckus with grunts and groans.
"You raise China Poland pigs?" There was more squalling and oinking. Patrick kept aggravating the hogs. "Are they speaking Chinese or Polish?"

Nell approached them with her hands on her hips. "These are fine hogs Da raises. It's not gloomy here. My

Ma loves picking the native walnuts since she was a little girl. Da's worked hard."

Uncle James interrupted her. "You that feisty youngest one? Bridget Ella?"

"Don't call me Bridgett Ella," she said. "Name's Nell."

"Pleased to meet you, Nell." Uncle James hammed it up, raising his voice. "Your neighbors must be used to the hogs squealing."

Patrick slapped his knee. "Why he didn't purchase better land while he had the chance, we'll never know. You don't make a silk purse out of a sow's ear."

Less laughter. Others concentrated on their work. Nell marched away with her black eyes snapping.

"He should've taken his walnut inheritance and chucked it off the ridge. Let those loud hogs follow." James wiped the tears from his eyes. "Ha, ha."

"Aye, that's enough jokes." Uncle Willie's mouth twisted to one side. "Let's do what we came here for and get along."

The men from the church shook their heads. Da listened for Reverend Webber's buggy and anyone needing help.

"It's about time I extended a word of greeting to you. You're Stephen, Sam Waring's foreman, and this man with you?" asked Da.

Stephen said, "This is Malcolm, Sam Waring's brother."

"I'm most pleased to meet you, Malcolm. I understand you're an instructor at a military academy?" Da's eyebrows lifted up. "I appreciate your help."

"Yes," Malcolm replied, "a shooting range instructor. My brother's foreman, Stephen, invited me."

Da thanked Stephen and Malcolm for their help. Short and stocky Malcolm nodded his head, with a friendly smile.

"Excuse me, uh, Mr. Glisson?" Stephen's knees bent low with the heavy wall frame. Malcolm rushed over to help. They both struggled with the weight while Uncle James and Patrick strolled by snickering at their jokes.

Da rushed over. "Let me offer a hand, Malcolm."

Uncle James and Patrick carried their tools to the opposite side of the construction site. When they crossed paths with church volunteers, they ignored them. Da shot them a stern look.

I won't let them ruin this day for my Da. Nell sighed. *Better return to those cookies.*

~~**~~**~~**~~

The girls returned to the work site with their arms loaded with food. Up in the rafters, Uncle Patrick's hammer blows crashed in the morning air. The steady hammering was an improvement over their griping. Instead of working with the entire group, Uncle James beside Uncle Patrick separated themselves from the others. If some of the members reached out a hand to them, they waved them off. Stephen offered Uncle James a board. James turned away and went around to the back of the pile to retrieve his own. He tucked it under his arm and rejoined Patrick.

Strong, and tough, Stephen grinned at him. "Walking with the board upright? Looks like you've got your own staff there."

"Aye, me own special shillelagh, is it?" James sneered.

With a grunt, Stephen went back to work.

Malcolm mumbled to Stephen, "Ignore them."

After an exchange of gruff looks, Edmond held a board in place for Uncle Patrick. "Say, where'd that other board go?" Patrick ran his hand down the length of the board. "This one's split. Who took…?"

"There are plenty of other boards. I'll grab ye' one," offered Da.

"Each to his own," said one of the men from the church. "I wish Reverend Webber would arrive soon."

Everyone complimented Ma and the girls' meal. The afternoon became hot and muggy. The girls carted out large platters of cookies. Ma kept crocks of cold spring water in the nearby shade. In the heat, several wiped their brow and stepped into the shadows on the ridge.

Listening in on pieces of Stephen and Malcolm's conversation, Uncle James asked, "Are you questioning some of my brother's building plans here? You think your ideas are better?" Tempers flared.

Jostling broke out between James and Malcolm, followed by pushing. Malcolm threw the first punch. That escalated into an exchange of blows.

Da's face turned ashen.

"Don't put up with his bull roar, James," cried Uncle Patrick.

James took a left to the jaw and reeled for a second. He was heavier than his opponent. Malcolm caught one in the bread basket. He tumbled backward over a log that made up the children's mansions. Distracted by a mouse, Cahoots scratched under the log. There was a terrible, loud yowl. Cahoots, focused on catching the mouse, was pinned by the log.

"My kitty!" screamed Nell. "It crushed him." *My kitty can't move.*
Distracted by Nell, James let his guard down. Malcolm got to his feet and rushed at James, with his steely gray eyes gleaming. He threw another punch. James fell hard. Charging out straightaway, like a heavy machine, Patrick joined the fracas. Malcolm never saw it coming.
Patrick swung at the off-balance Malcolm. A stunned pause followed.
Straining to lift Malcolm to his feet, the church men loaded him into a wagon.

The color drained from Da's face. He stammered out a request for the work to stop. He was in shock, and his hands shook at the violence. Shoulders drooping, he turned his back to the barn. His speech came in tight sputters as he expressed his sorrow that things had gotten out of hand with his brothers and Malcolm Waring. He cleared his throat and thanked them again for their hard work.

He mumbled words about hoping for a hasty recovery. He looked at his brothers and shook his head. He prayed that when Malcolm recuperated, they could show their appreciation for all Malcolm's help.
Da managed a smile for his neighbors. The men from the church gathered up their tools and left the property. Da

wandered around, with his head down and one hand over his mouth.

Uncle James and Patrick slumped on a log, chins on their chest. The uncles made no sound and established no eye contact.

"Why was there such an issue with the men from the church?" Da's eyes focused on his brothers, who were fidgeting on the log. "You must've been disappointed in me, not these men. Were you settling an old score? Who threw the first punch?"

Patrick's hands shook. "The Irish will be blamed for their roughhousing. We were joking and whatnot. Didn't you want family help?"

"They weren't family." James talked too much and too fast. "Malcolm shouldn't have let Stephen egg him on. That Stephen, he's the one I should've been fighting. But since Malcolm threw the first punch, there was no choice."

"Patrick didn't know his own strength," said Uncle Willie. "He never has."

Da kept saying he wished the Reverend would have been there. *I've never seen Da's face look so old and tired. Is he going to be okay?*

CHAPTER 11
Taking the Bad With the Good

The parlor shadows stifled all but the sounds of Da praying with an unfamiliar hoarseness. His mouth resembled a thin line. "Help Malcolm, Lord. How can we make amends for Malcolm's injuries?"

Nell said, "I'm waiting for you to say what you always do when we lose a crop, or a cow dies. Remember, Da? We'll have to take the bad with the good."

He didn't say it. But he did say, "You're growing up, lass." Nell held her tongue. *We're not in the same boat. Da's hurt bad. I lost Cahoots. But poor Da.*

Da's voice remained a faltering echo of mumbled prayers for Malcolm's recovery. His words spun like the dark circles of dirt and sweat around his eyes. With a shudder in the cool cabin, Nell tucked her blanket around Da.

A light rap on the door jolted everyone to attention. Da bolted upright and lifted his dusty jacket as though it weighed thirty pounds. His face was white. Reverend Webber's shadow filled the crack of light from the open door of the somber cabin.

The entire Glisson family was seated there in the evening shadows. The Reverend's gaze searched the group. "Michael, fresh air would do the family some good."

Da motioned everyone to follow.

~~**~~**~~**~~

While they were sitting on some tree stumps in the wood pile, with the ridge behind in the distance, a pinkish moon rose above them. The Reverend said, "It's the Easter moon. The Easter moon stands for the message of our salvation, and our forgiveness."
Unsteady, Da glanced at the sky, but he didn't seem to see it. He leaned forward for the Reverend's words.

Reverend Webber took a long breath. "Michael, and family, I have sad news." He smoothed his trousers with the palms of his hands. "This morning, I was called away to visit an elder church member. She died. Her funeral will be on Good Friday. I'll be officiating two services that day."
Morty sucked in a quick bite of air.
Ma started to weep.

"For I regret having to report that Malcolm Waring met with a terrible accident on the road late this afternoon. The wagon jolted on a hill, and Malcolm, who was still unconscious, rolled out of the bed of the wagon. The others believe he hit his head on a rock. He was killed in an instant."
Edmond let out a heavy sigh and gulped. Da grasped his heart and reeled on the stump. The Reverend caught him around his shoulders. Ed, Morty, and Junior surrounded him.

The Reverend said, "We must forgive Patrick and James. It's not their fault. They didn't knock him out of the wagon nor put the rock under his head."

With his face in his hands, Da was inconsolable. Any relief from the Reverend's words became twisted in his grief. He wept for Malcolm.

A long silence settled over the group.

Da peered at the ridge, deep in troubled thought. "Even though it's a boundary between our land and the Warings, it means something more now. A young man starting out in life's going to be placed nearby. My heart's breaking for Malcolm. Me croi. My heart. My family."

Edmond and Morty put their strong arms around Da's weary shoulders.

Edmond confessed, "We pushed our need for a barn too hard."

Morty pleaded, "I wish we never would've stopped at Uncle Willie's and asked for Patrick and James's help."

Ma mumbled an Abraham Lincoln quote. "The best time to stop a fight is before it ever gets started."

Da's words filled the still air. "They're men now. They know there's going to be heartache." He righted himself in his shabby boots. "This family's supported one another through every kind of sorrow and joy."

Edmond took a deep breath. Junior tilted his head back and blinked to avoid his tears. Da stood tall and thin before them in his raggedy work clothes and white beard.

Morty said, "Da, you've worked so hard."

"My thanks to all of you. Your mother and I have an inheritance for each of you. We know your dream, Edmond, to join your brother, Martin, and sisters in

Kansas. We appreciate that you've put things in order here. You're a good farmer. We know you will do well. There are too many of us to make ends meet here in the township." Da's voice failed him. His cheeks and lips moved as if with a mouthful, but there was one last thing he had to say. In a whispered gasp, he formed the difficult words, "Go after your dream. You have our blessing. Join your sisters and brother in Kansas."
Led by Ma, they all embraced Da. They told him how much they loved him before Da, exhausted, stumbled off to bed.

~~**~~**~~**~~

An uncomfortable cloud spread over the cabin for several days. With the sun barely up, Edmond left for town. The long-anticipated barn was forgotten.
"Come on," said Morty, rallying the younger boys. "Let's not sit around here. Let's go fishing."
Honora completed the housework but hung close to home all day. She mumbled, "What's taking Edmond so long?"
Nell was thankful no one came to hear articles from the newspaper. Ma's shoulders sagged, trying to focus on Nell forming her letters on a slate.

"How would you like to meet Mr. Skiles, at the school?" said Ma.
Nell stuck her bottom lip out, wagged her head no, and crossed her arms over her chest.
"I'm determined to attend to your education. I hope that you will fit in. Catch up. You've done well not being

so long to bed grieving for Malcolm, and Cahoots. There are still a few weeks left of the school year."

Nell asked, "But what about Da?" She gripped her cornhusk dolls close to her heart.

"Sh. Da and I'll talk about your breathing and school. He's busy today. He doesn't want you always behind," said Ma.

~~**~~**~~**~~

"Have you been at the Warings all this time?" Ma placed her arm around Da's shoulders.

"And to town." Da sank into a chair by the hearth. "Sam Waring said we've nothing to say." He said, "Hell's bells, and stood in his doorway with a terrible glare."

"I hear someone on the road," said Nell.

"Did you tell him we're all so sorry about his brother?" Ma ignored Nell. "It was an accident?"

"Yes, he stood there in silence, although Bud mumbled something about his dad wanting revenge. I told him I'm working on an idea for the ridge. Waring sneered. He said, 'There's nothing that will bring back my brother, Malcolm.'"

Ma nodded. "Malcolm's loss is a tragic accident."

"Waring cut me off. He wasn't interested in my ideas. His voice was like a snarling wolf. He said, 'As if some sentiment will take the place of a life. I don't make agreements with folks with blood on their hands. Now, I won't ask again.' Then his heavy oak door slammed."

Honora shouted at Nell, running out the door after her. "Oh! What a child with your wheezing over Cahoots."

124

Da and Ma followed, strolling arm in arm across the long grass. The younger boys were coming from the creek with their fishing poles. A wagon struggled up the drive. The old wheels groaned. They heard Edmond giddyap the horses. The draft horses panted. Their hooves clopped. *What was that weight on the team? Edmond didn't go for logs today.* Nell scanned the drive. *The wagon was out of sight around the curves. I can hear the team working so hard up the steep drive.*

The family waited for the wagon to come over the hill. Da blinked his eyes in astonishment. "What in the world?" A monstrous, dark black, shiny stove with polished metal handles glinted like a giant trophy in the back of the old wagon.
"Oh, look-ee! Yes, siree. Look at that. A stove!" Nell jumped up and down alongside the wagon, flapping her arms and shouting, "Look, Da! Look. Ma, Ma, come closer, quick. You got to see yourself in this shiny thing."

Ma rubbed her eyes as she looked up at the wagon bed. "Edmond, what have you done? We can't afford that. Have you spent all of your hard-earned wages? Have you lost your senses?"
Honora was skipping, her skirts swinging in circles around her. Nell was right behind shouting, "A new stove, Da. It's big. It's shiny."
That night, Honora got the tin corn popper hot on the unexpected gift. Ed paused in his nutcracking, and watched.

Da sat close to Ma with Nell on his lap. "I sold the northern acres sight unseen. I wired Martin the funds to purchase the remaining 160-acre homestead, on the same road as that of your older sisters and Martin, for Edmond's inheritance. This way, Edmond, Mary-Jane, Kate, and Martin will all be together on the same road in Kansas."

The sole sound was the pop, pop, pop of the corn on top of the gleaming stove. White kernels spilled out in abundance. Honora filled basket after basket. Da's face was at peace, gazing at his sons. "Morty, I realize how important finishing school is. Mike Junior, I'd be right proud if you went out there and helped your sisters for a season. This way, you'll travel with Edmond to Kansas, and get to know Martin. Morty and Jack will have to manage without you."

"I know why they're leaving." Nell lowered her head. "I'm sorry if I've been ornery."
Ed scoffed. "It might feel like there's nothing to be done about orneriness, but you came by feistiness for a reason. I'll need it where I'm going. Next time I see you, you'll be a grown lady. I already notice a change in you, Nell, but something tells me you'll always be feisty."

~~**~~**~~**~~

Where is Da? Today he looks like the saddest man on earth.
Nell found Da in the late morning sunshine, peering down the length of the ridge.

Edmond's leaving left another ragged hole. I want the best for my brothers, but I'm afraid they're pushing me aside and abandoning me. Even Da thinks he may never see them again. Is that why it hurts to breathe? But Da, Mike Jr. will return. Won't he?

With his hand shielding his eyes, Da gazed at something Nell couldn't see in the distance. "What is it, Da?"
"My pap's legacy."
Da left Nell's side and strode through the underbrush with its new spring growth. He broke off a long stem to chew on. "I've dreamt of a walnut grove. Aye, I know the younger boys aren't much different from the older ones about wanting to abide here." Da trudged further down the ridge. "Och, aye, it's the only way. I hear a small voice in me heart. It feels like my dream must slide to the side to make room for my new plan."

"A new plan?" Nell galloped ahead to catch Da.
They tramped along with only the tender sounds of nearby doves cooing. "Yep, I'll plant but a few saplings, and I'll let my dream of the gunnysacks of nuts nest underground. I'll plant the saplings well-spaced along the two lines of the ridge where Malcolm died," said Da, scooping handfuls of black soil. "You know the motto on the plaque from Ma's church?"
Da's voice sounds like the creek when the water flowed gentle around the rocks.

"Aye," said Nell, isn't it something like, *"Even if tomorrow I knew the world would go to pieces, I'd still plant my trees."*

Da clasped his hands together in front of his mouth and whispered a prayer. "'Tis fitting. Set a few benches and some odd trees in between. It'll be a park-like setting. Those trees'll grow tall and dignified. Their branches will fill out, not touching one another. This is what I'll do about Malcolm's death. I'll call the memorial, Peace Ridge.

"I'll leave the old gunnysacks in the nursery bed behind the stable. Can't bear to let them go. Aye, plans for returning peace between the two families come first." Da stroked his chin.

Ma, Honora, and the two boys joined them on the ridge. With warm soil, the ridge greened up. Colors of the first wildflowers dotted the margins of the fields. Again, a dove cooed.

Exhausted, Da explained his vision. "As the weather provides, I'll be digging up the best walnut saplings in the nursery beds and ones from the forest. We'll plant them on the ridge. My idea is to plant a memorial for Malcolm, with trees and benches spaced and grouped and a path in between them."

"I like that," acknowledged Morty.

Jack said, "No nuts. Just saplings?"

Da gave him a wink. "Time's important."

"At the cemetery, this morning I saw our uncles. We took flowers to the grave." Nell broke the silence.

"Did you go inside the fence with Ma and Honora?" asked Da.

"No, I stayed outside. They scattered the flowers on Malcolm's grave."

"A wagon approached with three men in it," added Ma. "We knew who it was. Uncle Willie waved. The other two kept their eyes straight-ahead. When we started back up the forest path, your brothers took their hats off. All three went in."

"They bowed and knelt down beside Malcolm's grave," said Nell.

I wish Sam Waring could've seen them. He'd forgive us and be glad for Da's dream of a memorial grove for Malcolm

CHAPTER 12
September 1888, Thirteen!

One Thursday morning, in September 1888, after days of overcast skies, the clouds rolled away, and bits of blue sky could be seen. The unfinished barn had stood colorless with the cool air whipping through it. Rain dripped off graying rafters, which were patterned with moisture stains. Da, Morty, and Jack, the last of the farm workers remained busy in the fields. Da didn't have the energy to think about the barn in the gloom.

In the late morning, the part of the roof that wasn't intact lay open to radiant sunlight. Thick, blanketing clouds populated the sky. Scattered clouds moved into the distance. Standing puddles reflected off boards and tools in the soaked barnyard.

Autumn began with lots of rain. The corn would have to stay in the fields for several weeks due to the muddy rivulets running off in every direction.

At the irresistible clinking sound of Da's cart, Nell and Honora licked the last of the cake batter from the bowl. Honora grabbed Nell's hand and yanked her outside. "Haven't heard that old cart for so long. The day's here. Since I've been little, I've waited for Da to dig up those three gunnysacks of Tipperary walnuts. Time to see his idea for a memorial with saplings."

They skipped down the path beside the cart to Da's cheery tune.

"What's that tune Da's singing?"

"May our hearts be light on Nell's thirteenth birthday."
As they caught up to him, he tipped his hat and greeted
his two merry daughters. "I presume the birthday girl
made peace with the chickens?"

Honora moved her feet faster than she moved her
mouth as she modeled Nell flinging her bent elbows out
like flapping wings, hunkering down like one of the flock.
"She tried to tiptoe around, but the old rooster came to
life. The coop's door will need new hinges the way she
hopped out of there." Da guffawed at Honora's jig.
"What?" spluttered Nell. *It's hard to tell when they
laugh if I'm coming up short.*
Da shook his head.

Not stopping for breath, Honora rushed on. "The rooster
brushed Nell's legs and bare feet, and then he broke her
skin. A peck."
"He did. It hurt, so I let him have it." Nell wrinkled up her
nose.
"Not a place for flapping your wings and kicking. Let
them relax as you gather." Da's chuckle delighted her
ears.
"Da, where are the three gunnysacks of nuts you've
been saving?" Honora searched the cart.
"Och, aye, behind the stable for now. The saplings'll
grow faster," admitted Da, admiring the work area with
twinkling eyes. "I'm grateful for new dreams. Nell's lived
to her thirteenth birthday. This is the birthday of the
grove."

The ridge had a fresh look of order with the cleared rows. Saplings were planted with a substantial distance to allow them time to grow to full size.

Morty said, "Da doesn't need us to gather any more saplings or nuts. He's already handpicked the saplings. Let's get to planting."

Jack nodded.

Da's rejuvenated spirits tickled his family. He allotted time to pause and enjoy his pipe. He considered each task ahead. He shook his head with pride at their progress. In high expectation for each row, he kicked up his heels. Saplings stood tall and upright like two ranks of soldiers. Now and then, he'd cry out, "Look at the beautiful root ball on this one. About nine inches for a leggy sapling."

A root ball rested in Jack's hands as he duplicated Da's method.

"Good roots mean an excellent yield. The saplings are three years ahead of any nuts we'd have planted. They're good specimens," Da said, shoveling a pile of black soil over the delicate rootlets. "Aye, they'll live forever with these root balls. Look at the delicate leaf pattern first for identification, which is shaped like an egg with an end tip. 'Tis the twig makes it easy to identify. Some shoots are a foot or more long with about twenty-plus leaves."

"What about in the winter when there aren't leaves, Da?"

"Always look at the ground. You'll find shells or nuts. Use your knife, and cut a twig the long way. Inside the twig will be rows of ovals like a honeycomb. Let's find a tree with a wide trunk. Step back. Look at the bark. It looks like gray diamonds. Always look up. They're the biggest tree around."

Da hadn't talked this much since Malcolm died.
"When you're transplanting reach into the heart of the tangled walnut roots. Find the taproot. The key is no bending. It's first in the hole. The tree'll grow one hundred feet tall." Da tamped the soil down with his boot, raked in manure, and watered it. "Like the pure stand of hickory, I want the Tipperary and the local walnuts to make this ridge home."

Morty set his pliers down, checking on Jack. "Da wants holes dug the appropriate size and place for each sapling. Then mix soil and manure over the top." He modeled Da's method. "Grand. Now water it in."
Jack said, "Morty, Have you ever wondered what other gifts of the world Grandpap could've blessed Da with?"
Grandpap knew what he was doing. Nell shook a mosquito off. *I can plant as good as Jack.*

"One nut grows a tree over a hundred feet tall," said Morty, tamping it down. "Takes one hundred years. Da believed that the walnut would prove valuable."
Morty sounds excited like Da does.
"In sixty years, we'll be growing high-quality timber!" Jack clapped Morty on the back. "I'll never forget the

stories of the Irish people's hunger. I see why Da likes Ma's foraging."

Who knows what we'll be like in eighty years? I want to help.

Da protected their tangled roots as he rearranged the taproot from the heart of the root ball. "My children are all welcome to plant saplings and seeds to grow into mighty trees."

"Wait, what's that noise?" Morty jolted to his feet.

"Nell? You should be helping Ma. I heard it too." Jack peered around.

"It's not twigs crackling. It's more like a rifle being loaded?" said Morty.

Da's face went white. "I saw it. It gleamed like a barrel. Pointing this way."

"Who's out there?" Da pulled Nell behind him.

"Whoever you are, you need permission to be hunting on our land." Jack spat on the ground. "If you're after a fight, we've got one for ye."

Running into the trees, Morty hollered, "There, someone is dashing off in a dark coat and hat." He bent down to pick up an object. "Look at this brass. It must be from a spent round."

Somebody's angry and frustrated. Nell shivered. *They are trying to frighten us away."*

~~**~~**~~**~~

With the sun setting toward the evening of Nell's birthday, Da lost all track of time. Ma held the meal. "Michael, your touch with the saplings reminds me of handling newborns. You were so tender, as you knelt above each sapling."

"Da's using a map," said Nell.

"It's like a map." Da sniffed his stew and smiled. "Delicious. I'm ordering the rows with nut trees and other trees. I'll take the top off of one sapling and put it on the roots of another. It's called grafting."

Nell's eyes spread open wide. Honora whistled.

"Out on the ridge, Da measured the space between the holes and eased his spade into the ground like he was breaking ground for a church," said Honora.

Da winced, holding his back. "Plenty of kneeling. We've got a long way to go."

"Your shirt's so crisp and white." Ma smiled. "It makes you look handsome and younger."

"Da's eyes looked like an inspector's when he studied his map," said Nell.

"It might feel like chewing your cabbage twice, but see how important it is to learn to write and cipher?" declared Ma. "I suppose I will make an exception on your birthday. You may put your unfinished work aside. I'm proud of you for working on your words and catching on for school soon. Wash up for supper."

Ma and Honora steered around the long-handled pots not wanting an accidental spilling of the wonderful-smelling beef stew. Ma was still in the honeymoon period with the new stove. She pricked the top of Nell's beautiful birthday cake. She fussed with a rag as she brushed the crumbs off the stove's shiny metal. Down through the holes into the fire they went.

The cake made the kitchen smell sweet and buttery.

Turning the damper down, Honora groaned, "Oh, where's the dripping pan?" Her teeth were set on edge. "I wish I'd put it under the boiling pot of stew." They kept the meal warm. It was easier with the new stove. On the window sill, Nell's cake cooled.
Honora eyeballed the table, which was still not set. Nell's clothes looked as if they'd been flung in a mud puddle. Honora pinned up the last of the laundry. In a hurry, and with a careless fling of her arms, Nell knocked the entire line to the floor.

"I'm thankful it will be another year until her next birthday," groaned Honora. "I've been with Nell all day, collecting eggs and washing. Where'd she go now? Oh, she's hanging upside down from the hitching post, waiting for Morty to return with the mail. But she's been acting better than usual."
Nell's thin legs were crossed over the hitching post, she stuck out her tongue to catch raindrops. She cried out, "He's here!" Nell hopped from one foot to the other. "What's that you brought from town?"

Morty handed Nell a small package. Nell sounded out the words on the address. "Nnn—ell! Oh boy, it's for me."
"Who's it from?" asked Ma. "Nell, look at this word that begins with *K-a-n.*"
"It says Mike, from Kansas!" shouted Nell. She ripped off the paper and inside found a bluestone ring. She

clutched the ring to her chest. Her shoulders shimmied back and forth.

Bill Drew followed Morty from the drive. "I couldn't forget Nell's birthday, either." His present squirmed out of his grasp.

An orange kitten made Nell's cheeks flush even pinker at another unexpected present. She wrapped her puny arms around a blinking and stammering Bill.

Unable to think of anything to say, Bill inquired about Junior.

"He's still out in Kansas, helping Kate and Mary-Jane," said Ma, "encountering an eyeful of the West."

Honora reached out to brush Nell's hair out of her face. "Happy birthday. The ring's a luxury around this homestead. A new cat to boot."

"I want a name that begins with 'z.' I've got it, Ma. Zeke." Nell broke off a stiff strand from the broom to correct the kitten. She swatted him. "No! Zeke! Don't scratch."

With a tutting sound, Honora returned to the stove.

~~**~~**~~**~~

The last of the tree-planting weather continued into late fall. Da enjoyed the long, serene days. He'd visit with anyone who'd listen about the memorial grove. Ma ladled the potato soup with narrowed eyes. Everyone enjoyed it, but Da merely took a few bites.

Before she knew what happened, Nell misplaced the bluestone ring Mike sent for her birthday. The boys complained that she kept hindering their way, digging up their straight, neat rows. "She's got her own idea of planting. We don't need her help," whined Jack. "This planting's serious. Not a job for a little sister, even if she's thirteen."

Nonetheless, Nell went ahead and dug holes.
"Served you right for losing your ring," shouted Jack. "At your age, you shouldn't lose a ring."

~~**~~**~~**~~

One Sunday evening, late in the fall, Da didn't touch his dinner. His shoulders rose and fell with his heavy breathing. Every sound caused him to flinch, and his eyelids flickered open. "Nell, your ring will show up. Grant it time. The crows have an eye for purty things. It's fortunate they didn't haul you off. Don't fret. It'll show up." Da sank back in his chair. He looked drawn as he crossed his lanky right leg over his left. His calloused hands lay limp in his lap.

Ma said, "I've never seen you look so tired, Michael. You're overdoing it. The extra work on the grove? You've made a good enough start for this year."
Da didn't answer.
Honora commented on his full bowl. "Should I wash the bowl, Da?"
"Ah, Honora," Da beamed at her, "never lose your dazzle."
Ma's eyebrows were knitted into deep furrows. "Michael, did you eat enough soup?"

With Da's eyes half-open, and his voice fading, the family had to lean forward to hear his babblings. "Splendorous, Sadie. Boys bone tired. Such good workers." Da's breathing was still labored. "Pushing that heavy cart." he panted. "Pacing off steps. Holes." He gasped even more. "Stakes."
Ma put her arm around Da's thin shoulders. Her face was pinched with worry. His arms drooped like broken wings in his good shirt. Da's mouth softened into a peaceful smile. "My girl, my Sadie."

His eyes closed and then fluttered open. He glanced around at his family. He spoke with a halted cadence. "If one or more of you agrees to put aside the land and not sell, please remember it's my dream for my grandchildren to have this as a legacy. Tall trees with straight trunks will bring a fair price. We're beholden' to my dear pap's gift." A long pause let Da regain his breath. "It is the gift of the world for generations. A grand man he was. Keep planting." Struggling to remember what to say, Da yawned and tapped his lips with his knuckle. "Keep planting. That's what pap would say."

Ma bit her lip. "With all of your ramblings, I think you had better lie down."
"Aye, Sadie," he mumbled. "I'm so thankful, so thankful." A long silence ensued, and he yawned. "Our children are the first generation to grow up here." He drifted off again. "Such good neighbors, the Drews. The others."
Ma shushed him.

Da taught us about the strength of the tap root. Poor Da, he's sapped.

"Let me finish." Da gasped. "This first generation of walnuts will need about sixty years to grow …, not overcrowded in a jungle but spaced apart in a grove."

Da taught us about the strength of a taproot.

Da placed his arm around Ma and dragging, shuffled off to his room.

CHAPTER 13
An Early Winter

Winter came during the waning days of autumn when the trees were still loaded with leaves. It was Nell's first winter without Da.

Nell kept reliving her memory of Ma asking Morty to go for Doc Simpkins. Ma's words went around in her head. "Tell him that Michael's already gone."

What could Ma mean? Da? Gone where? Something wasn't right. It's so quiet downstairs. I haven't heard Da's voice. Why don't I smell Da's pipe?

Nell didn't smell any cornbread for breakfast. She didn't hear any banging of pots.

Nell leaped from her bed. "Where's Da? Where's Da?" she screamed.

At the top of the loft ladder, Honora opened her arms to Nell. "You can't keep reliving this."

Nell waved her away and ran back to bed. Before pulling the covers over her head, she cried, "Did Ma send for Doc Simpkins?"

Later, Nell sat listening. She replayed the agonizing thoughts over and over again. "Why couldn't Doc save Da?" Most of those first days and weeks, she slept. Winter had come early and with a fury. The farm was all but socked in. She'd heard faint voices from beside the crackling fire. She turned toward the wall and covered her head with a pillow.

Sometimes when she woke up, she heard her family talking about a funeral. When the roads were better, the snow would melt. Outside it was gray. Gray. The snow was gray.

I hate gray.

Nell could hear scraps of conversation from the kitchen. Nell didn't even look at her embroidery. She dropped it to the floor next to her bed.

"Again," said Honora. "I've tried to tell her to keep her hands busy. She eats maybe one bite of her meal. I told her she can't lie there in the loft. With her face buried in Zeke's fur. She needs to come downstairs and be with us. I thought maybe her embroidery would help her. It's of a tree. Da's motto is lettered beneath."

I'm so cold. My fingers and my arms. Can't warm up. Da passed away in his sleep. Honora's worried about embroidery? It can't be.

Nell looked at the embroidery on the floor. She rolled over.

How can he be here one evening and then gone? He said I was purty? I don't care if I ever finish this needlework. Look at the tree branches, breaking under the load of snowy leaves. It's too much. My water looks frozen and gray in my cup.

"Thank you, Honora, but that's enough." Ma's voice was soft. "Let me feed her the next meal. Her stitching can wait. Nell needs time, all the time she needs. Allow her time to remember Da as the good person he was. He worked hard all of his life."

"It's hard enough for someone my age to let go. Da died with no suffering," said Ma. "Things are hard. We must be careful of Nell's breathing. Why the icy roads are too hard to travel on. Give her time to rationalize Da's death."

Don't they feel the same way? It doesn't feel like they do. Rationalize? Nell sobbed. *Why did Da have to go? I miss him. I wish he'd come in from the field. He's gone. That's all I know.*

"His old croi wore out." Ma tucked a blanket around Nell.

"When did he die?"

"It's been a few days."

What about my heart? How long can it last without him? Ma mentions her legs. Nell glanced down at her legs. *She says it feels like they've been cut out from beneath her. Everything's cut out from beneath me. I'm in a dark hole.*

Over a steaming bowl of oats, Ma's words fell flat on Nell's ears. Ma placed oatmeal on the table. She held Nell. She begged Nell to come downstairs and join the family. The oatmeal was gray. Ma's bowl of peeled apples turned a grayish brown. "Da's favorite pie will make the cabin smell good." Ma put her shoulders back. "I've been shedding tears for days on end, knowing that my other half's missing. Nell, your silence must end. Talk. Let's keep Zeke outside. Your breathing's labored."

Nell screamed. "No. Don't put him out. He's been good to me all my life." Then she wept like a baby, "Ma, poor, Da."

The days dragged on. Honora said, "Her face looks terrible, with the gray circles under her eyes. You're looking better, Ma. Maybe Nell will soon. It's been a long time."

"Thank you," Ma said. "We have to keep looking ahead. Do things that we're used to doing and clear our minds from sadness. Da was always cheerful."

Clear my mind of sadness? When every meal comes, and he doesn't. Nell surveyed the yard outside her window. *He's not anywhere in the fields or out at the ridge. I'm the youngest, and the others don't have answers, either.* "Drink something. You've got to. Eat your food. I don't want you lost in sadness. You've got to eat," said Ma. *I am lost. How do I get back unless I find him? Da, I need you. Come home. You're lost. I need you here.* Nell shook under the blankets. *I want to hug you. Call me your Nell again.*

Ma's sweet voice persisted as she completed basic chores. She made a point of asking each child for a hug throughout the day. She clasped Nell to her heart all night. Each night, Nell tossed in the blankets, kicked her feet, and thrashed around. With Ma and the family grouped around the table, there were plenty of chances for Nell to overhear conversations.
Honora waits 'til she thinks I'm sleeping. Then she starts her complaints about me.
Nell scrunched her face up, with her ears cocked to hear these evening discussions.

"Nell's too old to be clinging to you, Ma. We don't want her acting like a baby again."

"Yes, this might set her back. Before this, she was doing better." Ma scolded Honora. "It's normal after her hard birth, breathing problems, and losing the older children. And now Da. She feels abandoned. She's the youngest. It's us who babied her."
Oh, Honora. Why do you always have to think you're better than me?

Ma asked them all to be a comfort for one another. She said, "Consoling someone else will bring you comfort. Be kind to Nell. Don't let her feel pushed away. We don't want her battling to breathe. Let her grieve. She'll learn to cope and find her way."
I can't find my way without Da. My whole life, I've been pushed away. I'm small. I'm not capable.

Da's death was difficult for everyone. Then came tears, followed by Nell's withdrawal. Then loud, angry outbursts. She threw things. Stomped her feet. Hit. Ma's patience never wavered.
"Let's keep our words positive." Ma told the others. "If she claws and kicks, help her. It will take time before she's better. Da's life was a grand one. His biggest accomplishment's fulfilled, raising you all to adulthood."
Grand? Mine isn't. Nell sniffled. *I'm an adult?*

"He kept his goal to build a beautiful memorial," added Jack.
"He didn't plant his whole inheritance," mumbled Honora.

Nell's face turned red. She clenched her fists. She wanted to thrash and punch Honora. She burst into tears.

Morty said, "Da didn't want us to blink water when he died."

"What do you know about blinking water?" shrieked Nell.

"Da would have given anything to have completed that walnut grove. There was not enough time," said Jack.

Nell lunged for Jack. Ma gritted her teeth. She pulled Nell off Jack. Ma stooped over. Nell heard Ma's labored breathing. She clasped her arms around Ma. She cried, "You okay, Ma? I don't want anything to happen to you." Ma's prayers and hymns filled the cabin with her sweetness and warmth. Nell didn't hear as much sighing. Little by little, Nell forced a feeble smile.

After a few days, Ma's words caught in her throat. "We have to talk about Da. Remember how much he loved his life. He couldn't have dreamed land like this would be his when he left Ireland. His walnuts are the gift of the world."

There was a slight movement upward of Nell's lips. Ma stroked her hair and checked her breathing. "We'll say good-bye to Da soon. It'll be okay."

How will everything be okay? How do I say good-bye to Da forever? Nell's eyes darted around the room. *Ma's words float past Da's rocking chair, up to the rafters, and lock inside my heart.*

Honora and Morty organized a walnut bee for the funeral. "Da would've liked that," said Ma. "A group of people in cahoots, as busy as bees at a quilting and shelling walnuts."
The family stood tall and strong.
All except for me. I am short. I can't stand all the gray. The black. I hate them both.

Folks came and said such wonderful things about Da. Nell couldn't help but lift her head. She helped with the walnut husking. Da's brothers arrived, Willie, Patrick, and James. The uncles embraced each of Da's children. They reminded Nell of Da. She hugged them back hard. Ma's soft-spoken thanks for the Lord's provision brought a close to the evening.
It's all too much for me. But I'm breathing, each breath for Da. I take slow breaths, in and out. I'll do my best for him. Nell closed her eyes and exhaled. *I'll always be your "in-hair-a-dance," Da. I'll be your gift to the world.*

~~**~~**~~**~~

Seasons slipped by without Da. When another birthday signaled autumn, the wind howled louder and colder, lashing at the cabin windows. Nell begged for the lamp on low at night. Ma said she couldn't spare the oil. Nell tossed, turned, and snuggled into Ma.

All the darkness in Nell's life, with her older brothers and sisters moving away, made the hurting come that much closer again.
I can't think about any of that. How come a family doesn't stay a family?

These worries robbed her nights of healthy sleep. Anger grew from these fears that blurred her days gray. It added to Nell's agitation when Ma prayed for Morty and Jack's school attendance and finding enough time to manage the farm. "And for Nell, if she could catch up in school, but for now she needs to remain home," said Ma.

Nell overheard one neighbor's words as she patted Ma's shoulder. "A widow's difficulties are many."
Another said, "With almost all of your children grown, it's hard to have your youngest, ornery, and unhealthy and unable to attend school at her age."
"Can you manage the farm? Town's best."
"The newspaper subscription has to go. The high cost of buying coffee isn't a necessity," Ma replied with a brave nod. "I've returned to savoring my red-root tea."
Listening to the neighbor's remarks on Ma's difficulties without Da caused Nell more anxiety and breathing problems.
I'll start school.

Bill Drew's words helped her breathe. "We've both lost our dads. A few school years back, we read about a boy who never knew his dad, written by Charles Dickens."
"Don't you think I'd be too far behind for that book?"
"No, Nell. Not at all. You've got a sharp mind. Anyone can see that."
"Books can help you see further than all the way down the whole ridge, clear past Missouri."
Oh, no. School's almost to start. November's here.

Nell gritted her teeth and shivered. "Don't 'spec anyone to like me."

"Better give them a chance. They'd be crazy not to," said Bill.

~~*~~**~~**~~

The school year resumed in late November. The schoolteacher, Mr. Skiles, failed to familiarize himself with the names. He stuttered on the roll call. "Bridgett Ella?"

"Don't call me Bridgett," she croaked in her raspiest, grouchiest voice.

Nell, only the size of some of the younger students, kept her chin from trembling.

"That's not a respectful voice to use when addressing your teacher. Now stand in the corner, Br … I mean, El … you!" He steered her by her elbow. She fought him like a wildcat. Around and around the benches they went. The classroom grew noisier and noisier with the hysterics.

He thought he'd have it easy with someone as small as I am, Nell smirked.

"When I get my hands on you, I'll use my strap." Mr. Skiles threatened.

At twenty-two years old, Morty wasn't going to let anything keep him from attaining his eighth-grade diploma, including Nell. He picked her up like a sack of potatoes. He locked his arms around her. "Don't even think about escaping."

She screamed and spluttered.

I don't fit here. I've got to learn to calm down.

Morty's red, angry face looked older than the teacher's. She coughed, and took deep breaths, in and out.

"Breathe, Nell. Take your time. Good," said Morty.

I am Morty. It's hard in front of all these kids.

Nell listened as Morty apologized to Mr. Skiles for failing to remind him not to call her Bridgett Ella. "She goes by Nell." The room quieted down. The children filed out to recess. Morty stayed beside her until she breathed easier.

"Her wheezing scares us." Morty assured Mr. Skiles that *he'd* be there tomorrow. "But Nell's the youngest, and she's been pampered and spoiled. She's a little tyrant."

I was going to go to school, but I'll never forgive you, Morty, for saying I'm a tyrant.

Nell shook her head back and forth.

Ma says it's not my fault I'm spoiled. Da said I was born for a mighty purpose.

"Aha." Mr. Skiles stroked his chin. "Yes, I observed her on the playground this morning, doubled over, and laughing at an unkindness to a younger student, which calls for the strap."

Nell dragged her feet and flounced around, making it difficult for Morty to ride her home.

Morty's mouth formed a tight line. "Are you trying to make things harder for Ma? You've got to do your part, Nell."

"I love Ma. But I heard what you told the teacher." Nell stayed still on the horse most of the way home.

I'll never forget Morty's words or Honora's when she took Gertrude's side against me.

Nell gritted her teeth, seething over their spurning.
I'm sorry I let you down, Ma, Da, and our good name. I didn't even make it a half-day. If I go back? The strap. One thing's for sure, I'll get Morty back. Honora's not going anywhere.

CHAPTER 14
Bleak Fields

Early snow and drizzling lingered. The sun framed in fog paled and refused to warm the cornfields. Morty, although good with the team, said, "In all the mud and icy slush, we can't make any progress. Jack and I'll try the first colder afternoon to complete the harvest with what daylight we have after school." They bogged down in the cornfields every time. Morty slogged onto the porch and threw up his hands. "The fields won't dry out. Sorry, Ma. We waited too long to harvest the last of the corn."

The next morning, Ma said, "I thought of what Da would do. We'll pick all the frozen corn we can."
With her arms full of blankets, Honora pushed Nell toward the door. "I'll bundle these around Nell on the wagon."
Ma donned Da's jacket. Nell burst into tears. To keep the peace, Ma, with a quick thrust, shoved the patched jacket into a trunk. "Until you're older," Ma soothed.
When I'm old, I don't want anyone to wear Da's jacket.

All afternoon, Ma, Honora, and Nell worked in a whirlwind. Nell twisted off the ears with all her strength. Their frosty husks glistened with snow crystals and stuck to her hands. Nell threw the ears into the bed of the horse-drawn wagon.
I like that thump when they smack against the wagon box. Take that, Mr. Skiles, and your strap.

The draft horses jerked and pulled the wagon as far into the field as possible.

The rows went on and on, up and down hills and through gullies. Corn mounded in the wagon bed. The wheels were packed with icy mud.
The frozen kernels of corn look like missing teeth. Nell shuddered. *Brown teeth trickling through holes in the wagon floor into the cold ground. Oh, Da. You're in that cold cemetery.*

Nell looked across the frozen field. The cornstalks were gray and brittle. She bit her lip. "There's too much corn out here."
Honora staggered through the clumps, with Ma hobbling behind.
I still cry. I'm afraid when I can't see them in all these stalks. Nell tried to keep up. *I feel alone. My tears are freezing on the cornhusks.*

The brownish kernels caused Ma to tut. "Some might still shell." Mist hung pale in the tree line. The sun shimmered halfway down the sky of wind-whipped clouds. Bleak, early shadows crisscrossed the rows like railroad ties. On and on, their shoes popped and squelched out of the icy mud. They packed the ears back to the wagon and returned for more. Nell stuck with it, with her scarf around her mouth. It was hard to breathe in the frosty air. Ma and Honora traded off patting Nell's back with steady slaps to quiet her persistent dry cough.
There's that moaning sound again.

Nell took slow, deep breaths.

It's not the wind. It's Ma. I hate that she can't walk with her willow cane but trudges with her aching back and hip.

Ma nestled with Nell down in between cornstalks, out of the wind. "I don't want to call for Doc if we can help it." There they huddled, in between coughing bouts.

It's warmer here. I'm safe, with Ma close.

Nell and Ma made a game of it, hiding in various places. Zeke came darting between the stalks, and Nell scratched him under his chin.

Once again, Ma and Honora shivered through the dirty snow in their icy shoes, carrying the last armloads of corn back to the wagon, while Nell waited on the seat. Their breath hung like steam in front of their mouths.

"My children will learn how even without Da," panted Ma, "not to yield. We'll fight our way ahead and overcome obstacles."

Nell's smile was full of hope. Her clenched fists were full of the fighting part. She let Zeke look for mice. "Ma, about Mr. Skiles, and his strap ...."

"Nell, no straps," said Ma. "We all have challenges. If you remain patient, you'll be well soon. They'll be a new teacher before you return. I'll help you at home."

"Morty better be more accountable." Honora turned back for more ears of corn. The draft horses chewed on the cornstalks. "He's going to be ashamed that he gave up on this field."

"We all need to know what we're made of and how to take a stand for what matters." Some of Ma's words blew away in the wind. With the cold trip, riding the drag in the frigid air, even the team didn't need to be coaxed back to the stable. They made a straight path for home.

~~**~~**~~**~~

When they arrived home, Morty shook his head in disbelief at the wagon of frozen corn. "Thank you. That must've been miserable. Nell's breathing? How'd you do it?"

Honora stood with her arms crossed over her chest.

Ma told him of her dream that they'd all understand their capabilities and take a stand for the farm and for what's right. "Nell shouldn't be threatened with a strap after being sick, losing her Da, and on her first day."

Honora tapped her foot. "If we could do it, then you should've been able to take a stand to try harder for the farm."

"Jack and I'll unload the corn," replied Morty. "We'll prepare any extra corn for sale. I've taken a stand." Morty held his chin high. "I've asked for Bertha Webber's hand in marriage. I'm going to graduate and marry Bertha. It's important, and that's the stand I'm taking."

What is Morty talking about?

Her eyes rushed from Ma to Morty, to Honora. Nell couldn't believe her ears.

Marrying Bertha?

"I've been thinking about how many farmers are needed on this homestead. It's perfect for Junior and Jack. We've each got to take a stand on one thing and decide what matters most." Morty took a deep breath. "It's hard to state the truth. But in my opinion, the memorial grove on Peace Ridge is nothing short of foolhardy and sentimental hogwash. I know Da wanted it to be a tribute to Malcolm's death. I've no excuses about not wanting to farm, but Edmond said the ridge could be planted with a row crop. I want to leave the younger boys in decent shape. My future is in logging."

"What?" Honora cut Morty off, throwing a pan of biscuits in the air as she kicked a chair catawampus. "Let the memorial grove go?"
Nell put her hands over her ears at the uncommon commotion.
I can't think with all of their quarreling.
Nothing softened Honora's hollering. "Why would you ask for Bertha's hand in marriage before you'd honor what Da wanted? After all, I'm the oldest if there's to be a next one leaving."
Next one leaving? I've got to breathe.
Nell closed her eyes.
Breaths in and out slowly.

"Morty made it clear he never wanted to farm," said Jack. "I stand with Morty. If he thinks the memorial grove isn't the right direction for the farm, then he's the eldest man for making decisions now. He's smart."
Honora said, "I'm tired of listening. My face and frozen hands hurt, and I'm exhausted."

"I'm not leaving," said Morty. "I'd like to build a cabin for Bertha and me to live in on this land."

"How's that again?" screeched Honora like a broken saw. Her voice was shrill, and Nell never remembered it having a sting like this for Morty. Again, there was that sharp, stabbing tone in Honora's wail. "You're trying to receive your eighth-grade certificate. Why bother? I'm twenty-four, and you're still twenty-two. I won't be left behind as an old maid."

An aching silence fell over the room like a heavy blanket. Honora's fists were still balled on her hips. "I beg to differ about the grove. You boys owe this to Da. Why are you stubborn?"

Morty pleaded, "It's nothing against Da's idea of planting his legacy nor his declaration of peace to the Warings. It's not my dream. That's all. Why call it a memorial for Malcolm when we've got Bud or someone watching us down the length of his gun barrel? The Warings don't want it. We've got plenty to do. We're barely eking out a living."

How can they think about leaving Ma?
Nell bit her lip.
I saw how Ma struggled in the cornfield.
Jack stood up beside Morty.
Honora widened her stance. "Da planned for future lumber and nut harvesting for our inheritance, plus, a memorial to bring peace between us and the Warings."

With fists clenched, Morty hollered, "Criminy! And Bud or someone from the Warings is out there with his gun barrel glinting behind the brush for the next sixty years. Maybe you want to put up with that?"

"We're assuming it's Bud. I don't want to take his side, but I want Da's wishes honored. That's all," said Honora.

Keep breathing in and out.

"What about asking Martin or Edmond's opinion?" inquired Morty. "They'd plant corn or wheat on the entire ridge."

Honora glared.

"School always starts late." Morty stood firm. "After eleven-hour days on the two-horse plow last spring, and now the hardships farming without Da? My decision's made."

Family contention grew at the end of that first winter. Nell's frown increased the more she thought about Honora and Morty.

Who does Honora think she is? Not perfect, for sure.

Unable to hold her tongue, Nell joined the squabble night after night, sometimes on Honora's behalf, and then she'd turn tail and be on Morty's.

Morty must know we need him? That Morty. One more mention of Bertha.

Nell's fists balled up.

I've had a bellyfull. And Honora, I stand up for Da's legacy more than she does.

"Listen, children. We'll need to work together. These frigid days aren't for planting anything," said Ma.

Their bickering gave Nell plenty of chances to practice slow, careful breathing. She'd wheeze at any reminder of Da's death or uncertainty about who in her family might leave next.

My breathing's better. My ribs don't hurt. It's been cold, so long. I will get strong enough for school. For Da.

Ma told Bill Drew's mother that her former days of housekeeping and sharing the newspaper belonged in ancient times.

How many times a day have I heard her pray?

"Help us to conserve, Lord." Ma often whispered, "My dearest Michael, how you lessened the load." For now, Ma made ends meet and taught Nell at home.

A gray fog lingered around the homestead. Da didn't want them to "blink water," but how could they adjust without Da? Morty said his schoolwork suffered with the farmwork, but he must graduate. Nell listened as Edmond's questioning letters were read aloud, creating more tension about the grove and farming. Ma wrote to Edmond about what a big responsibility the younger boys shouldered. She asked Michael Junior to come home at Christmas. When the day grew long, she and Nell would be off to the fields with the crockery pitcher and a plate of baked goods for the workers.

~~**~~**~~**~~

"I'm thankful you boys learned many skills from Da," said Ma.

But, Ma, don't forget. We need them here, and Morty needs to forget his engagement plans. Nell stomped her foot. The idea of working full-time in timber. Breathe in and out through my nose and have peaceful thoughts.

"When Junior returns from Kansas, he'll have gained more experience farming. With him turning twenty, he'll be ready to lead." Morty stoked the fire. "I miss him. We all do. I'm counting down the days until Christmas when he arrives at the depot."

***~~**~~**~~**~~

The cold December day arrived, and throughout the evening, Junior's vivid tales of Kansas warmed the cabin.
"I sure miss Mary-Jane, Kate, Edmond, and Martin." Jack shook his head with fond memories.
"They're doing well. They called me Uncle Mike or Mike. No more Junior."
"Welcome home, Mike," cooed Honora. "That sounds good, Mike. Plain Mike, no more Junior."

Mike told them all about the day-to-day happenings on the frontier land in Kansas. He added to the stories each night.
"Picturing all four of them on the same road together comforts me," said Ma. "Tell us again. Every detail about all you remember. It helps relieve our despair and bridge the separation since Da died."

"That's a dry old country around Wichita. Driving those cattle up from Texas has made it a boomtown. It's tough farming out that way. But it's sure growing." Mike's voice purred like Da's. He shared enough to satisfy each family member's longings. The shy fellow told them all

160

about little quirks of loved ones they'd never met. He made them laugh. "Nell, you've sure grown. Your breathing's better."

"I'm learning to read and write," said Nell.

Mike doesn't think of me as a runt. Maybe the others'll stop. I can catch up.

Morty announced, "I forgot to mention I visited with Doc Simpkins at the train station about Mike's travels to Kansas. Doc said he traveled across that country. He said he'd stop out in the spring, but to let him know if anyone needed him for anything any sooner."

I don't want Ma to have to pay Doc. I can do this.

"I'm all the more convinced that I've made the right decision to go into logging," said Morty. "I know it's the right time to marry Bertha. I'm glad we'll both have finished our education."

Fingering the baby blanket in her lap, Ma said, "To make up for Da's absence this Christmas, I won't drop store candy down through the loft floorboards, but the girls and I made sorghum taffy and popcorn balls."

They enjoyed the season, and one holiday afternoon, Nell got a chance to try again at making a friend with Gertrude.

"Gertie helped me with my spelling. She taught me the letter *p*. Popcorn, pitcher, purty, and poor."

"What made her think of those particular words?" Ma released an appreciative sigh.

"Da said, 'purty.' 'Member, Ma?"

Oh, I hope Ma remembers.

Gathering Nell into her arms, Ma said, "Yes, I recall the night Da died. I remember he said the crows might have taken your ring. They liked purty things, and we're lucky they didn't fly away with you."

"I know I'm puny. But I'll always help you tote the water pitcher."

"Puny? Phooey! You're catching up. Remember what Mike said."

"Gertie said we're poor."

"Poor? Wrong. Never say that." Ma's jaw muscles tightened. "Do you have two arms? Two legs? Eyes? Ears? That's not poor. Da told me something special at your birth." Ma's voice was soft.

Nell's head jerked up from her slate.

"He said that if someone that small lives, then God must have a mighty purpose to complete. He thinks you'll be able to hold on."

I've no idea what Da meant, but it sounds capable and not needy.

Ma and Nell celebrated with store-bought cookies that Mike purchased in Kansas. They dunked them in red root tea with milk. "I can't fathom all your reading improvement. You'll soon be through these two old primers. We'll finish. I'll make cookies to rival these store-bought ones for big words."

"Let's work on your 'g' sounds. Like ginger and Gertie." Ma made a game of it. She asked Nell, "What's a word that ends with 'g'? Here's a clue. It's a missing object."

"My ring-guh!" shouted Nell, emphasizing the "guh" sound.

When the cold winds quit howling, Ma reminded Nell they'd take a summer break. "Let's learn your '*h's*.' Huh, huh, huh! Help. Help on the walnut grove."

I'll find my ring. Da must have meant I have a purpose like Mary-Jane and Kate do. But Da, there's no more land on their road in Kansas.

CHAPTER 15
Holding On

As spring storms intensified, so did the children's tempers. Ma said, "We must count our blessings. We own this land. I promised Da we'd hold on to his inheritance."

Known for her usual, good composure, Honora continued quarreling with Morty. "We're sure to lose the place like the neighbors did if you keep griping about the equipment and the unfinished barn. Wait until winter's over. Then plant crops, and the barn will come."

"Then *you'll* finish planting the memorial grove? With all your washing and mending?" asked Morty. "Maybe you'll see the emptiness in having a grove?"

"I won't give up on it, ever." Honora punched her fist at the air. "I've got plenty to do, but I'll add that to my list. With all the grumbling we have inside, maybe that's what we need?"

"What about Nell?" asked Morty. "Can you imagine the trouble she'll cause?"

With her teeth jutting out like a panther's, Nell wanted to growl, but she saw Ma turning from the stove. "Ma, you're limping," said Nell. "Is your hip hurting again? Do you need your cane?"

Honora rubbed Ma's back and legs. "We'll let her rest," whispered Honora. "Let's have a look at the grove. Ma needs quiet time. The wispy, little saplings are budding. This long winter without Da is over. Let's see. Did any of his saplings take? He rooted them deep in their holes."

"Maybe the male bluebirds are out? We'll see them swooping through the two rows about as high as the fence posts." Honora turned to the window. "Oh, look." "They're back." Nell gasped. She stood motionless at the window. They watched their bright blue feathers flitter over the gray fields, weaving their way around the Proverb tunnels. Nell pushed through the front door. She skipped along, with knees high, up, down, and around the tunnels after the fluttering blue wings, saplings stretched in rows from the steamy soil. Nell spread her arms wide.

~~**~~**~~**~~

One late March evening, with the sun well below the ridge, Nell sat on a stump, petting Zeke. As the afternoon grew late, she waited beside the road for school to be out. "Here they come." Zeke purred. Nell's eyes flashed with curiosity at how her brother's faces would look at the unmistakable ring of hammers. She dropped Zeke. She held her hands behind her back. "You'll never guess."
Their uncles Willie, James, and Patrick waved.

"They arrived early today with Charles McMinn, a hired hand from town. He's a stocky, red-haired man. Seems slow on his feet, and not that handy," said Nell.
"Oh, goodness, the barn." Morty whispered his thanks. "At last our nightmares are over." The uncles and Charles remained late into the evening. They continued to work long days on the barn with the boys at school. They returned on weekends.

Things are better.
Nell's mouth went slack.
The barn's almost built. The crops are greening up. The grove?

Chattering about the hundreds of walnuts she'd been planting everywhere, Nell frolicked back and forth across the rows.
"This is important. Please be quiet, Nell," Honora hissed. "I want to hear any tips the boys may've learned from Da on the grove."
I need to learn how to do it too.
Honora listened. She scowled at Nell. "Please sit still. If you keep demanding your own way, you'll always be behind, alone, and unable to make ends meet."
I'm tired of always hearing my shortcomings.

Nell's lower lip swallowed her upper lip. She crossed her arms over her chest and stomped her feet. "I've got my own ideas."
"Fine. But stop digging so close to my rows," said Honora. "Only the biggest ones make it."
I'm plum full of Honora. Doesn't she see how hard I'm working?
Nell planted like a feverish squirrel.
She thinks she's my boss. But I do love the soil on my hands. The breeze and the sun on my face.

"Time to help Ma, inside." Before leaving, Honora surveyed her plantings. Hands folded behind her back, she towered over her rows.
She resembles Da. If only pipe smoke circled her face.

Nell snorted.

Honora's foolish if she thinks I'm only searching for my birthday ring. My rows look good too. Who does she think she is, visiting with that Charles? Ha! I bet she wants a suitor? Then she can marry before Bertha does. Nell squealed at her little rows. She bent one knee into a high skip over the little saplings and nuts she'd planted. *Even if they're imperfect.*

~~**~~**~~**~~

"Hello to the house." That first spring and summer vanished without Da. Doc's gentle voice called, "Hello to the house."

Honora and Nell were coming around the cabin. Above them, a few leaves were turning yellow. Nell spun around to head back to the ridge.

"Oh, no you don't. We've gotten all washed up at the well. You're going to see Doc." Honora dragged Nell through the grass beside the cabin. "You heard me, young lady. Be quiet. Let's allow Ma a couple of minutes to visit with Doc. Sit down here by the window." Honora held Nell with a tight grip. They scooted closer to the open window.

"Aye, Sadie, you're squinting." They could hear Doc's barrel of a voice. They listened hard for Ma's reply.

"I have only a few spectacles with me today. If none of these work I'll bring some more next time," said Doc. "It'll make reading and all kinds of things better."

"It's not that." Ma's voice rose. "I'm concerned for Nell. She's been angry. All the bickering. Her breathing's still keeping her from school. She's fourteen years old. Her behavior's a drain on all of us. She was doing so much better before …."

Honora clamped the palm of her hand over Nell's screech. She held Nell down.
Is Ma talking about me? Ma thinks I'm ornery. Doesn't she still love me?
Nell twisted and turned.
What difference does my orneriness make? Hasn't Ma noticed how I'm trying to breathe better?

"Grief makes some people show anger," said Doc. "Her breathing and bronchospasms may be made worse by the heavy precipitation, which makes her more susceptible to every sickness that comes around. When you don't feel well, sometimes you don't act well. In her life, she's going to have to learn to cope."
"Sometimes it seems like her behavior isn't all about her breathing problems. I know you saw a variety of cases in the goldfields, and you may not have experience with this problem, but I'd like to mention something I fret over."

"Yes, Sadie Jane."
"I hate to say this, but what can I do if her prickliness drives family away? Have you heard of this before?"
Doc clomped across the parlor's plank floor. "No, my dear Sadie. I don't have experience with that." His clomping stopped. "Why, there's a linen over the picture on your wall."

"Yes, Doc. It's the portrait of Michael and me." Ma explained. "The grief has been heavy for Nell. We covered it to soften the blow."

"Da, such a fine man. An honor to have called him friend. Morty mentioned your oldest girl's at her wit's end."
"Yes." The only sound was Ma's sniffles.
"It's going to take all of you to keep this farm going. But I hope that Nell will outgrow her former ways in time," said Doc. "She'll pull her weight."
Silence from Ma.

"Do you still put the pine tar in the steam bath for Nell?"
"I do." Ma's voice sounded strained.
"I've got an alternative for that stinky, old pine tar," said Doc." Let's try camphor. In addition, I'd like her to drink a cup of black coffee to open her airways. Not a bland cup. Make it strong."
"Camphor in her steam baths? Okay." Ma agreed. "I'd be obliged to enjoy the cup of black coffee with her."

"Excellent. These feelings of rejection caused by family members' absence lessen her ability to contribute to the home. But, as she matures, we'll see. Something tells me that if too many more of your sons leave, it'll be difficult to make ends meet here. She needs to develop skills and confidence." Doc cleared his throat. "An idea's occurred to me. My patients tell me how you help folks in this community with their ability to read."

"Why, yes." Ma's voice brightened.

"I visited with Mr. Skile's replacement. I learned of her favorite book. It's *David Copperfield*, by Charles Dickens. She plans to read it aloud to her students. I've sorted out a dusty shelf in my office. Are you interested in this raggedy old copy of *David Copperfield*? It was never far from me, while at the goldmines."

"Oh, my yes, I'd love to read it," Ma gushed. "Years back, I read about Charles Dickens, the author of the book. He toured St. Louis. I am not sure he liked the prairie much. He'd have liked it up here in Shawnee Township in the trees."

"David Copperfield loses his father at an early age. Great turmoil ensues, but he overcomes his worries and fears with grand success. Like Nell, he feels rejected and abandoned by close family members. Please consider an evening reading group, with a few friends to read with."

"I've got Luella Coffman just begging me to read a chapter book," said Ma.

"Yes. In Nell's case, if she receives a double dose of the story, her confidence in school may increase. It'll show that conflict is everywhere, but *David Copperfield* succeeds, with no family or parents and in terrible conditions. And yet, he's hopeful, in spite of his fears and rejections."

"My fingers are trembling to turn the pages." Ma held the book over her heart. "My prayers are answered, Doc."

"Sadie Jane, Nell has strengths, but the weaknesses attract all the attention. The Dickens' book will improve attitude, grammar, and vocabulary. Shall I speak with her now?"

The cabin door opened with a bang. Honora held the latch with one hand. The other hand was clamped around Nell's hair as she tugged her through the front door. Loud snarls and thumps came from Nell. She fumed and pounded her heels across the threshold in Honora's iron-like grip.

"Get your hands off me," Nell griped.

Boy, I'll get you for this, Honora.

"Girls, stop this quarrel. Come inside."

With a few more heel thumps and howls, Honora led Nell into the cabin.

"Ah, yes." Doc beamed. "A course of physique training to build up those lungs." Doc dug into his bag. He produced a jump rope. Eyes popping wide-open, Ma checked her new spectacles.

"You won't tie me up with rope," Nell hollered.

With a gnash of her teeth, Honora plunked Nell on a chair by Doc. "What a great idea for someone intent on the demise of the walnut grove."

Nell's claws flew. "How dare you? You think you're better than me?"

I care about that memorial grove as much as you do.

Doc stretched his hands out. "Please, please, Nell. Calm down. I have a new prescription. If you follow it, I won't need to visit again."

"I don't set by that stinky pine tar." Nell howled.

Good riddance. I've seen enough of Doc anyway.

"Nell," Ma chided. "Hold your tongue."

Doc rummaged in his satchel. "I've been to new training in Chicago to learn about better ways to treat breathing. I've got a replacement for pine tar."

Doc cares about me when he's in Chicago?

Nell's mouth hung open. Her curiosity got the best of her.

"To train the physique with breath control is something to be accomplished over time, if added to everyday routines. It increases a restful night. It builds up the patient's lungs. Work leads to health."

"I work in the grove," Nell offered.

"Excellent. You must complete chores each day that other girls your age accomplish. In addition, you will drink a cup of coffee every afternoon and apply the new breathing salve."

Nell looked down her nose at her dirty bare feet, but her eyes leaped right back to Doc's face.

"Reading is important to your Ma's dreams for her children. Your Da was one of the most inventive men I've ever met. There are many distinct kinds of 'wisdoms.' School is part of my prescription, along with extra books."

Chin high, Nell didn't miss a word.

"You're familiar with the new teacher, Bertha Webber?"

Nell grinned. "Mr. Skiles is gone?" *Oh, mercy.*

"In this situation, with family members who move far away, and at your age of fourteen," Doc's whole body bobbed in the affirmative, "it's a hard-boiled cure that forming relationships with peers will decrease anxieties."

~~**~~**~~**~~

The neighbors became regulars at the after-dinner read aloud. No one missed a chapter of *David Copperfield*. A discussion followed the readings. Ma called on each one. "Fred, why did *David Copperfield* begin reading books?"

"The at-must-fear was controlled by Mr. Murdstone," Nell shouted.

"Atmosphere."

"Yes. Reading comforted him with his unhappy home life." Nell bounced high off of her chair. "Reading gave him a chance to dip into other people's lives and took his mind off his worries."

"I have one more question." Ma's face flushed. "It's Luella's turn. Why did *David Copperfield* feel ambushed?"

Nell blurted out right over the top of Luella. "Mr. Murdstone stood over him with a cane. Furious over Davy's bad grammar, he trapped him." Nell's gravel-like voice smoothed out. "Nobody's gonna trap me. I'll take a bite out of 'em."

The group burst into laughter.

"Yes, true enough, Nell. Thanks for your contributions. We'll start the next chapter on Monday." Ma's smile spread across her face. She waved good-bye to the reading group.

A piece of paper crinkled in Ma's pocket. "Listen to this."

Dear Mrs. Glisson,

Nell is a fervent listener of David Copperfield. She no longer bullies other students. She raises her hand. Her listening skills are so advanced that I believe she will catch up on things she's missed. We still need to work on her outbursts, but I'm tickled with her progress.

Sincerely,

Miss Webber

"Every time I read it, I'm overcome with joy." Ma clasped Nell in her arms.
This is important. Ma's proud of me.
Nell's arms tightened around Ma's neck.
This is my best day since Da died. I'm not feeling any breathing problems. I'm sure my orneriness will be gone forever.

CHAPTER 16
The Last Decade of the 1800s

Peeking over the bush, Nell glimpsed Honora, who was now twenty-five years old.

Miss Webber said we're soon starting the last decade of the 1800s. There'll be lots of changes in the 1900s. The twentieth century.

Honora weeded and pruned the saplings' lowest branches late into the afternoon. In the humid air, the saplings on the memorial grew straight, tall, and with a perfect crown on top. Nell ducked back down out of Honora's view. She snatched Zeke up close.

I hate to give Honora too much credit, but she does work on the ridge. She cares for Da's dream too.

The sun pierced the late spring evening's clouds. Since it was late in the day, Jack stopped to chat with Honora. "The boys are plain tuckered out, but I've got more energy." He circled his fists with a flourish at an imaginary opponent.

With a long sigh, Honora's shoulders fell. "I need time to think. Nell's behavior improves, but she still bickers. Will her feistiness ever end? I'm afraid she hates me. She acts so rotten, like she wants me to fail. I'm older. I don't hold to Ma's babying her."

They don't think I can hear them, but I can.

Shuffling around shadowboxing, Jack circled back to Honora. Honora's forehead creased. The corners of her mouth turned down. "Ma's worried we might crush

Nell's spirit. I dwell on how much some of her spirits *need* to be crushed."

Do you think my spirits need crushing? Maybe yours does?

Nell stuck her tongue out.

"What about if I take her in the boxing ring to wear her out a little?" offered Jack.

"That bony thing?" Honora grunted. "Do you know how scrawny she is? Her arms are as thin as the feeblest saplings are."

"Not weak, though," said Jack. "She needs skills to fight, combined with her fierce attitude. That jump rope Doc recommended will make her stick legs strong. She flies through the air with it."

"She needs work on being kinder, not how to knock someone's front teeth out."

"You two sisters are nothing alike. You're the best sister ever. You're even nice to that Charles."

Of course, Honora's the best. She's always been everyone's favorite. Perfect. Darn Jack.

Nell put her fingers in her ears. She made herself smaller.

"That's what I want to talk about, Jack. Please don't compare us. Nell doesn't need it. As far as Charles is concerned, why, he's a grown man, not a boy. He enjoys fun, not work, work, work."

"You've got that right. But Nell's behavior worsens every time we lose a family member." He bit his bottom lip. "Let's hope she doesn't wear us all out. Poor Ma."

What?

Nell dropped Zeke.

They haven't seen me wear them out, yet. What do they mean? At least, Ma knows I'll never leave her. It'll take the whole family to save the walnuts. I aim to keep the others from leaving.

"Isn't that right, Zeke?"
Robert Coffman and Ma were nearby on the cart path. Nell ran to Ma to tattle. She wiggled between them, trying to interrupt them.
"Yes, we're having better yields," said Robert. "Our land's flatter, with many fewer hills than here. There are not any forests nearby."
"Quite a difference," Ma agreed.

Interested, Nell paused to listen to Mr. Coffman.
"My cabin's rented to a young man, Pete Daniels. He's from the ag college. Pete loves hiking in these forests. He spends nights exploring the wilderness nearby. He made a friend, Bill Drew. He enjoys his harmonica.
"Bill shared details about the local farmers, and that your family saved many of their hardwoods. Bill told him how close he is to your family. Pete's studying to become a professor. His work includes research for the Illinois legislature. The legislature is considering a law to grant tax money to farmers growing trees."

~~**~~**~~**~~

Nell's laughter scattered across the farmyard. "Honora, swing me around." Nell sprang from right to left foot. Streams of lush summer light sparkled on the two girls in their long dresses. They squinted in the brightness

177

after taking shelter in the barn from a downpour. Steamy cornfields surrounded them to the east and south.

"Honora, try to punch me. Please. A few more times? Watch me slip away from you." Nell bobbed and weaved from side to side. "That's what Jack taught me. It takes practice."

Nell begged Honora to hit her hands with her fists. "Please try it." Hands spread, she turned away each of Honora's punches first a left, a right, followed by the puny girl jabbing her right fist into her big sister's shoulder. "Let me at you," crowed Nell.

"Are your chores done?"

"I'm almost fifteen. You don't need to check on me."

Clasping her under her arms, Honora got behind Nell. She swung her around and around in the midday air. "We're all grateful for Doc's new prescription," said Honora. "There have been plenty of arguments between you and me, but it's a relief to have a moment to enjoy you. You're still so tiny."

"Fun. Do it again. Swing me into the sky."

Will she ever stop calling me tiny?

"Honora, don't hurry it so much." Nell pleaded.

She's got plenty of time for that Charles but what about me?

~~**~~**~~**~~

In the fall, Nell turned fifteen. She struggled to be more like Honora. "My size makes me look like a little kid.

178

Please talk to Ma about my still having to spend the hot afternoons inside. Blah. Black coffee."

"We need to follow Doc's orders," said Honora. "Let's pick peaches for Ma's pies. That'll be a treat with your coffee."

"Aw, Honora!" Nell stomped her bare foot in the wet, tingly grass. "I *am* following his orders."

I'm not a baby.

"Nell, you remain on the ground, and I'll hand them down. I don't want them to bruise. This will be Ma's first crop of any size. Be careful."

"Yes, Mr. Murdstone." Nell enjoyed *David Copperfield* so much that it crept into her conversations.

"After this, we'll go right in." Honora ignored any complaints. "Ma will be excited to slice them. I'll make the pie crust."

"Okay, Peggoty-Pie."

On this hot, humid afternoon after the short thunderstorm, they sought relief from the sweaty dampness. The sky brightened. The rain smelled fresh on the wet grass. The thunderclouds churned away to the north. The last hint of a rainbow disappeared.

"I'll get the highest, ripest ones. I'm taller, and my arms are longer. Pick only the low-hanging ones. Don't go above the crotch of that tree. Hear?" Honora chided.

If only I could, I'd scurry right up there.

Too afraid to climb, Nell kicked her feet off the ground, pushing off the split trunk. She grabbed a branch. She placed her feet back on the ground.

Boss, boss, as if this is the workhouse.
"Imagine the taste of a fresh peach pie if you can?" said Honora. "How good of a job the new stove's going to do. Bubbly peach pie, fresh from the oven. It'll be perfect." Honora plucked a rosy-colored ripe peach. "Aah, better check if they're flavorful." She sank her teeth into its fuzzy, cool skin. "Oh, they're so sweet and juicy. Yum."

Both girls sampled the sugary fruit. The trees sparkled with the recent raindrops. Nell regarded her beautiful big sister.
She's so pretty, sitting among the branches, with the juice running down her chin.
Swallowing the sweet nectar, Honora stood on a limb. She reached for a sagging branch. "They're so delicious. Nothing quenches your thirst on a hot August day like a bite of a ripe scrumptious peach."

"Uh, excuse me." A stranger appeared beside Nell, standing under the canopy of Honora's peach tree. Nell hid behind some leaves. The man's voice startled Honora.
He glanced up. "Why, hello. Mrs. Glisson?"
"Oh! You scared me!" Honora scrambled for a thicker bough to steady herself. The thin peach tree swayed. Slippery, wet branches surrounded her. Honora lost her footing. The man stepped forward. He put his arms around Honora to support her before she tumbled out.

"Oh, my! Pardon me. Ma's inside. "Uh, the boys are mowing the southeast pasture," stammered Honora, dabbing the sweet juice on her face.

"Pardon *me* for startling you." He set her down. "I'm Pete Daniels. I'm a graduate student from West-Central Illinois Agricultural College. My research is on fruit and nut production." He stood out, tall and lanky. Pete wore glasses, and his hair was so blond that it appeared to be white.

Biting the side of her bottom lip, Nell couldn't take her eyes off of Honora.
Why's she so careful? Look at her pick her way through the long grass. She's proud of her pretty ruffles. Her sticky hands are hidden behind her back.
Nell frowned at her and snatched up her cat.
"I've become acquainted with a friend of your family's, Bill Drew." Pete followed Honora like a kitten. "I rent the cabin at Robert Coffman's."

"Uh-huh." Honora, who sounded like Ma, nodded. Nell's eyebrows shot up on her forehead.
Honora can't talk. Her face's so red that she's going to choke on that big bite of peach in the side of her mouth. Is there something in her eye? She keeps batting her eyelashes.
"I'm a student too," offered Nell.
"What college?" Pete laughed, reaching out to pet Zeke. "What a nice cat."
"Oh, never mind. He doesn't want you petting him." Nell cleared her throat in an attempt to alleviate her coarse voice.

Honora's beautiful smile dazzled in the sunlight like it did around Charles, Uncle Willie's hired hand.

Smoothing her hair down, Ma drew near from the cabin. "Good afternoon. I'm Mrs. Sadie Glisson."

"Pleased to meet you, Mrs. Glisson," said Pete. "I'm Pete Daniels from the ag college. This is a busy time with your crops, but it looks like a good year for fruit-and-nut production. I'm assigned to fieldwork."

"We do our own fieldwork." Nell's voice sounded loud and harsh. "What's *produkshun?*"

"Inside, Nell." Ma smiled at Pete. "Honora, we'll rest, and then *we'll* finish the peaches. Why don't you take Pete for a tour?"

"Thank you," said the graduate student. "I appreciate your hospitality, Mrs. Glisson. Thank you for your daughter's time to show me your land."

With the look in Ma's eyes, I'd better get inside.

Nell grimaced.

~~**~~**~~**~~

Soon the sound of Ma's soft snoring came from her chair. Nell crept back outside.

I'll hide and listen for Honora's voice.

She heard Pete say, "What an interesting land choice your father made. The trees flourish."

"Yes, that tree by the drive is what led Da to turn his wagon up this road." Honora tipped her head back. She peered overhead. "I'm so happy he picked this place."

"Ah, now I understand why the farmers didn't clear more of this wilderness. It's pretty here."

They walked side by side out to the ridge. Honora's brown hair caught the rays of sunbeams. Nell observed the scene filtered through leaves.

Look at the way Honora's arms swing. She thinks she's done everything herself.

"Is this Peace Ridge, Honora?" He scanned over the ridge that stretched and cleaved the southwest view all the way to the horizon, lined with trees.

Silence.

"Yes. My Da brought his walnut inheritance from Ireland. Before his brothers discarded theirs, he put all three of them as padding around his fiddle." Her skirts brushed the tips of grass blades. "These trees are a mixture of my grandfather's walnuts and the native ones here in Shawnee Township. Da picked them up everywhere, and each pocket contained at least one. Folks laughed at Da because he saved them and then planted saplings. My mother collected walnuts throughout these woods. She met Da here. He always said her black-walnut cake, oatmeal-nut cookies, and dried-apple turnovers with nuts were the best."

"I'm wondering about a memorial grove, which is a tribute to a young man who died nearby. A neighbor informed me it was out here somewhere?"

Through her long, thick eyelashes, Honora nodded.

They dropped the subject.

"Aren't these English walnuts," inquired Pete. He fingered their important characteristics, with the leaves laddering up the twigs and the green nuts.

Honora said, "My Da wanted to cross different trees. He called it grafting."

"Aha! Brilliant." He bent down and touched the slender trunks.

That's it.

Nell crashed through the brush. "Honora, what about the pie crusts? Do they roll themselves?"

I'm going to get rid of this man if it's the last thing I do.

~~**~~**~~**~~

Seizing his sketchbook, Pete squinted and grinned at the walnut mansions. The big logs were wide enough to stand on, and about twelve feet remained.

"All the kids rolled the logs across the ground and pushed them together until they formed squares for rooms. See the openings for doorways?" asked Nell.

"This land's like a park," affirmed Pete.

Boy, wouldn't Da have appreciated that?

Nell sneaked another peek at Pete.

He can't be all bad if he likes our mansions.

Skipping from room to room, Nell was delighted that a future professor took the time to sketch their mansions.

"Choose any room. My Da said there won't be any 'no-trespassing' signs on his land."

"Signs are all over west of here." Pete scratched his head. "Ah, I forgot to tell Honora something. A young man, a descendant of a former slave, mentioned his mother holed up in a place with logs formed into rooms on the ground."

"What? A slave? That can't be. Sounds like how some people were treated in *David Copperfield*."

"Worse, I'm afraid. Tomorrow, we should quiz each other on what we love about that book." Pete smiled at Nell. "The name of the young man I met is Asa Reynolds. His mother escaped from Kentucky. I met him at the cabin I rent. His mother told him how she camped in logs on the ground formed into rooms, like a child's playhouse. I bet she followed this ridge from the south until she got to your mansions."

Wait 'til I tell Honora.
Nell gave a low whistle.
Pete's stories are exciting. He likes David Copperfield.
"I wonder if she ever thought about coming back here?" Pete took in everything.
I doubt she would want to stay here by herself at night.
Nell shivered.
If I was her, I'd run.

"When the weather turned too cold, Asa's mother found Robert Coffman's cabin, and then continued on to the Underground Railroad. I live in the cabin now."

"On the railroad? Underground?"

"No, Nell. Years ago, it meant a secret place where slaves would be safe. Sometimes they hid in wagons with false bottoms. This runaway slave bore a son, Asa, at the cabin I rent. He works in this area where he was born. Years ago, your Ma helped his mother in birthing. Your Ma's like a hero to him, helping someone on their way to the Underground Railroad."

This Pete has taken a real shine to us.

Nell's black eyes popped open as big as walnuts. "I've missed quite a bit of schooling. But I'm catching up. I never met no Asa. A peace offering for Malcolm Waring is part of what my Da sought. His dream was to have this become a nut grove. He wanted the trees to be spacious and in nursery rows."
"It's too bad he didn't finish."
"He hoped one of my brothers would do it. Honora's trying to help. Me too."
"Peace? Why, wasn't a man killed here?"
"Near here." Nell nodded. "But Cahoots, my white kitty, died on this spot."
My sweet kitty. I wish Malcolm wouldn't have died on our land.

"I'm sorry that happened, Nell."
"I've got Zeke now. There's been someone in the brush with a gun. I help plant trees. I take seven big running jumps for the English walnuts. But, oh boy, for the blackies, I take about twelve jumps! Honora said it's the right way." Nell's light hair rippled up behind her.
I'll show him the way to measure.

~~**~~**~~**~~

The next morning, Pete came to the cabin. "Mrs. Glisson, your daughters made my time here most enjoyable. Thank you for the hospitality and wonderful pie."
Tucking her hair into her bun, Sadie Jane said, "I hope nothing's wrong. You're not going to camp here tonight?"

"I would've liked to. The mansions are unique," said Pete. "My day got off to a rough start. I bumped into a man shouting and waving his gun around for me to leave the property. He warned me not to return. I'll let him cool off. I'll be back."

~~**~~**~~**~~

That night, Nell talked Honora's ear off. "That college man better keep his promise. He said we'd talk about *David Copperfield*. He loved the mansions and knows a slave girl's son, Asa Reynolds."
"Pete's nice." Honora smiled. "I'll bet he'll be back."
"He's my friend too," scowled Nell.

Those blasted Warings.
Nell sighed.
I might be the puniest and the feistiest, but I'm ready to keep this family together. What land are they after? Honora says she's not sure it was Bud. Stephen, the Warings' foreman, isn't nice. He could've been involved in Malcolm's death. I'll join Jack in the boxing ring tomorrow. I'll be ready to run anyone off who bothers Pete again. I'll find the man with the gun. He won't want to tangle with me. The legislature is considering a law to grant tax money to farmers growing trees. It must have something to do with the coming twentieth century?

CHAPTER 17
Morty's Plans

"Ma, we got word from Kansas." Morty slapped the envelope on the porch railing. "Edmond Glisson, Wichita. I don't expect this is another letter to check on corn and hog prices. It's been almost three years since Da died. Wouldn't we be amazed if he moved his entire family back here?"

Scraping the last of the scraps and milk into Zeke's bowl, Nell listened.

Edmond return? Oh, Edmond. I want to find a way to keep us all together. Of course, we'd get along.

"I don't know, with Lizzie in the family way. It would be hard to uproot the children," said Ma. "You did right, though, to write to him and inquire about his interest. I'm not surprised by the questions he's asked regarding the family. How would we get along with a sister-in-law and nieces and nephews underfoot? Nell's almost sixteen years old."

Ma always puts others' feelings in front of hers.

Nell's eyes lit on Ma's face.

It's strange that she worries about us all. We'll get along. Me? I'll be easy to get along with.

"We'll work it out." Morty hugged Ma.

Ma patted Morty's shoulder, "I agree. Nell won't know what to think if Edmond returns."

Even if Edmond returns, I want Morty to stay too. He says Mike and Jack are strong, capable, and trustful.

Nell shrugged.

He doesn't say any of these things about me.

"What would you think about us building a cabin for Bertha and me? Fall's arriving soon," remarked Morty. "It'd be good to learn from Uncle Willie. Like Da, he loves to do the joinery on log cabins."
"Wonderful," said Ma. "Da would've loved the idea."
"We've got the fieldwork caught up. We could work with Uncle Willie and Charles who is still unemployed. He accepted Willie's room and board." Morty stood tall. "This'll be an important addition to the homestead and get Charles off his duff to boot."

But we need Morty around here.
Nell sauntered around behind the cabin.
Bertha, I won't allow you to take Morty from farming. If Edmond comes back, maybe the others will follow. Honora and Pete love to explore the forest. They choose trees for the grove. They don't plant many of Da's seeds on the ridge.
Nell ambled down the cart path and into the forest.
She listened for their voices. *They don't need me. I thought Pete liked me? Why don't they plant more of the three gunnysacks of walnut seed? Morty doesn't say anything when he hears Honora's giggles in Charles's company.*

My breathing's okay even with chores.
Nell kicked a rock in the dusty road.
They're all so busy. The older kids always helped me before. Now I'm on my own.

She tramped around the homestead, scuffing her shoes in the dust. There was a snore from Ma's rocking chair on the porch in the warm afternoon. Nell tiptoed away. *I've got to find my family.*

Jack's homemade boxing ring was empty.
The boys must've joined the neighborhood children as they flocked to the swimming pond to cool off. I want in on the fun.
Nell frowned.
Another humdrum day. They left me out again. Bertha can't have Morty all to herself. I'll fix her.

~~*~*~~*~*~~*~*~~

Excited voices drifted up from the pond.
"Yeah, want to see me swim across?"
"You can't swim that far."
"Don't bet on it!"
Whoops! Hollers! Splashes filled the air. Kids. Fun. Nell shook her fists. She peered in the direction of the swimming hole, with shouts of joy. The water looked green, cool, and deep. Foxlike, she sneaked along in the trees. Clothing draped over bushes disappeared as Nell's arm darted out. She snatched and hid the swimmers' clothes. Her brothers splashed and dunked. Everyone had a wonderful time.
What about me? They're unaware I'm here.

Three older girls ran out of the water with their arms wrapped around one another's shoulders. They searched everywhere for their clothes. The girls flung their arms out and shouted. They ducked back into the water. Morty offered to help them find their things. Small enough for him to miss her in the brush, Nell rocked back on her heels gleefully and muffled her cackle.

My own brothers don't include me. No one called for me to jump in. They didn't even offer to help me swim. Edmond would've.

On the road home from the pond, Nell plotted her next move. She spotted a familiar figure.

"Hi, Nell! How was your swim?" asked Gertie.

"My brothers have been at the swimming pond every afternoon these last few days, without me," complained Nell.

"I remember how they used to egg you on to come in and try it," gushed Gertrude. "You're still not afraid, are you? Morty's so patient. What a good brother."

"Me? Afraid? Oh, no, I've been to the pond." Nell circled her toes in the dust. "I didn't want to bother Morty skinny-dipping. He thought it was a grand old time, helping the older schoolgirls find their clothes."

I hear Ma's words in my mind. "God hates a lying tongue."

"A grand old time?" Gert's eyebrows rose high on her forehead. "Morty? Skinny- dipping with older girls? He retrieved their clothes? Did he hide them? Isn't he engaged to Miss Webber? He's crazy for Bertha."

With a shoulder flinch, as if she didn't care about Morty or the girls, Nell batted her eyelashes. She stalked away. Her story was full of holes.

Several evenings later, the black trees patterned the orange sky beyond Peace Ridge. Morty and his brothers debarked logs. Their backs were sunburned from the day's heat. Nell toted one last crock of water to the new cabin site. The brothers worked in a rhythm with their draw knives. Shavings piled up.
Tuckered from the long day and all set to go, Mike called, "Ready, Mort?"

Waving good night, Uncle Willie shouted over his shoulder, "'Tis a tight cabin for you. Excellent work. Let's keep the draw knives sharp. The bark peels back better with each log."
The wax-bottle lid between his lips, Morty nodded. "I'll be along after I seal these fresh-cut ends." He rubbed the wax into the log's rings. "This'll keep the bugs out for years to come."
The others finished their debarking and left.

Scooping up more globs of paraffin, Morty scanned the sky as a crow flew over with loud caws. He rubbed the waxy goo in deep on each log. The sun was low. Dusk approached, and shadows lengthened. When he'd finished the last one, he jumped at the arrival of his sweetheart, Bertha.
"What a treat you stopped by." He took her hands and led her to a seat of cut logs. Fireflies flitted all around them. Their bright green light reflected off Bertha's white apron. Her face was rubbed raw.

"What's wrong, Bertie?" he asked.

"I got an earful of information in town. It's in regard to skinny-dipping. I'm certain it's plain gossip. It concerns me that the older girls and you were skinny dipping at the swimming pond."
"Okay," whispered Nell from her hiding place.
Maybe we'll get rid of Bertha.

"Now, wait a minute here. We've been courting for years, and I've never skinny-dipped with any of the neighborhood girls in all that time." Morty bit his lip. Nell strained to hear. "My two brothers dunked me so many times, but I do recall them, and Nell's yellow, corn-silk head between the thick green bushes. I suspect she hid those girls' clothes. Maybe she started this rumor to hurt our engagement."
"Nell, Nell! I'm so sick and tired of her orneriness," shrieked Bertha.

The chirp of the crickets' song stopped in the daisy-sprinkled meadow.
"As one of the oldest ...."
Bertha interrupted. "I realize your family's been a credit to the community. And I've sought to improve Nell's conduct in school. She's mischievous and doesn't expect to receive any discipline for her uncontrolled behavior. She'll never change."
I don't need to be controlled.
Nell continued scheming.
I don't want my family to leave.

"What are you saying?"

Embroidered hankie in hand, Bertha blew her nose. "I've taken my time to think this over. I don't want to live here, next door to this day after day. Plus Sam Waring."
Good. Let her go.
"This is childish."
"My heart aches for my dad. Maybe he's all on whom I can rely. This rumor made me sad. I worry about your true feelings. I miss my father. He needs me in Missouri. I'll wait for you there."

"But, Bertie, our cabin." His arms fell at his sides.
She sobbed. He cupped her chin in his hand. "Don't let Nell's childish falsehoods ruin our engagement."
"This is something you need to hear. Your sister needs discipline. She'll always be an ornery old tyrant."
Oh, is she going to be sorry!

"Your father isn't all the family you have." Morty placed his hand on Bertha's knee. "You have me." The crickets' chirps paused for a brief moment. "Missouri will be good for both of us. Besides, my older brother Edmond is coming."
I can't believe my ears. Everything turned sideways.
Bertha's tears coursed down her face. "You'll go with me? Thank you, Morty. I do miss my father," she sobbed. "We'll still be together then?"
Wasn't no falsehood.

"You're a good teacher, my dearest. We'll find a new position for you in Missouri."
Wiping her eyes, Bertha dabbed her nose with her lace hankie. The crickets' chorus resumed. Zeke wound

around her ankles. "Whose cat is this? It's not a barn cat."

"Oh, no," Morty said. "If Zeke's around, then so's my sister. Nell, I know you're out here. Scat! You're not allowed to eavesdrop."

I thought so. You don't want your family, only Bertha. That must be why Bertha put me in the corner so much.

Nell spat.

You won't see me. I need to breathe so I can scream.

~~*~~**~~**~~**~~

The shiver of fall in the air, and the smell of overripe apples would forever be linked in my mind to the farewell hayrack ride for the Drew family.

The Drews' land up for sale seemed about as possible as hearing a skunk sneeze. Nell's distant memories of William Drew's walnut milk and Bill Drew's friendship tasted bittersweet.

People who never considered leaving are going.

Shawnee Township buzzed with concerned rumors regarding Sam Waring's low offer for the Drews' land.

Trying to cheat a widow lady and her children.

Nell fumed.

Sam will never win with Da's memorial to Malcolm, or they'll have me to tangle with.

"What finery for a hayrack." Honora helped Nell ready herself. "I'm glad the dress fits well." She fashioned a strip of the pretty fabric into a bow to adorn Nell's straight, blonde hair. "You're sixteen now."

The draft horses' reins were guided by Bill's delicate touch and clucking sounds. A rickety stack of hay bales towered on the rack.

The hay's stacked too high on the rack. It looks tippy.

The happy jibber-jabber of the folks already seated on the hay bales didn't relieve her tension. Her new ruffled, rust-brown dress flapped in the breeze.

"Come on, Nell," hollered Mike.

Nell didn't know where to look or go.

I don't care if my face looks mean. I might take Mike's hand, but I won't take Morty's hand, that's for sure. I won't sit up there so high off the ground.

Nell turned her back to Morty and Bertha.

Soon to be Missourians, fancy that. He mustn't have told Ma how I treated them.

Honora's regal appearance flashed beside Pete. From the woodpile, Charles McMinn's axe stopped in midair as she climbed aboard. Bill dropped the reins and sprang off the wagon. He hoisted Nell up. She stammered her thanks.

Bill greeted a stranger. "Hello, Joe. How're things at the Robertsons? Sorry about our land. I wish we could've accepted your offer. We already promised it to the Warings."

Ma seized Nell's hand. Nell tried to smile with her eyebrows woven in consternation. She squashed herself in tight between bales on the floor. Ma sat on a bale beside her.

The hayrack rumbled down the road. Everyone was in high spirits. The Drews,' some close neighbors,' the new fellow, Joe Robertson from Pea Ridge Township, and the Glissons. The colorful leaves floated down on the fall evening. The freshly scythed hay smelled so good in the cool air. The horses' hooves kept a steady rhythm.

With their arrival at the Drews everyone circled around the blazing bonfire to warm their hands. Bill's harmonica and Ma's apple pie made for a fun evening.
Bill found Nell beside the fire. "I'll remember this night all of my life. Do you remember my pap's story about the old Indian couple?"
Her teeth chattered. "It scared me to pieces."
"Did you enjoy the music? We'll go slow all the way back. We'll drop folks home. Ready to go?" Bill helped her to her feet.

On the return trip, Nell sat on the floor again. Her dress covered her ankles. Her chin rested on the backs of her hands. With her elbows between her knees, not one wheeze escaped. The old tunes spun in harmony around the well-wishers. Bill kept tabs on Nell after he'd played several refrains. "Are you comfortable? We're not too far. I hope the ride's gotten easier for you?"

Mike held the reins as the horses trotted up one rolling hill and down another. The red, yellow, and orange leaves swirled in the evening breeze. The moon silhouetted the trees in the sky.
"All those new critters in Kansas," said Mike. "Wonder what a body'll find across the river in Iowa?"

Nell let herself relax on a hay bale when a loud crack and an acrid taste of gunpowder filled the air. Rifle shots exploded in a flash of fiery red from the roadside.
Where did the bullets go? What happened?
The horses were spooked. They whinnied and nickered with the rumbling distraught pace of the wagon.
Mike's steady voice quelled the confusion. "Those were blanks, but it's a good thing we kept control of the hayrack."

With both hands clapped over her mouth, Nell sank between the hay bales. Mike paced the team, but they'd bolted far from the scene by the time he'd calmed them down to a trot. The hayrack was quiet, and Nell crouched low. The tall trees looked like scary figures bending in the breeze. Then Bill's Irish lullaby calmed the air. Jack plucked along on the fiddle.

Ma stroked Nell's hair. Her wheezes were quiet. They pulled up the steep drive home. Before Bill turned the hayrack for home, he took Nell's hand. He placed there a little nest he'd woven of grass with three, tiny, whittled eggs inside. He hugged her farewell.
The folks I care so much for are like nuts that fall from the trees in the breeze.
Nell made a tutting sound.
They let go of their roots. Roll where they will.

~~**~~**~~**~~

She tossed and kicked, trying to sleep while the bright morning sun cascaded into the loft. Nell heard Morty

and Ma downstairs. "Bertha said she saw glimmers of hope in Nell. But there were occasions when she was at her wit's end. Bertha commented that she wouldn't abide Nell's orneriness. She couldn't live here."
Straining to hear more, Nell pressed her ear to the floorboards.

"My energy runs low with her behavior." Ma fretted. "I will warn her again about her cantankerous ways. It's time to pray for the next teacher. She's never handled her feelings of abandonment. I couldn't hold her like I did the rest of you."
I'll never forgive Bertha, nor Honora. She chats with Bertha about marriage. Will it be Charles? Or Pete?
Nell felt a tightening in her stomach.
She talks to Bertha like she's her real sister.

Nell's mind wearied with the harm she'd caused Morty and Bertha.
How do I talk to them about my fears? I can't lose another brother. Memories of Mary-Jane and Kate, the boys heading West, Da dying, and Bill Drew leaving make me want to hold on to Morty more. Isn't anyone a part of my life forever? Anyone?

Chapter 18
The Boxing Ring

With a whomp, Jack sunk into a heap in the woodpile boxing ring. "Where'd that right jab come from? What do you mean, *you* need help? For a sixteen-year-old girl who resembles an eleven-year-old that's quite a wallop."

With her stiff right arm out, Nell giggled at Jack's antics. "You ran right into this."

He stuck his fist out. "Say, I'm the teacher. Ma wishes you got along with Honora and Morty. It won't be long, and they'll be married."

The old padding Jack wrapped around her head slipped into her eyes. "I don't care, and I don't want that old scratchy lamb's wool around me!" She whipped it off and threw it onto the ground. "It smells stinky!" panted Nell. "Honora said she'd take care of the walnut grove. Always."

"Shoo, have fun, and quit worrying. See? I've got padding wrapped around my head," gasped Jack. "Honora hasn't the time to plant those gunnysacks of nuts. She'll marry, like the other girls. She's fond of Pete. She always giggles with Charles McMinn."

You don't know what schemes I've got planned.
Nell shook her fists.
Honora wouldn't leave me.
"Put Uncle Willie's old gloves on. Put up your dukes. Put your chin down. You should treat Miss Webber better. What did she do? Nothing."

Nell changed the subject back to padding. "No, the newer pair. Not the one with the stuffing hanging out. That's your reason for wanting the black pair, Steerforth."

"Who in the world is Steerforth?"

"He's in *David Copperfield*. He takes the best of everything."

Like Bertha, Charles, and Pete are after my brother and sister.

Nell undid her head padding and flung it away. "I want the black pair. Nothing? Is that what you think? Bertha Webber, the favored teacher is moving to Missouri."

"You're so ornery."

"I haven't been *that* ornery. I, uh." Nell stopped and pressed her lips together.

Jack'll scoff. I won't mention how much Morty hurt me when he called me a tyrant to Mr. Skiles.

"Listen here. I'm bigger and in charge in *this* ring. So, get into your padding."

"Keep your boots on." She ran to the wash line and unpinned a feather pillow. She stuffed it under her dress. "How's this?"

Hooting with laughter, Jack practiced his footwork.

"Gertie, when did you get here?" asked Nell, surprised to see her approaching the boxing ring.

Gertie giggled as Jack pretended to pummel Nell's stomach. They all doubled over in laughter. Nell flung the pillow into Gertie's arms. "Hey, pin this back up for me."

"How've you been, Gertie? My right jab's better." Nell demonstrated with a quick punch. "Don't worry. I didn't get clobbered. I had the pillow. Aye, one good thing about being small. It's easy to twist away from Jack's punch and time the next one." She ducked under the rope. "Jack has a fancy name for twisting yourself away from the punch."

Gertie didn't ask.
"What? You mean rolling?" Jack wove around his sister. He winked at Gertie. "Uncle Willie taught us to watch our footwork. He's the one who taught quickness. Soon as your opponent cocks his elbow back. Pow!"
"Bless my soul," cooed Gertie. "I'd jump out of the way too. You look like a professional boxer."
"It takes good anticipation for a jab," said Jack. "You counter it with your hook. Bingo. A knockout."
"Are you going to become a boxer?" asked Gertie.

Nell pulled Gertie away. "Want to help whitewash the trees? It keeps the bugs from eating the bark."
"I caught Honora and Pete strolling hand in hand. They crossed the bridge downstream. Pete swung Honora up into his arms like a baby. He lifted her up on the bridge railing." Gertie's eyes sparkled.
"What's he doing that for?" gulped Nell. "Aren't they working on the grove?"

"He leaned way out over the railing as if to throw her in the water."
"He wouldn't dare," said Nell.

"Pete lifted Honora back over the rail and onto the bridge. He held her close," confided Gertie.

This feels different than the joshing around Honora does with Charles.

Nell's belly churned.

Doesn't she remember my poor health when the others left?

~~**~~**~~**~~

The saplings planted on Peace Ridge thrived with groundwater seeping around their roots. Spaced forty feet apart in anticipation of growth during the next sixty years, their limbs, like umbrella ribs, opened flat above their sturdy trunks. They appeared strong and courageous like soldiers marching in formation. A memorial for Malcolm Waring.

Nell talked Gertie into whitewashing the thicker tree trunks. They fought over the stirring stick. They sloshed the mixture on their hands, clothes, and bare feet. They laughed and played. Nell's arms encircled the bucket. "Don't waste it. Be careful. Don't step on Da's walnuts that I planted."

"What are they doing out of their rows?" asked Gertie.

The two girls dipped their brushes into the whitewash. They swished it on thick in places, hit-and-miss in others. Nell bossed Gertie. "No, don't start at the bottom of the tree. Reach up high, Gertie, and paint down. We've got to protect the trees from bugs."

"If you want my help," retorted Gertie, "I'm starting from the bottom." Then she bent far over and stuck out her rear end. Nell daubed it white.

"Nell, you should act like you're sixteen," said Gertie, noticing Honora and Pete had joined them.

"Da wanted lumber with large diameter trunks," explained Honora to Pete.

"I'd have grafted trees with fruit that would be easier to husk," replied Pete. "He was a smart man to value the timber. That should be in my textbook."

The two whitewashers gawked at the tree planters. With a closer view, they admired Honora's tall, graceful stance. The breeze tossed her auburn hair around her glowing face.

Honora and Pete aren't working again.

Nell's lips curled down in a frown.

Not planting Da's nuts?

"The English walnut grafted onto the rootstock of the hearty local black walnut will be the next trial's theme." Pete's voice soared with joy. "Perhaps next February, we'll begin."

Honora placed her hands on her hips. "Next winter? What about this fall?"

"Next semester's written work must be completed before more fieldwork is accomplished." He puffed his platinum-blond hair off the top of his spectacles. "These new grafts will be part of my semester essay, *New Species on Borrowed Roots*."

For half a second Honora's chin began to tremble. Then her voice became shrill. She held her palms up, hands in front as though holding a textbook. "By Jove, we'll select a black walnut root ball with a main stem the thickness of my thumb."
Giggling at her no-nonsense tone, Nell and Gertie exchanged looks.

"We'll have done with this upper-budded stem from an English walnut of the same thickness. With the application of sap, they shall be united." Honora's fingers, steady as those of a surgeon, splayed the bark on the green stem of the root ball of a black walnut, folding back small flaps of bark. She inclined her head to Pete. Honora and Pete discussed which top cuts would be attached to which root sections.

I can tell she's hurt.
Nell nibbled her thumb.
Not fooling me.
Not to be outdone, Pete took over. "The flaps must be safeguarded to enclose the attached green twig within, thus, using the sap, we'll apply this cloth as a wrap."
Honora's laugh was irresistible. "Suppose we shall have our upstarts."

Pete circled his arm around Honora's waist, and they both plopped to the ground in hysterics. "Excellent discourse," said Pete between guffaws.
"Will the new tree be an English tree or a black walnut?" asked Nell.

"Yes!" Pete twirled Gertie around followed by Honora. "If the English walnut twig or scion is a strong variety, like your Da hoped, the black walnut tree will take on those characteristics."

"Ma says it's to be a memorial grove," breathed Honora. "Let's make memories."

Pete whirled Gertie and Honora around again in a spontaneous big round dance on the ridge top. Pete named the species of walnut trees after the girls. "On my left, are Honorable Honoras, and the ones on my right, are Gorgeous Gerties."

"What about mine?" cried Nell.

"Oh, that's easy. Mini Nillies." The happy dance went on. Silly Pete reached his hands behind him. Honora grabbed them, and they skipped high on their toes, tamping the dirt around the little trees. Gertie joined their train, and the excited laughter continued. Nell did not crack a smile. She crossed her arms over her chest.

Mini sounds like a ninny? And Nillies like silly dillies.

Nell's breath became raspy. She bared her teeth, gulping back tears.

Gorgeous Gerties and Honorable Honoras? Mini isn't much better than little. Sillly's an idiot.

With his hands behind his back and palms up, Pete danced by. "Nell, you have to let things go. I fathom that it's difficult, feeling like you're enough. Please take my hands."

Nell bit her lip at his smile, she seized Pete's hands, forgetting her orneriness.

"Where are my grafts?" fumed Honora. Another year had flown by, and Honora had worked hard. She turned in every direction looking up and down the ridge. "That's funny. I know this is the right place."

The sun filtering through the leaflets made a lacy pattern on the ground. Water droplets shimmered in the wind. Honora swallowed. "I declare, I don't recognize the walnut saplings I grafted. But I'm sure this is the spot." She squinted into the sunlight. "There's been no hard wind. What happened? Nell, did you?"

"No. I noticed them the day you flirted with Pete." Nell raked in another row.

Honora screamed so loud that cows scattered on the fields.

"Honora, what's wrong? I promise I didn't touch them." Honora's long auburn hair framed her fiery face. "If you broke my grafts, that's it for you. Did you? We grafted so many. Look at them." Honora flung her arms to her sides.

No," said Nell.

In tears, Honora threw her hands up as a breeze whirled and scattered her muttered words. "All our work." She scanned the rows of trees. "I'm tired of Bud or someone from the Warings on our property. This isn't their land. How dare they cut these!"

"Revenge for Malcolm?" asked Nell.

"Nell? Where are you going?" The hem of Nell's dress disappeared under the fence. "Stop right there." Honora stomped down with her foot. Nell's hem tore. "I'm the oldest, and I will handle this my way. Stay put."

Morty, Mike, and Jack ran over from the cornfield. "What's all the yelling? Is a body hurt?"
"Do you see any of the grafted trees for Pete's trials?" Honora pounded her temples with the heels of her hands. "This is serious."
"Last warning, Nell. Come back," screamed Honora.
"Easy. Lots of Irishman are known for their red-hot temper," said Morty. "Not the Glissons."
Wiping her tears, Honora grabbed one of the cut tops of a graft. "Would you look at Nell? The hem is out in her dress. She's still running. "Stop!"

~~**~~**~~**~~

Sam Waring's wide frame filled the doorway from side to side. His eyes sparked. "Leave my property, Miss Glisson. This 'lit-tle' girl has no business at my home, either."
I'm not afraid of him.
Nell inched forward.
This is how he treated Da.
"Get." Honora glared at Nell. Then she shoved the lopped-off sapling in front of Mr. Waring's face.
"Listen to me. I'm not little, and this is my business," said Honora, pushing Nell back.

Sam's chest thrust out with his booming laugh, he waved Nell away as if she was a gnat.
"We've worked hard on Peace Ridge Memorial for Malcolm." Honora's hands shook. "You're a banker.

You're aware that farmers in Shawnee Township are struggling. Someone from your property has destroyed our grafted trees. They've been sliced with a knife."
A look of recognition flashed in Sam Waring's eye.
He's guilty.

"Peace Ridge Memorial," said Sam with a leer. "Trees for an offering of peace for the life of my brother, Malcolm. I told my foreman to cut any branches close enough to re-seed our land. We don't need any of those dirty trees sprouting on our place."
"Aye," said Honora. "Malcolm's loss was a tragic accident. But this will ruin our ability to …."
"The grove is our legacy," interrupted Nell.

"Walnut trees? Legacy?" Sam spit the words out.
"This needs to end." Honora caught her breath. "Peace doesn't have to be in the past. I remember as a little girl, there was peace."
"I don't care about little girls, or this little girl." He pointed to Nell.
Nell's face reddened. "We've got walnut mansions."
Don't call me little.

"My brothers have been tormented and bullied. Bud or one of your hands has caused enough trouble. There have been sightings of someone on our property with a gun, a university student harassed, and now trees vandalized." Honora's voice regained its fervor.
"Let your mother join the rest of those vagabonds who moved away on covered wagons." Waring's ugliness continued. "Hell's fire, the symbolism of that ridge has

no meaning. My son's been at a preparatory school and soon off to military college for four years. He'll be back. We'll settle our claim to half of that ridge. As I told your Da, I don't make agreements with folks with blood on their hands. Now, I've asked you once to leave my property."

"Half the ridge?" Honora's words faltered.
Nothing could stop Nell. "There are no halves on that ridge. It belongs to us."
With her pretty hand stretched out to stop him, Honora reasoned with Sam.
"That's our land." Sam slammed the big heavy oak door in her face. Honora flung the slashed off sapling she'd brought with her on the threshold. Bud watched from an upstairs window.
Bud, what can you do?
Nell shook her head.
Nothing. I almost feel sorry for him. Why does he look so sad?

Honora turned away from Nell as they met Morty and the boys. "He made it sound like we don't own all the ridge?"
"The church permitted Da to graze his cattle on it. An old story circulates about only half of it belonging to Da," explained Morty. "Nothing worth getting in the ring for."
Wiping the hem of her apron across her dirty face, Nell said, "You're not a Glisson if you don't think the memorial grove's worth fighting for."
"How dare you speak to your older brother like that," said Honora. Your rotten behavior is worth a fight. Still

wiping your dirty face with your apron. No matter how many times I've scrubbed it? I learned what you said about Bertha. Pete's a good friend of mine, no more than that. And Charles? You act like I swing through the trees from one to another."

Labored breathing and sniffles were all Honora heard in return. "Listen here. You're my baby sister, and if a fire spread through the roof one night, I'd grab you out of your bed and run from the loft with you. Ma doesn't want your spirit broken, but we don't want any more of your ornery spirit."
"Hah! Save me in a fire? Baby? I'm sixteen. You'll be gone, anyways." Nell fumed.
I know what's going on. The others left too.
"Ma asked me to help you in the grove. You and Morty don't care about me, or you wouldn't leave."

Honora snatched Nell up by the apron strings. Then she dragged her to the pump. "Nell, you don't talk about Morty or me like that. You must obey your elders. Wipe your face on the rag at the pump, not on your clothes."
I'm glad for the boxing Jack's taught me.
Nell lobbed her straw hat into the mud.
Does Honora want to fight?

"Get that hat back on." Honora meant business. "As if you're not my baby sister. You're wearing my outgrown shoes. They look like they've been through the "War between the States.'"

"There's mud when you work in the shade! I don't need my hat or you," hollered Nell. "The only one who listens to me is Ma. She'll never leave."

Honora slammed the hat on Nell's head. "You're not *planting* the walnuts right. It looks like a child's work. What help is that?"

How dare she say that?
Nell howled.
Will everyone always be so much bigger and stronger than I am?
"Watch your tongue and wash up. Ma isn't young. You need to listen to her. She needs real help, not play. No one else escaped consequences for this behavior. I told you not to go to the Warings. You disobeyed."

"It's not my fault, Honora," shouted Nell. "I want to help. You're not my Ma."

~~**~~**~~**~~

I'm sorry about your grafts." Ma's voice sounded weak behind the mound of bread dough. The shiny woodstove gleamed behind her. "Thank you for all the help you've been. My eyes are so blurry, with more spots than clear places to take in the loaves."

"There have been plenty of tough jobs on this farm." Honora punched the dough for Ma. "The loss of my grafts is almost unbearable, but Nell's worse. I'll finish the bread. I'm sorry to hurt you, Ma. But I can't abide her anymore.

"I bet your Da would be proud that the homestead includes this second cabin. It's taken us another year. With winter coming I'm glad we're almost done. I'm proud of you for teaching Nell boxing." Uncle Willie patted Jack on the back. He gazed around at his brother's property. "The great boxers in Ireland learned more by teaching it to others." He ruffled Jack's hair. "Now here, we've got a real talent. But it's time for the champ to return to his carpentry skills."

"Jack's teaching me a cinch." Nell bent her knees like a boxer. "Watch this."

"A clinch?" snorted Uncle Willie. "Jack's top-notch at coming in close to his opponent, tying him up. Not letting go. But that's not all the defense he's got. Your brother has a real gift. He'll be a champ at bobbing and weaving. It's hard to hit a moving target. And Nell, going on seventeen."

I wish Da could be here, Uncle Willie reminds me so much of Da.

Nell's face turned to the side and rested on Uncle Willie's arm. She folded her hands under her chin and half-closed her eyes in contentment.

"What have you in mind for the rest of the new cabin? With a solid barn and this second cabin, Edmond won't recognize the old place." Uncle Willie peered around the worksite. "What did you call this thing you designed?"

"A gin pole. But I didn't design it." Morty's eyebrows wrinkled. "A neighbor gave me the idea."

"A neighbor?" Ma looked puzzled.

"Yes, er, I didn't want to say much about it, but Bud Waring loves machinery. With the draft horses, it makes quite a difference."

The fresh water made a glug-glug sound in Ma's crock. She poured Morty fresh spring water and asked, "Bud? Clever with machinery?"

"Old Sam wants Bud to follow in his footsteps, military school and all," said Morty. "Sam's not interested in any of Bud's ideas with machines. Bud thinks it won't be long, and there'll be machines that fly."

Ma's eyes widened.

"Bud's not a bully now that he's grown-up. He observed my struggling with the equipment. He's mixed up on life. Sam's got a tight grip on him." Morty lowered his voice. "Sam doesn't listen to anything Bud says."

We're receiving help from Bud

Nell twisted her lips to one side.

An enemy? What can he do? I know how it feels when folks don't listen to anything you say. Morty's for sure leaving us. That's plain as day. But in cahoots with Bud?

"My next problem is Bertha. She asked me if I'm certain about Missouri," replied Morty, frowning.

"You've sent her a passel of letters." Ma refilled the tin cup. "I'd say the wedding's on."

"Fancy that," said Nell. Her mind raced with anger.

Pete and Honora strode up to the new cabin. Pete returned Morty's graduation essay. "Your inclusion of the timberwork diagrams for the growing forestry industry is brilliant. I'm intrigued by your skills. You've gotten a great education here. It seems to exceed the requirements of an eighth-grade diploma. This community should hang on to these innovative instructors, teaching botany, astronomy, and geology."

"Yes, student behavior makes it hard to keep the good teachers around." Honora eyeballed Nell.

"Take a gander at this cabin's big, square beams." Pete whistled in admiration.

Attaching the ropes around a log to a gin pole he'd put together, Morty tugged on the draft's lead. The horse responded to the slightest syllable that Morty uttered. "The gin pole uses horsepower to lift the logs, with the central pole connected by ropes and pulleys to the block and tackle. The neighbor gave me this tip."

"But you're the one making it work." Pete's mouth hung open.

Slapping his hat against his thigh, Uncle Willie said, "Using a block and tackle to pull three-hundred-pound logs up a ramp, is the way to go. The cabin's done in no time."

Pete said, "Morty, you've got an understanding of the give and take of wood and communicating with these big animals. The notching you've done is an art."

"I don't think the joints will pull apart. They're finger tight. A stout cabin for Edmond," added Morty.

Morty hasn't said two words to me since the swimming-pond incident. Does he know how that hurts?

Running his hand over the debarked logs and flat stones, Pete remarked, "Who's the stone mason?"
"The only expert we have is Mike. He selects all the stones," said Honora.
"Remarkable. Colorful pattern. Flat. All about the same thickness. What an eye for masonry."
Don't try to tempt Mike to quit farming.
Nell scowled.
"I like the feel of the stones. It's close to mining. Closer than farming," explained Mike.
He's next.
"Why are the logs numbered?" inquired Pete.
You're going to be a professor?

"If they're ever taken down and reassembled, it's easy to follow the numbers." Morty showed Pete the four white oak sill logs on large cornerstones and patted them with his rough hands. "Aye, one through four, and the other logs will layer right up on them."
"Yup, it's putting itself together," said Uncle Willie. "Black walnut floor and ceiling joists."

A hush fell over all the workers as Pete got to the point of his visit. "You're a talented, hardworking man, Morty. With your calm voice you're able to demand control. You'd make a good leader of a logging company."
Pete continued, "Honora's mentioned your ciphering and problem-solving ability. Uncle Willie indicated your eye for assessment and your ability to calculate the

wagonloads of dirt that come off of a site. I understand you're not interested in any more schooling, but I'd like to honor your work with a letter of recommendation for when you arrive in Missouri."

"Bertha and I'd be much obliged." Morty's face split with a big smile.
At Bertha's name, those ripping-the-family-apart ideas leap like flames to my mind.
"With Missouri's lumber industry booming, you'll be in demand. I have a timber associate there. You'll meet all the requirements."
"Thank you, Pete," said Morty.
"Why don't you speak with your family about this?"
"Family?" interrupted Nell. "Oh, he's not interested in our feelings. Bertha's are all that matter."
Morty's jaw dropped.

"He might have trouble working for a logging company, if it doesn't fit with Bertha's plans, like this cabin." With a flash of her eyes, Nell stuck her little pointy chin out at Morty.
How does it feel to be the oldest brother leaving us?
Dropping a stone, Mike stood next to Morty.
Refusing to let Morty's character go undefended, Jack joined them. "He does care about family. He's leaving for Missouri later than planned, so the cabin's ready for our older brother, Edmond."

"All three of these nephews and my nieces make me a proud uncle," said Willie. "Let me try to repair this muddle. Nell's the youngest. Her substitute mother left

on a covered wagon, and perhaps her love comes out sideways when she's fearful of another sister or brother leaving." Uncle Willie shook his head. "The truth is, she thinks the world of Morty."
Returning to the job, Morty picked up the leads. The others muttered under their breath.

"Chester, giddyup, boy." Morty's face remained scarlet, and his tone was off. "Git on now, Chester-boy."
He let Chester's rope run through his hands as the log turned on the gin pole. Mike and Jack waited on the wall to put the next log into place. Chester's steady pulling lifted it to them. They settled the log into position. Uncle Willie turned away, answering Pete's questions. Charles claimed Honora's attention.

Lost in thought, Morty went through the motions of lifting the logs, when, without warning, one of the wooden pulleys broke on the gin pole. The log fell, pinning his left leg. The weight of the big log split the bone. Morty's cries of agony filled the worksite. Morty collapsed with sharp screams of pain because his twisted leg, was caught under the log. The sounds of Morty's suffering pierced the worksite. Reaching him first, Pete and Uncle Willie carried Morty to Pete's wagon.

As the wagon pulled up on the drive, Ma hobbled from the cabin, with her eyes almost squinted shut. She put her face down toward Morty's breath. Her hand covered his heart. "Please take him to Doc Simpkins right away.

My poultices and whatnot won't be enough. My eyes aren't good."

"A man in Rushville needed his leg amputated in a similar accident," said Charles.

Nell looked around for an opening to run to.

My legs are giving out from underneath me.

Instead, she froze. Her mouth was open, and her tears flowed. Pete drove Morty to Doc Simpkins. Uncle Willie supported Morty in the wagon bed.

~~**~~**~~**~~

Ma trudged up to the loft. Nell lingered upstairs for the better part of two days after Morty's injury. There was no crying or any sound.

Finally, Ma's going to discipline me.

Nell's thin face was drawn, and her eyes were dull. She didn't respond to Ma's knock.

"Why don't you tell me what you're going through? It's only a few months until your seventeenth birthday."

Sitting still, not moving a muscle, Nell remained silent.

Ma's wrinkled face tightened with her concerns for Morty. With all the patience she could muster, she said softly, "I'm trying to understand."

With her head down, Nell sat like a frozen stump. It was hard to detect her breathing.

I 'spec Bertha's right. Ma's sweetness is wearing out. I've caused plenty of trouble.

Ma resorted to pinching Nell's arm when she wouldn't respond. Nell sat up and blinked at Ma. Her bottom lip pushed out.

"Nell, the only way to stop all this fear of letting go of your sisters and brothers is faith. But your spoiling's over. I've been too gentle. Did Morty ever hurt *you*?"

"No." Nell sobbed. Her stomach cramped. She swallowed. "Pete praised Morty for his essay. He encouraged him about working in Missouri forests, but then, I knew we needed him...."

If I hadn't been so cruel.

Ma waited.

"I said something bad about Morty."

The thin lips parted. Ma sighed with relief.

"I told Pete that Morty's a farm boy, not a forester."

"Oh, Nell." Now it was Ma's turn to be quiet.

"I said that he might not be able to handle the crew since he took all of his orders from Bertha."

Closing her eyes, Ma folded her calloused hands. "Folks think I'm not strong enough for you, a ninth child. I don't want any part of your going, but would you like to go and let Bertha finish raising you?" Ma cupped Nell's chin in her hands. "As good a teacher as she is, it's likely she'd have a better chance with discipline. Would you live in Missouri?"

"No, never, Ma."

"Lord, help me find a way," said Ma. "Do you think I still love the oldest four living far away?"

Of course, Ma. You always have.

Nell nodded.

"Folks ask me if I love all nine of you the same. I answer no. I love the ones who are sick and the ones who are out of my sight more. Nell, you're healthy now." Ma's

voice sounded tired. "There are things that must be spoken. Love doesn't stop no matter how the miles add up. Or poor health. It grows stronger."
Sucking in short, rapid breaths, Nell panted.
I don't want them to leave me. That's all, Ma.

"Morty will always love you. Even if he goes, his roots continue to grow. Honora, Mike, and Jack too. Your job is to love them back no matter what choices they make." Ma's beautiful, smiling eyes teared as she lifted Nell's chin. "That's called unconditional love. That means love with no conditions. That's family. That's blood. Da left all of his family in Ireland. They loved him, even knowing his plans might be forever. They wanted the best for him. Real love causes sorrow when we say good-bye."

"Oh, Ma, I'm sorry. I'm so bad," moaned Nell.
"It's time you told yourself you're good and that you're loved by God. He doesn't want our perfection, but he wants us to long to hear his direction. At your baptism, the Reverend drew a cross on your forehead. The cross means love."
Hot tears continued to slide down Nell's nose and patter off of her pointy little chin.

"Your love wasn't offering your family any grace. I've allowed you too much freedom."
"I've got it coming," spluttered Nell. "I've been a tyrant because I wanted the family together. I didn't want them shoving me away. This accident makes me want to change. If Morty's leg is amputated, they'll all leave because I'm not good enough, Ma."

Ma's voice changed pitch, "Is *that* what you think?"
"Yes." Nell nodded.

"Do you think that's what happened to Da when he left home? He wasn't good enough?"
Her voice was soft as a whisper. "No, Ma."
"Da's parents let four of their sons go. They've never seen them since. Do you think his family loves them any less?"
"No."
"That's why we endure. We keep working and doing our part, thinking of the best for loved ones, not ourselves, with no mind for how difficult it is. Do you understand?"
"I'll never leave you, Ma. I'll never be mean to any of my family.   Tattling.   Eavesdropping.   Interrupting. Falsehoods. Playing pranks to keep my brothers and sisters from leaving." Nell massaged Ma's hands. "I'm ready for the woodpile."

~~**~~**~~**~~

At the woodpile, Ma's eyes watered more than her daughter's did. Afterward, Nell's breath came slow and steady. Her inspecting eyes glinted softer, and humbler. She took Ma's hand back to the cabin. Nell didn't credit anyone's comment about how the pulley would've broken anyway.
Morty would've spotted the rope if I hadn't insulted him. If his leg's amputated, I won't know how to be sorry enough.

Any time the family discussed Ed's coming home, or Honora's actions, Nell kept quiet.

222

A sister needs to work and love her sisters and brothers by giving them hope.
"Ma, please. Let me care for Morty. I don't have any breathing problems. Please trust me. I'll do whatever's needed."

Struggling with her disbelief, Ma couldn't help but say, "I wonder how long this behavior'll last?" Ma wasn't alone. They all had incredulous looks. But Nell's defiant posture toward them ended. Her demeanor with her loved ones changed. Determined to do the best she could, she brought Morty's compresses and followed Doc's orders. She mailed all Morty's letters, including her heartfelt written apologies to Bertha and Pete.
Just when I think I've heard everything. Bud's helping our family? Look at how much I've grown up. I'll be ready to let them go.

CHAPTER 20
Honora's Strengths

One small figure, seventeen years old, got up at daybreak. Nell continued working hard. She tended to livestock, laundry, and cooking with no grumbling, or banging of doors and pots, or scowls.

Jack's pleadings could be heard from the boxing ring over the bawling of the milk cows. "Can't you take a break, and make time for one round?"

"No, thanks. I've got work to do. It won't be long before our nieces and nephews will arrive. Think how fascinated they'll be."

I want them to see my cordiality and hard work, and that I'll never leave Ma.

"What? Are you not going to call me a name from your book? How about Uriah Heep? Don't be afraid to put your dukes up. Come on, Nell," pleaded Jack. "Morty will be okay. You're no fun."

"No thanks," she mumbled.

"Where's that fierce scowl?" chided Jack. "Nobody but me would miss that."

With great care, Nell hung up each piece of laundry on the wash line. Jack went into the ring with his stuffed grain sacks that took the place of a speed bag. "This guy doesn't know where the direction of the next strike is coming." He pounded the bag with a flurry of punches. "Take that! You're not in the workhouse prison, you know."

No time for chatter. Nell's forehead was beaded with sweat and a red flush.

Ma needs to sign the paper she placed in the Bible for Pete. I should take Morty for his morning walk. It won't be long before Doc's visit. Clean the parlor, kitchen, and outhouse. I can't skip rope or dance with Honora and Pete. I must polish the stove.

"Watch where you're going, Nell," hollered Honora.

"I'm looking for Pete," replied Nell.

Honora unpinned a towel from the wash line. She wrapped it around three sandwiches. "You're breathing so hard. I'm not sure about Old Blondie. Have you checked if his wagon's here?"

That's strange. Old Blondie

Nell went around the corner of the barn.

Honora's preparing a picnic basket without Pete.

"Nell, watch out for my books!" Pete jumped out of her way. "Say, you want to dance again?" He spun her around.

Holding Ma's paper out to Pete, Nell turned to hurry away.

"Hey, how *is* Old Blondie?" Charles McMinn sauntered into the yard. Honora patted her hair into place and grabbed her basket. Charles took her arm. He guided her up the cart path.

"Honora? You gonna say good-bye or tell us where you're going?" A lump grew in Nell's throat.

"Oh, I'm sorry," said Honora, absorbed. "This day's planned. A picnic before fall's gone. Ma's aware of it.

Nell, would you please be a peach and finish my chores?"
Honora and Charles disappeared out of sight. Pete and Nell frowned, speechless.

~~**~~**~~**~~

As the sun dried up the dew, Nell finished several chores. She made time for her late morning walk with Morty. She wrapped her arm around his back. "Jack's practicing at the boxing ring."
Morty hobbled on his crutch.
Jack hauled back with a left. The punching bag swung out and away. "Watch my combination." He stopped in midsentence to acknowledge his brother. "You're getting around on your cane? Your leg must be improving?"

Grimacing with pain, Morty plodded on.
"Uncle Willie gave us time off from Edmond's cabin." Jack shuffled in the dirt. "He's taking me to a boxing exhibition. I'm glad you're up and around," hollered Jack.
"Watch my improved clinch for the big match." Jack's voice sounded primed. "No one else'll fight. I'll teach this old punching bag a lesson. Ground hard enough for you?" He shuffled around the ring with his fists thumping the bag. "Knockout time, buddy."

~~**~~**~~**~~

"My, she's been gone all day." Ma's fretting outpaced her creaking rocking chair. Morty drifted off to sleep in the warm parlor. "Nothing when you checked?"

226

Nell bent over her embroidery. The needle went up and down through the fabric. "She's twenty-eight."
I want to tell Ma what I saw at their picnic.
Nell squinted and wrapped a French knot.
I've made a vow. I won't tattle. I wish Ma could walk better. She'd know for herself.

Quiet filled the parlor, except for the ticking of the marble mantel clock.
"Nell," said Ma for the fourth time. "Did you see anything?"
There will be no more of my blaring and bleating like a ram.
Nell shook her head no.
I made a promise that I'll treat my loved ones better, I'll never again hear about the possibility of my moving to Missouri with Bertha.

Still blaming herself for Morty's injury, Nell pondered Honora's whereabouts.
I've always wanted attention, but my actions often lead to hurting my sisters and brothers. After what happened with Morty, I need time to think it through. I don't want my nieces and nephews knowing me as a tattler. Seeing Ma pat her eyes with her handkerchief makes me want to tell.

"I believe it's twenty-year-olds being twenty-year-olds," said Nell.
"I don't want to regret saying this," confided Ma, "but I don't care for Charles. To me, a pair of shiny boots

doesn't mean he's worked an honest day in his life. But you're right, she's twenty eight years old."

With her eye on the loft ladder, Nell kissed her mother good night. "I love you, Ma." Exhausted, Nell hauled herself up the rungs of the loft ladder.

I hope this is your will, Lord. I did turn back at the pond, but it's hard to know when or how to obey elders.

She tossed and turned, afraid for her sister. The night grew late. It was stormy with a chill in the loft. She could've sworn she heard Ma's rocking chair creak.

This late?

Tiptoeing down the loft steps, Nell found Ma wide awake. Ma shushed her before she could speak. "Don't wake Morty." She reached her arms out to Nell. Nell sunk to the floor. She laid her head on Ma's knees. Her eyes were red. "What did you witness, Nell?"

"I've tried to think this through before blaring out, but Ma," Nell's bottom lip began to tremble, "I don't like Charles, either."

"What is it, Nell? This isn't spreading stories. I'm asking you because I need to know. Please!"

"I'm sorry. I've been ornery for so long that obeying elders is hard. Ma, don't send me to Missouri."

Ma's mouth hung open.

"Charles chased me away when you sent me to check on them. When I went back, I found an empty pond. Charles ...." She shut her eyes. "He was angry and yelling."

"Again, I turned back. He chased me. Honora tried to stop him. He acted fiercer than one of the old bulls. He called me names. He said crazy things like, 'You've no business spying on us all the time.'

"When I ran, he caught me. I kicked him hard in the shins. A bottle of whiskey fell out of his trousers. He swung his hand to grab me, but he missed. So angry. I ran hard all the way from the pond. I wanted Honora to come home with me." Nell's voice broke. "It's so hard to know how to obey."

Loosening her grip on the arms of her rocker, Ma embraced Nell and kissed her face. Ma combed her fingers through Nell's hair until she stopped crying. Nell knelt in front of Ma, and there they harbored, wrapped in each other's arms.

~~**~~**~~**~~

Unloosening herself from Ma's arms, Nell stirred. She went to the parlor window. *What?* Jack and Mike came out of the barn. They pulled sheets over their heads. Then, in the moonlight on the drive, they disappeared around the corner like ghosts.
What kind of joke are those mischievous boys up to? Mike and Jack will help Honora.
Nell figured they were scaring some sense into Charles, he would never keep Honora out this late.
And if I'm right, his drinking's obvious to the boys. They don't want her to have any part of it. They must be hiding in the cemetery to run out and scare him.

Not wanting to wake Ma or Morty, she tiptoed out of the cabin. The cool night air felt damp. She shivered. She ran down the drive and turned on the road toward the cemetery.

I must look like a ghost in my long white nightgown.

The darkness engulfed her. She listened like a night creature. Nothing moved. She kept going. She stumbled in a hole in the road. She found her way to the cemetery. Startled by loud voices up the road, she ran toward the sounds of fighting. It was too dark to see. Yet Nell glimpsed the outline of three men in the back of a wagon. Fistfighting and slugging made her stop in her tracks. There were thuds, yells, and harsh words.

"Ow! Ow!"

Mike and Jack must be roughing up Charles.

"Whomp, Oomph. Ow," someone groaned. There was another oomph. Smack and a banging. Then a crunching sound. Then more sounds could be heard. Sounds of slugging. Terrible thumps, and a body crashing occurred. A body slammed into the wagon side. There was heavy breathing.

"I said I'm sorry." A man's miserable voice cried out in pain.

The voice sounds funny, not like Charles's.

Terrible thumps. Bodies crashing.

I can't tell who that was. Jack? Or Mike?

More thuds, thumps, and yelling.

Nobody's going to hurt my sister or brothers.

Nell strode closer.

"Who's that?" hollered Jack.

"It's only me," said Nell.

"What in the world?" Jack jumped over the wagon side. "What are you doing here? You need to walk Honora home. We're all right. We've got this drunk knocked out."

Nell tried to peer into the wagon bed, above the yellow spokes of the wheel.
Mike's knee pinned a man's back below the wagon's sideboards. "Go ahead, Nell."
"Help me. I need you, Nell," begged Honora mournfully.
Mike lowered Honora down into the waiting arms of Jack and Nell.

Nell placed one arm around Honora's waist.
I feel so afraid. I love Honora. We all do. I hope she stays away from Charles.
Her other arm supported Honora under her left elbow. Honora hobbled along, but at her side, every now and then she cried out in pain. Nell braced for each sob and labored step. Honora's head slumped over to the side.

~~**~~**~~**~~

Several nights later, Morty's voice sounded like Da's in the hushed cabin. "You've got to speak to us. What happened that night at the pond with Charles?"
"Morty, I don't know," moaned Honora.
It didn't sound like Honora's voice.
Nell's eyes widened.
Honora looks older and tired. She'd been in bed the last few days.

"Morty, you need to save your energy for your Missouri trip." Honora's next words were even harder to hear. "Doc'll advise you that your leg's ready for travel. Morty, you've gotten the cabin pertnir done." Honora mumbled, "Please, concentrate on joining Bertha."
 "I'm worried about you," said Morty. "Not the cabin. Bertha's fine. But you're not. I understand part of what happened that night. I remember when Mike asked the teacher what imbruted meant, which is when a person lowers himself to the standards of a brute. We'll have justice."

"Morty, no. Please keep this quiet. Charles McMinn has agreed to marry me."
Morty's fingertips made a tent in front of his bowed head.
"He has no land." Honora's voice trembled. "McMinn's not a good name. There's no inheritance, or steady employment."
"Shh. No, I'm not worried about Charles at this time," shushed Morty.
Not worried about Charles.
Nell sat up in her bed.
I will be. Forever.

"Honora?" Morty's voice sounded older.
Honora's voice was muffled, covered by her hands. She sobbed.
"We know what happened. The man took liberties. Jack and Mike hid in the cemetery to scare Charles in the wagon as a practical joke. They recognized the wagon,

and, well, um, they didn't expect the situation that occurred. They want revenge for the assault."

Honora's flood of tears sounded as though they were choking her. "Charles wouldn't bring me home. Tired of his drinking, I decided to get out of there." Her voice changed to the faintest mumble, "Nothing could happen in two short miles. I took a ride from—" voices garbled. Morty pleaded with her to keep her voice hushed.
With a soft voice, Honora went on. "Mike and Jack didn't realize the problem from their hiding spot until I screamed, 'Stop it. Stop it! Please stop it! Leave me alone. Get off of me! No! Stop it.' The boys hid to scare Charles, but when ...."

Honora's words blurred together. "The boys threw their sheets off and came tearing down the road to his wagon and then, the fight started. The boys are so strong." Honora's body became racked with sobs. She fell into Morty's arms. "He hurt me," she cried. "My brothers. I needed both of them."
Both? Charles can't whip Mike or Jack.

"Mike flew into action, with Jack right behind him. I tried to fight back. They threw punches, trying to get him off me. There were sickening, cracking sounds and cries of agony. Sobbing and shaking, I tried to brush off my torn clothes and mend my dress. It's ruined."
Honora sighed again. The words rushed out. "He said he wanted a kiss. That's all. After the fighting I remember he cradled his arm, writhing in pain. 'Sorry,'" he said. Honora buried her face in Morty's shoulder.

Finally, Honora spoke again. "Aye, Morty. No revenge. Charles will accept me the way I am."

"A bad injury occurred during the fight," said Morty. "Mike flung him off of you, and he crashed against the wagon box. He broke both bones in his right arm above the elbow. They say he'll lose the range of motion to rotate his palm. Farmwork will be difficult for him."

Farmwork? What work won't be difficult for Charles?

"But no more violating my sister," said Mike.

Violating? What's that mean?

Easygoing Jack's voice filled with wrath. "Let him try to deny it. He'll have me one-on-one next time!"

"Please, Morty." Sobbed Honora. "I don't want any more bloodshed or revenge. I know it's impossible to have Da there, but I wanted Ma and Da to stand up for me at the courthouse. I'll never forget the older girls' wedding. Charles is working to pay for the license and such like."

"I'll stand up for you. I'll postpone leaving. You're the loveliest sister. Ma and I will stand with you. I've got the money for the license."

A wedding like a funeral. Poor Jack always punching his punching bag. Nell backed against the barn wall. Mike working on a walnut cradle. Poor Morty. Another delay. I want Morty's bones to knit together stronger than the boards are in that cradle. Did Honora's head get hurt? Nobody could've acted any stupider.

CHAPTER 21
The Crooked Arm

Sam Waring deliberated about firing his foreman.
Stephen won't be half the man he's been. I need a foreman who's up to par.
Sam paced.
But this information could harm my reputation. Hmm.
"Doc Simpkins, I called for you because of the terrible crook in my hired man's arm. The pain, and the infection." *I'll see what Doc can do and then decide on Stephen's future.*

"I'm asking for a reasonable explanation of what happened," pressed Doc. "After what I witnessed in the goldfields, I'd say he's been in a bar-room brawl. Not a wagon rollover. The scratches on his face remind me of a smaller person trying to defend themself. Where did this take place? Were there any witnesses?"
"Since when does a country doc need to ask all those questions?" roared Sam. "Doc, we'll call another doctor to attend to him." Sam Waring kept his lips pursed together in a stern line. "What difference do facts make? As a doctor, aren't you going to treat him?"

"You go ahead. Call someone else." Doc clutched his bag. "I believe a neighbor of mine mentioned other brawls this foreman of yours has been involved in. That are reputed to include women." Doc's nostrils twitched. He let his breath out of his nose like a bull letting off steam. His eyes gleamed with fierceness. "As a doctor, I'm responsible for informing the sheriff."

With a cruel twist of his mouth, Sam spit out his words. "I'll take Stephen over to Rushville. Someone there will do what they can for him. I sent for you only because of your proximity. I won't forget this incident. You don't have to include this with the rest of the scuttlebutt circling in the township. This matter is to be confidential, Doc. Understand?"

"Scuttlebutt," exploded Doc. "The law needs notification. There are inconsistencies in this fellow's story. I've been called to the assault of a young lady from another township. I needed time to get to the bottom of that ugly attack. She moved away. I'm not sure Stephen's arm will ever heal. This should have been immobilized and treated. One thing's for sure, no military, he won't be able to hold a rifle in his right arm. I would recommend light work."
Don't worry about Sheriff Rippon. We're good friends."

~~**~~**~~**~~

Stephen's right arm never healed.
That's it. He's not someone I need around.
Sam chuckled.
I've got a campaign to run. I'd like nothing more than the commissioner's job.
Rumors around town didn't change, regardless of Stephen or Sam's testimonies of Stephen's wagon rollover. "What a grand opening for a bank president? Future employees? He's got a black eye with his neighbors," said one resident with a scowl at the others.

"Curious. The foreman's bruises and scars didn't look like a wagon rolled over him. He should be banned from Brownsville County. What about jail time? And Sam? Leading the county and employing criminals? Speaking of futures, who's our next commissioner?"

~~**~~**~~**~~

As the unhusked walnuts thumped out of the bag onto the rough worktable in the barn, Nell stared at them. Everything had been a whirlwind.

I still envision Honora as a bride gliding across Peace Ridge in soft slippers and a long lacy veil trailing out behind her, a princess. Her outspread skirts would be lifted off the ground. Her auburn hair would be piled on her gorgeous head.

In reality, when they left for the courthouse, she wore an old dress with a gray shawl around her thin shoulders. Honora's words from the last day at the pond still plagued Nell.

"Whatever suits you, Charles, tickles me plum to death."

I'll stay strong.

Nell comforted herself, clutching the familiar wrinkly shell of a walnut. *Honora's right.*

The only shoes I'm ever going to need are army boots. Never cry again. I won't tell a man, "Whatever suits you tickles me." Without Honora, what'll happen to the walnuts? Honora did care for them. But she left them.

Nell smashed a shell with all of her strength.

The walnuts aren't an inheritance given but a legacy inside me. I vow to safeguard them, forever and my family but not Charles.

In the peace of the late fall afternoon, Nell and her brothers husked walnuts one after another. With the unmistakable rustling of the shifting of hundreds of shells, Mike hoisted another full bag. He poured them on framed drying screens. At the sound of a wagon, they all looked up. Morty greeted Pete and congratulated him on the completion of his fieldwork. Morty mentioned his trip to Missouri the following day. Pete presented him with several letters of recommendation.

Shuffling the last of his papers, Pete said, "I appreciate Ma signing the contract, but the college canceled your project site after the destruction of the grafts."
"We'll settle this with the Warings down the road," stammered Morty.
"Speaking of down the road." Pete removed a photo from his wallet. "This is my twin sister, Esther. She named her little girl Honora. I'm an uncle."
"Um, Pete." Hesitant to share the news, Morty bit his lip. "We held a wedding for Honora at the courthouse. It all occurred pretty fast."

Nell's stomach lurched for Pete.
"She married without the white dress and veil," explained Morty. "With her gone now, we're not sure of the ridge's future."
"The grove will always have a future." Nell's voice sounded strong and resolute.
I'm not sure how without Honora and the others. I'm puny and incapable without them. How can I forgive Honora? It'll take more than this century.

"You folks have helped me so much with my research." Pete cleared his throat. "I'll never forget you. Always promise me one thing, even when the world's going to pieces. I still want you to plant your walnut trees. Isn't that what your Da would say?"

I wish I could tell Pete, but the walnuts aren't an inheritance for me, Da's baby. They're inside me, part of me, forever.

Mike first, and then Jack, shook Pete's hand.

"I'm glad to see you're up on that leg, Morty." Everyone glanced up in surprise at Bud Waring's arrival. "I want to warn you my father's filed a court case against you."

"Court case?" Morty looked incredulous.

"My father's goal is to be rid of the memorial grove," said Bud.

"Bud, why warn us?" replied Morty.

"Da's family couldn't forgive. He broke away from your Ma's church group long ago. That's why my grandfather wanted the Reverend's church off their land. The church elders voted against him to allocate that land to your Da for his livestock."

"Can't it be settled outside of court?" Morty kicked at the dust.

"Dad's not going to surrender," said Bud.

"There are proposed laws in the legislature for landowners to receive credit on their taxes for tree groves," said Pete. "The Illinois forests are not all cut. The idea is to help farmers and west central Illinois's economy. It would be good for the community to have the trees."

"Dad's used to what he *wants*." A vein throbbed in Bud's neck. "It has to do with revenge for Malcolm's death. I don't agree. I'm confused about Malcolm's death. I'm sorry about Honora. Her leaving's changed things between my dad and me. I won't have any part of an assault. Er, uh… I know she and Nell worked hard." Bud looked out toward the ridge.

"We're sorry for the loss of your Uncle Malcolm. These trees hold a special meaning for us. If we got rid of the trees, would that be enough for your dad?"
"*Nothing* is enough for him," cursed Bud.
Bud needs our friendship. I feel bad for him. He doesn't fit. He feels alone and abandoned by what little family's he's got.

~~**~~**~~**~~

Heavy clouds chased away the late fall day. Nell'd taken a short stroll out to the children's walnut log mansions before the evening meal. She recalled early memories in the mansions of Honora bossing her around.
A year since I've seen Honora.
Nell veered west from the play area. She crossed the fence, and followed twists and turns, and bent under branches. Nell entered the Warings' dusky yard. The high windows, framed in thick draperies, spelled grandeur.

"Oh." She gasped, "Waring Mansion. Honora'd love these beautiful tapestries on the walls with the lovely floral fabrics."

Honora's leaving came at a terrible time. Morty needs to go. How will Mike and Jack's boxing, and the walnuts fare without him?
"Your tears won't do you any good," said Da. But Da, I've caused so much trouble. Ma's eyesight and limping. How could Honora leave?
Nell sniffled.
Honora, the prettiest girl in Shawnee Township, on hearing about Morty's engagement, dove right in and married Charles, a bum, with no job and no land. He's a poor excuse for a husband. A shiftless drunk. My sister, tall and lithe, isn't mistaken for someone half her age. She outshone the sun and then shook us off like ticks on a dog. But what about Da's legacy? How can I carry on without her or the others? I loved her more than anybody.

Nell's view from the shadows went straight into the Warings' window. The air was full of a roasted meat aroma. A butler reached between the tall candlesticks. He ladled a rich brown gravy before a lone diner Sam.
This is the kind of table I dreamed of for Honora. I must protect the memorial grove. Doesn't he eat with his own son?
Nell turned for home. "The last thing Waring needs is our land."

Ducking under the fence behind the wagon with the yellow spokes, she caught a glimpse of the back of a tall, muscular man. His limp right arm hung down. She heard the low growl of a dog. She shivered under the sunless sky. She hurried away. She imagined Honora's loud whistle calling her home.

The walnuts should've kept Honora here. I can't bring her home, but I'm looking for a way to let her know I'd do anything to get her back. I'd even forgive her for leaving.

Honora's absence reflected the emptiness of the small harvest and the forgotten wild plums. Her voice was forever gone from the kitchen and loft. The family and the groves thrived under Honora's steady, loving hand. *The nuts would drop again, but what would be the point without Honora? I miss you so much, Honora. Why did you have to go?*

~~**~~**~~**~~

The evening grew darker as Nell found the path home. She hurried toward the light she saw in the darkness. Jack peered through the steely night. He held a lantern in the cool western breeze. Honora always waited until we were all together and served dinner. Now Jack. *How much time do I have left with Jack?* Zeke meowed from below the porch and dashed out. Nell scooped him up. "Zeke, at least you're the perfect homebody."

The lantern flame flared as Jack tweaked the wick.

"I smelled that pungent fire inside." Nell stepped into Jack's yellow orb of light. She warmed her hands under her apron.

Sensing her sadness, Jack murmured, "I bet you're missing Honora."

Nell nodded.

"We all do."

With the secondhand newspapers, Ma kept the family up on current events. "Thomas Edison has invented an incandescent lightbulb. It will light up the night. I'd love to have one for my reading group. The paper states Thomas Edison is completing designs to light up entire cities."

I wish they could light up the darkness in Honora's city.

With her face full of a loving sweetness, Ma continued reading. "Oh, no!" Her loud outburst startled everyone.

"What is it, Ma?" asked Mike. "Is it another neighbor moving?"

"The land-purchase section lists all the sales to the Warings of Shawnee Township," replied Ma. "They've bought so many." Ma squinted even with the paper close beneath her nose. "When Edmond left, Da sold the northern acres to the Monktons. They've now sold to Sam Waring." Ma's hands trembled. "There's a court hearing on the deed for a section of Pea Ridge this Thursday."

The brothers' eyes met.

"The land known as Pea or Peace Ridge belongs to the widow of said, Michael Patrick Glisson Senior." Ma gasped.

"I hate bringing up this troublesome letter." Morty reached into his pocket. He handed it to Ma. "We received a summons."
Sitting up on their stools, Mike and Jack leaned forward.

With empty, glassy eyes, Ma folded her hands in prayer. Then, she clasped the official-looking envelope in front of her chest. "Sam's pert near got us stuck in a muddy carrot draw."
"He will not take Da's grove." Nell's tone made all heads turn. "Ever."
With a crackle of paper Ma unfolded the crisp sheets. She peered at the summons. The print was too small for her spectacles.

The family waited in silence.
"They want me to appear. My hip. My eyes. I can't see." She lowered the paper. Her rocking chair was still. "Me? Appear in court?"
"As the oldest, I'd go for you." Morty volunteered. "But I'd need help with my leg." He peered around the room. "Nell?"
I'd do anything for Morty.

Nell's eyes sparkled. "The vegetable soup and cornbread are cooling off on the stove. But there'll be plenty to last for the next few days."
"I'd like you to write in your wedding information beside ours," said Ma, signing over the documents to Morty. Right here, beneath Charles and Honora, and now the birth of little, Edmond McMinn. He's called 'Ned.' Please."

Ma handed the Bible to Morty.

"There are a couple of unopened envelopes here."

"Yes, those are Mary-Jane and Kate's wedding papers."

"Shall I open them?" Morty asked.

"Please do," said Ma.

"This one's Mary-Jane's. The other one belongs to Kate. Why look! There are also land documents from the members of Pea Ridge First English Church stored with Kate's first marriage."

Mike and Jack sat on the edge of their seats with narrowed eyes. Morty skimmed over the ancient paperwork from top to bottom. "Oh, my. One is a letter from the church, attached to the original deed, signed by all the parties in 1850. Da paid them a fair market price. The other is from the Brownsville County Clerk, asking for copies of information regarding the ridge. It states that the ridgeline is deeded to Da to run his livestock on as long as he fences the boundary between the church and his land."

"Da and I secured all our important papers in the Bible." Ma's voice quavered. "When Nell was born, why—?"

"Well, I'll be. Tonight of all nights," said Jack.

"It deems the entire ridgetop in Da's name. It is signed by the church members, the original farmers, including, one Elder Waring." Morty's lips pursed in a thin straight line. "This deed has never been recorded. There's no notary stamp. The county has no record of this. These farmers are gone."

"Tried doing the right thing," whimpered Ma, "keeping all these legal papers in the Bible. The deeds have been here all along. They were never recorded." Ma's tears fell. "Morty, I'm sixty-four years old. We've worked so hard."

"There'll be justice," said Morty. "You've read to us in the Bible about not tampering with a widow's property lines." Morty's hand hammered the edge of the table. "Da built this farm. He started that memorial for the Warings. They know that."

It's all because of my birth they didn't get the papers signed. It's as if a cyclone hit.
Nell brushed the hair from her eyes.
My poor parents did everything they could to keep the place going, but most of all to keep me alive.

~~**~~**~~**~~

Once again, Morty postponed his wedding date. However, on court day, the entire family witnessed him wearing his wedding clothes out in front of the cabin. They all gasped and said how handsome he looked. Nell was right beside him in one of Honora's outgrown dresses. Morty exclaimed, "Nell, the dress looks lovely on you. We've got the old deed with the church members' signatures. That'll increase our faith."

With Morty's guidance and patient directions to the draft horses, Nell drove all the way to town. She helped him on and off the farm wagon and with navigating the stairs.

Judge Camean noted the courtroom attendees' names as they were read. "Employees and staff of the courthouse, Sam Waring, Mortimer Patrick Glisson, Bridgett Ella Glisson." He paused. "Bridgett? That's my wife's name. She claims that name stands for power and strength. Did you know that?"
I believe that's something I'm going to need.

Taking a few deep breaths, Morty calmed himself over what Nell might say about being called Bridgett.
She surprised him. "I did not realize that, Your Honor. Thank you. I'd like to remember that."
"This courtroom recognizes the deed you have presented to the court as never being notarized. Also, in regard to the court's paperwork, due to the Recorder's Office by November 1, 1875, the deadline is far gone. Your father was a member of the local militia, I understand? Not mustered at that time? What barred him from filing this document?"

"Your Honor, that year, my mother fell from a tree," said Morty. "She experienced a severe injury, and a surprise ninth pregnancy. My sister, Bridgett," he nodded at Nell, "was born early in the pregnancy on September 8, 1875. My parents wouldn't accept that their baby would die. They fought for her night and day, as did my sisters, and brothers, and me. We're all close because of being born at home, all of us grew special connections with Nell, because of all of her birth difficulties and Ma's injuries." Morty choked on his words. Coughed. He found it difficult to clear his throat. "Bonds, hard to break, sir."

Nell, dazed, managed to raise her hand.

"Yes, Bridgett." Judge Camean nodded. "State your age for the court, please."

"I turned eighteen years old in September."

"Yes, please continue. I mistook you for someone younger. Please pardon these old eyes," said the judge.

"Doc Simpkins said I had zero chance of living. My mother's injury caused her to remain in bed. My father cared for me late into the night after long days of farming."

"The medical issues at home kept your parents from filing the necessary paperwork?" asked Judge Camean with surprise.

The Warings' attorney stood. "Objection. Not pertinent to the matter at hand."

"Overruled. I understand there's a memorial grove on said property."

"Objection. Not pertinent to the dispute over land ownership."

"Overruled again. Please continue, Miss Glisson, Bridgett."

Morty smiled.

"Yes, my Da received an inheritance from his pap, I mean my grandfather, in Ireland. Three gunnysacks of walnuts."

The courtroom broke into snickers.

"Order."

"Da wanted to plant nuts and saplings as a memorial for the accidental death of Sam Waring's brother, Malcolm.

The ridge is to be planted like a grove or a park in the hope his grandchildren would inherit the grove."
"The court will call a brief recess to examine the evidence."

Later, Judge Camean returned with a sad sigh. "This older document is not a working deed regardless of the accidental misplacement during a time of duress. It's invalid. The Glissons will be recompensed for the current value of their property on the western half of said ridge. The Warings will be the new legal owners of said western half of the ridge. The Glissons will own the eastern half."

An eerie silence surrounded the handful of neighboring farmers, board members, and officials. Judge Camean smiled with sympathy at Bridgett. With the smack of his gavel, he cleared the court. "This court will proceed with the next case, involving the stolen bull on the old Camden Road."

~~**~~**~~**~~

The crisp breeze filled with the smell of burning leaves as the horses trotted along past harvested fields. On the last hill, Nell pulled back on the reins at Morty's request. "Doc Simpkins gets wind of all patients, comings, and goings. What a major surprise he'd have if he heard talk about you speaking up in court. This is another confirmation of what a good fighter he delivered, a little one he found with zero chance to live. You're sure not little anymore. Thank you for being such a good sister, and for vowing to protect our half of the walnut grove.

Right now, you don't look four feet ten. You look like your five feet tall."

No words were ever sweeter to me. I said I could handle him leaving. How? Something has to change. The walnuts aren't an inheritance given, but a legacy inside of me. How do I remove what I could never move away from?

"When's the last time the youngest four of us worked together, digging out stones?" asked Jack. Coal ran along the creek at the base of the ridge behind him.

"Once I heard Morty's future father-in-law say stones represent truths in our paths that are hard to accept," said Mike. "I tried to figure out what he meant. I've learned that a hard truth sometimes comes with suffering."

Morty agreed. "We've lived through our share of hard truths."

"The coal mine is on the ridge's eastern side, where all the foundation and fireplace stones came from. This is now our half of the ridge." Mike wedged the corner of his spade under a stone. "I'm thankful we've this half of the ridge."

"I'm thankful we've got half of Da's walnuts." Jack shrugged. "Hate to see Waring with the others but, we planned for a memorial for Malcolm."

Full of stones the cart rattled all the way to the new cabin. Jack and Nell carried them inside. The dust from the stones sparkled in the sunrays from the windows. Nell mixed mortar. Morty tapped off their rough spots. Mike smoothed the edges to place them. All four children worked together in a whirlwind of dust and materials on the final job—the fireplace.

Weighing each stone in his hand, Mike surveyed their lines and curves before setting them. The intricate stone arch curved like a lovely eyebrow over the firebox beneath. They lined up the rocks that didn't quite fit into the fireplace along both sides of the cart path. This formed walls on both sides of the path.

"This will be a lined path for Edmond when he takes over the farm," said Jack.

Nell kept out of her brothers' plans, thankful for Morty's healing.

"There's plenty of room at Kate's house in St. Louis. Henry's new job there is going well." Jack cleared his throat.

The others stared at Jack, waiting.

"I decided to try out for the St. Louis Semi-Pro Boxing League," confessed Jack. "Uncle Willie thinks I'll make it."

Recovering from the shock of Jack's news, Morty gulped.

"Will you wait until Edmond arrives?"

"That's my plan," acknowledged Jack.

"What about you, Mike?" asked Morty.

"Ed'll need me. He won't appreciate our old equipment. I'll be here until he doesn't need me."

"The ridge?" asked Mike.

The brothers were silent.

"It might take me a long time, but I will follow Da's map and plant the ridge," stated Nell.

~~**~~**~~**~~

"Good-bye doesn't mean I won't cherish you in my thoughts each day," promised Morty. The family gathered around the hitching post.

Morty's leaving is hardest of all. After all his delays, I thought he might've been thinking about staying. His leg's better. Soon he'll be able to ride a horse.

Mike drove Morty to the depot in the wagon. Mike arrived back home with a headwind. It changed direction and howled through the log walls. "Morty was born on a night like this almost thirty years ago," recalled Ma. "God's favorite word is impossible."
"It looks like it's kicking up a big storm out there." Nell shuddered, standing at the window.

Later that night, a mighty burst of wind swept across a large swath of land around the ridge. All the walnuts clinging to the branches flew from the trees. Submerged in a layer of rainwater, many rushed down eroded gullies onto the walled cart path that headed straight toward the homestead. The stream of water cushioned, soaked, and channeled them.

The rain pelted down, and the stream on the walled cart path lined with the extra fireplace stones made a canal in the soft dirt. The swirling water filled with walnuts washed from the forest floor. The streamlets formed a rivulet in the cart path flowing with walnuts. They accumulated in a low spot behind the barn.

"It's as if Morty planned to line the path with stones. It worked grand. All the nuts rushed into the stream and collected into a pool behind the barn," cackled Ma. "Da always believed they'd husk better if soaked first.

"For years, the walnuts have been the extra we've used for trade. The neighbors are eager to barter for fresh-shelled nuts. The remaining nuts clung to the branches until Morty's departure." Ma wiped her eyes with her apron. "An opportunity for gunnysacks of walnuts still goes a long way."

~~**~~**~~**~~

On a Saturday morning in February 1895, as the sun sparkled down Main Street, in Brownsville County, Mike and Jack sparred on the train platform. It was cold enough to see their breath puffing. Ma clutched her newspaper. She was off to meet her grandchildren, with her hamper and small satchel at her feet. Nell stood beside her.

Mike twisted his hat. "Morty sensed you and Ma would leave soon, Jack. That's why he delivered the last of the walnuts before he left for Missouri. It'll make it easier for Nell and me to gather 'em."

"It's hard to believe the stream the cart path's stones made. The stone walls along the sides held the rain runoff in and made a stream," said Jack. "Walnuts delivered."

The big engine arrived at the station with a hissing of steam and clanging bell. The plank-board sidewalk vibrated. Helen Keith, Nell's new teacher, had spotted the Glissons at the depot. She hurried over to tell Ma about Nell's remarkable progress in school. She also wished Jack good luck. Before leaving, she gave Mike a pretty smile. Her last whispered words to Nell were, "I hoped you'd be here. Don't be afraid to let them go."

Keeping the water behind her eyes, Nell's brow wrinkled with worry.

I'm not anxious. I don't think Ma or Jack will be away from home for long.

With a mock uppercut, Mike tapped Jack's chin. "Soon, there'll be young'uns at play in the walnut mansions again."

"Yours?" said Jack with a laugh. "All aboard" could be heard in the background.

"No. I'll always remain a bachelor," said Mike.

"You're sure the ridge won't be too much with the farmwork?" Jack couldn't think of any other way to ask.

"Nell and I'll do our best. Jack, you're the complete package. You're tough." Mike hesitated. "But, how could anyone make it without you?"

"You're a great boxer, Jack," agreed Nell. "We'll keep the place going."

"If only we'd be together in St. Louis like a pair of draft horses. If we'd be any happier than we've been, why, we'd have to be...." Jack searched for an ending.

"Hog-tied." Mike finished for him. "Once brothers, always brothers."

"When did you say you wanted me to knock you out?"

"Take your best shot," Mike teased. Their laughter rang through the expectant crowd of passengers. Ma shushed them.

"Next time you're here, you'll be congratulated on all your wins. People will circle around you," said Mike.

"'Bout time to go." Jack grabbed his and Ma's things.

Ma hugged Mike and Nell. "I can't believe I'm meeting my grandchildren."
Jack wrapped Nell in a huge embrace. "We'll be back, Sis."
Surrounded by silence, with no one wanting to say goodbye, Mike reached his hand out to his brother.
Jack enfolded Mike in his arms. "See you soon, brother."

~~**~~**~~**~~

For part of the two-mile walk to school, Mike accompanied Nell. "I'm glad you've got a hood on your cape. The wind's cold. That was a good dinner last night. Your smile reminded me of Honora's when you gave me my plate."
Thanks, Honora. You taught me to smile when I serve. I'm the only face Mike has in front of him.
Nell scanned the horizon.
I'll make sure my face is a good one. If not, I reckon our days will creep along with loneliness hiding in the corners.

"I can't come right out and agree with you that they'll be back soon," said Mike. "Ma's sure tickled you're catching up at the school."
"Miss Keith is a good teacher," said Nell. "She's intrigued by my creative writing."
"Have you told her about the walnut grove and how it's part of your heart?" Mike winked. "Let her know why it's important to you. I'll make extra time at the end of the month. We'll prune the ridge."

"I don't want to lessen your time at the coal mine."
Mike needs that. Ma needs to visit her grandchildren.
Nell folded her hands in prayer.
I know Ma'll be back and Jack too, with all of his talent. There's been plenty of leaving. It's left holes in my heart. This time, two'll be back. I enjoy the work with Mike. He's so quiet.

Wanting to ease Mike's workload on the farm consumed Nell's thoughts. The demanding work matured this nineteen-year-old girl. She'd grown in skills and patience. With all the school she'd missed, could she, like Morty, graduate? She used every bit of her four foot ten inches to rake around the saplings, the cookstove, and all manner of farm and housework. Her size didn't matter. She managed new chores. Without her, Mike said it would be unbearable to farm.
This grants me hope, instead of thinking of Honora, her growing family, and disreputable husband, Charles.

"About time for me to return to my fireplace stones. I wish I could've gotten my eighth-grade diploma," said Mike with a sigh. "I know how far behind you were. Your progress is something Ma couldn't have dreamed of."
Waving good-bye to Mike, Nell hurried to school.
I only promised kindness to my family. I've had a bellyful of rumors. Others will find my ornery attitude if they push too far. I'll try to forgive Honora for moving a great distance away. It might take me until the turn of the century to relieve my anger and disappointment with her.

Ma's letter said that Honora mentioned her family sometimes goes without. Charles drinks up the money. Trouble skulks where and when he finds employment.
We could've been part of the experimental station with the college with half of the ridge. Honora left the walnut grove behind. For what?
Nell kicked a rock with all of her might.
That no-good Charles. I never wanted to attend school. Now I've got a teacher I'm learning from. Mike's always dreamed of another gold rush. He's tired of a wagonload of corn earning a dollar. Honora did so much for us younger kids. She helped Ma, grafted saplings, and scrubbed laundry.

Nell glared at her spindly arms.
I can't wash clothes like she did. Now, she and my nieces and nephews go to bed hungry. It isn't right! How am I going to do it without Honora? She left me with all of this. Why didn't Ma tell her she's made the biggest mistake of her life? Wouldn't Honora miss the walnuts? I loved her more than anybody, much more than that old Charles. I miss her. I know she'll never get home, like Da said about the Kansans. I'd do anything for her to return. I'd forgive her for everything.

Endless questions from Nell's classmates tested her resolve to be kind. "Have you received word on Honora? I bet Honora wanted to marry before Morty married Miss Webber? Is Morty in Missouri with Miss Webber now? Is Jack going to box in St. Louis? Do you miss your Ma?"

It took deep breaths for Nell to adjust to their questions. She bit her tongue. She kept her answers short. "I'm not sure. Jack's always been a great brother."
Gertie looks as though she might burst. She wants me to lash out at them.

Grabbing Nell's arm, Gertie pulled her away from their questions. "I know you've been worried about your family. I'll let them have it if you can't. Honora's such a beauty. How dare they? Morty's a fine and just man. Jack's loved by all."
"Thank you anyway. I know what's important to speak up about," explained Nell. "I like Miss Keith, at Ebeneezer School. The superintendent couldn't hire a better teacher if he swam naked and blindfolded across Crooked Creek in January."
"I heard Miss Keith's friendly with your brother Mike." Gertrude backed out of Nell's reach.

There was a sharp clap, and Miss Keith claimed their attention. "No more talking, students. Attend to your poems. All of you must develop your own style. There's a lyrical rhythm to Nell's writing. I, too, am familiar with farm life. But, I can spot verse that's full of heart."
Nell scrunched her eyes shut and held her stomach tight. She thumped her fists up and down beneath her desk in joy.
I fit.

Helen Keith didn't squint her eyes and wrinkle her nose at Nell's raspy voice. Instead, she said, "Never taught a student like you who smiles so with her eyes."

"That's how my Ma smiles, ma'am."
I love to hear this much more than the folks who comment on my inspecting eyes and glower.

~~**~~**~~**~~

The preparations to be completed for Edmond's April arrival stacked up in Nell's mind. As two years flew by, Ma remained in Kansas, helping Edmond and Lizzie. Mike completed the chimney all the way to the roof.
I'll sweep the dust and mortar. But I won't be doing any work on the roof, because it's too high off the ground for me.

A steady hum kept Nell's thoughts in order.
My Kansas brothers and sisters fight over Ma, as does Morty in Missouri, and Jack and Kate in St. Louis. They all say there isn't a place where she's not welcome.
Nell hoped that Edmond wouldn't be as pushy and forceful.
I hope he notices all the good things Mike does. Perhaps he'll realize I'm doing better? Only a few more months to graduation! Helen Keith can't believe I've soared through one exam after another. Ma said, "Surely Edmond's matured after all these years." I know how Ma'll smile with her eyes when she receives my diploma.

Morty urged Mike to keep records on the farm. He said, "Edmond might notice our outdated procedures." Jack thinks Mike's like the draft horses restrained. "He maintains self-control, but there's power underneath."
I wonder what Jack would think now?

Nell, who was preoccupied with the complications of family and chores, didn't notice a buggy stopped at the end of the drive. She cast a sharp look up the hill and across the fields for Mike.

Is he still putting last touches on the fireplace in the new cabin?

Reining in his horses, Sam shouted his greeting. "I'd like to have a word with your mother. I'm the new county commissioner. Seems quiet around here? I've taken over control of the fiscal operation of this county."
Nell's mouth gaped.
"I saw your mother boarding the Wabash the other day."
"How's my mother boarding a train of interest?" said Nell with a glower.

"I make anything in this county my interest. As bank president, I'd like to advise Mrs. Glisson on setting up a savings account. Then she'd be able to set aside funds for the taxes. It's not wise to wait until they're overdue. I discovered a new dwelling on your property. Each building poses additional tax rates. County laws are catching up with the times. There's no tax break on trees."
"My brother will pay the property taxes." Nell regained her voice.

"Your mother must trust *her* son. I wish Bud's head was on straight. Always tinkering with mechanical things."
"Mike keeps excellent farm records. He's finishing the chimney on the new log cabin for Edmond's family."

"It's close to the turn of the century, Miss Glisson. A log cabin is dated. You should be able to pay up this year's taxes with funds from the wood you've left to clear on your side of the ridge."

Sam Waring's going to counter everything I say.
"Your dad's dream with only half of Peace Ridge isn't practical for the twentieth century." Sam's face was a portrait of smugness.
"Edmond's eyes are on the twentieth century."

~~**~~**~~**~~

Sam Waring surveyed the primitive place as he drove out. *I remember Nell. She'll get right in the middle of a fight. That runt doesn't know what she's up against.*
He eased the team down the steep hill off their property.
The east side of the ridge and surrounding land are loaded with coal. It needs a new name. Waring's Coal Hollow is much better.
Sam chuckled.
If that no-good, lazy son of mine would obey. Bud's head is wrapped around the story of a couple of guys in Ohio with a glider.

Sam mumbled his calculations of the land value. "This ridge widens and narrows as it runs from the northwest to the southeast, cutting Pea Ridge Township at a diagonal. It stretches beyond Brownsville County's north and south borders. Mose Johnson reared his family of five off a small section of this ridge. The old west-bound train used to go right by there. A reliable miner, Mose

262

saved his money to pay his taxes. He's known as an authority in the area on all mining questions."

At least my boy, Bud, did something right to close that deal on Mose's section of coal. Mose enjoyed the whiskey Bud provided before he signed the paperwork. The land is in Bud's name, but that's simply for the record. He's collected my rent on properties all over this county. I told him I'd have Stephen piece out the storage of stolen walnut wood on my various holdings. Bud's reaction to Stephen's assault on that Glisson girl, surprises me.

Sam shook his head.

Bud doesn't need to know everything. Next thing I know, he'll care about their wood. He's like his mother. I'll tell him the old storage buildings near the train tracks aren't part of the deal.

Sam snorted.

Mose sold the storage buildings to the train company. He'll never suspect that's where I told Stephen to store the Glissons' hardwoods. I'll break the Glissons. They'll go broke like the others. Soon, I'll have them all bought out.

The coal varies in thickness. Plenty of mining remains along that eastern side of the ridge. The land's too hilly and rough for farming. Drift and strip mines are the only way to work these hills.

Sam gave a low whistle and said, "Bloody Hell."

Six-foot-wide passages can easily be dug out to twenty feet. If a body only has the means to remove these remaining farms. I'll feel that old familiar delirium the day the last Glisson moves away.

Chapter 23
Edmond's Cabin

With knees bent high, a thrusting kick, and a swing of her arms, Nell sprang from Ma's rocker. She'd fallen asleep behind her pile of mending. She dreamed of Ma's joyous face, playing with her grandchildren, and helping with Honora's mounds of laundry. "It's late? Mike hasn't returned from his delivery of wood staves to the Keiths?" *I know he enjoyed discussions about the election of the new president with Helen Keith. Miss Keith read the results at school. Ma did so much for all of us. She said she believed in me and that I could do it. Something's not right.*

"Fire? Why do I smell fire?" asked Nell.
What's that smoky smell?
"What fire can that be? We've been working so hard. Everything's almost ready for Edmond's arrival."
No time for daydreaming. She glanced at the stove and fireplace. The fire burned down to a few coals. She threw open the front door and sped around the homestead cabin. In the distance, the orange sunset above Edmond's cabin included a fiery tree. What?

The smell of burning wood filled her lungs. She coughed and spluttered. She jerked the two milk buckets off the back porch. The burning tree so close to the new cabin horrified her. Choking in smoke, with her heart beating like a blacksmith's hammer, she ran toward the fire. The crackle of the flames sounded like devil's play. The burned branches swung back and forth in the dusk overhead.

My heart feels like it's beating out of control.

Nell flew to the spring. She filled the buckets. She ran in circles. She bolted for the back of the burning cabin. The back wall caught branches on fire. Nell sprinted to the spring.

I wish Honora were here. She's strong. She could help keep this fire from more destruction. Oh, why did she leave me with so much? Mike?

Bucket after bucket, Nell heaved the water on the flames.

Panting and scared, Nell's thoughts billowed like the flames.

How could I fall asleep? Oh.

She watched as the flames sizzled and leaped up the back of the new cabin. Heat washed over her body. She choked on smoke and flames.

All the beautiful hardwoods are going up in smoke.

What happened?

Mike must've forgotten to check the fireplace's draft. Perhaps it caught fire and burned the back wall of the cabin. Oh, look at the roof.

With a wrench of her arms, Nell tottered back with more full buckets. Her aching legs tugged up the incline to the new cabin. Black branches dropped all around her. She screamed. They missed her by inches. She hopped up and down. Nell cast a grim look at Honora's old, worn-out shoes.

On this night, I could've used army boots. My torn nightdress is black with soot. Honora would've been angry.

At the spring, Nell lurched headlong over a stump. The muddy water drenched her blackened dress. Gasping for breath, she yanked herself up and slammed into a man. Water splashed out all over the front of them. Too exhausted to speak, Nell regained her footing and kept going.
I don't care who he is as long as he helps. One thing's sure. It's not Mike.

~~**~~**~~**~~

A high-wheel, westbound bicycle turned around. The cyclist, Joe Robertson, sniffed.
Oh. Smells like smoke?
With a snoot full of fumes, Joe had to hop off his bike, while coughing and sneezing.
Is that fire on the north side of the road where I made an offer on that property?
Joe slapped his forehead in disbelief. "It couldn't be … no, is it?"
Is it the little house on the forty acres? Burning? But no, mercy, it's on the south, a little east of the land that's for sale.

He steered his bike off the road to the south. He raced down the cart path through the trees. Joe's eyes burned with smoke. He choked and gasped. He came to a burning cabin. His vision weakened. He sized the situation on the fly and charged right into a girl in her nightdress who was carrying two heavy buckets. The remaining water she tossed onto the flames. He peered at the burning cabin. He tore off his outer jacket and inner vest. With one in each hand, he began to smother the flames.

The young girl made trip after trip. She sprinted back and forth from the spring. Joe continued to slap the flames. The girl doused them with the milk buckets. He bent right, left, and behind, beating the flames down. The relentless sloshing continued around him. The two of them worked side by side at breakneck speed. From the corner of his eye, he glimpsed a wagon jerk to a sudden stop.

~~**~~**~~**~~

Mike knew the route home as well as the horses did. He chewed on his plans about what remained to be done around the farm after he delivered the order for Miss Keith's father.

First, I've got to ….

Mike caught the smell of smoke. "Oh my! It can't be. No. No. Oh my goodness. Lord!"

I promised the family I'd never leave our puny sister alone. Is she always going to need looking out for?

He whipped up the horses, headed the wagon off the road, and crashed through the brush. Mike leaped off. He charged in the direction of the ridge.

Ed's cabin? I checked the firebox for sparks. What sparked? I put a whole bucket of water on the ashes. The same thing could happen to the rest of the wood I've stored in the storage shed for Ma and Nell. Hardwood piled to the west?

Mike barreled on.
Oh, mercy. It's nowhere near the woodpiles.
"Oh, no! Oh, no! Not Ed's cabin."
There's Nell, running in her nightdress.
Mike's heart pounded.
There's a man smothering flames with his jacket.

While she was filling her buckets at the spring, Nell's pointy chin stood out, smeared with soot. Mike snatched a couple of gunnysacks, dampened them, and smothered more flames. He recognized the other man as Joe Robertson, from Pea Ridge Township. Demonstrating plenty of power and strength as the other two tuckered out, Mike kept going until the flames were extinguished.

He hugged his exhausted sister. At a loss to understand the ruined cabin, Mike bent all the way over, with his hands on his knees. It looked uninhabitable for man or beast. He wiped the sweat off his brow. Consumed with coughing, he nodded his thanks to Joe. He clutched his frazzled sister to his chest. Nell sobbed in breaths of air.

Mike scrutinized the cabin. "Hard to take in."
He smelled a suspicious odor. What? That's impossible. Kerosene?"
Better take a look at the foundation where the fire started."

Joe crouched beside Mike. Nell followed in a daze.
"What are you looking at, Mike?"
"Oh! What's this? Why, it looks like dog tracks in the dirt.
Don't remember any dogs around?" Mike shook his
head. "Joe, thank you. Anyone driving the road?"

"No, I couldn't see anybody from my bicycle for a couple
of miles either way. The steam singed my eyebrows. I'm
still coughing from the strong smoke. I detected a
strange gassy smell when I arrived. But no, I didn't notice
anyone."
"I fell asleep in Ma's rocker. I woke up to the smell of
smoke," reported Nell. "I didn't spot or hear anything."
"Was anyone near here?" Mike kept pushing for some
recall.
"I didn't see anyone on the road," reflected Joe. "I
recognized the glowing sky and the branches with
orange and red flames. I ran to check on everyone's
safety."

Mike ground his teeth. "We got the fire out, but the
cabin's ruined. Poor Edmond. His family's new Illinois
home is ruined. Someone set it ablaze on purpose."
"A shame. No reason for that." Joe cringed.
Too exhausted for a debate, Mike wanted Nell to return
home. "I don't want you to catch a lung infection. Go.
Put dry clothes on. Please go. We'd love a cup of coffee
in the morning. I'll be on watch all night."

"I'll hole up with you," added Joe. "I thought someone
lit a bonfire for our new President McKinley."

"No. If this fire isn't bad enough?" queried Mike. "The election didn't favor the small farmer. But tonight, I found out about McKinley's victory. I respected poor Bryan's ideas. I'd like to be celebrating Bryan's victory. Lots of us in the rural areas of the Midwest needed him. Bryan wanted to mine silver for economic improvements."

Nell washed up, made coffee, and sliced bread and ham for sandwiches. It was difficult to sit still. She returned to the burned cabin. Mike and Joe sat together. They came up with a plan. They'd salvage what they could from the cabin.

Later, they carried the beds from the new cabin into the loft of the old homestead. Nell got the linens. They made a partition at one end of the parlor for Edmond, Lizzie, and the baby. Mike mumbled with a peg in his mouth, "We've got to take the good with the bad, and we'll let Edmond know about the destruction of the new cabin. At least we didn't lose anyone."

It took Mike several days to write a letter to Morty. "It's difficult to let Jack know, also. He worked so hard. There are so many unanswered questions. Will Edmond still come? Ma will care only that we're okay."

~**~~**~~**~~

A few weeks after the fire, Joe returned for a visit. They shared their noon meal with him.

Mike mentioned his concerns. "I spotted Sam Waring's buggy from the roof of the new cabin on the day of the fire. The fire didn't start in the firebox but in the logs on the new cabin's back wall. I found rags that smelled like kerosene in dry wood stacked at the base of the foundation."

Mike battered on the charred walls with his fists. "With the family due here soon, we'll have to drag the burned cabin into the woods with a couple of teams. Spring's around the corner. We're too busy to redo that shell of a cabin."
Joe's help made transferring items from the burned cabin to the homestead's loft easier. He mentioned his quest to purchase a few more acres to farm. "I made an offer on the land, to the north across the road."

"Good," said Mike. "Farmers are selling out to Sam Waring."
Someone set the fire. How can we ever find the culprit? Ma always says, "We'll. have the Lord's justice.

Chapter 24
The Plum Harrow

After splitting some logs for kindling, Nell fired up the woodstove. With the fire down to low coals, she kept the ham and beans simmering for Mike's arrival.

I've got enough time to run to the mailbox.

Not far down the road from the mailboxes, Joe Robertson rambled along on his high- wheeler. He saw her and waved his hand above the handlebars. "I'll race you," he yelled. He made a U-turn on the big wheel in the middle of the road. Joe gestured for Nell to speed up. "Try to beat me to the mailboxes."

Nell pumped her arms, ran, and slowed down. With a wide grin, chin high, she maintained a more ladylike pace.

"The way you ran at the fire, I knew you'd win." Joe circled around.

"Mike and I appreciated your help, Mr. Robertson," replied Nell. "I don't know what we would've done if you hadn't appeared. You're pretty good on that high-wheeler."

"I've been in races over in Adam's County. My name's Joe. I'm glad to get acquainted with my neighbors. Met you once on a hayrack ride. You're still in school?"

"I'm graduating!"

I can't believe I can say that after all those years of being so behind and such a runt. This Joe doesn't notice my small size. I'm not that short. I'm tall enough to reach out and take my diploma from the superintendent.

~~**~~**~~**~~

Nell returned from the mailbox. The two letters with their distant return addresses created such a sensation that she and Mike could hardly take a bite of their ham and beans.

"They are from such faraway places," said Mike. He opened Bill Drew's letter from Idaho.

"Bill mentioned his family in Iowa. They think of us often."

"Did he ask how *all* of us are?" interrupted Nell.

"He mentioned the Forest Service work he's doing on the border between Montana and Idaho. They've got to replant groves after logging."

Mike's lips moved as he reread Bill's letter. "He mentioned the church plaque Da admired. He called Da 'a man ahead of his time in conservation.' There's more. Listen to this. 'Have you allowed that old farm to take over your life, Mike? Gold's been found along several Washington rivers.'" Mike whistled. "Bill sends his regards to you. He hopes you're doing well and Ma's fine."

Nell fanned the second letter in front of her nose. "Here's the fancy one. The return address is from Putney, England. That's where David Copperfield's wife, Dora, lived." Nell angled her eyebrows. "It's perfumed and written with a feminine touch."

Dear Glisson Family,

"That's tomorrow," gasped Mike. "We'd better make a trip into the depot and meet this Elsie Powell's train."
Elsie was nothing like Nell pictured her. She was polished, but slightly tarnished in voice and mannerisms. She glowed on every topic about Seattle. She'd been hired as a dance- hall girl. She wanted freedom before she settled down with a family. She claimed she'd been a schoolteacher at an early age. The little urchins tried to turn her hair white. Now, she's on her way to the "American Wild West."

Throughout the next several days, Mike's face turned red. His eyes pretty near popped out of his head at Elsie's speech and the way she conducted herself.
"Oy, here you go. Grab some of these lily bulbs for your mum," Elsie cooed.
"What do I do with them?" asked Nell.

Coo, just put them in the ground any old where," chirped Elsie.

Mike folded and unfolded Bill's letter. "Bill's letter came about the same time as yours did, Miss. Here are both addresses. Bill works on the border between Idaho and Montana. The Drew family resides in Iowa. If you continue going West—you'll meet your aunt's family, on your way to Seattle, and Bill, when you're almost to Washington."

Elsie danced, instead of walked. She wore flimsy dancing shoes. She kicked up her heels. Nell fingered one of her silky fishnet stockings from the wash. She didn't come down the loft ladder like anyone on which Nell'd ever set eyes on. She sashayed down in her skimpy skirt with high-flying kicks that sent Mike to the barn in a hurry.

She asked Nell about her beau? Nell, who was too nervous to mention anyone, hid her flushed face.
I don't want to say anything about Joe Robertson or anyone else. I wish Honora could advise me.
Elsie showed Nell how to primp and curl her hair. She jazzed up Nell's old dresses with bright ribbons and colorful bows.
"In two days, I've wrapped Mike around my little finger," said Elsie. "He jumps for my every need. He makes a headlong rush to take me to town each evening to check out the nightlife.

"After a few rough evenings with a group of hired hands fighting over me, one rambunctious one in particular,

Stephen, poor Mike got worried. Your brother said, 'If I were you, I'd keep away from Stephen. He's been let go as Sam Waring's foreman. He's dangerous. I suggest you're on the next train west.'"
Elsie's giggles filled the parlor. "He isn't the best dancer with that right arm of his. But he makes up for it with his wicked smile."
I never thought anyone like a dance-hall girl would stay at our cabin.

~~**~~**~~**~~

A few moments of alone time at the coal mine were something Nell knew her brother treasured. "I didn't mean to interrupt you." Nell poured cool water from Ma's crock. "Wonder if Elsie's made it out West?"
Mike wiped his sweaty brow. "This is my prayer place for all of my family's happiness. Jack's boxing. It might be easier odds than me ever striking gold, but the Lord may let Jack succeed. For me to work alongside Edmond would be enough. And if there's another gold rush why, I tell the Lord, 'I'd be obliged.'"

"Are you thinking about goldmining?" asked Nell.
"Let me dig out this spot." Mike tapped away at an outcrop washed away in the creek. He used his pick to break it up. The pick sank a couple of feet. "This is more coal than I expected."
Nell remained quiet.
"The hillside goes back horizontally. It'll be easier to mine than digging a downward sloping tunnel. This coal vein must travel the length of Pea Ridge and pertnir to the horizon."

Mike continued, "Da said a person would be able to take it out in lumps in any place underlain a couple of feet thick. There are clay and rock but give me time. I'll hit black coal. Do you think that's why the trees grow well?"
"A bushel of coal looks easier than a bushel of corn does."
"Wouldn't it be a shock to discover yellow rock in a vein? I know you're worrying about the memorial grove. Tomorrow we'll work there. I won't borrow trouble, but with Edmond's strong opinions, we'll need it to look as good as it can. He's against it."

With plenty of time before Ed's expected arrival, Mike kept his word. They weeded, raked dead branches, and cleaned up around the remaining walnut trees. "I'll return to the ridge within the year and prune. The lower branches are scraggly. Several need their tops defined." First, Mike cut unwanted branches off. Then he perched on the edge of a log. He leaned close, and with his knife, like a surgeon, he helped nature by scraping away at the fresh cut to make a clean flush diamond shape around the damaged area. "The scrape allows the bark to grow back evenly as the cut heals."

"It's perfect," said Nell.
"It improves on the price of the logs." Mike nodded.
"Thanks, Mike." She gathered a large armload of smaller branches.
"Edmond wants to make the Glisson farm like many others in the county. With row crops that extend from boundary marker to marker. Some of the wood I've

logged hasn't only been for rails and staves. I've hidden some large, valuable logs in that old storage shed. They're not perfect, but the long boards'll bring a good price." Mike stared at his hands. "If something happens to me, it'll be like money in the bank for you and Ma. I've got a few more marked."

~~**~~**~~**~~

Mike searched through the thicket of wild plum trees. "Ah, this'll do." He cut down a medium tree in a tangle that needed thinning. Then, with his ax, he hacked off some thorny limbs. He cut a ring around the trunk and connected a chain for a makeshift plow. Then he hitched it up behind the horse. "There, Chester. It won't hurt you. I got you."

Nell watched fascinated. "You carried that tree all by yourself. Last June, you carried the plow across the swampy ground. Your heart must be three times the size of most men's?"
He's like Da.
"I might be strong, but I need your help today for this oat field," said Mike. "If all works well, we'll plant these oats for the horses. Ed's not crazy about oats, either. As small as you are, you'll fit on the harrow. You're tougher."

I'm not as scared as I used to be when I didn't have all of my sisters and brothers. How high off the ground is this harrow? Mike's easy to work with, kind and gentle. I want to keep him on the farm. After Morty and Jack left, I've got to let go.

"Are you ready, Nell? All you're going to do is ride the thing. I figure your ninety-seven pounds will be enough to keep the tree's cut branches digging into the soil like a harrow."

"This reminds me of Joe's high-wheeler, but not as high." Nell set the cool water crock in the shade.
Mike's thinks I'm enough.
With a click of his tongue, Mike prodded the horse. "That a boy, Chester. You've got an old tree behind you. It won't hurt you, boy. There's a real purty gal riding on it. Giddap there. Let's get underway."

I'm amazed. Mike creates something out of nothing. We've both worked since dawn. The field's harrowed. We don't talk. The hours disappear. There's no mention of gold explorations. He does mention how he wants Ma and my life to be easier and happier. Maybe he'll abide here? He says I'm important to the homestead.

A thick branch off the top of the trunk made a perfect place for Nell to hang on. Mike had wired handholds for her to grasp. Her weight pressed the chopped-off limbs into the ground, which acted like teeth in place of a plow. The old tree seemed to work like a harrow. It was a bumpy ride, but she hung on with all her strength.

Up and down the hills, Mike shouted. When he came to sharp turns, he called, "Hold on tight."
Trying to be funny, Nell widened her stance and put her hands above her head. "Whee, whee."

"Whoa, there, Chester." Mike's face turned white. What do you think you're doing on these turns, Nell? I don't want you killed. You scared me to pieces." He stoked his pipe and took a few quick puffs. "Okay, ready for more excitement?"

"Git up there, boy!" Mike struck his hat against his thigh. Nell laughed while she bounced along. He flicked the reins on Chester's back. Then they slowed down to a reasonable speed. He plowed up and down each row in the field. They gazed back at their work. The plum-tree harrow removed the clumps. The field was ready for oats.

"What fun," gushed Nell. Her eyes roved across their work. Afternoon sun bathed everything in soft light. Mike strolled behind the horse and harrow, with his head tilted to the side. He maintained control of the draft horse with the lightest touch on the long reins. Now and then, he clicked his tongue for the horse. It was quiet work. The draft, with his silent power, pulled them across the field.

Nell's weight helped the harrow dig in to smash the clumps, breaking them into soil. They jounced over and across another field. The tree's branches, like tines, checkered the acreage with sun and shadows. The iron harrow now in demand shared with three other farmers who couldn't wait—wasn't needed. Nell searched for the right words to describe Mike skipping down the furrows and scooping up handfuls of soil. "My, you're kicking up your heels like Elsie did."

"One way or another, the oats are sown." Mike unhitched the horse and looked up to find a visitor. "Speaking of kicking up your heels," said Mike. "Aye. Good evening, Mr. Robertson."
Joe tipped his hat. "Well. I'll be. That harrow looks like a tree trunk. Dag-gum if that old tree didn't do a superb job as a plow. Even the thorns helped crumple it up."
"Nell, if you can climb aboard this big contraption, you can manage my high- wheeler," Joe said softly.
Nell recognized the wrinkle in Mike's brow at Joe.
Doesn't he trust him?

After an uncomfortable silence, Mike said, "Aye, I couldn't have done it without Nell. The steep hills were a little scary. But we've got our rhythm now."
Unsteady on her shaky legs, Nell swayed as she stepped off the harrow. Joe grabbed her hand. She glanced around for Mike. His back was to her, as he led Chester to the barn.
"I bet you need a break. Would you like to stretch your legs?" Joe took her hand. She turned back to look, but Mike didn't tag along.

~~**~~**~~**~~

They strolled along in silence, along the margins of the fields on the cart path. Nell spotted the little domed archway over an old forest path. "Oh, let's go that way. I love how the branches spread over the path are like a small doorway."
"The trees in front of the house I bought look like they'd do the same thing. It's time to cut the clutter," said Joe.

282

"Cut them? But they add so much beauty. Trees are valuable."
"Nell? Is there anyone courting you at this time?"
She shook her head, swallowed, and took a deep breath.
It feels as though I'm trying to swim across the pond underwater. I wish I could talk to Ma.

"Do you think your Ma would approve of me?" asked Joe.
Nell nodded.
"Is it okay with you?" Again, Nell nodded. But this time, she smiled.
"Well, I'll be." Joe laughed. "I remember you at the hayrack ride. You spoke your tongue. Now you're so quiet. What was that? I thought I heard a tadpole gulp?"
As the trail narrowed to a single track, Joe led. He put both hands behind his back, with his palms up. Nell hesitated, thinking of Pete dancing on the ridge. She reached out and put her hands in his. With gentle pressure, he squeezed. Nell bit her lip.
It feels like I'm swimming across the pond underwater, and the water's murky. I can't see my way. It's emerald, green with white rays of light.

CHAPTER 25
High-Wheelers

There was one more day of "plum harrowing" because a few more hilly fields remained. After a while, Mike sat down in the shade. "Nell, I need to talk to you."

"But Mike, right now?"

"Yes, Nell." Mike plunged right in. "Joe's interested in how much land we own. He inquired whether you have an inheritance."

My legs feel as if they are going out from under me.

"I asked him what his intentions are."

Speechless, Nell swallowed.

"He stated he wants to increase his acreage."

A heavy silence fell between them.

"Mike, you don't want me hurt. I know that. I wish Ma was here."

"Yes, me too. I think of Honora. I want more for you. I know you want to protect Da's legacy. I'm not a good one on romance."

"I know you say you'll always be a bachelor. But Miss Keith?"

That'll never be." Mike shook his head. "There's one thing Ma shared that might help you. She said this about Da. "If you make a commitment, don't focus on your sweetheart's weaknesses but build their strengths."

"Thank you, Mike."

"Of course, you're not married yet. But let's try to finish the...." Their fieldwork came to a sudden stop. Uncle

Willie's wagon rounded the bend and pulled up with Edmond and his family!

Cries of joy came from the wagon. Mike and Nell embraced their brother's large family. "It's been a long time. I don't know whom to hug next?"
Edmond, and sister-in-law Lizzie, couldn't get enough of Nell and Mike. "These are your nieces and nephews. It's a long train trip for them."

An older boy, with a bright-blue cap, and three little boys in pants with suspenders peered over the side of the wagon. One tall girl, and two younger sisters in darling bonnets and long calico dresses, grinned from behind their mother. Lizzie held a tiny infant wrapped in thick blankets. She made introductions all around.

Catching up this one and setting them each on the ground, they got everyone unloaded from the wagon bed. They didn't miss one of them with their big hugs and joyful welcomes. Nell glanced up and smiled before she spotted the disgruntled look on Edmond's face.

"Don't tell me that's the best we've got for harrowing? What happened to that old iron rattletrap we used to share with the neighbors?"
"It's in great demand," replied Mike.
"Let me settle into the old homestead. Then everybody out of my way. I want to take a gander at that burned cabin." Edmond retorted. "I understand the sheriff needs evidence. Have you heard anything from the neighbors?"

"Joe Robertson was there that night. He spoke to Bud Waring one day in town. Bud said if he ever learned of any of his dad's men involved in the fire, he'd call the sheriff."
"Bud's changed?" asked Edmond.
"Bud doesn't want any part of wrongdoing. He'd like to end the revenge."
"If I could prove someone started that fire. Is that …?" A distracted Edmond gaped. "That isn't a wild plum you used for the harrow. Is it?"
"Um." Mike opened his mouth.
"You mean to tell me those wild plum trees haven't been cleared off the place yet?"
I won't let Ed mistreat Mike.

"It works dandy, Ed. Watch this." Nell hopped on.
The family enjoyed watching Nell ride the plum harrow. Her legs spread out, and her long dress flapped around her ankles in the breeze.
Let them see how creative their Uncle Mike is.
Edmond's children whooped and hollered. The older ones wanted a turn.

"I couldn't be more tickled," said Nell. Her nieces and nephews said they loved everything about the homestead. They romped around in joy at the homestead cabin that Da built.
"This cabin reminds me of a fairy tale with a house hidden in the woods," said Kathryne. "The nuts falling with a rat-a-tat-tat on the roof make it mysterious. I want to play forever in the log mansions."

I wonder if the homestead speaks happiness to them after the windswept Kansas prairie?
Nell smiled.

"It's well-loved. It looks like it's been here since the beginning of time. They said there are more trees on Grandma's land than in all of Kansas. There are layers and layers of trees." From the farmyard, the children spotted the ridge disappearing over the horizon. The burned cabin set their hair on end with their made-up wild stories of Indians burning it. The old cart path wandered off into the forest and added to the drama.

I can't imagine my Da traveling with our big family across the miles Edmond's family came. I hope they treasure it here for a long, long time and never leave.

~~**~~**~~**~~

After everyone settled in, Nell helped out at the recently built old folks' home next to the almshouse. She wanted to let Lizzie have the run of the cabin. Besides, this would allow Nell time to visit her aged Uncle Willie. He lived there now. Mike waited for Nell to come home. Ed's children flocked around and waited for their Aunt Nell and Uncle Mike to entertain them. They often led the children to the ridge to build mansions or to Crooked Creek. Mike taught them about geodes, hardwoods, and coal. Mike demonstrated what he knew about mining. The children's eyes grew big with their Uncle Mike's desire to mine gold.

"You, children, inside now," grumbled Edmond. He smirked in the direction of the original farm equipment, which was still scattered along the margins of the field as if it had been for years.

That evening, Mike and Nell strolled along from the creek.

"I told you we needed to plant those oat fields before Ed got here," said Mike.

"Yep, he's like Joe," agreed Nell. "Both are full of strong desires to bring the place into the twentieth century."

"Last week, Joe asked me if he could take you dancing. I said yes if he didn't arrive on his high-wheeler. Edmond's all for it."

Nell placed a hand over her mouth.

"Did I embarrass ye?" asked Mike.

Nell's face turned a pinkish shade. "I like him. He's nothing like Da." She waited a few minutes and said, "It's like another chance to be with Da when I help Uncle Willie."

"How's Uncle Willie adjusting to his new home?" asked Mike.

"He said, 'my old croi's not the best. The old noggin works as well as ever.' He insists he won't let his land be sold to Sam Waring. He spends most days on a porch rocker, wrapped in a blanket. Sometimes he talks about our ancestors' castles in Ireland. I told him about my difficulties of being born with breathing problems and being so behind and then catching up."

"Does Uncle Willie know about Joe Robertson?"

"Yes." Nell spun away, with a red face. "Uncle said if Joe asks me to marry, will I have Edmond give me away?"

Mike made a sudden shift in his posture. His fists tightened.

Nell said, "I told him no. I'll have my big brother Mike give me away."

Reaching for his pipe, Mike cleared his throat. He stared at the ridge.

As if someone could hear her, Nell lowered her voice. "Mike, you know the land I inherited that's on the grove. Would you trade me? I wish the walnuts were in your name. Joe's like Edmond. He wants row crops."

"Consider it done." Mike stood tall. "Write out a paper and sign it. I'll go to the clerk and recorder's office. We'll both protect the memorial."

"There's something else, Mike. I can't stop worrying about Honora."

"Charles is a poor husband." Mike looked up from his boots. "Joe's an excellent businessman. He's a respected farmer. He knows all about yields. His fields are picture-perfect. You wish Honora married better. That makes two of us. But there's no comparing him to Joe."

"Since she's got such a bad husband and sold her inheritance, I pray the dream of Da's legacy creates enough hope to bring her back," said Nell.

"Don't let Honora's poor husband make you lose Joe. He's the kind of man who won't leave. You'll never

starve. Life should be easier. He'll have plenty of acres and we'll protect the ridge."
Mike approves of Joe.

~~**~~**~~**~~

The entire Glisson family gathered on the porch in the evening shade. Joe stopped by and asked Nell for a walk. All the children wanted to come. Lizzie wisely told them no. Nell wrung her hands after her conversation with Mike. He'd reminded her of the importance of the walnut grove in her life.

I'm so glad to spend time with Joe. Would I forgo the grove in an attempt not to lose him? No. I don't want him to think I'm like Honora, telling Charles, "Whatever suits you tickles me plum to death."
Nell gritted her teeth.
Not me. Instead, I told him I'd take care of the grove. I've got a little saved from my job. Now, I'm so mixed up. I don't know how I feel.

"Let's not say any more about the walnut grove," said Joe on the way back. He took Nell into his arms.
Before she melted like candle wax, Nell stepped away.
"I've got a question," said Joe.
"Oh, not now, Joe. Let's spend time with Edmond's family."
"How about a ride on my uncle's old high-wheeler bicycle?"
"No. Too high for me." Nell scrambled away from him.

All the children laughed.

290

"Mike, can you help?" asked Joe. "You can stick your feet out and catch the evening breeze as you go down the drive."

"Oh, no, not that steep hill," balked Nell.

"You'll be easy to heft from my shoulder up onto the seat." Mike said, "Joe, can you hold the bicycle on the other side? I've got this side."

Up Nell went.

"No. I can't reach the pedals," said Nell.

Joe's broad shoulders. Ma said she believes I could do anything, but maybe not this. That front wheel's taller than I am. My legs are so short. Where do I put my feet?

Scurrying from the porch, the children screamed and laughed. Nell bounced along on the high seat, her legs straight out. A male cardinal flitted in the brush along the drive. It was Da's favorite. Nell laughed.

Da used to say cardinals are a clear sign of a romance.

Nell let go and extended her arms with her legs. "Whee, whee."

This man's in love with me, or he wouldn't have put me on his high-wheeler bicycle. I think he's in love. Am I? I can't believe it. If it isn't so, I don't want to know. Don't let go of me, Joe.

~~**~~**~~**~~

Nieces and nephews crowded around as Nell demonstrated how to rake one of the vegetable mounds and spread out the manure and debris. "This tunnel is the way Ma preserves fruits and vegetables. Preserves means to keep them from rotting through the winter. Ma said her mother called them 'Proverb tunnels.' A

291

wise woman knows the Lord'll help provide food for her household all year. She'd want you to consider the ants. They store food for the winter."

Joe twisted his cap and frowned at the tunnels.
"The potatoes, apples, and cabbage need manure," explained Nell to the children. "This fall, we'll cover the potatoes with straw, branches, soil, and manure. The fruit or vegetables will make it through cold winters."
"Children's work. Messy piles everywhere." Joe cleared his throat. "Their aunt might busy herself with other jobs."

Nell stood with her hands on her hips.
"I don't want my future wife crawling in tunnels and bartering walnuts."
Bouncing to her feet and not catching her breath, Nell said, "Our ways look mighty poor to you. But where my Da grew up, they counted on every potato." The dirt clung to her sweaty face in the humid air.
Why doesn't he say something?

The bark and soil under her nails from raking the manure embarrassed her. "You think we're a bunch of grasshoppers?"
"Nell, please. You've sure been flying off the handle. Can you stop raking with your nieces and nephews?"
With a thrust of her chin, Nell ignored Joe.
"By golly, you're driving a stump right into this proposal."
"Proposal?"

Joe got down on one knee. From his pocket, he slipped out a gold ring.

Nell gasped.

I feel like my legs are going out from under me.

"As I acquire more acres for crops, you'll consider me a better man. I've tried to find a private moment to ask you to marry me." Joe's hands wouldn't settle. "You sure know how to make a fellow look like a muttonhead." His voice softened. "Would you do me the honor?"

He's the type that won't leave this area. He'll come around.

"Yes," Nell said, breathing steadily to the tune of her nieces and nephews' cheers.

"Fine, then. I've got the county papers for the marriage. I think it's a safe risk to fill in the names now."

"That's the wrong thing to say. I wouldn't want you to waste time on the names on the papers." Nell turned back to her raking. "I don't want to hear about safe risks and paperwork. I'd like to hear you say you love me several times a week even in things we don't see eye to eye. We could meet in the middle."

"Sure, the way you're all glued together. You might as well bring that little Kathryne and some of the others on our honeymoon." Joe fumed.

"Honeymoon? You'd want me to wear my work clothes under my bridal dress to save time."

Me? Someone wants me? Not just anybody. A gem of a worker like Joe.

One evening, the sun hung low in the sky behind the barn. Edmond meandered around, appraising the farm equipment with Joe and Nell.

At the back of the barn, Nell pointed out bags of husked walnuts hanging from the rafters. "Morty's special delivery. He left for Missouri, and a storm swept them here in front of the barn. There's a purpose in the fact that they're stored here. They're safe and lasting."

"After we husk them, we let them dry. They hang from the barn rafters. The Missouri buyer comes in late November. He buys them. Yep, Mike's got hardwood logs stored in the storage shed and coal from the ridge."

Talking right over Nell, Ed said, "What do you think, Joe? Clutter that takes up space for new equipment?"

"Clutter?" said Nell.

"Those pioneer days." Edmond rolled his eyes. "We'll need room in our buildings."

"Joe, don't we have room for the ancient high-wheeler?" asked Nell.

"Right," said Edmond. "No old rust buckets left to stand around like dead warriors. Not Joe's new place."

Oblivious, Edmond grabbed at a dangling rope. A bag of walnuts hitched to a rafter rained down. Nell and the children laughed. Edmond mumbled something to Joe about Nell's feistiness. "We've always known she'd need to be cared for and wouldn't be able to do much on her own. Small and frail but born with a *mouth.*"

Nell sighed.

"I'll sew up the bag."

"Can we sew it together, Aunt Nell?" asked Kathryne.

"Yes, 'Kath-Wren.' Would it be okay if I call you Wren, like your Ma does?"

"It's fun being with you," said six-year-old Wren.

Taking the little girl's face in her hands, Nell kissed her forehead.

"Wren sounds good to me, Aunt Nell." Wren looked down at her brown boots and slid them through the dust. "You're the best aunt I could ever have."

While the equipment inventory was completed, Mike bent over the bag. "Joe's antsy to ask more questions about the price of Uncle Willie's land."

Nell's eyes met Mike's. She chewed on her fingernail for the right words. "Edmond acts as if he bought each of our inheritances, it would still be a pittance. He wants everything big and looking like a polished penny. Is that what makes a good farm?"

"He knows your inheritance's not a pittance," said Mike. "Joe must care for you. He made sure you didn't take a spill on the bicycle, didn't he?"

"Or wreck it," countered Nell.

"Uh-oh," said Mike. "More trouble."

Ed cast scornful looks at the old cart and the farm wagon. "That eyesore of a cart's got to go."

It wasn't hard to see the change in Mike. He took Edmond's guff, but Nell observed the sweetness in farm life disappearing for him.

*He's happiest when Edmond's children flock around him,
and when we worked together. Like me, they believe he
can do anything.*

"Your Aunt Nell relies on this cart." Mike's voice
sounded upbeat. "Let's grease the axle for her. We'll
check for any splits."
The children circled around.
"Let the cart wait," ordered Edmond. "There's more
important equipment to work on to keep this farm
aboveground."
All of Edmond's list of priorities were completed. Several
things still worked better than Edmond admitted. Mike
did his best. He continued checking off items on
Edmond's newest list.

Days later, Mike told Nell his reply to Edmond's pressing
orders. "I said with the mud drying up in the field, I'd
better harvest. Then I'd finish the equipment repairs. He
answered that maybe I better forgo my free time on the
coal mine."
It takes everything I have to bite my tongue.

Nell knew how hard Mike worked. He needed a break,
with mining. Her sigh whistled over her bottom teeth.
*I love all of my sisters and brothers. Mike's different.
Morty was right long ago. There's something about the
meek that deserves a tender touch.*

CHAPTER 26
Headlines

Slumped in one of the old chairs around the family table, Mike spoke tersely. "Edmond's grumpier than ever to farm with. He's short with his wife and children. He doesn't take time to delight in them. He praises Joe and his modern farming. His mind's torn between better land here or cheaper land elsewhere. He wants to make this farm successful with more pasture and hogs. A sure moneymaker."

The dishrag went swish, swish as Nell kept her eyes on the sideboard.

It doesn't feel like a family table anymore. There's division. It's important I don't step on Mike's dreams. The words on the plaque—go and plant your trees. It's important to remember this but not easy to keep my mouth shut.

While finishing the first page of the newspaper, Mike gulped down his tea. He went out to work. Nell picked up the April 1898 edition.

"Take note of that huge headline, 'Gold Rush in the Klondike.'" Lizzie entered the kitchen. "Mike's having trouble with attention to his work. Living for the day, but now, we discover him planning for tomorrow."

Nell's voice shook. "His plans are different than Edmond and Joe's."

Lizzie said, "With that faraway look in his eyes, Mike remarked, 'Time's perfect and everything's come

together. Nell's happiness. Edmond's boys growing up.'"
Lizzie fanned her face. She flopped into a chair. "By the
way, congratulations on your engagement."
"Ahem. I got a bread crumb stuck." Nell coughed. "I
appreciate your approval of Joe."

~~**~~**~~**~~

It was easy for Bud to spot all the Glissons from the
ridge. *If I had a friend, I'd wish for Michael Glisson. But I
know how my father feels about them. My father's
revenge has blinded him with hatred. He's making
decisions I can't abide.*
The big family gathering at the Glissons must include the
grandchildren? A reunion? Wedding? Dad's right about
these binoculars. They make quite a difference.

Dad's foreman reported crocks of flowers, pickles, and
other foods, chilling in the stream.
Bud noticed the extra time it took for his father to step
down from the wagon one decrepit leg at a time.
Sam had aged. "It must be a big shindig. They still need
to keep food cool in the creek in April. Primitive. If one
of these hicks marries, I'm certain it'll never be that old,
crusty bachelor they call Junior."

"His name's Michael," said Bud.
"Clodhopper, Michael, Junior, whatever. Isn't he the last
man left of that classless clan?" Sam stood with his arms
behind his back, and the tip of his tongue behind his
teeth. "No gumption."
*I'm only praised when I make things tough on the
neighbors.*

298

Bud adjusted the binoculars.

It's the only good I've done in Dad's eyes. I don't want Dad to know how lonely I've always felt. Michael's a fine neighbor. All of them are.

"Their family must be related to the northern backwoods Ozark bumpkins, who aren't able to farm a small acreage like theirs," retorted Sam. "To ask his older brother to return from the West as if *he'll* make something out of the run-down place."

"You've never forgiven them, Dad. But their trees are looking strong." *I want to cover my ears. I'm so sick of the hating.* "Dad, I want to talk to you about Stephen coming back. It's a deal breaker for me. How could you?"

"What?"

"I disagree with having any connection with him. He's made a bad name for himself. Suspected of involvement in assault and possibly the Glissons' fire. I won't work with him."

Sam studied his paperwork from the wagon seat. "Son, how do you like those high-powered field glasses I purchased? Your Uncle Malcolm mentioned those would be worth looking into. They save me time on acreage estimates. And I can keep an eye on what the employees are up to."

"Dad, do you not hear me? I'm asking you about Stephen?"

"Stephen's my business. He's already completing projects for me. Perhaps he's ruthless. But he owes me. He'll do what needs to be done."

I wish you could be proud of me for something other than being your puppet to increase your profits.

Bud smacked his hand to his forehead.

Can't Dad realize I know the difference between right and wrong? What about my interest in machinery?

"Perfect time for my own little present to the bride," crooned Sam. "All their wasted land. They never cleared those scraggly trees."

"Enough about their logs and trees. You, don't even know what you have, or where to stash it." Bud peered at the horizon. "Dad, I'd like to talk to you about a project with machinery and engines. Will you listen? I won't be involved with stealing their lumber."

"Are you back on that swill? You follow my orders. I don't have enough eyes to watch all of my holdings. You collect the rent payments and keep our business going. But one-by- one, we will strip them of that lumber."

No wonder I drink. I don't want what he wants. I don't want my name on all of the properties that he swindled farmers out of.

"We *will* harvest their hardwoods and bring 'em to ruin." Sam's steely eyes gleamed. "Before Stephen heads for the Northwest to follow that woman, he needs to earn funds. That's all. He'll finish surveying the Glissons' buildings. He could find another storage shed full of big black walnut logs. He followed my orders and stashed some on separate holdings. There are plenty of logs left. Stephen owes me. He follows orders."

"You mean the good hardwoods Mike's got marked in the forest." The binoculars thumped on Bud's chest.
"This big celebration down there'll be the perfect time for us to help them de-clutter, before they have to sell more of their land. Plenty of other farmers in Shawnee Township have moved on. I've got hired hands I can keep for the physical work. You keep Stephen busy."

"Oh, I see." Bud turned his back on his dad. He patted his pocket, making sure his flask was there. "Dad, listen to reason. We don't need to make money off of their logs. I've got an idea involving these new engines. Mike Glisson made a harrow out of an old plum tree. His sister's the one who rode the harrow. I've got an idea for a mechanical harrow. You always gonna' seek revenge for Uncle Malcolm?"

"Don't tell me where I can make money. Don't ask me about any more machinery projects. I know how you feel about the Glissons."
"But Dad, not many Glissons are left. They've worked hard."
"Indeed. Earn *your* keep. It won't be their property for long. The land will be sold. It's as simple as that when taxes aren't paid. Let's remember who's boss. These logs need to be cleaned up, but they're mere tiddlywinks compared with the real irons I have in the fire. You have my orders."
It feels like I'm going off a cliffside.

Bud shook his head. "You think that ridge's all yours? What about all the acres you put in my name?"

Sam swiped his sweaty palms down the front of his pants. He chuckled at Bud. "You want a roof over your head? Do what I say."

~~**~~**~~**~~

The afternoon brimmed with music and laughter. The fiddle, banjo, and guitar melodies drifted through the trees. The salads and desserts had kept cool in the creek. Family members assembled in front of the cabin for pictures. Mike, Edmond, and his family of nine lived right there. They didn't want to miss a minute. Ma traveled from Kansas with two of her grandchildren—Mary-Jane's oldest, Mary, and Martin's youngest, Martin Junior. Mary would soon be in a convent in St. Louis. Kate, with her family of six, traveled from St. Louis, Missouri, to Illinois with Jack. Martin Junior loved the homestead and the fishing. An older schoolmarm friend, Maude, accompanied Jack. Morty and Bertha stayed home in Missouri with their four children. Mary-Jane and Martin and the rest of their children remained in Kansas.

Uncle Willie, James, Patrick, Doc Simpkins, Helen Keith, the Coffmans, Joe's relatives, the neighbors, and others got reacquainted. Would Honora make it? And her big family? Ma's grandchildren took center stage. Kate announced her family's plans for another move far from St. Louis to Montana. Ma clasped these little ones extra-close. With Mary-Jane unwell, Ma would soon return to Kansas. Never a dull moment for Ma. She delighted in

the antics of the thirteen grandchildren thronged around her.
I'm a bit nervous with this big turnout.

Nell twisted her hair around her finger.
Honora has always stolen the show.
She did once again, but not in the expected way. At first, folks didn't recognize Honora. Her eyes looked hollow. Nell turned away but not Nell's two youngest brothers. Their eyes were filled with love, eager to give Honora a hand. Honora's seven unruly children, with their dirty faces and hands, and old, torn clothes—erupted out of Uncle Willie's wagon. Their entrance outdid a small hurricane. Honora dressed them with what she could, but they were no comparison with Lizzie's brood, with their shiny hair and good clothes. Joe greeted them with a wrinkle of his nose. He frowned at Honora.

"I didn't recognize you, Honora," blurted Joe. Honora held him close.
I'm so embarrassed.
Nell sensed the awkwardness.
What'll Joe's family think? Such well-respected farmers.

Like a band of monkeys with their cousins, the McMinn children ran ragged and unruly. Honora, who was worn out and unable to stand for extended periods, was expecting another child. Charles's didn't try to corral them. He waved them out of sight.
Kate had made a recent visit to Honora's. Kate fretted over Honora's surroundings, the poverty, illness, and

home that remained dank and dark. Kate confessed, "I love her so."

They whispered words of the crumbly shack in an alley with no grass or trees. The lack of proper ventilation made Nell bite her lip. Honora and her children went hungry. The children mentioned they ate robins at times.

"I encouraged her to use what sunshine there is to purify her clothes, towels, and bedding," explained Ma.

My stomach is lurching. I'm mad at her one minute and sorry the next. Poor Honora. No wonder they're all unhealthy.

Bolting in every direction, Honora's children gobbled food by the handfuls. Lizzie and Kate encouraged them to be seated. Honora sought a moment to talk with the bride.

"I've a question about Joe's intentions," Honora said with a long sigh. "It appears Joe's interested only in land. But, please, Nell, you can change your mind. There's someone meant for you. If Joe's love isn't there, it's not too late."

You're the last person I'd take advice from, Nell wanted to tell Honora. But she wasn't the last. Charles pried his way into the conversation. Nell wouldn't hear a word he said. *What a disgrace. I dread the minister's question. Does anyone harbor any objections?*

"The youngest Glissons turned out as well as the oldest ones did," remarked Honora. "Morty manages a logging crew. Mike runs the farm with Ed. Jack is a boxing success."

I wish Honora could utter a word about my fine clothes and hopes for the ridge. What she thinks about Joe's wrong.

After the service, the wedding guests looked relieved that Nell landed a respectable man. Their scuttlebutt that he'd soon be one of the richest landholders next to the Warings flustered Nell. Honora, out of breath and hoarse, squeezed close to Joe. Charles was beside her. "I don't want Nell's spirit damaged. She's born for a reason. That's how I raised my oldest son, Ned. My Ned's a hard worker in St. Louis."

It wasn't easy for her, but Honora admitted she'd sold off her own inheritance land. "But Joe, I'm proud of Nell. She values the ridge land."

It doesn't feel like she's proud of me or my choice of a husband.

As Joe fidgeted, Honora raced on. "She wants the walnuts to remain."

"Yes," said Joe's cousin, Lana. "This is the last place where a person can purchase shelled nuts with all the work done for you."

"Mike wants to keep them too," said Edmond. "A place to return to. He must be joking."

"No worries," added Jack. "Mike'll be richer than any old farmer."

Calm and unruffled, Ma straightened her scarf. She smiled at her grandchildren's mischief and sweet voices.

They competed for her rippling laughter. Her smile never wavered throughout the wedding. She expressed her pleasure that the chicken, desserts, and fiddle music lasted until the end.

After all the congratulations, the guests began to disperse. Mike announced to friends his plans to leave for the Klondike. "Yep, it's time. Edmond and Joe will improve things here."
The word spread. They all congratulated the shy fellow. Darkness closed in on the evening. Guests departed. Joe mentioned early-morning milking. The honeymoon would have to wait for the offseason. He whisked Nell away.
I'm glad I don't have to hear any more from Honora.

~~**~~**~~**~~

Trying to keep a low profile, Mike attempted to leave without any fanfare. But family and friends gathered near the wagon. Edmond and Lizzie, knowing his plans, surprised him with a gold pocket watch. It was engraved with the names of all his sisters and brothers.
"I'll be with you step-by-step every morning, reading about the Klondike." Ma hugged Mike close. "Write often."

Threading the watch chain through his buttonhole, Mike tucked it in his vest pocket. "In Da's rucksack, I've stuffed an extra pair of coveralls, Da's old jacket, and knitted woolens."
"Good luck. Hip, hip, hurrah." Nieces and nephews cheered. "We'll miss you, Uncle Mike."

"This is what you always wanted. Do it," said Jack with a pleased smile.

"It's your life. Go for it," cheered Edmond. "You'll be known for your resourcefulness."

Old Doc Simpkins, who struggled to walk, rode back out from the county home with Uncle Willie to say good-bye. Although tired, they wouldn't miss this moment. With brave waves and clapping, they all cheered, "All the luck in the world, Michael Patrick Glisson!"

Doc said, "I won't be needing this waterproof coat on my rounds. I'd be honored if you took it to the goldfields."

Nell never took her eyes off of Mike. She hung on to his last words. "I'll be back. Thanks for being my right-hand man, Sis."

He thinks I'm enough. Not a runt. Her lips trembled. *I'll miss you, Mike. Things'll be okay with Joe.*

"Write soon," pleaded Ma.

"Let us know about Bill Drew and Elsie Powell," reminded Nell.

Edmond's children shouted their farewells. "Good-bye, Uncle Mike. Good luck. Bring home the gold."

The next morning, before Ma and Jack boarded their return train for St. Louis, Ma suggested, "Honora, plaster mustard poultices on twice daily. Use them for any of the children and yourself. I don't like that cough. Then, next time you're here, and you're better, we'll have time for the walnut grove."

CHAPTER 27
Joe's Farm

Northwest of the Glisson homestead sat the little frame house Nell now called home. She sat on the front porch, making a tutting sound.

My brothers and sisters got a long ways away. I'm just across the road.

Behind her, the ferns she'd acquired from Joe's cousin, Lana, shimmered in the sunny windows. With Ma back to Kansas, as midwife for ailing Mary-Jane, Nell delivered her first baby with Lizzie's help.

Packing baby Lee on his shoulder, Joe strode onto the porch. "My big baby boy," praised Joe. "He's healthy, beautiful, and sure got a pair of lungs on him. I'm crazy about the little bruiser."

"Lee's fussiness keeps us busy. That's for sure," remarked Nell.

Every day since their wedding, Joe's cough worsened. He griped about taking spoonfuls of Ma's elderberry syrup and other herbs. "This old-fashioned stuff's cockamamie." Nell packed his chest down with mustard poultices as many evenings as he'd let her after his long days in the fields.

Lee's colic continued. Nell listened to Joe's cousin, Lana, about current methods to supplement Lee's food. "You're a small woman. He might need cow's milk."

Soothing and patting his little back, Nell did all she could for Lee. She walked the floors and the path to the mailbox each afternoon for word from Ma or Mike.

"Lee, little Lee. Lookie. Let's see if we got a letter from your grandma or Uncle Mike. Your Uncle Mike is up in the Klondike. He's going to come home with gold nuggets."

A letter from Mike came after several more months. Joe coughed and stammered, "Why I'll be dogged. This return address is Canada. It's 1901. It's dated 1900. I can't believe he made it. He's so quiet, but …." Joe bent over with a round of sharp coughs. "How's he handling those frigid temperatures?"

At her wit's end with colicky Lee, Nell's face split into a huge smile with Mike's letter.

It's enough to know he's there.

Between Lee's fussiness and Joe's continued illness, Nell soon forgot the letter. She skimmed it and shoved it in a drawer for later. She couldn't walk or comfort Lee enough. She distracted him by pointing to things from the porch. "See the birdie." She whistled. "Lookie, Lee." He stopped crying. "See the dairy cows. Moo, moo."

I wish I'd time to chase them away from the swampy creek bottom.

Lana's words circled in her mind.

"You're small. You may not have enough milk for that big boy. He's about the size of an eight-month-old."

Gracious. All my tricks are followed by Lee's loud cries.

"It'd be okay to heat up a little warm milk? Would that suit you, Lee?"

Joe's forced breathing, severe cough, and exhaustion after lunch frightened her. Someone must complete Joe's chores. Nell did. Every afternoon. Joe asked Tom, his older uncle, to come by and help Nell. Late afternoons, Joe spent on the porch, rocking Lee. Nell and Uncle Tom worked hard.

One evening, they noticed the quiet. Nell jumped up. "How long has little Lee been sleeping in the walnut cradle? He's doing so well with the extra milk."
They both rested and were glad to have a little break from Lee's tears. Later, they found Lee still in his cradle, not breathing, cold and ashen. Joe and Nell, as frantic new parents, did everything they could think of. "Is anything in his mouth? Pat his back, and slap the bottom of his feet," cried Joe in desperation.

"I listened for his heartbeat. He's not breathing. I put him on his tummy and on his back. Look at his color. We've done everything. I can't think of anything else we can do. Run. Ask Lizzie to come. We need help." Nell sobbed. She clutched little Lee to her chest, patted his back, and pinched his cheeks.
"Hold him. Talk to him. Keep him warm," begged Joe.

It didn't take Lizzie long to arrive from across the road. She tried. They knew there was nothing else they could do for baby Lee. "You've got to realize that countless women have a baby die. You must try again," said Lizzie. "If my baby girl hadn't died, we'd have ten children

now." Lizzie wiped her hands on her apron. "You'll have plenty more. Nell, it's important to let him go."
No matter what Lizzie says, I don't feel any better.

Inconsolable, Nell asked the new doctor to stop by. "He was big and strong? Why did I fail? He would've lived. My Ma and Da raised all nine of theirs to adulthood and never lost a one."
"Listen to me." The doctor jammed his hands in his pockets. He bit his lip. "You gave him cow's milk. There's snakeweed in parts of Illinois and Indiana. Dairy cows feed on it. It grows in swampy areas. Did your dairy cows graze in there?"
To blame me for not ever seeing my little boy's smile? Little Lee is all alone in the Robertson Cemetery. I can't even sleep. Lord, I believe you're not even here. I wish Doc Simpkins hadn't moved into the old folks' home with Uncle Willie.

"My child's gone. He was alive, but now he's gone." Nell wept. "There's no way past this pain. I wish the earth would swallow me up. I can never watch him crawl."
"It's going to take time to heal," advised the doctor. "Give this love to something else."
"I've cried so much. I can't cry anymore."
I know how David Copperfield's heart broke when Steerforth took Emily. My angel, Lee, is gone. My Da's old croi quit on him. My heart hurts so bad that I can't go on. No, I won't pray. I've suffered so much. The guilt. If only we'd not offered him that milk.

Over and over, Nell blamed herself. She looked in the mirror and turned away in anger. She thought of Honora's bruised arm years ago. She left the same little half-moon circles on her own arm. Joe tried to talk to her. Nell wouldn't listen to him. She buried her face in the bedding and cried, "I wish the earth would swallow me."

Joe couldn't finish a sentence without coughing. Nell snuck a peek at Joe. He knelt beside the cradle. In his arms, he clung to one of Lee's little gowns. This set her back a few more weeks. Between the coughs, she saw Joe cover his mouth with his hand, and his whole body shuddered. *This death's made him sicker. My poor, poor Joe.*

After months of self-pity and turning away all help from those who'd come in to wash and cook, Nell knew she'd better rise and help Joe.
I'm not going to blame myself anymore. Ma and Lizzie said I could do it. I've got to stop losing Lee and save Joe.
Fitful coughing came from Joe's side of the bed.
I figure he's coughed so much, he could cough his life away.
After long months of sadness, Nell spooned the elderberry syrup throughout the night. "You've got to take this since you refuse to see a doctor. Let me put another poultice on, Joe."

Bent over with hacking, Joe spit up blood. His forehead was beaded with sweat. He pleaded for more syrup.

"Can't talk. I've coughed my throat raw. I've got to tell you …," more coughing, "the logs in the storage shed …." His severe congestion made it difficult for him to talk or breathe.

"Let me give that back of yours a pounding." Nell cupped her palms, her hands flew with a fervor, pounding Joe's back. "You need two of these spoonfuls from now on. Rest on the porch. Keep your handkerchief around your mouth to keep soil out. I'll weed the fields. Rest."

"But Nell. This is important. The storage shed's pertnir' empty. I've spoken with Edmond and his family. They don't know anything about Mike's logs. Edmond said he'd have the sheriff out. Who would steal those big logs Mike stored inside?"

"With Sam next door? They're black walnut, Joe."

"Yes, Nell." He said between coughing spasms, "They're important."

"You mean, you don't think we should let the ridge go?" Always strong, Joe buried his face in Nell's shoulder. "No." He sobbed.

"Don't say any more, Joe. All I want is your health."

~~**~~**~~**~~

Bud peered across the ridge.

It's time for me to talk with Dad. I can't do this any longer.

"I want to keep thinning out the remaining hardwoods. That's final," said Sam.

"I disagreed with taking the walnuts out of the Glissons' storage, and their marked ones in the forest. What are we doing? Are we going to keep going until they're all gone?" Bud let out a long sigh. "I will not. They're not ours to take."

"I've mentioned before that your having a roof over your head means doing what I say."

"I don't need a roof over my head. I'm moving into Mose Johnson's cabin."

Sam spat. He barreled back to his new buggy.

My dad's consumed by his own power and greed. I've got to figure out what to tell these workers.

Bud walked right into Da's newest foreman.

"Your Dad said to talk to you. You want us to collect the tagged logs in the forest? Nobody's around. Grab everything going to the mill to be planed? Drag 'em out of there?" asked the foreman. "Where do you suggest we store them this time?"

"No more logging," said Bud. "Change of plans."

"Your Dad hasn't left yet. Let me see if I can catch him. If he wants to clear-cut the walnuts, we'll keep 'em cleared."

"Don't clear-cut them," yelled Bud. "I need time to negotiate with my father."

Old man Glisson was right. They're the biggest trees. Think of what old Mike would think if he owned a pair of field glasses. Old man Glisson. They called him Da. It feels like I'm choosing him over my own dad. But I don't care how much these logs are worth with Dad's friends at the mill. I know how much they're worth to the Glissons. Dad'll want the hickories next. Then the forest will be a mix of overgrown junk trees before he buys it all up. It'll never be enough with the revenge burning inside of him.

"What about those logs arranged like rooms?" asked a worker. "They're junk aren't they?"
What next?
Bud gulped.
Dad must've told them that those rotten, worthless old logs are filled with maggots. Dad is always spouting off his motto, "As your commissioner we'll clean and modernize our county's backwoods' hollers.'" But he doesn't own us all.

"Leave them for now. Did you hear what I said?" bellowed Bud. "Let's think. Surely dad's got plenty of projects ahead of rotten logs."
"Leave 'em? Your father hates all those nuts around there. They roll around on the ground. They hurt his ankles when he comes out to hunt."
"*Hunt?*" Bud snorted. "When's the last time you saw him enjoy what he has?"

The foreman's nostrils flared. "We've got plenty of other orders to follow. Sam's right hand doesn't know what his left hand's doing."
Loyal workers?
Bud swallowed a sip of whiskey.
Dad's never taken the time to understand me. It's time to make my glider wings, build a runway, create a gin pole like Morty's, and hire a worker. Dad, you think you've got irons in the fire? It's time for some tinkering.

~~**~~**~~**~~

Tragedy struck. A telegram came to Mr. Edmond Glisson, Brownsville County, Illinois. "Mary-Jane died in childbirth. Wichita, Kansas.

"We're so sorry to deliver this tragic news so soon after the loss of Lee. Ma's going to be tied up in Kansas for a while with Mary-Jane's little ones. Sorry about Lee." Edmond patted Nell's shoulder. "It's hardest on you with a son and sister dying."

Nell swallowed. She sunk into a seat.

My Mary-Jane.

"It's hard to believe Mary-Jane died." Lizzie glanced around Nell's parlor. "Your house is so modern with big windows, lots of light, white walls, and no log walls. It's peaceful here, Joe's coughing seems to have died down."

After Edmond and Lizzie left, Nell got out her stationery. "Dear Ma. Oh, my dear Mary-Jane."

She was my substitute mom when I was a baby. My sister. There's nothing worse. Prayer is no use. Little Lee. Now Mary-Jane. They are both gone. When's the end of inconsolable? Ma? When will you be home? Ma must wonder why no letter has come from me in months? I've been unable to tell her about Lee and Joe. Take deep breaths.

Nell picked up the pencil.

Dear Ma,

We've both lost a child. I lost Lee. I gave him cow's milk. The new doc said the snakeweed the cows fed on killed him. I can't cry anymore. I've cried so much. I don't want to go back into all that pain. I've got to look out for Joe. He's been sick.

I'm sorry for Mary-Jane. It's hard to believe she's not there, banging pans on the stove. I'm sorry, Ma. You've been a good Ma to all of us. I miss my little Lee. I'm having headaches and stomachaches. I'll never hear Lee say, Mama. Joe's been coughing a lot, he's better today. I keep going.

Love,
Nell

Unfolding and refolding the letter, Nell stared at her words. She held the letter tight to her chest. She set it down, clenched her pen and wrote a shaky line across tear stains that fell on the crooked words at the bottom. *Ma? You said I could do it. Ma? Ma…. The question mark disappeared in the salty water.*

~~**~~**~~**~~

Stewing over who would manage his property in Kansas, Edmond said, "Now that Mary-Jane's gone, Dennis isn't able to farm both his property and mine anymore. We're trying to decide what to do.

"Joe, you're still young. You've rallied back from illness. We remember you said if you owned additional acres to farm, you'd have no worries. Losing your son's been a big loss. We want to offer the acres we bought to you first. Then we'll return to Kansas."

"Your health does seem better. We're so glad you're not coughing into your handkerchief," said Lizzie. "But please, don't worry about the old homeplace. We can sell the homestead's acres to someone else."
"I'll take out another loan with the bank. This way, I won't need to outbid Waring." Joe tried to hide his shakes. "The neighbors say Sam'll buy up the area. I've got a loan on Uncle Willie's land that I'll sign this one against. You're free to return to Kansas."

No one asks me how I feel—which hurts. To me, it feels like falling.
Nell's hands shook.
Joe's been so sick. We need time to gather our thoughts and make plans. How do I tell him? But I want him better.

~~**~~**~~**~~

Nell kept up a determined pace with the farmwork.
Joe's improvement is lasting. It's been months now. I'm elated. I'm still unable to pray, but I'm thankful. I'll never forget losing Lee, but I've got Joe.

Weeks went by after Edmond and his large family moved all the way back to Kansas. The old homestead had never felt so empty.

I thought returning home meant staying. Edmond's leaving has left another gaping hole. Kansas seems different now. I picture poor Dennis, searching for a wife to replace Mary-Jane. How can he replace Mary-Jane? Ma'll have to remain in Kansas and run the Dillons' house.

With all the pressure Joe put on himself with all the new land, he didn't take time for short rests. When dust flew off the fields, he relied on his handkerchief throughout the day. Nothing helped at night. He was unable to sleep. The dry season continued. The coughing never stopped. Nell washed out bloody handkerchiefs every day.

The blood made me gag at first. Now I hold them like tender prayers to my face. I'm used to them.

She pleaded with Joe to rest.

I'm afraid.

Joe repeated, "I'll be dag-gummed. I've got work to do." She soothed him when he tossed and turned under the blankets, his forehead feverish, trembling, and chilled. *He's known for his youth and strength. I walk the floors each night, worrying if there's anything more I should be doing. I've got plenty of pillows propping him up. Must I pile on more blankets? He's in so much pain. All our security is in this home, which is signed against bank loans. He coughs and barks which scares me.*

She pressed her fists against her quivering lips.

I'm applying Ma's tonics and salves. But he's racked with pain. Joe you were made so strong. I have nothing to cure this. I've contacted that doc again.

~~**~~**~~**~~

"I don't need no, doc," said Joe.
The doctor sat down beside Joe. "Have you been exposed to TB? Something's settled in your spine. I know it's painful. It's a terrible complication."
"TB? No," said Nell. "He's not been around anyone with consumption or tuberculosis."

The doctor bit down on his pipe. "Perhaps the loss of your son decreased your resistance? Combined with this infection, it settled into your spine and lungs. I'm sorry. There's but one recommendation. I suggest a sanitorium."
"A what? Why? Where's that? For how long?"
There's that feeling of my legs going out from under me.

"In St. Louis."
"Doc, I've got acres that need tending. St. Louis?" Joe's voice was so weak. His coughing flared. He gasped for words.
Nell's devastated mind raced.
The earth's about to swallow us.
She mustered a brave face. She stood beside Joe.

~~**~~**~~**~~

"This'll work out great. You're the man I need." With that, Bud hired Asa Reynolds, who needed work.
"Mr. Waring, if...."

320

"Call me Bud, please."
"I'm interested in machines."
"You're a good hand, Asa. Never met a quieter tinkerer."

"There's no end in sight for the demand we can fiddle with. I'm thankful you don't ask too many questions. I know it sounds bizarre, but I want to clear the air. I know my father's gone crazy with greed."
"You're someone I can learn about machines from."
"My heart's for flying. Asa, have you ever dreamed of flying?"

~~*~~*~~*~~

Going to the sanitorium proved expensive to the young family. Honora's oldest boy, Ned McMinn, visited his Uncle Joe in St. Louis every day. Mary-Jane's oldest daughter, a nun in St. Louis, prayed for Joe. No one told Nell to forget the loss of Lee by trying to have another child anymore.

Not eating, and wanting to remain in bed, Nell got up to wash the dishes. She washed the same one over and over. She had thoughts of Uncle Willie's words, "Stay in the fight until the final round."
I'll do my best for Joe.
She didn't allow herself thoughts either way about Joe's living or dying.

I'll have the sheriff out here for the stolen logs when Joe gets better. Mike hauled those in here for our future. Sam helped himself. If only the world would swallow me up. I've never been able to sit with the thought of being alone. We love each other. I'm so sorry I argued with Joe over the grove.

Joe did not linger long in the sanitorium. He died of TB.

With the sun hidden behind low clouds, Ned McMinn made a quiet arrival onto the Robertsons' farm from St. Louis. He hated the idea of his Aunt Nell being alone. To find out about Joe's death via a telegram? His mother, Honora, an invalid herself, urged her oldest to go. Ned took the train to Brownsville County. He rented a livery horse to ride out West to visit his Aunt Nell in person. He found her home all shut up. He left the long letter from his mother in the box in the mudroom with the other mail. He introduced himself to Joe's uncle, old Tom Robertson.

Tom Robertson struggled to hold down a job. He welcomed Ned and put him to work. "Been here since Joe took sick, there's plenty of work." Tom taught Ned how to milk cows, care for the chickens, and all about the hoe.

"My experience is in city alleys," explained Ned. "We lived between two saloons. I know how to joke and swear up a blue streak."

"I know a bit about that myself," confided Tom. "You could say I've spent plenty of time along the tracks."

"This farm ain't no place for swaggering. My connections in St. Louis put me in Brownsville County. I'm thankful to be closer to my invalid mother, Honora, Aunt Nell's sister."

"Your Aunt Nell's been in bed for many months. She said no visitors. I put eggs, milk, and produce on the back porch. I'm not able to manage all the land my nephew owns. Put a large wooden crate for all the mail. I didn't know what else to do this week. I did a lot of cleanup in these buildings and across the road. The old homestead's empty. I piled musty old things by the burn pile."

~~**~~**~~**~~

One quiet day, Nell listened to the rustle of the cornstalks on the edges of the field. She arose from her dark bedroom and went to the back porch. She pushed aside two envelopes from Gertie, piles of bills, and bank collections. She found Ned McMinn's scribbled note on the side of the pile. His spelling and writing were terrible. She ciphered out that he played checkers with Joe each day before he died. She read his last words, "I'm working here on my days off. I can help you, Aunt."

Inside Ned's note she found a letter from Honora. Nell read it from the rocking chair in her room where she'd rocked little Lee.

Spring 1907

Dear Nell,

I love you so much. I didn't mean to hurt you at your wedding. I wanted you to have the best. I couldn't bear anything less. I didn't know I had

TB. It's contagious. Mine's developed over a long time. I've been able to raise most of my children. I've lost three of them. None of them saw a doctor until the last one. Emmett died. The doc said it's TB. Poor Joe. Imagine my guilt. I've struggled with this disease. I'm so thankful that strong, handsome Joe didn't suffer long. With what's left of my large family, I linger on.

Looks like we swapped places. Now I need help with my breathing. With Mary-Jane's death and Kate's move to Montana, I'm your closest sister. I knew a fighter when I saw you. You were born for a purpose. Hold on. I've something hard to say. I know you've hated Charles. But Charles married me out of kindness. Charles wasn't the man that Mike and Jack fought with that night in the cemetery when I was assaulted.

I couldn't let you find out. I begged the family not to tell you. Even though you were the youngest, you had such a fire in your heart. Da noticed it. Doc Simpkins did too. But this might be the

Throwing the unfinished letter down, Nell fell to her knees. She glanced at her wedding picture in the little cardboard frame. She ripped the picture out of the frame. She tore her head off. The scrap floated to the floor. She relaxed with short puffing exhales, her lips pursed. Her tears burned.

I remember Charles's arm. Uninjured? He didn't fight. Yellow wheels? What? Why am I seeing yellow wheels on a wagon?

"Wagon?" she whispered. "The night of Honora's assault?" Nell gasped. She felt her eyes burn with his name on the letter.

Oh, dear Lord. No, no, the same wheels as those on Sam's wagon? On the driveway that night? Stephen's arm hanging down, not Charles'? Stephen hurt my precious, sweet, capable sister Honora? Her life's been so bad—Honora, a beauty, kind and sweet. Charles isn't guilty. Yet I condemned him. As if being a lazy bum's not enough? I put a burden on his back he shouldn't have carried. He cared enough to marry Honora, even if she'd b...been assaulted.

Ripping the letter to pieces, Nell ground the paper into the floorboards. A new strength boiled inside her. She ran from the house. She couldn't resist the urge to run. She ran as far as she could from this. She needed to pump her arms, and bring her knees up high. Run. She flew off the steps.

Ma said when I'm angry, I only hurt myself. She also said the Lord'll help you.

She tore across Joe's land, down the road, across her empty family homestead, down the cart path, and under the pretty archway into the wilderness. She ran, panting, crashing through the brush, with her head thrown back, her feelings catapulted behind her. Branches slashed at her. She stumbled. She ran. Turning toward the ridge, she shouted. She screamed in the direction of walnuts reaching thirty feet high.

I'm thirty-one years old, Lord. What are you doing to me? Are You leaving me to plant the grove?

Overgrown weeds choked the bushes, and neglected trees. She flung herself face down on the ground under a tree, gasping for her breath, with her body stretched out.

My Honora. My precious, precious sister. Married in your old gray shawl. Me in my proper dress? Oh, Honora. I was embarrassed by you at my wedding. I didn't want advice from you or Charles. Your poor, dirty children, who starved and ate robins.

Nell sobbed. "All this suffering, Lord? Ma said you're a good Father. You'll never leave or forsake us?"

Oh, Honora. Honora. My precious, precious sister. I'm so ashamed of how I treated you. I'll take care of you and give you something to fight for. I'm sorry. Please forgive me. Please, Honora.

My heart's pounding like those locomotives hurtling down from Chicago. Lord, I don't know you. I don't talk to you. I don't pray. You've made it too hard. Ma said you wouldn't give us anything we can't bear. I can't bear this. I want revenge on Stephen and Sam. Isn't this from you? Couldn't you have helped Honora? No answer? I will never pray to you again. I never will. I'm all alone here. There are no loved ones or family nearby.

Except for her fingers, Nell lay still. Her nails like spades dug into the soil. She raked it and clawed it. Her hands clenched the earth. She fought the aching emptiness within her. Her teeth wanted to bite the soil and yank off the blades of grass.

"Dirt," Nell screamed into the ground. "Dirt! It's all the family I have. My clothing be cursed." Then, she spit out the taste. She moaned. "Ah, Aah. Stephen. Sam." She spit. She pounded the dirt with her fists. It felt like hours, but she continued to lay in the dirt.

I won't come out from under this tree. Lord, I won't come out. Please, show me something?

"Show me! Show me!" She shrieked. Her screams came from deep inside her soul. She didn't sound like the young bride or the spoiled youngest daughter of nine children. At this moment, she cared about no one or nothing. After what seemed like hours, she made more silent pleas. *Show me something, Lord. Please, hear me. Hear me, Lord. Please hear me!*

Her wailing screams pierced the sunset, with no thought of the sound. Lying on her belly forced her to struggle for air. The squirrels rustled in the dry leaves nearby. A frog croaked. "Ahh, Aah!" More screams. Her heart raced. Her words were like hiccups in her throat. Her shoulders shook. Then her whole body shuddered.
I'm like Davy Copperfield. All alone. My dress filthy.

It took forever, but over time she lay there as quiet as the dirt she tasted. Sounds blended into a dull silence. She listened with her fingers deep in the soil.

~~**~~**~~**~~

A man crouched down behind branches.
I shouldn't have stumbled up here on their property. If I can keep from making a sound, the woman will leave. She'll never sense she had an observer.
He looked down. His hands trembled. His knees knocked together. His breath was loud.
She must hear it. I can't let anyone see me. I'm so tired of their cruel names.

He looked at his filthy shabby clothes.
I need to wash myself.
He remembered when he used to bathe in the nearby creek.
One day, I'll be ready, but not yet.
People don't like a mooch, on their property who is not working or improving.

A scream that only can be recognized by God. I know that cry. I screamed that way in the fire. You know that sound, Lord? It is the sound when our heart is being ripped out of our chest. Help that woman. Help her. Lord, grant her peace. Show her like you did me. You are here. You hear these cries that are like our fingerprints. Which are different from all others. They are the deepest sounds of our being, and from heaven, you recognize each of us in them. Come, Lord, Jesus. Come.

I can't help her, Father. My eyes are bloody. My clothes and body are unclean. My beard is long. My stench will scare her. Help her, Father.
Hidden in the heavy brush, the hermit stood shaking. His body tensed with fear.
If I could go to her, but I'm afraid, but deep in prayer for her.

~~**~~**~~**~~

I won't move from here unless something changes. I'll nest here all night.
Nell let the soil compressed into wedges, drop and crumble from her sweaty palms. A little circle of shiny metal fell out.
"What is it? It's my ring. My sweet Mike." She sobbed. "I'm not a child anymore." She made a fist around it and felt goose bumps. After a long time of breathing with pursed lips, a feeble twitch began at the corners of her mouth. It spread like cool water through the grime.

It's been so long. I know what this is, Lord? It's peace. I can't remember when I felt it last? With Da on the ridge? My Da. Mary-Jane holding me? After I hurt Morty? With Mike on the harrow? Oh, my Mike. On the high-wheeler?

My Joe. Holding sleeping baby Lee? Lord, protect Lee and remain with me. Don't leave us.

She pushed on her knuckles. Shaking, and with her elbows up, she came to her knees. She dropped the tiny ring in her pocket.

Tiny? It was for a child.

She brushed the leaves off of her.

Oh, what's that? She crinkled her nose at an unfamiliar scent. I thought I saw something in the brush? A man in old, filthy clothes. Do I know him? No. I'm not afraid. Peace fills my body.

As calm as a mushroom on a stump, Nell swallowed. Crickets chirped all around her. She walked in the twilight, to find her way.

I feel at peace. I am at peace. Thank you, Lord, for lighting my way. To think Honora thought it would be hatred that would make me fight. It's the opposite. It's something far grander than hatred. It's love, Lord.

~~**~~**~~**~~

When she got home, she lay on her bed. "What is it?" She hissed. "What is it? What is different? It's peace. It's peace, Nell." She calmed herself.

It's peace, Bridgett, it's peace. Peace. Justice will be mine for Sam. A rudder of peace and love you'll be to your family, and experience no more thoughts of the spoiled runt. My grace is unfolding for you. You're no longer a child. Follow me. Oh, Lord, I'm sorry. I'm sorry I didn't pray to you. I didn't obey you. I'm sorry. Help me to be where I hear you.

Then, she slept. When she awoke, she didn't want the peace to go away. She saw the walnut cradle and the empty frame from her wedding picture. And there was the little nest with the whittled eggs. She held the nest tenderly.

Lord, I beg you that this peace won't leave.

She continued to beg to hang on to the peace she felt. "Please don't go. Don't leave me. I won't be ornery unless You call for it."

"Stay. Stay," she begged. She fought for the peace to remain with each deep breath, with a bite of bread, and a swallow of tea. "Stay, please don't go."

"Angels guard us, and they watch over us." She sang to it and danced around the kitchen. "It's His peace. He came. He cares. He'll never leave me."

Later came a knock on the door. She took another deep breath, full of peace. "It's okay to open the door."

"Ma?"

"Oh, Ma, Ma. Oh, dear Lord, thank you. Ma, Ma." Nell's eyes shone. She hugged her mother close. She choked on her words. "My, What's this? Wren? What's Wren doing here? Ma?"

"It was Wren's choice," said Ma. "Wren asked her parents if she could come. Edmond and Lizzie said they've nine children. That's plenty. They want you to have Wren to raise her in a loving home. They all agreed that she's a remarkable little girl to want to comfort her

Aunt. All alone. With their big family, they want to do this."

"Let me stay, Auntie," pleaded Wren. "I like it here. I liked going to school here. I'll fit right in with my friends."

Nell's throat hurt to swallow after all the screaming on the grove. She reached into her pocket, where she'd rubbed the ring smooth. "This is for you, Wren." Nell's lips cracked but formed the most beautiful smile beneath the premature white strands in her blonde hair. She stooped to her knees but not alone. Ma and Wren came down with her. They knelt together on the kitchen floor, with their arms around one another.

"Oh, Ma, it wasn't poor Charles. Poor Charles. It was Stephen. He had the cruelty to hurt our beautiful, beautiful Honora. And Sam …. Oh, Ma."

"We'll have to forgive them too. Hush, Nell. You look so different. Your face is full of light. Hush. Look at Mary-Jane's recipe card. On the back, I scribbled something on the train for you. It's from the Bible, 'He gives us new strength.'"

Ma said, "Hush, now. We've got a girl to raise. We've also got Honora's boy, Ned, and his brothers and a sister to help. We've got Tom and Martin's son, Martin Junior. Martin Junior wants to come and fish along the creek. We've got plenty of family to think of."
I hear your peace, Lord. Do you have enough strength for all of us for each new day?

Dearest Honora,

I'm so sorry, Honora. I've always loved you. I'm sorry for my jealousy. I'm sorry for how I treated Charles and frowned at your children.

I denied Joe's death for months. I was so angry at him for leaving me. I've learned to pray again. I can try to explain the peace. To be still and hear the Lord, I want this for you, Honora. Depression lifts. It's through the loving of others.

Your Ned's good to us. Do you remember how I loved David Copperfield? I realize it's all about perseverance. What that poor boy in the book went through to find his "family." He didn't quit. I'm not going quit on you, or Da. Ma said she loves the sick and the ones far away. I laughed the other day at the joy of sending a child off to school. I gave Wren my ring I found on the ridge.

May the Lord give you new strength for each day.
Love,

Nell

"I didn't want to interrupt your letter writing, Nell, but we need a younger hired man. What about Asa? He's the boy I delivered." Ma sat down beside Nell. "Tom thinks Bud hired him? I know we'll have to sell land. There won't be much time for the grove or money for an extra hand."
Asa working for Bud? I thought Bud worked for his dad?

Nell said, "Ned mentioned he would work when he's off from his deliveries."
"Yes," said Ma. "Ned likes to fish too!"
"He's a blessing for Tom," said Nell.
They found Ned bent over the cart's axle. His tanned arms gleamed. Brown hair circled his face. "Good morning, Aunt Nell. Not the city boy you thought I was?"

"We need you Ned. You're an answer to prayer."
Ma's right. The only way to hang on is to sell off the land, and protect the ridge. I'll protect the ridge for Da and Honora. It's a lot to be thankful for, Lord.

On Thanksgiving, Nell and Ma's eyes sparkled with joy. Ma's little portrait of Abraham Lincoln was rehung in Nell's dining room, above her marble mantel clock the family below. Tom, Ned, Wren, Ma, and Nell.

~~**~~**~~**~~

Bud glanced back into the sun which was angling into the barn at the approach of a horse. Bud squinted at the spruce lumber he'd turned into wings.

I feel like a child, caught with my toys.

Bud's newspaper fluttered in the breeze. The headline predicted the rise of airplanes in farming, ranching, and forestry.

Sheriff Rippon will notice all the scraps on the floor that didn't fit the bill.

Bud kicked some wood under the table.

"It took me more time than I thought to complete this case." Sheriff Rippon eased out of his creaking saddle. "I'm anxious to close a case that Edmond Glisson filed on stolen logs. I've covered almost the entire county."

"Hello, Sheriff."

Sheriff Rippon scanned all the inventions and equipment with a raised eyebrow. "Bud, you're living out here?" The sheriff's keen expression held a knowing look. "Your dad's changed." Sheriff Rippon peered across the field at the railroad tracks. Then across the brush in the shadow of the cliffside. "That's Mose's old cave visible there in the rocks? Hasn't been a train rumbling down those tracks in a while. I'm retiring, but I've worked these county roads for years. Heard you're a machinist? Hired Asa Reynolds?"

"Yep. He's a good worker," said Bud.

"Folks in Shawnee Township aren't afraid to hire a colored man."

"Asa's quiet, honest and strong, and a great employee whatever's his skin color, is Sheriff," Bud said. "I'm on my own now. Working on parts for machinery makes me want to be a better man. I know you've taken my father's side on things."

The sheriff barked a laugh. "I'd like to turn over a new leaf myself. I've got some regrets. Sam behaves like he's the only one who matters in this county. But that's no excuse."

"He's swindled farmers and widows." Bud's voice sounded bitter. *I might as well get this off my chest.* "An evil's grown inside him these last years. It's like a disease. His revenge toward the Glissons is unstoppable. I know he's harvesting their logs. I don't know where the evidence's stored."

"Your dad's all about progress. How many times have I heard, 'No more of this one-horse county? These wilderness areas are a harbor for problems. Other communities have clear-cut theirs.'"

"It's gone on since Dad's brother, Malcolm, was killed."

"Son, I worked on that case. It was nothing but an accident," said Sheriff Rippon. "And these missing logs … changed my feelings for Sam. To sink this low. Those Glissons worked hard. Your dad signs my paycheck. I'm not proud to say that I've turned my back on some of his tomfoolery. But to let him roll over this county?" The sheriff kicked at the dirt. "I've built up feelings for these farm families. One of them is that little lady, Nell Glisson, her, and her brother. I 'spec you know her brother's in the Klondike? They packed that homestead on their backs for a few years. She's all alone and forced to sell off her acreage. If I wasn't retiring, I'd do something. Yep, I'm glad we're both on the same side." The sheriff fumbled with his wagon reins. "I've had enough. This county deserves better."

~~**~~**~~**~~

News of Jack's victories delighted Ma and Nell. They didn't want him to uproot his family home in St. Louis. But Jack assured them that if Mike didn't return soon, he'd come back and buy the homestead and the last of the farmland.

They anticipated Mike's return as they did Elsie's rain lilies from Putney, or the long-ago sought-after grafts that Honora planted on the ridge. They reread Mike's first letter from years ago. Mike compared his experience in the blizzardy whiteouts to Wichita's dust storms, driving cattle on dry trails all the way to that big, frozen country.

Dear Ma and Loved Ones,

It feels like forever since I left Illinois. It took a long time to backpack over those mountains. The snow was waist deep. Our gear was bundled on our backs. Bigger load than gunnysacks of walnuts. Heavier. All to reach the Yukon River after it broke up.

We waited all winter. We sawed logs into planks and built a raft on the lakeshore. Years ago, Morty and I tried to whittle a rudder of slippery elm. The rudder I made is out of red alder. When the ice broke, our raft held together on the Yukon River. You wouldn't imagine the sights we've seen and the adventures we've had.

In Dawson City, we pushed our way through the crowded town filled with wooden lean-tos. Aye, as Doc said, there were too many men and ramshackle cabins. All the good claims were taken.

Searching up and down the river we saw stake after stake taken. Before it turned too cold, we joined up with a company. Nell, you asked about Elsie. She's up here too, and Sam's foreman, Stephen. We set timbers to support our digs into the riverbanks. We rock the rockers and sluice for gold. "Lookie" in the bottom of this envelope. I put a pinch of gold dust for ye, Ma.

Your fourth and loving son,

Michael

"Grandma, catch all the sparkles," said Wren softly. "They're gold." In the kerosene lamplight, they glimmered. She cried, "Pretty, oh, so pretty."
"This letter's dated. But miners still work hard for that gold dust worth priceless dollars an ounce. Please, Lord, protect Mike," prayed Ma.
"He, and thousands of men he went in with, are having the time of their lives. I pray the creeks sparkle with fine gold. Then he'll return," said Nell.

We'll have to slog on without him.

"There's nothing he'd like better than rocky banks to dig gold from." Ma cackled. "But, we're thankful for his letter, Lord."
It's enough to imagine all of my brothers and sisters' dream adventures, excluding Honora. Lord, I trust that Lee will have one with Joe. They'll plow together up in heaven. Joe's not sick anymore. Lee doesn't cry. His granddad's dandling him on his knee.

"Ma, have you ever heard the bluebird's love song so much?" Nell peered from the open parlor window.
"No, Nell. Never. When I sit on the steps out back, they're trilling in the spring leaves all around me."

*** ~*~ *~* *~*

Several weeks later, they received a sorrowful letter from Sister Mary Glisson in St. Louis. *"Our dear Honora died on May 7, 1908. She mentioned the May ninth anniversary of her parents, but she died at peace two days before. Her oldest daughter, Nellie, brought the younger ones in at lunchtime to see her. Honora looked beautiful for them. Before she died she said to tell Nell to use the ridge for crops."*

A heaviness fell over the home. Ma said that a blackbird flew up as she sat on the porch steps.
I wish I could be a little girl in Ma's arms again. I won't think like that.
Breathe, Nell.
I want to breathe.

Grateful for a few hours before Wren came home from school, they grieved for what they'd known to be inevitable.

"I'm sure we can collect walnuts from the forest to sell every fall."
"Yes, Ma. The nuts'll help Ned support his sister and brothers. We could sell more acres of cropland. Perhaps Edmond's right about row crops on the ridge. We've protected it a long time for Mike."
We'll never let Sam and Stephen exploit us.
Nell sat beside Ma.
Sam keeps us so busy that we can't plant the Tipperary walnuts. Lord, I trust You. We'll hang on to the grove longer.

"Ma, I pray Honora will wait for me on a stump before she enters heaven. Then she can show me the way. We'll be together."
They rested in each other's arms.
Later, they heard a knock at the door. Kind old Robert Coffman came to check on his friends. "We're sorry for the news of your daughter Honora. Luella told me that she died." He wiped his forehead with his handkerchief. "A real dandy, she were. A real dandy."

Ma gestured him to the best seat in the parlor.
"No, I'm obliged." He cleared his throat. "Let me kneel here by the door a minute. I'm all dirty." He wiped pipe ashes on his coveralls. "I want to allow you ladies time to grieve for Honora. But it's never the right time to check on folks. Ned and your hired hand mentioned

they've seen a vagrant around these parts. Have you womenfolk spotted any vagrants around the homestead?"

"Yes, Tom's mentioned a hobo around," said Nell. She went to the window. "Wren hasn't mentioned anything on her way to or from school."
"I've seen an old man with a long beard." Robert cupped his chin in his hand. "Your Ned said he's the one."
Not a word did Ma utter.

"I've got a notion he's still in these parts. We don't want to encourage him. We should put a notice from the Shawnee Township's residents in the paper. 'Vagrants aren't welcome.' Would you consider this?" Robert raised an eyebrow.
"Let me think about that," remarked Nell, with her hands behind her back. "I know it's wrong to live on someone's land and not work for it."
I remember a faint outline of a man in the bushes that was somewhat familiar. But I know Ma lives for the helpless.

"One other thing. No offense, but I'm on the County Home Board. We're in need of an evening custodian. Light-duty. You can't run this farm by yourselves. Years back, Nell, you worked at the home."
Offense? It's an answer to prayer.
"Yes, I'm interested."

"With Doc Simpkins, your Uncle Willie, and many others you've known all your life living there, I thought it might be a good fit. My Luella's a breakfast cook there." Then, with a polite tip of his hat, Robert let himself out.

I'll try to keep us out of the almshouse next door to the County Home. We'll help Honora's children. Afterall it's not the almshouse I've read so much about in David Copperfield.

CHAPTER 30
The Home Residents

After the first week, Nell became an immediate favorite of the residents not because she kept the place spotless—but since she knew the importance of visiting with the old folks. Many residents waited for the petite ball of fire to arrive. They'd heard about her losses. Their friendship touched Nell.

She jabbed with the broom and mop into all the corners. She sided with the residents. She ignored the rule of the hated manager, Thomas Camean. "No meddling with the residents."
Rumors circulated that Thomas sold out to the corruption surrounding the County.

"Corruption?" inquired Nell.
"Yes, the commissioner, the honorable Sam Waring, controls the decisions of a generous portion of the county government. Thomas Camean is a good friend of Sam's. Since Thomas partnered with Sam, he and his brother, the former Judge Camean, are on poor terms."

Lord, I hear you call me to use my feistiness to keep track of all the things I've learned about Sam Waring. I acknowledge You in my part. It fills me with peace. The walnuts are my legacy, but also for others. As soon as things get easier, I'll plant the grove. The residents long for my pats on their backs, jokes, and hugs. They need them more than they need the scalding hot water and sanitizer on the floors. The floors can wait for blankets to be tucked, steady hands to spoon the last of their broth, and patience to catch drips off their chins. It makes me appreciate Ma, Wren, and my growing family.

Walnut planting waited. Notes on corruption grew. Nell figured she'd give the job a year. Ten years went by. More years and more expenses piled up, with Ma's need for new spectacles, Honora's children, Wren's musical talent, and ever-rising taxes forced her to sell off more acres. Nell didn't need to look for work. She windmilled in all directions. She listened and made the good folks snicker at her jokes. She heard more than once, "Boy, she's got a mouth on her."

"Let me take a look at that sports section there in the newspaper. My brother's a boxer in St. Louis. He can knock 'em out just like that." Nell snapped her fingers. She shuffled around like she was in the ring. The more antics she acted out, the more they laughed. If she saw a long face, she sat down and showed them how she used to collect eggs.

Over the years, they grew to trust her. They admired Nell's grit. She held on to her Da's legacy when all of her sisters and brothers left. They shared their knowledge of local corruption. Anger burned toward Sam. Several stated their amazement when the little lady thought their words important enough to write down.

Alice, a longtime resident, and former bank employee, saw plenty of shady dealings cross her desk after thirty years as a secretary for Sam Waring. "I typed up questionable forms. He never did put much by you folks out in Shawnee Township. His own neighbors!"

"In what way?"

"You lived next door to the Warings out in the boonies? You're the youngest, the one they called a little ty-runt." Alice cackled. "You were given zero chance to live."

"I struggled with breathing from being so undersized."

"Your Ma nursed many folks to health. I met her years ago. She's the salt of the earth. She get around okay now?"

"Yes, she's back from Wichita. Almost blind, she uses a cane. We live together."

"The state investigated, but Sam's so slippery they couldn't catch him. With his beguiling smile and charm, he always hugged mothers and children all over the county. Folks are tired of his inflated tax assessments of farmers and widows."

Alice at times reverted to her juvenile behavior and called out for her mama. On other occasions, her observations were sharp. "With all the wealth and land old Sam accumulates and his speeches about progress, one day the papers will be full of the most crooked county in central Illinois. Inflated taxes, indeed."

I hear a still small voice tell me to "document." I'll ask for Helen Keith's help. No wonder I can't make any headway with Da's dream. Help me, Lord, pay off our debts with this job. Wren's such a good musician. I thank you, Lord, ahead of time for sending her an organ. There are Ma's eyes and so much more.

Keeping an eagle eye for a chance to chastise Nell, Director Camean barked, "Don't poke your nose into others' business. Get busy with your broom and mop. Your disrespectful glower will be on my report. You should be fired! How many times must I remind you of your duty roster?"
With a growl, Nell went outside to rake sticks off the sidewalk.
Holding the door wide, Director Camean glared at Nell. Then he voiced his grievances. "Evening custodians do indoor work. The day person rakes. You must cease from opening and closing these drafty doors. The boiler already works overtime. I need quiet to prepare this institution's budget for the county assessor."

Leaves circled Nell's feet. She pushed through the front door past him. He slammed the door closed. Ledger pages blew off the counter. Nell muttered, "It's cold in here now. Common courtesy outweighs rules."
"Stick to your duty roster, Mrs. Robertson."
The folded paper crinkled in her apron. "I don't need it. How many years have I worked here?"
"Follow it." He fumed.

~~**~~**~~**~~

During the warmer seasons, Ma sat outside most afternoons. Almost blind now, she "saw" with her other senses. "Is someone there? What's that smell?"
Ma's voice trickled in through the open window.
Who's she talking to?

347

Ma, stiff and feeble, hobbled closer to the little gate.
"Hello," she cooed. "Can I help you?"
Nell saw ragged and dirty clothes and a long gray beard.
Head down. The man acted kind and patient.
"Are you hungry? Wait one moment." Ma tottered
inside. She got a crock of her peach preserves and warm
clean cloths.

Keeping out of Ma's way, Nell watched the old man from
the window. Ma pushed things into the poor man's
hands. "Here," she said. "Use this cloth for your eyes.
They'll heal."
"Thank you, ma'am."
Ma felt her way back to her chair in the sun.

"Ma, why do you help him? Next thing we know, you'll
invite him to family meals." Nell approached Ma's chair.
She realized Ma was snoring. She tiptoed away.
*She's a good soul. Da said she'd doctor anyone in need.
But if he doesn't work, should we offer him handouts?
He doesn't look strong. He could live at the almshouse?
I should be kind but I'm too busy working to make ends
meet. There's no time for the walnuts. I wonder how
much money we have left to earn for Ma's needs? She
has to hold the newspaper close to read. We must find
out if Mike's coming. Wren's organ? The taxes?*

With a flick of the reins, Nell was off to work.
*The old smells and taste of collecting walnuts course
through my veins. When I see the little green nuts hiding
in the branches in midsummer, I can picture the tree's
sap flowing. Then the nuts fall. I want Wren to hear,*

"Katy did, Katy didn't," from the katydids in the walnut grove. Every fall, I long to teach her that the nuts must be picked up right after they fall on their own.

~~**~~**~~**~~

One year followed another as April 1917 arrived. Nell still concentrated on the older residents and her personal concerns. She'd invited Ned McMinn's brother, Smoke, to a picnic before he went off to fight in the war. *I'm a fool, worrying about the hoeing and the encroaching trees on the ridge rows. It seems so unimportant, with Honora's son going to a place where the world's going to pieces. Then she paraphrased the plaque, "Even if the world's going to pieces plant your walnut trees." These words are so important. Wren'll need to learn to plant the legacy.*

As did most residents, Uncle Willie and Doc Simpkins fell asleep in front of their suppers. Nell's mop flapped around the corner of Uncle Willie's bed. He laughed. "Aye, here's our breath of fresh air."
A ruckus filled the hallway. "I miss my mama. I miss her."
A bedpan skittered across the floor.
"Custodian," cried a nurse.
"I miss my mama," hollered Alice Orr. She entered the wrong doorway.

Mopping up the hall, Nell followed Alice into Doc and Uncle Willie's room. Alice mumbled in a disgusted tone, "The bank president, now Commissioner Waring, always got what he wanted—to control the bank. Now he's got

349

his big mitts on the treasurer, assessor, appraiser, and sheriff. Even his own lawyer."

Hearing a male voice by the door, Alice said, "Papa? Is that you? Papa?"

In seconds, she returned with long-lost memories of troubled times. "Waring thought little of my secretarial skills. He stored all those deeds in the vault because of his greed. Secret notes and files were tucked here and there. It's wrong to increase taxes from their real assessments. All those farmers sold out. Sam's bank called the loans. All decisions went in the bank's favor." Nell led Alice back to her room.

"My folks stopped by here yesterday. I hear a team of horses on their way. It must be them." Alice's childlike voice whimpered, "Bye-bye."

Holidays rolled by. Seasons blurred. Nell kept taking notes on Sam whenever she heard his name mentioned. Ned gathered around the table with Tom, Wren, Ma, and Nell. *I know Ma thinks of the vagrant out in the woods. But I've got all I can handle. Mike? I'm sorry, Da and Honora. All my busyness. We're still a community out here. The grove'll be nice enough for everyone.*

~~**~~**~~**~~

Too feeble to come for the holidays, Doc and Uncle Willie rallied for Nell's first day back. Uncle Willie waited for Doc's snoring. "Doc isn't doing so well. He's having spells. He stops breathing. He's been ailing for a time. I know he's got his wits about him. But perhaps nearing the end."

"I'll come more often." Nell slopped her mop out of the bucket.

She tiptoed out, peering up and down the hallway. "Has Doc seen a doctor?" She knew Director Camean was close to firing her. "I want someone to see Doc? Today. He's suffering."

Always eager to see her, Doc waved her over to his side. His voice was feeble, but his mind was strong. "Since it's not confidential medical information, I've a few more facts regarding Sam Waring. I remember your Ma's words. 'God loves the word impossible.' You'll be able to use your notes to protect yourself and others from Sam. I'd like to say a little more on the night of Honora's assault.

"Sam knew what happened to Honora. Sam's an accessory to crime. Stephen's suspected of an arson in another county. Out of my fondness for Da, I don't want you or any of your family around Stephen. Stephen's in deep with Sam's obsession with a coal mine on the ridge. There's more than one snake in the weeds out there. Stephen's being blackmailed by Sam. I'm also concerned about my estate. This establishment is under Sam's authority. Bud doesn't want any part of any of this."

A pinched face appeared in the doorway. Thomas Camean. Nell knew Camean's look. "What are you doing, visiting again? How many times have I warned you?"

"Recent research vouches for a person to be able to mop and visit at the same time." Doc winked at Nell, with a clever change of the subject. "Jack's the best middleweight boxer who ever set foot out of Brownsville County."

Camean scuttled away. Doc said, "Nell, the way you've protected the ridge, you've done the township honor."
Camean seemed to be everywhere at once that week. "Nell Robertson, rules are rules. The residents don't need to hear your stories. Are bedpans sitting in the hall? Written reports will be turned in on this. Return to your duty roster."
Director Camean has no idea how I've befriended these people and listened to their stories while cleaning for over ten years.

~~**~~**~~**~~

A few weeks later, Nell watched Ma nod off to sleep in the shade of the porch after supper. Nell wiped off the last plate in front of the open window. Ma's newspaper riffled in the cool breeze. Her face was so peaceful. Then Ma arose. Nell heard Ma's cheerful hello. "Would you like the news?"

In the dusk, Nell observed Ma shuffle to the gate. She handed the paper to the same old raggedy man.
"Thank you, ma'am. Delicious peach preserves." He possessed a well-educated voice. He remained in the shade of the trees. His clothing blended into the shadows. "I enjoy something to read more than

352

anything. Another lady gave me a Bible. I sure do appreciate your friendship, ma'am."

"I hope your eyes are better," Ma said. "Not such a fiery red. Come back. I'll gather you more herbs for that infection."

As the hermit disappeared into the trees, Nell swept across the porch. "I'm sorry I haven't had the time to make sense of this friendship, Ma."

"There are less fortunate than us. He's a hermit. That's all there's to unravel." Ma sounded tired. "The newspaper states that they're still looking for a new sheriff."

~~**~~**~~**~~

Slumped over his big oak desk in his office with the premier black walnut paneling, Sam addressed an envelope in between coughing episodes.

I feel my age. The medicine does no good for my spells. I'd turn this all over to my son, but he's turned against me. Hiring a slave's son. He's taking trips to New York, and now Louisiana to learn about airplanes. Is Indiana next? It's time to clinch my victory.

"I'd like this envelope delivered to a railroad employee at the depot, by the name of Sparks."

"Yes, I'll put that with today's mail." His secretary handed him two notes. One was Director Camean's report from the County Home to be delivered in person. The second was for approval of Sheriff Rippon's retirement plaque. Sam looked at the large mantel clock. "Oh, bother." He sighed. "I'm tired. Not today."

Director Thomas Camean peeked around the door. "I've my report here, Commissioner. I've included several past warnings about an employee not obeying rules."

"Is this something that I need to address?" The commissioner cleared his throat. "Thomas, you're aware of policies on employee expectations?"

"Yes. I'd like to put this item on the agenda for the board. This employee's been with us for years."

"How's this employee's quality of work been up to this time?"

"Excellent."

"The name of this individual?"

"It's our evening custodian, Mrs. Joseph Robertson."

"I don't care what she's been. Terminate her at once."

After many years at the County Home, Nell lost her job. *I wonder if I dug up too much info with the residents. I feel like a caterpillar on the fence post in the cornfield.* Nell crossed the yard to the barn, while the late morning sun was high overhead.

"Tom, I'm checking for a letter from a former reverend, who preached here years ago. He drove around in his wagon with an organ in the back for services. It's been stored all these years. When he grants me permission to buy his organ, would you accompany me to pick it up for Wren?"

"Why, yes, ma'am. Wren's sure going to love that."

"We'll have to take the farm wagon out to the property. The former Reverend Webber is my brother Mortimer's father-in-law. I think Ned will be gone for the next day or two. We'll wait for his strong arms. It'll be a long day."

"Won't you be late for the Home?" asked Tom.

"I've been fired. You'll find me doing a lot of cleaning up. I will work around the homestead. This way, I'll be able to keep a better eye on Ma. But most of all, filing bankruptcy or not, we're going forward with Peace Ridge."

"I'm sorry to hear about your job, Nell. Word is, that you've been doing wonders for that place," said Tom. "But I've always wanted to see your family dream planted."

"Thank you, Tom."

Nell worked hard all day on the few acres left. She saved time at the end of the day for cleanup. "My, I've never seen the place so organized. Tom, do you remember seeing a hole behind the stable dug up? With old gunnysacks in it?"

"I recall placing them by the burn pile years ago when Joe died." Tom squinted. He thought back. "But there are new ones left as well. Saplings of every size growing there. There are nuts scattered all over. I always wondered what happened to the rest of them? Squirrels must have gotten in there."

I can't let this stop me.

Nell let her breath out with a long sigh.

I know those saplings are offspring from those original nuts. That's the main thing.

Nell received the letter she'd waited for. She shared the news with Ma and Tom. "Morty's letter mentions Reverend Webber would be honored for us to have his old organ. The last time it carried a tune was when we had the girls' double wedding. Then it was stored on the old Mose Johnson place. His letter states, 'I'm sure it's still on the large shelf beneath the hayloft. Even with all of its travels, you can't beat the sound.'"

Wren's graduation? At least, she'll have her own organ, and Ma will have her new spectacles. I've lost my job at the County Home, things will be tough. The old sheriff's retired. It's not too late to ask him for any news about the logs.

Nell glanced up to heaven.

~~**~~**~~**~~

"This ground's been waiting for this," said old Tom. Ned and Nell worked side by side with Tom. They prepared the ridge for planting the long anticipated walnut grove. "Thanks for being part of this ridge, Tom and Ned."
"What's making all the racket?" They turned around, puzzled. A gas tractor chugged toward the Glisson homestead. Big steel wheels churned. Bud Waring sat on a seat, gripping the steering wheel. Smoke puffed out of the exhaust.

As it got closer, Asa Reynolds, Bud's hired hand, strolled across the ridge. "Yes, sir. Bud spotted you all clearing with hand tools yesterday. It looks like you've got all the stumps and rocks out." Asa stopped talking. The loud tractor rattled their senses.
Nell cackled.
I thought I'd never see anything again like Elsie Powell in her fishnets, but this machine takes the prize.

Asa said, "Old Sam's not partial to engines. Bud needed a spot for a test field."
"I thought you were a ten-year-old boy stooped over like a farmer, Nell." Bud shouted over the spitting and ticking of the tractor. "Is it only you three? Are Ned and old Tom trying to clear these acres by hand? This

machine's about the price of four mules, but it can go all day. As long as you keep water in the radiator."

"We've got the big stumps out." Nell panted. "I've wanted to plant this since my Da died."

"This tractor'll save you hours of time. I see you've met my assistant, Asa?" Bud smiled. "He'd like to work while I'm gone. I'll be out of state the next several days. Sorry about your job at the home." With a thrust from the bottom of the crank, Bud gave the handle a clockwise half-turn. He released it. The engine started to sputter. Bud climbed aboard. He put the tractor in gear. The mechanized tractor dragged the big plow. It kicked up soil and picked up speed. It made loud popping and ticking sounds. With more puffs of black smoke, it bucked and snorted. The tractor warmed into a steady rhythm.

Surely Asa must know how much of the corruption Bud's father's involved in?
"How do you feel about planting trees, Asa?"
"I'd like that," Asa said. He tipped his cap. "I've got a proposal, ma'am." His round face beamed. "With every opportunity, I'd like to trade work for that high-wheel bicycle in the back of your barn. I'd enjoy riding those back roads from the old Mose Johnson place to my church down this way most Sunday mornings."
"Asa, that's a deal. I've got another deal. I believe there's an organ stored in an old building at Bud's. It's owned by a former reverend."
"There's plenty of old clutter," said Asa. "I'll help find it."

"I know Joe'd love to see the bicycle ridden." Nell squinted at the plowed field out over the yellow wildflowers waving in the breeze.

Thank you, Bud. We don't have much acreage left to justify a machinery purchase. But what a difference this machine made.
"There's no clumps to start the new rows of nut seeds."
"Bud's been talking gadgetry for years," said Tom. "Fast and loud. Never heard such a racket in these parts. That tractor might've scared the poor hermit to death."
"After Uncle Joe died, the hermit showed up," remarked Ned. "He's shy. He's Grandma's good friend."
"Ned and I used to keep an eye on Ma. The hermit wouldn't hurt anything," said Tom. "She's been giving books, medicine, and food to him for years." Tom's veined hands shook. But his praise of the hermit was solid.

~~**~~**~~**~~

The next day Nell wiped the cake-mix-like soil on the back of her coveralls. She paused and admired her spacing between each nut on her rows.
Thank you, Lord, for the peace of having this field ready.
Tom, Ned, and Asa alternated transplanted saplings they dug from the forest with nuts. Three decades ago, saplings like a line of soldiers marched down sections of the ridge. Nell's shoulders relaxed as she realized Peace Ridge was making a comeback!

"I've dreamed of this day for so long." She laughed. "Over the years, Da's seeds have multiplied into enough for many rows." Placing her arm around old Tom, Nell said, "Thank you, Tom. You too, Ned, for protecting Ma when I'm gone. Dusk's coming in a hurry. I thought I caught a glimpse of a bird with a white face."

"That old barn owl's back, eh? He's a message to deliver for someone that needs it. That's what my grandfather told me," said Tom.

~~**~~**~~**~~

With her apron holding the rosy tint of the sunset on a Tuesday evening in October 1920, Aunt Nell agreed to a word alone with her nephew, Ned McMinn. She found a seat on the porch steps and with a tender pat indicated the spot beside her.

"All of our lives, my mother's cherished memories were of the walnut grove," said Ned. "No matter how busy I am, you can count on me to help plant the ridge."

"With your brand-new automobile you must appear wealthy to the farmers," responded Nell.

"I've an offer for you regarding my delivery job. Just when business picked up, it's as if someone's trying to horn in on my route. I need help."

"Is this in regard to the trunk of your new automobile dragging, packed full of the 50-proof corn extract that poor people use in their baked goods?"

"Yes, Auntie, the automobile's a must. I need help with deliveries when I'm gone. It's a gamble. If only you could drive."

"Ma taught all of us a quote: 'Even if I knew the world was going to pieces, I'd still plant my trees.' We must go

360

for our dreams, and if we fail—we can come back and at least we'll have tried."

Ned's voice trembled. "The farmers can't make ends meet by storing corn in their silos. Corn extract earns a better price than hauling their bushels of corn to town."
"But they need a still?"
"Yep. Bud's built stills for several and others of them copied his design. I don't want Grandma to know that's what my deliveries are. She's sure proud of me for owning my own auto. I don't want to be the black sheep of this family. I believe in the walnut ridge for Granddad. I'll help you plant the ridge."
"But, Ned, how can I help you?"
"I've got to find additional ways to support my brothers and sister. All I need are a place to store the whiskey and a fill-in driver." Ned removed his cap. "The location here's perfect between the Mississippi and the Illinois Rivers. Lots of backcountry."

Nell's face looked grim.
Thank you, Lord. Keep my mind at peace.
"Aunt, this is my opportunity to aid the farmers with stills. They require someone to bring them supplies, and store their product, and a deliveryman for the bigger cities."
After Ned left, Nell explained Ned's need to Ma. "Are you thinking what I'm thinking, Ma?"
"Yes. It's time for us to help our boy and time for your driving lessons. Wren will be too busy teaching you to worry about her graduation present. Then you or Wren'll be able to drive me to one of the town meetings

on the new laws with women voting. If only I could've voted sixty years ago."

"I would've voted for Abe myself."

Ma never ceases to amaze me. What will she think of next? Voting? Ma will enjoy the music. Ma's one of the few who said I could do it. You're right, Ma. We've continued to protect the ridge. Our rudder, Mike hasn't come home yet. But now, at last, I'm returning to the grove after I help Ned.

CHAPTER 32
A Timely Arrival

"Doubts are casting weird shadows over my desk." Sam Waring stabbed his finger on some maps.

I'm filled with dread. Life's best is passing me over.

"Pardon me, sir? You wanted to sign these letters?" asked his secretary. "It's past five o'clock at night."

"Yes, and you are?"

"Miss Maclaren, Commissioner Waring. This is my fifth year as your secretary."

Sam grasped a pen but shoved the letters across his desk. "I don't want to hear any more about Doc Simpkins' estate going to a former employee of the County Home. Inform Camean there's nothing left after his bills were paid." The evening train was pulling in. "Whoo-woot." He hobbled over to the window. "Oh, my, look at this. Well, I'll be. Jack Glisson, the semipro boxer is back in town."

"Sir, the paperwork...."

"Life's passing me over, Miss." grumbled Sam. "Everything's been in my favor to own that section of land for access to the coal mine. It's a shorter road to build. How can that woman make it with the inflated tax assessments she's had to bear for years? Clearing the hardwoods her family prized?"

"Mr. Commissioner!" Miss Maclaren's voice exploded. "May I be excused?"

"Oh, yes. Would you take a quick gander at our little depot? There's a crowd forming." Sam gasped, "Oh, no.

They couldn't be?" Sam stared. "As if *he's* a hero of this county. Nothing surprises me after these fickle voters elected a new sheriff from Wyoming. He'll be another fizzle in the pan, just like this Glisson. Don't you agree, Miss?"

The secretary's eyes opened wide. The whites of her glare glowed in the dim overhead bulb.

Sam went on as if he were addressing the brick wall. "Maybe the newspaper had it right when they questioned my mental stability, due to signs of senility. It's common knowledge I own over half of two townships." He looped his thumbs in his front pockets. "My son thinks because his name's on the deed, he owns one of my holdings. It makes me so angry. I worry there's too little oxygen."

"It's late. You're not feeling well again, Commissioner," admonished his secretary.

"That Glisson Klondiker has surpassed his deadline for payment. But his sister's the one that inherited the ridge."

"But, Commissioner Waring," said the secretary, "you had me pull the records. They traded that land over twenty years ago."

Sam shook the cobwebs from his head. "Let me see that document." Sam spun around in his chair.

No, no, no. It can't be happening. Nell can't pay. It's almost mine.

"Mine," he repeated over and over. "It can't be. This land'll have to be sold for the cost of the taxes. This'll break their spirit."

"Good night, Mr. Waring," said Miss Maclaren, with a shake of her head. She gathered up her things. She tiptoed out of the room.

Sam put his feet up on his desk. The sound of people cheering outside the building alerted him.

It's time to sell those logs and close the deal on her land on the ridge. We'll have us our road to the mine.

"Jack Glisson's too late. He acts like he doesn't have even a twitch of fear for his family. Their situation'll soon rattle his composed, happy demeanor."

I suppose he's here to help his sister and nephew? His presence alone pushes me into a sense of urgency.

Sam gathered the last things he wanted from the building and opened his office door.

~~**~~**~~**~~

Pumping his knees as if preparing to skip rope, Jack whistled a chipper tune. "Hello, Sis. Give me a hug. Hello, Ma. Hello to my beautiful niece. Wren, is it? Remember your Uncle Jack?"

I can't believe it. I've got to keep my composure. A faraway brother returned. Is he real? Two nieces? A sister-in-law? I don't want to scare them off either.

Nell smoothed her hair.

I wish I'd have put on my best dress. Ma's overjoyed. But, all of a sudden, I too, can't resist the urge to kick up my heels and skip around my brother's truck in joy.

"Big news. We're here to stay. Nell, your letter stated you need my help with something on the old Mose Johnson property?" asked Jack.

"Er, right."
Stay? Forever because of moving an organ? I should've tried to acquire the organ sooner.
"Things are a little crazy, but they'll improve now that you're here. I can't believe it, you're truly here. I'll explain what I need from the Mose Johnson place later."
Nell gulped. "Of course, we're thrilled you're back."
I've given Jack no clues of what I've been up to the past couple of years since losing my job and Ned going to jail.

"You're still the same old Jack. It's been so long. Uh, um. What a nice truck. This is such an unexpected surprise. Did you move everything? You've got the whole family?"
"Yes, we're out of the big city and all the law-breaking. The Model T's army surplus from the war. It's a 1919 model, that's a couple of years old. I bought it this morning in town."
"It looks almost brand new."
He's so cheerful.
Nell swallowed.
He won't care what I agreed to help Ned with.

"That's always been you, Jack. Never let anything put you down. The townsfolks will hold their heads high that a champion's come home."
"Yes, Nell, this *is* home," replied Jack, all smiles. "A small town's bound to have some excitement. We're leaving behind saloons, corruption, and the hustle and bustle of St. Louis. Everything's changing with all the automobiles in the big city. People are in such a hurry. Too much excitement in the city. I thought you'd be more surprised to have us back."

If you think this small town's quiet, wait and see. He's so handsome, with his three-piece suit, and large mustache. He's fit and strong looking. I noticed a slight limp.

"We want to take it easy, be semiretired, and purchase an older model tractor."

Nell hid a twitch. "You'll be surprised to know we're underway with planting the walnut grove. We plowed with a tractor."

Why is Jack thinking of peace and quiet? He's forty-nine, riding a tractor all day? We've been waiting for him so long. Jack's easygoing. It's hard to ruffle his feathers but, if they do ruffle, look out. But Maude walks like a woman accustomed to getting her way. Let them settle in. I hope Maude likes the old family homestead with all of its quirks.

"Jack, please." Maude sighed. "Can you help me with the children?" She plopped four-year-old Anna Lois into his arms.

"My dear sister, life is what you make of it. I've seen enough of the city." Jack spun Nell around, making Anna squeal. "We came home to be together. Now let's give auntie and grandma a welcome-back hug." With a big wink, Jack pumped his fists and stood in the stance of a champion.

"Jack, Marie needs assistance to find the outhouse. Do you mind?" Maude marched eleven-year-old Marie over to him.

Easygoing or not, I don't ever want to be far from his big hug again.

"It's so good you're all here."

That boxing might have crippled him a little, but Jack's solid as walnut wood.

"Marie, do you want to see where I scratched my name on the wall when I was your age?" asked Jack.

"Yes, Papa," mumbled Marie.

"Ladies, I'm tickled that you're all here together. This parlor looks wonderful. All the ferns, tasteful rugs, and beautiful pink lilies under the window." He gave Ma a warm embrace. "And look at the family pictures on all the walls. Your cozy chair." Jack spun, a little unsteady, on one twisted leg. "What's that big space being saved for in the corner?"

"Wren's graduation organ. Remember the Reverend's organ at Mary-Jane and Kate's wedding? We're hoping to bring it here from the Mose Johnson place."

"Oh, is that what all the fuss is about? Aye, we saw each of Kate's three daughters' recitals in St. Louis before they moved to Montana. And, Wren, what a treat that you're going to have your own organ!"

"With Wren playing the piano and organ playing all over town, she earns one gold medal after another," said Nell.

"I could play my fiddle with Wren," suggested Jack.

Maude, exasperated, had more instructions for her husband. "Jack, our traveling bags. It's sprinkling outside. Didn't you mention there have been sightings of a vagrant?" She shuddered. "My heavens, I don't want our things stolen or damaged. On our way up the drive, a young colored man about scared us off the road riding an old high-wheeler bicycle. In this neighborhood?"

I hope Ma doesn't mention her friendship with the hermit. Jack remains easygoing and calm. Like anyone raised on a farm, he knows the value of work, and a vagrant is another mouth to feed. Jack's like Da. His cheerfulness is ever-present. But Maude might not appreciate the hermit or Asa.

Jack and Anna stepped outside. They grabbed their bags. "No boogeyman out here, right Anna?"
"No boogeyman, Papa." Anna giggled. Rain glistened on her dimpled cheeks.
"There, we have them, and not a moment too late." Jack laughed a big laugh that filled the room with warmth. "Marie, are you ready to make a quick dash into the wild to find the privy?"

All aflutter from the coolness of the rain, Jack returned with Marie and began with the long-awaited news from the Klondike. His voice was calming and rhythmic. "Aye the beauty, and the grandness of the Arctic. Wolves howling, ow-whoo, whoo-woo wolf, wolf."
"That's enough. To create such a stir. Jack, please." Maude pulled her shawl around her thin shoulders. Jack reached in a bag and brought out a package with broken string. He read the enclosed letter from the Northwest Territory authorities.

"The letter inside this package states that Michael Patrick Glisson, from Dawson City, a clerk for a Wilson Mining Company, went missing. A fine clerk, with excellent records. Talented in equipment design for the company's many needs. A well-thought-of and trusted employee."

"Did they check to see if he went on to Nome?" interrupted Ma.

"No, Ma. It doesn't say their investigation included the authorities in Nome. After searching for Mr. Glisson for more than a year, we're sad to report he's still missing."

"It's such a big place. Do they have enough manpower?" Ma queried. "I imagine there's still gold left behind."

"It states there are thirty-three posts in the Yukon Territory. They all maintain safety and enforce the law, including looking for missing people and working together with all law enforcement agencies."

"Maybe they overlooked something," said Nell.

"It says the police force have acted with diligence, efficiency, and strong moral principles."

"They took so long to let us know," Ma said.

"Ma, they sent the certified letter with a copy of Mike's will. Wills were drawn up for all the employees of the mining company for which he clerked. They mailed his last paycheck per his request for taxes on his inheritance to the authorities of Brownsville County, Illinois. In the case of his death, absence, or injury, his land is handed over to Mrs. Nell Robertson, his sister, and his mother, Mrs. Sadie Jane Glisson. This check should more than cover all taxes."

"Oh, Michael." Ma cried.

"There's a postscript scribbled at the bottom from a detective. I can't read it, but it says, 'I'm sorry to report we found nothing more.'"

"My Jack, you said if you and Mike were ever to be separated, you'd want to be hog-tied to Mike. Thank you, Jack." Ma wiped her eyes.

"I know you were counting on Mike coming home."

Sitting on the sofa arm, Wren piped up, "Uncle Jack, we've been waiting for Uncle Mike for a long time." She sniffled. "I don't want him to be missing or dead."

"That's not what Uncle Mike would want us to be thinking. He'd want us to know he's having the greatest adventure of his life," said Jack. "What I picture is him on his way to the next gold field, happy to be mining. I don't think of him as a missing person. When all the gold rushes are over," Jack's big bushy moustache and wink softened their worries. "We'll see there were too many men up there to know everyone's exact whereabouts. Aye, has anyone told you, Wren, how much you look like your Aunt Honora?"

Sunlight gleamed around the pretty parlor.
I see Maude's ladylike. She's fussy about her daughters. A firm Christian lady and an outstanding pianist. She looks like she'd been a strict school teacher with iron rules. Is she turning her nose up at us, or does she always look like that?

"Shall we have tea now?" asked Ma. They passed their best cups, saucers, creamer, the sugar bowl, and a plate of Ma's delicious cookies.

I see Maude's white gloves, and I'm embarrassed by my calloused brown hands. The little girls are so delicate in their matching pink dresses and muffs.

"Are these cookies homemade?" asked Maude. "They have a strange fruity, nutty flavor."

Bounding off the window seat, Jack got his bride another one. "They're Ma's specialty of oatmeal with raisins and black walnuts."

"Oh, no more, thank you. But what an interesting flavor," said Maude. "Did Jack mention my three rules?"

Ma's eyes shot open. The corner of Nell's mouth curled down. They shook their heads, no.

"I told Jack that if we're to farm, none of the womenfolk are to do manual labor. In addition, I asked that our home remains private. All of you lived there once. It's our home now."

"Of course," said Ma. "Is that all?"

"No alcohol is to be on our property." Maude tapped her fingers on the table. "We came here for peace and quiet with no more fighting for Jack."

I hope she doesn't notice we used corn extract for the vanilla. We can't afford vanilla. I agreed to help Ned with deliveries and store his moonshine here. But Jack looks so happy, I don't want to change that.

Nell grimaced.

Dag-gum, Maude. Oh, dear, I remember what happened with Bertha. Please, Lord, grant me another chance with Maude.

Jack sprang from the window seat. His legs did a stiff jig. There were hugs all around. With a merry twinkle in his eyes, Jack and his family crossed the road to the old homestead cabin.

CHAPTER 33
Maude

As soon as Nell heard Ma's soft snoring, she sat back hard in her chair.

I don't want to forget the folks in the County Home. They didn't see me as puny. They thought I could do something about the local corruption. One thing I can do is pursue Sam for stealing Mike's logs. I wonder how Jack will feel about our involvement?

Lowering her feet from the potbellied stove, Nell saw a uniformed sheriff peering through the screen of the parlor door.

"Hello, I'm Sheriff Tiffany, trained as a Revenuer. I'm Brownsville County's new sheriff. I'm from Wyoming. I'm checking on sightings of a vagrant."

"Is that so?"

"I'd like to verify some information."

Nell's bottom lip trembled.

Uh-oh. He's sure to be after contraband liquor.

Sheriff Tiffany lowered his voice. "Mrs. Robertson, I'm here about your nephew Ned McMinn. I'd like to see him released from jail and the moonshine business. It's off to an ugly start. We've got a hunch plenty of moonshine's stored on this property. The vagrant's involved?"

"The vagrant isn't your man," said eighty-nine-year-old Ma, appearing from the bedroom. "Couldn't be a nicer, more trustworthy person, who reads his Bible and is good to talk with. He's shy and is seldom seen."

Poker-faced, Nell waited.

"Do you folks know the location of any stills?"

A rustling came from the front porch. Jack and Maude's noses were pushed against the screen door. Nell gasped. *They must've forgotten something.*

"We had to turn back when we saw the sheriff's car," explained Jack.

Now I know I've got a brother nearby.

"The girls are asleep in the truck," replied Maude. "Are you all right?"

"This case involves you too," said Sheriff Tiffany. "It's critical to a much bigger case, involving Sam Waring. Sam's gotten so much power in this county. My predecessor informed me there's a likelihood his big mitts are part of the corruption in local tax assessment. Sam's become more desperate. He's got accomplices who owe him money. He owns about everything in Shawnee Township."

"He's after us. For revenge." Nell shook her head.

He's likely the one taking over Ned's extract sales.

"I don't want Ned McMinn in competition with Sam's cohorts." Sheriff Tiffany grimaced. "Sam's got connections to the big city."

So does Ned.

"I'd like to know there's an end to this bootlegging involvement with the Glissons." Sheriff Tiffany glanced from Jack to Nell. "Ned's delivery van was seen behind the Rushville Tavern the night it burned. We believe

Ned's story. He testified that he took the train to Jacksonville to attend his brothers' fiddle performance."

"I know he wanted to attend," muttered Nell.

"He stated that he returned to the depot the next day. He suspected his vehicle had been moved and parked funny. He found rags and empty kerosene cans in the back."

"Ned wants out, and he wants the Glissons' good name to be cleared. He regrets that he can't return the money and goods to the farmers and still owners. The farmers are afraid to lose their goods. It's too dangerous."

Maude's face turned white.

"What if someone finished Ned's business for him?" asked Nell.

"Yes, but…." Sheriff Tiffany cupped his chin. "I don't want anyone hurt. It's too risky. Ned mentioned that Sam's head man has returned penniless from the Klondike. He owes Sam. He's no doubt the one who found Ned's storage locations."

"I'm certain you're referring to Stephen." Nell's eyes widened.

Sheriff Tiffany nodded.

"An arson happened on our property more than twenty years ago. It was the same scenario. Stephen worked as Sam's foreman. No evidence was ever found. The culprit was never identified." Nell tutted, "It's very suspicious that the same person's linked in both incidents."

"If we handle this right, and go slowly, we can bring down Sam Waring's entire empire. We need hard evidence against Sam and his friends. We could bring him in for something smaller than the tax corruption he's involved with."

Leaping from her chair, Nell's voice rose. "How about the theft of hundreds of dollars' worth of black walnut wood?"

This is my moment. Right, Lord?

"I'd like evidence to verify that he's involved in the stolen lumber case. We've been hoping that someone will testify against Sam. Everyone is too afraid of his power. If only a witness would come forward."

"Oh, I'm your man!" In her exuberance, Nell about knocked the sheriff over. "I've got documentation on Sam. I'll be right back."

"Even if your information can be cross verified with statements we've received, there's but a slim chance it'll hold up in court. Do you have solid physical evidence?"

Sheriff Tiffany took his cowboy hat off. He wiped his brow. "Have any of you worked with the vagrant?"

Vagrant? Dead-end trail. Oh, Lord, help me locate the solid physical evidence.

Nell squinted her eyes at the Wyoming man.

This is a young, daring new Sheriff, not bought into Sam Waring's corruption. Green? But, I'll bet he's a good one.

"Mrs. Robertson, I appreciate your enthusiasm to help. We need to wait until we have a couple of strong men."

"What about my brother Jack?"

"We're not involved in what's going on here." Maude sounded perturbed.

"Let me permit you folks some time to think about the illegal activities on your land. I'll return." Sheriff Tiffany donned his hat and left.

"Ned McMinn's a criminal? Are stills operating on our property? Are cars and wagons pulling up to the place at night?" asked Maude, choking.

Jack offered Maude a sip of tea. He patted her back. "Don't start thinking about taking the girls and heading back to St. Louis."

"My grandson, Ned's been a big help here." Ma set her head back. Her Adam's apple stuck out. She held up a bottle labeled vanilla extract. "We substitute corn extract for the vanilla. It doesn't come from mobsters. It's folks trying hard to hold on to their land. In our case, we couldn't have made it without our Proverb tunnels."

Startled faces greeted Ma's next words. "Maude, it's time to explain some things, dear. For years, we've tried to keep Jack from feeling obliged to end his boxing career and come home."

The rhythmic even tone of Ma's voice filled the room like nourishment. "Many of our friends and neighbors have left the area. The farm yields are down. We're fighting for Da's dream."

"And Honora's," whispered Nell.

"You mentioned Proverb tunnels?" Maude blew her nose with her handkerchief. "It reminds me of my grandma's farm. I love that this family," Maude squeezed Jack's hand, "my family, believes in the Proverbs.

"So long ago, and after years of city teaching, I'm glad to be in a rural area." Maude continued. From beneath her lashes, she acknowledged Nell with a nod. "I'm sorry. I made it sound like I couldn't forgive the alcohol. It played a devastating part in my upbringing. Please forgive my airs. Perhaps we could start this relationship over? Ma Sadie, would you include me in the Proverb tunnels?" Maude asked for seconds of Ma's cookies and tea.

"We've never done anything illegal. We've been experiencing special necessities for years, such as selling off land, Wren's lessons, and friendship with the hermit." Ma blotted *her* eyes as Maude sipped her tea. "I believe in helping others. I can't abide by the hermit being stripped of all of his dignity." Ma rose from her chair. She hobbled to the window.
"Is he there now?" gulped Maude.
Ma's telling Maude that her friend's a hermit. I guess I should confess my bootlegging.

"He disappears when he hears anyone else around. He's called, 'Old Red Eyes,' by folks who've caught a glimpse of him. They're afraid of him. He's innocent and kind. But yet, they run from him." Ma turned from the window with her chin high. "Nell's another one. Folks ran from her orneriness. She's suffered plenty. She's a big reason we've got what land we have left. Nell's never met the hermit. She's never said a word to criticize me. She's too busy working.

"Around his eyes, eyelids, and eyelashes, it's hard to see where the whites of his eyes should've been under his long, mangy hair." Ma's voice began to break. "The scars circle around those red, red eyes. He has a huge beard and filthy clothes. The wilderness is his home. My eyes aren't the best. My hearing might be going, but a man reading all the time is no ne'er-do-well."
Ma said her piece. Maude's mouth gaped open.

Jack put his arm around Ma. He held her for a long time and then Nell. "Thanks, ladies. I'd like to find this hermit."
"I've got things to finish too," said Nell. "We'll put the organ on the back burner. After we're all caught up, the organ's ours."
"My next direction will be to search the forest." With a tip of his hat, Jack placed his arm under Maude's elbow. Maude turned back and hugged Ma and Nell to her.
I feel at peace with Maude. Thank you, Lord.

CHAPTER 34
The Hermit

It's easy to see all of Nell's hard work, clearing the ridge.
"Say, I'm not too far from my old boxing ring." Jack chuckled.
I'll be doggoned. Nell's fought for Da's legacy. I could never forget this route if I was blindfolded. The timbered ridge rolling to the southwest.
"She sure knows how to land on her feet." Jack ducked through an archway into the forest.
My idea's to search near the burned cabin. It's way back in the deep brush, overgrown, and choked with briars. It helps to have grown up here. That was no deer path I traveled on. I'm certain a man uses this trail.

Jack circled around behind the blackened timbers of the cabin. Not a trace of smoke existed. Light and shadows played through a gap in the jumbled branches. A perfect breeze allowed a mix of color and an aroma of food cooking to signal Jack that he wasn't alone. He muffled his movements. He followed in the general direction of the thick brambles. He wove his way through briars, snapping twigs, but not disturbing the old raggedy man hunched over the fire.

"Hello," called Jack, who was creeping closer. "I'm a Glisson. Our property's next door. It borders this land on the east."
There was no answer. The startled man sat up. He glanced back toward the burnt cabin. Then with a shrug

as if it were too late to make a dash, he crouched back down.

It's uncanny. But I know him. He's filthy, gray, and burned, and yet, I know him. He's thin and frail. There's something dignified, gentle, and almost graceful about him.

"Do I know you?" asked Jack, easing onto a stump.
The hermit flinched at what must have been his first conversation in his sanctuary. He trembled. His gaze drifted away.
Jack, the boxer, knelt on the ground. He waited for the hermit. "My sisters, and brothers, and I used to have houses made out of logs rolled together." Jack's eyes blinked. "I think I know you."

The other man didn't move. "Why, you're Bill? Bill Drew?" said Jack, staring. "Bill, it's you. Isn't it?" Jack couldn't believe it. "Bill Drew," gasped Jack. "Bill, it's been forever since I've seen you. Oh, Bill." He stood and reached out to clap the frail shoulders.
"It's been a long time." Bill ran his hands through his long beard. "I don't want folks to see me like this. Don't mention anything to Nell. She doesn't want a failure hanging around."

His voice was pleasant and rhythmic like Da's. The only thing that kept Jack from being overcome was keeping his own voice steady. "I've been gone for over twenty years. I became a boxer in St. Louis, with lots of people, cheering, and crime. A conductor on the trolley for years. I'm home now."

"I know," Bill mumbled into his beard. "I went to the Klondike with Mike. Your brother always said he didn't want to be alone on the adventure. He needed companionship. I needed him as much as he needed me. There were plenty of experiences to change a man. After that, things got sidetracked."

Creeping closer to the bent-over shape of the hermit, Jack couldn't hide his eagerness. "Have you made a place for yourself in Morty's burned cabin?"

Any attempt for Bill to maintain his pride shattered. Bill wilted toward the ground. His face on his knees. A torn and filthy shirt hung on him. His bony elbows poked out of ashy gray holes. His shoulders shook from his pain.
He's like a box turtle, pulling in tight.

Jack knelt in the grass. He placed a strong arm around Bill's shoulders. "There, there, Bill. It's okay. I know how hard life can get. It can become twisted like these deer paths."

Crossing his legs and keeping his hands close to his sides, Bill attempted to make himself smaller.

"But Bill. It's me, your old friend. I'm older, but I'm still the same Jack Glisson."

"Michael and Sadie Jane's youngest boy?"

"Yep. You came here for refuge. That you'll have." Jack's voice comforted. "Don't worry. We'll bring you whatever you need."

"I don't need for anything." Bill shook his head. "I live off of the land. I thought it was a shame about those walnuts on the ridge," he stammered. "I found the old gunnysacks of your Da's."

Clouds scuttled by. In the brush Jack saw a pair of sparrows light in their nest.

"I've started a new memorial grove to the southwest. It's down off the ridge, where it drops down into thick trees in the creek bottom," explained Bill. His voice broke.

"Amazing, Bill. Nell's wanted that forever. She's so busy. What a huge blessing to the family legacy."

Bill acknowledged the praise with a sad smile.

"You've spent so much time in the forest. You always were known for your kindness and gentleness. Did you enjoy your work for the forest service on the Montana-Idaho border?"

Not able to answer every question Bill turned away.

"Do you have things to read?" asked Jack.

A bumblebee buzzed. Crows cawed followed by silence. The creek bottom seemed to be waiting for something.

"I came back to flee from crowds." Jack broke the stillness. "I presume you're doing the same?"

Bill's head tucked down into the long, gray beard. He rocked himself for a few seconds. Then, he knelt. He stirred the coals on the fire.

Jack's voice quavered. The big, grieving boxer sank onto a stump. "Bill, Mike's been missing for a long time. Can you tell me your story? I don't mind your eyes. Ma said they're improving. You were saying you went to the Klondike?"

The hermit jerked upright in confirmation. The man bent over the kindling, fingering slivers of wood and hunks of bark. He paused with reverence over their design before reaching for another log from his woodpile.

Trying to make Bill feel at ease, Jack pressed on. "Nell's life has been steered in a hundred directions to keep the homestead afloat. With the losses and corruption, she's decided that it's never going to be the right time. Everyone called you, 'the vagrant.' She never thought you'd stay all these years. You could've been a much-needed friend to each other."

With tangled hair and beard, scarred, dirty, thin, and broken, Bill Drew, the hermit? My heart breaks for the sadness in his eye and for Ma, sweet Ma, applying salve to his burns and treating his eyes with patience.

Placing his hands on his thighs, Bill sat up. A determined look filled his face beneath his red, sore eyes. "I've received stacks of books on the rock in front of my shack and a surplus of food. The books are a comfort. The food's like a lift, but the books I consume." His eyes fastened on the horizon. "Why do these folks care about the life of one man? A complete failure."

"Many of them enjoy your company," replied Jack.

"I came back to where I grew up. My favorite place, where people cared."

"All the leaves of this forest cushioned and protected you from all the staring eyes and cruelty you've suffered."

Bill's long, unkempt hair and beard fluttered in the breeze. Then, after a long pause, he cleared his throat. "I was a piano player in a saloon in the Yukon. Your brother Mike always waited for me. Got off early due to the severe cold. Elsie had the night off."

He looked at Jack with a tortured face. "We heard a ruckus up ahead. Stephen and two other men hit Elsie. They pushed her to the ground. They yanked her inside our cabin. Her desperate shouts alarmed us. I remember saying it's too dangerous. There's three of them.

"Mike struggled through the deep snow and ice. He kicked in the back door. I followed Mike. He punched one and swung another around. Stephen and the other two pounded him. In the mix-up, I took a blow to the back of my head."

Bill paused.

"Much later, I woke up in the snow. Inside, terror and blood were everywhere. Elsie and Mike were nowhere to be seen. The coals in the fireplace had long burned out. The cabin was a shambles, ransacked, and abandoned. They'd even found the hole in the floorboards under the bed where Mike and I hid the few nuggets we'd saved."

Bent over double, Bill held his head in his hands.

"Tired and frozen, I searched for Mike and Elsie. I couldn't go on anymore. The severe cold made me desperate. Word was those men cleared out of town. They took Elsie with them. No one offered any information on Mike."

I can't hide the heartbreak glistening in my eyes. Jack's head hung down on his chest. *I always wanted to be at my brother's side.*

"I'm sorry this happened, Bill."
"I'd no idea how to search for Mike in that immense country. I kept at it." Bill continued. "After three weeks, my efforts became mechanical. They'd been gone so long, I couldn't find answers. I'd been replaced at the saloon. There was no trace of Mike. Other miners helped in the search, but no clues were found.
"I left." Bill threw his hands up. "It took a long time to find my cousin Elsie in Seattle. Many of the Klondikers mingled there, reliving the glory days. No one knew about Mike. One of them directed me to Elsie's hospital bed."

Digging into his coat pocket, Bill held a tiny photo. "She didn't know where Mike was. This is Elsie's infant daughter. She gave me this photo. It's yours. Elsie's sickness scared me. I left my cousin to rest."
"I've been carrying this story tight to myself." Bill groaned. "The only place I could think to go was to return to the forest on the border of Montana and Idaho. I'd worked there before the Klondike."

Bill, like a man condemned, covered his head, and moaned. After many heartbreaking minutes, he continued his story. "I've never spoken about this. The forest was a black, burned abyss. A fire had roared through miles of my old job site. I stumbled around, in a dazed state. Places were still burning, charred, and black. Destruction was everywhere. I reached the little settlement of houses where my fellow seed planters and I lived.

"The massive forest fire annihilated everything. I sank to my knees beneath a tree, not knowing what happened to everyone. I must have fallen asleep. A burning branch fell on me. My eyes filled with hot sparks. I cried out in agony. My eyes felt like they'd burn out of my head. The pain knocked me out."
Bill took several deep breaths before he continued.
"I was in so much pain and shock that I could only stumble to the south. I wanted to disappear."
He held his head in hands. "My eyes needed care. I held a rag to one."

Jack leaned closer to catch the muffled words.
"During my endless walk, I could see only a little out of one eye or the other. I withdrew from the sound of voices. I avoided all connections. My sleep was full of nightmares of that hot, burning limb falling on me. I staggered on through the nights and rested in the day.
"I recalled the atmosphere out here on Peace Ridge, where your Da planted the saplings for a memorial grove. I needed that sense of peace. It's taken a long time for me to feel safe.

"I've memorized Isaiah 32:2. 'A hiding place from the wind, and a covert from the tempest—the shadow of a great rock in a weary land.' I've taken to planting new nut trees and others along the creek. Behind your Da's stable, I found some walnuts in ragged, burned gunnysacks. They're thriving. Might be a suitable place along the creek, compared with the ridge.

"I needed to be alone. I do not understand the emotions that engulfed me. It had to do with my grieving."

He couldn't seem to stop wiping his eyes and nose. "Doc Simpkins was right about how hard the goldfields can be. I've been to the cemetery. Doc's buried between Da and Malcolm. He'd have liked that. I should tell you that Mike often commented on how safe he felt in Da's jacket, with Doc's coat over it. I've dealt with substantial guilt. I was such a coward and didn't stay longer. People run and scream, 'Old Red Eye,' when they see me. I remain here by myself.

"I told myself to stay isolated. I couldn't spend time with people or bear the shame of how they would see me. They never stopped with their cries of, 'Old Red Eye.' At first, I made piles of brush, straw, and leaves, after which I found a woolen blanket. Next, I moved into the burned cabin.

"But I do hear things that scare me in the forest. Stephen's returned as Sam's foreman. He must owe Sam something fierce. I've heard him say he's got debts to pay. That's why he's back from the Klondike." Bill shuddered. "He and his rough friends are the ones who hurt Elsie and fought with Mike and me. Frightening things are going on now. Some nights they're at a still on the ridge, where the old log mansions were. They make plans and talk about jobs. They've got more stills.

"They're involved in bootlegging to make money. I've disabled many of their stills. I hear them talking about an important job. It involves the transportation of stolen walnut logs from Mose Johnson's place by train. They're busier than ever because Sam's son, Bud, is out of state. Then, the logs will be milled in another county to hide the evidence. Sam took them, so as to bankrupt Nell. I've heard them say, 'Wednesday night, March 23, not long before sundown.' They've got strong men to help them."

"That's less than two weeks away." Jack shook his head. His mouth was set in a tight line. He shook one big fist inside his other hand.
"My cousin Elsie and Mike shouldn't have been treated like this. If there's justice for Stephen and Sam, I want to be part of it." The hermit closed his eyes.
"Also, they took jugs of corn whiskey from your storage shed. They've driven off with some. Others they've hidden in your Proverb tunnels."

"You've got to be methodical and in control. Take each step like a machine with a pattern. The truck'll work." Wren smiled. "That's how I handle my organ recitals. It'll work for your driving, Aunt Nell."

"Oh, so you're the expert after your exploits of driving around with Willard McCoy, the area sapling salesman?" The sun shone through the clouds over the old farm road. *I grimace at the thought of my little Wren leaving.* "That's the way Willard shifts when he's going down a hill." The old truck made a wrenching sound. "Your foot on the accelerator has to be steady and controlled. It's a smidgen at a time when you put your foot on or off the clutch."

"Yes, Wren, mother hen." Nell winked at Ma. "I don't want to make Ma's head whip around the turns."

"I'm glad to be here for all of my grandchildren," Ma said.

Step-by-step, Wren reviewed the shifting process. "Do it again. I know you want to help Ned. It takes time to learn."

It took Nell a long time. Her fear of machinery almost outdid her fear of heights.

"I'm proud of you. Do you realize we've got three generations of women in this truck? I'm afraid you won't be good at quick getaways." Wren grinned at Grandma Sadie. "I hope Auntie won't jerk your neck, stopping and starting with the engine spluttering and coughing every time. My poor Grandma."

Jack's Model T leaped forward. It bolted backward through the wide-open barn doors. They all hooted and cackled. "To think my Nell is driving," remarked Ma.
"You call this driving?" Nell chortled.
After all the days of practice, Nell drove well enough. Wren said, "I don't think you're ever going to roar out of the coulees with control or come up the hills without popping the clutch. But never give up."
"I can't tolerate the graveling, grinding rocks on the undersides of this tin can. It takes all I can muster not to floor it." Nell steered around some thick branches. "More delays. All I want is to work in the walnut grove."

"Uncle Jack'll be shocked at how you drive his truck, Aunt Nell. We're both surprised you haven't injured yourself or anyone else." Wren scoffed. "You're so fond of speed. This is going to spoil you. I remember when I was little, and we saw you and Uncle Mike. You were riding on a plum tree he used as a harrow." Wren moaned. "Aunt Nell, Grandma, I'm sorry I brought Mike up," muttered Wren.
"Somethings we've got to wait for," said Nell.
"That's thinking positive," said Ma.

Hugging Wren and Ma, Nell went over the plan. "We won't miss any of Wren's performances. Uncle Jack wants us to use his truck for her recitals. Before and after them, we'll pay the still owners, split up what supplies and jugs we've got, and let them know we're out of business. We don't want Ned to have any connection to Sam's ring. This way, we're out quick with no enemies. We'll return the money we owe, and all the merchandise in the storage shed. We'll finish Ned's route. Don't worry, Wren. None of Sam's men will recognize Ma or me in Joe's old coveralls and caps—not when we're coming and going from area schools and churches. That'll be our cover. Oops, there's Sheriff Tiffany's vehicle."

Sheriff Tiffany angled his black vehicle off the road. He tipped his hat to Ma, Nell, and Wren. He threw open his door. He swiveled around, so both cowboy boots lined up on the dusty road, before arising. Then he loped over to the driver's side of Jack's truck.

"I've been visiting with Jack. He's gleaned valuable information." The sheriff's voice grew softer. "I understand your feelings for the hermit, Sadie Jane. It's with his help, that we'll solve this case."

The hermit? How can he help us?

"We've got to produce some innovative ideas to stop Sam. I've read your documents. Excellent job, Nell. They're journal entries, but they're enough to infuriate an officer of the law. I'm certain Waring got away with the things in these folks' testimonies to pave the way for his coal mine."

Sam's made us suffer by paying inflated taxes. But, Honora's assault is the worst.

Nell's chin dropped to her chest.

I'm relieved that Jack and Sheriff Tiffany think the hermit's all right. I'm ashamed that I've been too focused on making ends meet to help the hermit.

"I suppose the farmers couldn't stand together against Waring?" Sheriff Tiffany asked.

"Well, I've thought about that too," said Nell. "Most of these fellows bartered before banks came in. With low taxes at first, they thought they had some catching up to do. Most didn't know to appeal the inflated cost per acre. They were too busy surviving."

"I see you're driving, Nell," said the sheriff, tipping his hat. "I'll stop by in the next few days with further updates." Sheriff Tiffany nodded at the three women in the Model T.

"Yes, I, um, thought we'd better catch up with the times."

~~**~~**~~**~~

Too exhausted to sound powerful, Sam could only babble his motto. "Progress, progress. No more one-horse county. Big. Modern. Have you seen all our new roads? My constituent's comment on my light burning late into the night in my wing of the courthouse. It takes plenty of work to run this county."

"Dad." Bud hesitated. "The taxpayers might not see your light, when they can't see your integrity."

"I question your logic. Your sobriety? Term after term, I'm voted in."

"Dad, you've gone too far. I mean, inflating taxes on widows? Why?"

Charming most reporters came natural to Sam. Today, if it wasn't for Bud, Sam would've been too weak to push by them. Outside his office, Sam's hair was uncombed, and his three-piece suit was untidy. He tripped on a painter's bucket in his haste to escape from the reporter. The painter cleaned up the spill and resumed his stenciling. The gold filigree Sam had demanded, lined his office window and his door, which was labeled, "Private."

Sam's large calendar hung crookedly. It was loaded with foreclosure dates. Down the long dark hallway, Bud led his father outside.
The reporter followed, grilling Sam. "So the county's under suspicion?"
"Yes, did I mention an interesting part of our remodeling?" replied Sam in a daze. "The original walls—"
"Are you all right, you seem to be off-topic. I'm sorry I didn't even notice the remodeling."

"Made of the finest black walnut."
"Ah, yes," said the reporter, with a bewildered shake of his head. "I'm working on a story a citizen sent into the paper, seeking information on a black walnut memorial grove. The design is speculated to include a parkway that loops through forest land adjacent to an Indian cave? This could be a real draw for state tourists on their way to the springs in Adams County."

"Adams County? Walk in the woods?" raged Sam. "We'll soon be entering the next decade. No time for a trek through the woods unless it's after a golf ball. There are plenty of city parks."
"Yes, sir. I couldn't make much headway on the topic of county corruption. I thought this memorial would be a

better topic," said the stunned reporter. "I thought I'd straddle your motto for county progress with building recreational parks to benefit the taxpayers?"

Sam couldn't keep up with the reporter. His head spun. "You're focusing on a topic of unlikely interest to my constituents. They're behind me on progress. Conservation of trees? A hiking trail? As commander at the helm, I can say there's zero chance of any of these issues carrying any weight in Brownsville County."
The reporter's tone sounded strange. "I *see*, Commissioner."

"Thanks for your time." Bud steered his dad away and led him to his car. "Dad, I've got the biggest news I've ever had."
"Listen, I've got a meeting with Stephen and Sparks." Sam jingled his automobile keys. "Yesterday, three crazy drivers followed me in a plain Model T. I've even seen them on the lane to the farm. I'm being followed. Do you think they're revenuers? Whatever news *you* have can wait."
As his father roared away, Bud scratched his head. "Oh, boy, Dad. You're losing your grip. But when haven't I expected something like this?"

~~**~~**~~**~~

Sam roared past the Glissons' chickens in his rumble seat roadster. He spun gravel and feathers everywhere, careening onto his drive. He smiled at the ornate radiator mascot on the hood, the jaunty wooden-spoked wheels, and the shiny, black exterior. It was time for another meeting with his foreman, Stephen, back from the Klondike, and Sparks, an acquaintance who was employed in the area as a handyman for the Chicago Line.

"We're in agreement about Wednesday, March 23, at 5:19 at night?" Sam puffed himself up to full height. "You both know where the old Mose Johnson place is located? There's a train spur there. It crosses 500 West into Brownsville County after the creek crossing."
"Haven't taken a coffee break there for years," said Sparks.
"There'll be no coffee break the night of March 23."
"No." Spark's chin jutted out. "We'll make a stop at that old siding, where those storage buildings are at the scheduled time on March 23. I'll have a friend, a fireman, on board with me."

Rubbing his hands together, Sam jerked his head at Stephen. "Our men will be on the south side of the tracks."
"Of course." Sparks raked his fingers through his hair. "How long will it take you to load? I've got a few men I play cards with. They could come along for extra help."
Sam waved Spark's offer away. "The train's loading shouldn't be more than a half hour. We'll have the logs there and plenty of men to load the cars. We'll need freight to store in front of the timber as a false front. We'll be early and out of there by 5:50 in the evening."
"Consider it done," agreed Sparks. "See you then."

"Stephen, you've heavyweights lined up?" Sam gnashed his teeth. "If they have friends who know how to keep their mouths shut, have them bring them along."

"Don't worry about any extra guys," replied Stephen. "I've got enough strong men lined up. Don't worry. They'll keep their mouths shut."

"The pay will be worth their while. The logs must be handled with care. Their length increases their value."

"Is that all?"

"No. On the morning of March 23, check with me first before you leave. The wagons will leave deep tracks. Sweep over them. Make sure there's no trace of our presence there. They won't be able to tie us to the wagon route out to the tracks if they're cleared."

"Everything's handled on our end. What about at the mill where they're being delivered?"

"I've got connections. It's all taken care of. No one will know the origin of the walnut logs," said Sam with a snort. "They'll be transported in covered freight cars, instead of on open log cars."

"There are local mills." whined Stephen.

"No. The one I've contracted with is an old friend, one who owes me."

"Those roads will be a grinder on the wagons."

"You've got the rest of the day after you check in with me. Stack the logs on the siding. The sheriff suspects nothing about the Mose Johnson place. Get those logs secured in the freight cars."

"But boss, those long logs are a lot to handle."

"Load them. They're being shipped the size they are."

"Whatever you say." Stephen cracked his knuckles. "We'll handle them like gold. We'll stack the crates in front of them. We'll make sure our tracks are covered."

"It's a big job to load. They'll be paid well. That knucklehead of a new sheriff will be rooting out bootleggers." Sam bit his lip. "Stephen, no northwest officials have anything on you, do they?"
"No, Boss. Mike Glisson's out of the picture. That Elsie wench was expecting when I last saw her. She was sickly, living in a hole in a Seattle alley. No more kicking up those purty little legs."
"What happened to Mike Glisson's partner?"
"Never seen again." Stephen shifted his weight. "After this, I'll have you paid up."
"You'll always owe me." Sam's head swung toward the door.

Stephen snapped. "No, Sam. Do you hear me? No!"
Sam tipped back in his chair, breathing hard. His bald spot gleamed under the chandelier hanging from the elegant, plastered ceiling high overhead. "I'm not worried about your loyalty, Stephen. I'll see you early on the twenty-third."
Stephen scowled. He yanked the big oak door open. Sam shuddered as it slammed shut.

Nell pulled the truck over to the side of the road.

"Hello, Ma, Nell, and Wren," cried Maude. "I'm glad it's you. A few angry farmers have been driving the road. A man stopped and visited with us. He said he'd been hoodwinked by one of the Glissons taking over his livelihood. He's a well-dressed, older fellow. He's driving a shiny, black vehicle."

"Maude," said Nell. "That's Sam Waring."

"Oh," gasped Maude. "No wonder he asked for our backing. He seemed like such a lonely man. No more sweets for the girls."

Nell called to her two nieces. "Lookie, lookie. See Auntie driving a car, Anna. Your Grandma Sadie's in here and your cousin Wren. Would you like to jump in with us, Marie, to one of Wren's piano recitals?"

"Nell," Maude tutted.

"Would you all come to my graduation? I'll be playing there." asked Wren.

"Of course, that's why we're here." Maude grinned.

"Watch Auntie's new driving skills. I won't scare you. I'll ease off the clutch and roll away. And honk the horn. A-roo-guh, a-roo-guh."

Catching her foot with the wrong pedal, Nell's showboating ended. The truck coughed and spluttered. Gears clashed. She pressed one foot pedal, and the engine shrieked. The truck shook. After a few more mistakes, she tried again. At the same time, Nell hooted and jabbered wisecracks about newfangled machinery. The two girls giggled. Maude's eyes opened wide, and her head moved forward, the gears ground again, and the truck bucked. Nell left Maude and the daughters behind in a cloud of dust. "I'm not quite finished with my last driving lesson. Sorry about that." Nell waved to them. They drove away. Wren and Grandma covered their mouths.

Further up the road, Nell came to a sudden stop. "Wait," yelled Nell. "I'm stopping right here." The clutch, and the brakes squealed. "There's snakeweed growing alongside the road."

"Aunt, what are you doing?"

Jumping out of the truck, furious, Nell thundered into the borrow pit. She ripped out her fierce enemy— snakeweed. Wren gulped. Nell flung the mutilated weeds into the truck bed. Grandma Sadie said, "She won't let those weeds alone. She pulls them out wherever she sees them. I've bided my time before. We'd better rest our eyes."

After she'd pulled all the snakeweed out, Nell hopped back in the Model T. "I never let poison grow on my watch. If only I could rip out all of them."

If only I wasn't so busy with all of Ned's business, we'd have more time for the walnut ridge. A few more deliveries, and we'll be back to working on our legacy.

~~*＊~~*＊~~*＊~~

"It's difficult to believe," said Bud. "But I'm going to be flying my own plane back to my place." He scanned the pretty red sunrise over the Ohio countryside. "I see plenty of opportunities for crop dusters everywhere I've been." He patted the door of the plane. "The plane's tight. She's in decent shape and not beaten up."

"No, sir. Not too many hours on the engine either," replied the instructor. "With all of your mechanical skills, you'll be able to keep this little Jenny in flight for a long time."

"Look at her. What a sweet little biplane with a wooden frame, and all those cables for additional support."

"It's got a lot of wing area. It can handle a good load. The wooden propeller's laminated spruce wood. That's what you wanted."

"I'm so thankful you had one surplus warplane left. It's a fair price. It's well worth five hundred dollars. I love my little Jenny."

"As you learned in your lessons, she'll be easy to control. Turn the engine on and off, speed up, and slow down. That's how they flew those dogfights. There's not much more I can offer you in lessons. You're a good pilot and a great mechanic. You'll be home earlier than you expected."

~~**~~**~~**~~

Nell and Ma waited until the dark of evening to start their work. They wore men's coveralls, handkerchiefs, and caps low over their faces. They bounced along over ruts to the first storage shed. "No liquor is stored here. It's empty." Nell backed Jack's truck up inch by inch, with grinding gears. With a big, arcing, turn, hand-over-hand she steered the Model T toward the cart path.

I can't leave Ma at home. This is her way of helping her grandson. Bootlegging's dangerous. No place for a ninety-year-old. Jack would skin me alive, but she's insisted on helping.
"Ma, there will be no carrying. We don't have Wren tonight, with Willard bringing her home. You can't use your cane. The ground's too uneven." Up the cart path, the truck made steady progress. Gnarled branches swiped at the sides of Jack's truck. "Easy, easy," said Nell. "I forgot the moon's waxing."

She steered the truck up the bumpy path. They twisted and wriggled all the way to the Proverb tunnels. "Park as close to the tunnels as possible," said Ma. "We'll have some carrying to do. Let's hope Jack's right. Perhaps the jugs of moonshine are stored inside the tunnels."
With a shake of her head, Nell set to work.
I remember the first time I had my head inside one of these. I was so tiny that my whole body fit.

"Ma, what's that you're saying?" Nell struggled to hear over her digging sounds. "It sounds like you're picking up the crates. I told you no carrying."
There's no one else here unless a wild turkey lit on the tunnel.
Sticking her head further into the brambly, thorny tunnel, Nell dug out pint and half-pint jugs. She set them behind her toward the entry, emptying the tunnels.

I warned Ma to stay in the truck. But what are those noises? Oh, well. It won't hurt if she wipes off the dirt from the jars I'm pushing behind me. That clinking sound must be her arranging them in the wooden crates.

"So much for a lookout," said Nell, backing out of the tunnel. She didn't see any jars.
Where are the jars?
She got to her feet and gasped. Someone dressed in black, with a black cap, jerked Nell around by her coverall straps and threw her into the brush. Before she could scream, her attacker rushed at her. Nell noticed his right arm hung funny.
It's Stephen. Sam's foreman.

"I spotted you a ways back through the old man's binoculars." Stephen's voice snarled. "Trespassers. Thieves. Who are you? You, puny runt, a friend of Ned's, taking our property?"
Although short, Nell crouched. She remained agile. She leaped onto an upturned crate, spread her legs, and made herself look tough as Jack taught her.

I've still got my boxing skills.
Jack's training flashed through Nell's mind.
Stephen must not have seen Ma.
With knuckles on his hips, Stephen calculated his next move. Branches snapped, and a muscular, smaller man, with head down, burst from the brush and rushed at Stephen.

Stephen's eyes darted off Nell. He took a big hit and fell hard. Stephen wobbled to his feet. Stephen turned toward the smaller man.

I've only got a second to think back to Jack's lessons. I'm strong enough for this one move. I've got the perfect opportunity. How many years have I waited for this? Bounding from the crate with all her wiry strength, Nell put everything into her clinch. She pinned Stephen's arms down.

Now maybe he'd better think again about assaulting a Glisson. This is for my darling Honora.
With a heave-ho and a mighty thrust upward of her knee, she kneed him with a crippling force. Rolling through the grass, Stephen howled in pain. He staggered to his feet. He ran cursing through the woods. The smaller man brushed himself off. He had a strange helmet-like hat with large goggles that looked like eyes on top of his head. He reached out his hand toward Nell.

"Bud? Is that you?" asked Nell.
Bud embraced Nell. "You didn't need me." Bud patted Nell's back. "Good job! That was quite the clinch you put him in. That knee of yours made quite the knockout strike."
"I needed you, Bud. With you here, he ran. Thank you." Nell pointed at the truck. "My right-hand man is knitting baby socks." The top of Ma's head was visible above the dashboard.
"Your nephew's a good man to have around on your farm. I hope Ned's cleared of all charges. Poor, old Tom.

He does well for his age, though. Those two have been reliable workers over the years."

Nell nodded. She was still shaking and breathing hard.
"Let me help you with these heavy crates." Bud fished the crates out of the brush where Stephen had stashed them. "I still care about dad. I'd like to help him before it's too late. He's in a lot of trouble." Bud loaded the crates in Jack's truck. He crawled into the tunnels and started emptying the last of the jugs. Nell loaded the crates of alcohol into the truck.

"Ma and I are delivering these to their rightful owners. It's going to take a few more trips to finish the job."
"Since you were little, you've always battled, haven't you? Dad doesn't know how much Stephen's involved with the bootlegging. I want my dad out of this wrongdoing. He's failing."
"Do you think your dad can ever forget his thirst for revenge?" asked Nell.
"I don't know. It's more than that. He's developed a compulsion of greed and power to own all of Shawnee Township. This sickness could cost his mind. He's a bitter old man," said Bud, with his eyes shimmering.

"Things went well on your trip?" asked Nell.
"They sure did. You'll have to come by one day. I'll take you for a ride."
"I'd like to pick up an organ at your place. It belonged to the former Reverend Webber. I've been so busy, but I've got my brother Jack and other help lined up."

"If there's an organ, you're welcome to it. I remember the Reverend. But I've never searched through all the storage sheds. There's a lot of clutter."
"Oh, I promised my niece, Wren I'd purchase one. The Reverend said a friend stored it out there for him years ago."

"Come on up. Look around. If you find it, take it. Maybe you've got better eyes than I have. I tried to stop at dad's a few minutes ago, but he must be in town in his office as usual. On my way out his road, I saw lights through the trees. I wondered why someone was out here at this time of night. I wanted to let dad know how my training went. He's not expecting me back for several days. I thought he might be proud of me for finishing so early. I'm glad I heard the ruckus and ran down here. Stephen can't be trusted."
"We're thankful you did too. Good night, Bud."

~~**~~**~~**~~

Their voices still sounded jittery over the washboardy dark roads. But Ma and Nell drove home to the sound of a hundred crockery jugs jingling down the cart path. "This load is our last one, Ma. It was good to know you were there."
"I won't knit on our last run," Ma assured Nell.

I heard the crickets and frogs and they quieted for a moment. I heard Ma's jaw pop. She's so excited to accomplish this for her family that she can't swallow. She thrust her tongue against her bottom teeth, sucking air in her nose. I've known this motion all my life' 'Tis to

407

summon all her courage. One more night, and we'll be out of the bootlegging business. We'll be back to planting the ridge.

March 23: Early Morning

Back and forth from the old farm wagon to the Glisson homestead, Jack added the last items he needed. His plan included more than securing Wren's organ.
Oh, no. Nell shows up now. What timing? Keep cool. I don't want her catching on.

"I came over to say good-bye," said Nell, who was snooping around.
"This old wagon'll be best. It's a big load all the way out to Mose Johnson's old place. Imagine! Wren's beautiful music will fill your parlor, with Ma safe and sound in her rocker," said Jack, with a nervous chuckle.
"You're sure you don't need the truck?"
Jack didn't make eye contact with Nell.
I thought I convinced her about the farm wagon.

"It's been quite the wait, but we're tickled you're home." Nell clapped her brother on the back. "I appreciate your taking this trip up to Mose Johnson's place. Are you jumpy? You've been so quiet?"
"Oh, I've got plans I'm chewing on. But this is the perfect day to find the organ." Jack's voice changed pitch. He stammered, "The ...the boys and I can check on... er, the spring squirrel-hunting conditions. It's been years since I've hunted in those parts."

"Hunting? And picking up an organ?" Nell's brows knit together.
"I've told the others we could spend the night in the cave up there." Jack shuffled his feet. He kept his eyes on the ground.

Nell's face stiffened. "Goodness, squirrel-hunting."
"I'm suffering from curiosity myself. When I checked the tires on the truck this morning, I found mud and leaves. I think some of Wren's recitals must be in a forest?" Jack tapped his fingers on his arms folded across his chest. *Nell's so smug. She doesn't fool me.*

"Oh, have fun with the fellows. Bring back the organ from Mose's cave and plenty of squirrel meat." She cackled. "Wren will have her organ. This will be our last run."
I better not say any more. I don't want Nell to know what the hermit told me about the stolen logs. Sheriff Tiffany said it could get ugly. We don't want bystanders in the way of a brawl.

"Jack, do you have enough strong guys? Just you, Willard, and Tom? Tom's not that strong. Asa and Bud might be working away from the place. Bud said to come on up and look around."
"If anyone's out there, we'll ask them to lend us a hand. Everything'll be fine. I don't think we even need this many men to load an organ."
"I know what you're going to say. You and Mike could've done it with only the two of you. Somehow, I think he's with us, Jack. He knew that country and all those

interesting rocks in the cave. Remember William Drew's Indian story?"

"Aye, I've been there years ago to explore the cave. Those outbuildings will be good places to keep the organ's wood dry. It's a good-sized cave under an overhanging ledge with a dry rock floor in it. We'll spend the night in there if need be and arrive home tomorrow with the organ."
"It's quite a ways up there to the northwest."
"The road's beautiful, yet treacherous along those creek bottoms. We wouldn't want to drive it at night, although tonight's a full moon. All the water meanders to the big rivers. It's like a park."
Nell said, "I remember driving by there with Da and the older boys years ago. The road becomes a two-track cart path further northwest."
"Be careful, Nell."
"Watch your sore leg lifting that heavy organ."

I didn't think she'd ever let me go.
Jack flicked the reins on the wagon, and they were off. The road descended a steep pitch out of a rocky creek bottom full of mud, and then back up and through the next drainage.

March 23: Midmorning

Jack and his crew drove for an hour, and the trees got thicker, growing over the road the further they drove to the northwest of the county. The land disappeared in the dense growth. The road was in danger of being reclaimed back into wilderness. A remote forest was forever advancing.

When I was a boy, I remember Da fighting the trees back from his crop fields. No wonder there are hillbillies in these uncivilized areas.

Another hour passed, and the road wrapped and rolled around streams heading to creeks. The impenetrable, rutted road was filled with puddles, potholes, and a few dead snakes as the road coiled and the wheels spun. "There 'tis," said Jack. "We're here. The old Mose Johnson place. Now, Bud Waring's."

Jack's group poked around for a while. There was no organ. Asa and Bud weren't anywhere to be seen. "Let's take dinner and then explore the last storage shed closest to the railroad tracks for the organ. We'll see if it got buried behind something. We can check out the cave before company shows up."

Stephen and his gang will arrive about suppertime to load the train about twilight.

After their meal, they circled the stable area. They pried open the adjoining doors on the building closest to the tracks. The doors creaked and groaned on their hinges. Light scattered over the clutter.

"Amazing," said Tom. "There's the organ on that shelf like the Reverend's letter said. It's behind all of these ...logs? There's the organ and all the logs!"

"The logs? Oh, my. Look at 'em." Willard whistled.

"Look at all the logs my brother saved. My, my, Mike. They are all the ones he marked in the forest." Jack held on to the door for support.

None of them could believe how many logs Sam and Stephen had stored there. It was beautiful, stacked, dry, and ready-to-load like no other.
"Hello, Willard? What? Are you ...? Tom, Jack?" Asa peered into the storage shed. "I got home and thought I heard voices." Asa nodded to all of them. "I suppose you've found the organ. What? The logs? We didn't have any idea that all these logs were stored up here. What beautiful wood."
"Never mind that," said Jack. "Let's get in the cave before the wagons start coming. Stephen and his crew are going to load these logs into their wagons. They'll move them onto the train siding and load the freight cars."
"Not the train? Impossible?" Asa looked incredulous. "The train hasn't used that spur in years."

"Sam Waring's capable of it with all of his conniving. He's going to load those logs out of here by train. If any man's got the power, he does. Let's hide in the cave," said Jack, panting. "We've got to wait on the organ. Let's go. We'll watch Stephen's men load the logs from inside of the cave. That's all the evidence the sheriff'll need."
"Oh, mercy." Asa bit his lip. "So, they were out here all along? We had no idea they'd been stolen from the Glissons."

"They're from my brother Mike's log piles he cut in the forest and logs from Pea Ridge. Sam's stored them here all these years," said Jack, sighing.

After they scrambled through the loose rock up the side of the cliff, Jack's voice grew loud and animated, echoing off the cave walls. A few rocks rolled onto the tracks below them. All four men crept in and crouched further back inside. The group fit comfortably into the large room of the cave.

"Perfect time for a short rest," said Jack. He yawned and kept his voice from thundering.

The sheriff will have his evidence soon. Like Ma says, the Lord will have his justice, even after all of the years it might take.

March 23: Late Wednesday Morning

The sparkling sun shimmered through the picture window of Waring Mansion. Across the pond, a pair of flapping tundra swans slipped into the water. Sam scanned the drive for any sign of Stephen.

Late. Where is he? I told him to be here early.

At last, Stephen arrived, late in the morning. Sam cornered him. "I said early Wednesday morning. You're already on shaky ground with me as usual." Sam turned on Stephen. "I heard you lost the contents of the tunnels in a fight on the Glissons' land? Some mysterious 'Little Guy' got the best of you?"

"Yes, sir. He's wiry and quick. It was dark. I didn't see the other guy who helped that runt."

Poking Stephen's chest with his thick finger, Sam said, "Well, that 'Little Guy doesn't stand a chance over this 'Big Guy.'" Sam flipped his thumbs inward toward his own chest. The measures we're taking spell power, not some flimsy patchwork plan."

"Right," Stephen said. "He's tough, though, Sam. He's skilled at the clinch and dart. He weaves, bobs, and moves right and left quicker than a whip."

"Of course, I haven't heard your excuses before. He dances around like a checkered butterfly, does he? Stephen, I hope you haven't dirtied my name in *your* bootlegging operations. I know you're trespassing on neighboring land. The little guy must be a friend of Ned McMinn, whom we've got in jail. He's got to be from around here. He knows these farm roads so well. My name's not to be tied to the bootlegging."

Sam raised his voice to make another point. "You're already running late. The logs are a big enough problem. I want that wood loaded. Make no mistake. No evidence will connect us to Mose's place. Sparks will take that old spur in a roundabout way out from the cliffs onto the flats. Then he'll run the train on the main line out of the county. I can't think of any loopholes, except that you're already behind schedule. That train will be coming in there at dusk. You should be on your way. Stack those logs up next to the tracks. Bud won't be home for several more days. The place'll be empty."

Stephen's face fused into a cunning leer. "I've got my crew. We'll be there well before dusk."

"Sparks is worried they don't use that spur anymore. He questioned how well the tracks have been maintained. They've sat there twenty years on the side of the cliff. He mentioned a drainage issue under the cliff."

"Aw, like you say, Boss. Hell's teeth. It's hogwash that the track could break down." Stephen snorted. "As if there aren't other tracks under drainages. Don't you want this over? It's been years since we emptied Mike Glisson's storage places. All the train needs is to maintain a slow rate of speed through there. A real engineer would agree. What bull!"

"Sparks knows that spur. If it wasn't safe, he wouldn't take it." Sam clucked his tongue. "You're right. Bull. What does Sparks know about the water draining off the cliff? It softens that ground along the tracks. We haven't had the spring rains yet. Have the crew there ready, Stephen. Get those logs loaded on the freight cars."

"Stack the logs in back. Got it. Stack the crates of cookie tins from Chicago in front of the logs. Check. No one will suspect the logs behind the cookies. I know all of this, Boss. Can't I get my wagons rolling?" With a frustrated wave of his hand, Stephen left the mansion. It didn't take him long. Empty wagons soon rumbled down Sam's drive past the pond and the napping swans, with their heads tucked under feathered wings.

Later this afternoon, I'll drive out to my son's place. I'll drive to the tracks myself and oversee my operation. I'll see who's the fireman Sparks hired. I'd bet it's some old bum he plays cards with.

March 23: Afternoon

Asa, Jack, Tom, and Willard kept watch from the cave on Mose's old property. They observed Stephen and his gang hurrying to stack the logs alongside the siding. A short time later, the locomotive arrived at the siding with a hissing of steam and brakes. Several rocks rolled with the vibrations. Rays of dust shimmered down with the locomotive's power.

"What's this?" Startled, Jack sprung back as Sheriff Tiffany and his deputy ducked into the cave. The train was easing to a stop next to the logs. The sheriff and the deputy had arrived undetected. Jack explained all that had happened. "I'm so thankful you're here. Sam's men look like a mean bunch. They're hurrying to unload the wagons. They're just going to beat the train's arrival. Now, we've got six to their nine." The men in the cave grew quieter. They watched the proceedings.

Loading of the cumbersome logs took longer than any of Stephen's men anticipated. When Jack, the sheriff, and the others knew Stephen and his sweaty gang were at the end of the loading, Jack said, "I figure it's time we intervened."

March 23: Late Afternoon

Sam neared Mose's place.
I know my son and his hired man aren't around, but how I'd like to run into my son, Bud. Good walnut wood is becoming more and more rare. After we've succeeded, the Glissons'll be finished. That property will be mine.

Nell Robertson won't have a prayer of paying the taxes on the ridge with black walnut lumber.

I'll make some money off that valuable wood with no splits, no water damage, and the heavy, good-sized butt ends. The crates had better be stacked in front of the logs. It's a perfect false front with the valuable logs behind. It's innocent enough. A train of several freight cars from the American Biscuit Company will be underway from Chicago to St. Louis, hauling freight cars of cookies. Sparks is aware of all the arrangements we've made. He wants to be paid. He'll stop the train for a half hour to let them load. Then on they go.

They had better know enough to chock those logs with heavy blocks. As long as there are no other sudden stops, they'll be okay. It'll go without a hitch. For twenty years, I've waited. I've made all the arrangements and connections. This will keep those hillbillies from ever seeing their dream of that memorial grove or that Wyoming sheriff from solving the case of the missing logs.

Parking his shiny-black car close by, so he could save the walk up to the tracks, Sam jolted to a stop.
But? What? What's happened? Who, who are they fighting with? Stephen and Sparks are throwing punches. It's Jack Glisson. Is the man fighting on his knees? The fireman stood off to the side. He isn't helping Sparks or the others.

March 23: Early Evening

Nell and Ma eased out of Jack's barnyard for their last run. Nell was relieved that they'd have the last of the farmers on Ned's list paid and accounted for. "We'll pick up Wren as soon as we finish this last big job." Nell and Ma drove up the long-rutted hill to Paddy Fitzsimmons's place. "It's almost dark up here, Ma."
"Yes," Ma said. "I know I must look a sight when I see you in your coveralls and cap slouching over your eyes."
"I'm glad this is the last stop. It's scary out here. Someone could be following us." Nell's voice sounded eerie. "At least we'll make good on all the farmers' agreements."

Paddy Fitzsimmons's jugs rattled and clinked in the back of Jack's truck. They bounced over each rut in the hilly drive. "It's dark. He's not home." Nell pressed her lips tight. She sat up as straight and as tall as she could, peered over the steering wheel.
Thanks for giving me the peace, to do this, Lord.

She turned the truck lights off and got out. Scurrying over to the bench under the tree, she set the last crates of moonshine underneath. She did the same with the bag of money they owed Paddy. All debts were now canceled. She slid back into the truck and ground down on the clutch. Her foot slipped because she was nervous. The truck shot back in reverse. Branches snapped. The truck jounced over bushes and roots.
"I let off the clutch too fast. Doggone. Doggone. I'll pull us up, out of here."

"Wait, Nell," whispered Ma. She pointed to where a sweep of lights coming up the hill shining through the brush. Tires crunched on the dirt road.

Nell and Ma spied on the two men from behind the bushes. "What do they think they're doing? They better not have followed us to all of Ned's locations. Perhaps they think they can help themselves again before the farmers got their pay. Shh, let's watch them."
A strange low grunt was all Ma had for a voice. "They're not pulling this off. Not on this Wednesday night during Easter week."
"Shh, Ma. Let's wait."

Nell didn't miss the man reaching for Paddy's moneybag. She tiptoed closer. "Stay here, Ma." Nell approached in her bulky coveralls. Her cap was low. Her handkerchief was positioned over her mouth. Nell glanced back.
Ma had exited the car! She hobbled along with a labored gait, stabbing her diamond willow cane into the grass. Ma was sneaking up behind the first man! She adjusted her scarf over her mouth.

"Ma, get back in the car," hissed Nell. Ma's long, faded dress was partially tucked into the coveralls. It made her look much larger. Her hair was pulled well back off her forehead. Her cap sat on top of her white hair, which was poking out from beneath the brim. Ma's only ornament was the dark-red scarf tied around her mouth.

Ma's tiredness could be heard in her sore throat. She stooped a little with her cane.

The man must've heard her approaching. He turned, jumped, and paused. He said, "Oh, I don't think we need to worry about this guy. He can hardly get around on that cane. He's grunting like an old man."

Ma growled in a twisted, awful voice. "Set that money down right where you found it." Ma had her yarn, with a knitting needle stabbed in it, jutting from her large coverall pockets right at him. "My partner and I've got our weapons leveled on you. You'll get worse than what your cohort Stephen got."

"Stephen's not here. Take it easy, Mister! Say, I'm just a guy Stephen met at the bar in Rushville." The lanky man held his shaking hands up. "Stephen hired me to run this route for him. He had some big job tonight he was pulling off at a cave or something that was all about some logs. Let me go. Please, I've got a family."

"Set any money you've picked up along the way on that sawhorse—now!" said Nell. "I know how much was at the other farmers' houses. Now set it down. Get in your car. Get out of here as fast as possible or you're going to be in the biggest hornet's nest of your lives."

The man never turned around. He dropped the moneybags and pivoted in the direction of the car door. He slammed the door. His partner was right behind him. The car roared away.

"Ma. Get in. We're not done yet."

Logs? Cave? Oh, no! Jack? But at least, Paddy's got his money and jugs back.

"But I thought you said we were going to a party? What were they talking about? Cave? Logs?"
"It'll be like a party at Mose Johnson's old place. On the way, we're going to pick up Wren at Asa's church. She won't be able to stay for the full evening. It's a good thing she's one of the first musicians."

After she picked up Wren, Nell drove right down the middle of the road as the sun was about to set. Dirt and dust boiled up on the road. Nell knew all of this country, as well as the homestead land. She slowed down as she saw children playing outside the almshouse.

March 23: Midevening

When Sam observed that Stephen and Sparks were losing the brawl on the train siding, he became enraged. "I'm not wasting any more time. These guys don't know what's at stake. Those logs are evidence." Sam got as close to the fray as he could. He spotted the fireman beside the engine. Sam shoved the fireman's back. "Close those doors. Get aboard." The fight was still going at full tilt. The locomotive engine throbbed beside the fighting men. With hisses and creaky squeaks, the train eased forward. The men stopped fighting when the train jerked from its position. It inched ahead.

"Hey, wait a minute," shouted Sparks. "What are you thinking? Sam?"

Sam Waring didn't heed any of the warnings from Sparks. He cursed the man for bungling his operation.

March 23: Nightfall

Holding his heaving sides, Asa stepped away from the fighting. He'd heard an engine. It was a small plane. Could it be Bud? Before Bud could bring the little Jenny in for a practice touch-and-go, Asa hopped on his high-wheeler bicycle. Asa rode out onto the makeshift runway. He flagged Bud down. Bud acknowledged Asa with a wave. Bud landed the plane. He taxied up close to the high-wheeler. Asa jumped off his bicycle and climbed on the wing. He got up close enough to Bud to explain what was happening. Bud's expression changed to panic when Asa repeated the words, "Sam's driving the train with the stolen logs."

Bud taxied the plane across the fields. He bounced over the furrows. He crossed the drive as Nell, Wren, and Ma turned off the road in the old Model T behind him. "Nell," he shouted over the sound of the engine. "She'll never hear me." He throttled the plane back, scrambled out of his seat, and stepped down on the wing.

Jumping onto the drive, he ran back to Nell's truck. "Get in. I need a copilot, Nell. Dad thought you were so puny and that you could never win against all of his power. Jump in the front seat. Those are your logs. You need to claim them. Let me grab a small crate from the truck, so you can see out of the Jenny."

"I can't. I can't go that high into the sky," said Nell. "I'm afraid." She glanced back at Ma and Wren. *They've done so much to help me.*
Ma flapped her red scarf out the window. "Nell! Nell! You can do it!" Ma thrust the scarf into Nell's hands. Bud grabbed her elbow and rushed her to the wing. He hefted her up.
But… but …I just learned to drive.
"It's too high. I can't."

Bud placed the crate beneath her in the front seat. "I don't want you to miss the view." He pulled a helmet and pair of goggles over her head.
There's no way we can stop the train. But, Sheriff Tiffany didn't want Sam to cross the county line. I remember long ago when Pete Daniels offered me his hands. He told me there are times you've got to let go.
"Bud, what would I do without you? You learned how to fly this thing?"

Bud had no time for answers. The plane bounced up the drive, headed straight for the tracks. Bud tapped Nell on the shoulder. She turned back to see his smile. "Here we go!" They picked up speed, lifted off, and were airborne. "The evening breeze is bearing us right up." Nell's hair streamed out from under her helmet. Ma's red scarf flapped in the breeze. Nell screamed as the plane climbed. She felt like she could touch the sky, "Whee!" *It's peaceful up here. Thank you, Lord.*

~~**~~**~~**~~

Sam drove the train too fast in the loose sections that hadn't been maintained. He heard the doors and walls of the freight cars rattle and bang with explosive sounds. "What's that?" Sam questioned the source of another suspicious noise. "Strange." He looked all around. "It feels like something's over the train?" Out the window, he saw the tail of a small airplane. It kept buzzing the cab of the locomotive. Sam was furious. He shook his fist out the window. The moon shone down the tracks. Starlight sparkled on the side of the cliff above. The loud plane's engine buzzed the locomotive again and again. "Stop that." Sam's mouth gaped open. "That looks like Bud! Who's that little girl with him? A woman? That looks like the puny Glisson gal. Nell?"

"Stop, Dad. Dad, please!" yelled Bud. "Stop!"
"It sounds like he's yelling, Stop!" Unable to pay attention, Sam was too busy shaking his fist out the window. The small airplane continued buzzing the cab of the locomotive. The moon was full. The locomotive started to lurch.
"Step it up," yelled Sam to the fireman. "We're going to outrun that plane. We're not going to be found with this evidence."

Sam shouldn't have put so much speed on the unmaintained spur. He zoomed past the shiny rocks that jutted out below the cave. He barreled along the side of the cliff toward the straightaway east of the cliffs. "Ahhh, Hell's f... fingers! I'm losing control of the train!" The fireman bailed out on the flats.

There was a great deal of load movement. Big heavy logs rolled in the cars that weren't chained or roped down by the required methods. The earth bed beneath the rails had shifted so much that the rails weren't stable. The wheels jumped the tracks. There was a noise like an earthquake's massive roar. The train derailed with a crumpling sound. It smashed to the ground in a cloud of dust. The poorly loaded freight cars dominoed into one another. The locomotive lay on its side, three freight cars behind it. The doors of the three freight cars of logs had split open like tin cans.

Crates of cookies flew in all directions, with logs half in and half out of the car doors. What a spectacle! The logs spilled without the chains and ropes Stephen and his men had halfheartedly tied down. But the false front of crates of cookies broke open with the force, and crate after crate of store-bought cookies flew out, leaving a wide, littered path.

People from Asa's church and the almshouse heard the loud crash. They saw all the crates and logs tumble away from the locomotive. Children playing at the almshouse ran toward the big, monstrous locomotive lying on its side. No trains ever used this spur? They'd heard the locomotive tooting its horn on the side of the cliff west of the almshouse.

Many of the people from the church were impoverished fieldworkers. Those in the almshouse were penniless. Feelings of oncoming tough times were being felt in the countryside long before they hit the city folks. The locals hadn't planned on many treats for Easter. It was a miracle. People were grabbing and shouting. Not one person went away without at least half of a case of cookies to take home for the Easter holiday. Hundreds of tins of cookies tumbled everywhere along the tracks. The people cried out for joy at the crates of cookies.

~~**~~**~~**~~

No injuries were reported. During the derailment, Sam Waring's death was the only one. All the logs would be returned to the Glissons.
This is the day we've been waiting for! What joy I feel. Thank You, Lord.
Nell gasped as she and Bud bent over the logs.
After all these years, these are them. Thank You, God

"The logs show signs of Mike's care. His clean cuts where he severed the lower branches and smoothed out the bark in a diamond shape, so it'd disappear. I'd know these markings anywhere with the pruning methods Da taught us." With tears running down her face, Nell thanked Bud over and over. Then she caught her breath and put her arms around Bud. She offered words of consolation. "I'm so sorry. I'm sorry for the loss of your dad, Bud.

CHAPTER 38
Unexpected Gifts

The belated birthday picnic for Ma included many friends, family, and neighbors. Asa loved Ma. He brought a lady friend from his church to introduce to Ma. "I didn't make her ride the high-wheeler. I borrowed a wagon. It appears, that a lot of your children are here?"

"Yes," said Ma. "I know almost everybody here. And there's someone from all nine of my children, except the two out in the Northwest. Let me make introductions. I'll go in order with my other seven. This is Edmond's Wren. You know her because Nell raised her. My oldest daughter, Mary-Jane died. She was Sister Mary's mother. This is Sister Mary. My son Martin went to Kansas long ago. This is his son Martin Jr. You've worked with Ned, he's Honora's son. You're about the same age as my son Mortimer. And this is my last son, Jack, and his family. Nell's my baby."

"Grandma and Aunt Nell," cried a young woman. She and a little girl came forward from the guests. "I'm Ellen Webber, Kate's daughter. I'm all grown-up, and now from Montana. Your neighbor, Robert Coffman, brought us out from the depot. Nell, it's been years since you and Joe married, but I was here as a little girl."

Ellen circled her arms around her Grandma Sadie. Everyone grew quiet as they heard Ellen's voice breaking. "My mother, Kate, your second daughter worked hard on our Montana homestead. Kate wanted to be here for your birthday. She'd been ailing with stomach cramps for months. A few weeks back, she took ill and passed away."

"Oh, my darling Kate." Ma cried softly for several long minutes.

I see my chest rising and falling. I breathe in and out. It's not the time to try to keep water behind my eyes for any of us. I see Ma's quiet look, and I heard Ma's jaw pop with a dry swallow. Ma thrust her tongue against her bottom teeth, sucking air in her nose. I witnessed that a night ago. I've learned that motion. 'Tis to summon courage. Our poor sister Kate is buried in Montana.

"Last week, before my train departed, the strangest thing happened." Ellen wrapped her arms around the little girl. "This eight-year-old girl, Arlie, arrived on the train out at Bowdoin Junction, Montana. Her mother, Elsie Powell, suffered an illness out in Seattle and died. Elsie sent Arlie to us. Elsie's letter stated that her daughter, Arlie, was to be given to her Aunt Nell. She's got Uncle Mike's pocket watch with her."

Jack knelt beside his mother. The big boxer's hands shook as he removed a tiny photo from his pocket. "Here, Ma. This is the time to give you this."

Clutching little Arlie's hand, Nell reassured her. "Don't worry. I won't let go of you. I'm your Auntie." Nell bent and kissed Arlie.

Her little head is bent down. I know that feeling of abandonment, but no more.

"Ellen, I'm so sorry about your Ma. My dearest sister Kate. What a loss for all of us."
My last sister. Oh, Lord.

Nell continued with a tender tone of reassurance. "And I'm so sorry for Arlie's mother. Elsie and I enjoyed visiting. She was a pretty lady. Her legs were filled with vim and vigor. What a dancer! I'm so glad you're here tonight, Arlie. Your mom, Elsie, would've liked this beautiful evening."
Once again, the warm sun brought a joy back to the party.
"You Glissons have a strength in numbers." Asa laughed. "I wouldn't want to be on anyone else's side in a bad fight, but Jack's. Even with his injury, he kept them all busy that night of the brawl on the train siding."

Neighbors sat around the tables. Over their sips of coffee, they shared their views of some of the recent happenings. "It's sad Sam Waring lost his life. All of his conniving." Nell's soul must've been filled with iron to leap into that plane. She always had the orneriness, but what a purpose she was born with. Sam Waring sought revenge against the Glissons for years. We're glad it's over."

Nell's eyes glistened.
At last, we're celebrating Ma's long-overdue birthday. She's lost another daughter but gained an unexpected grandchild.
Everyone was tickled with the beautiful April weather. They gathered around the tables in the yard as they'd

done many years ago for Kate and Mary-Jane's double wedding. The tree limbs swooped up and up. The limbs scalloped the sky while their formidable roots grounded them to the homestead. The branches were starting to blossom. Their fragile buds bounced on the warm breeze and netted the sounds of happy voices, singing, and clapping.

Nell glanced around as folks departed. She reached out her hand to each in thanks.

I'm so relieved we got all of the farmers' money and jugs back to them.

After the last farewells, Ma and Nell stacked plates. "Where's the rest of the family, Nell?" asked Ma.

"I think the others have a surprise." Jack smiled.

They heard the draft horses nickering at the hitching post. "I've got the old farm wagon hitched up. Come on, 'birthday girl' and the rest of you. Let's ride out to the ridge and down to the creek bottom," suggested Jack helping them on the wagon.

Nell held little Arlie's hand secure in hers. Ma, with her arm around her granddaughter, Ellen, oohed and aahed at the line of erect saplings on Peace Ridge. Below the ridge, along the creek bottom, came the sounds of excited voices. Jack eased the wagon down the cart path.

Bud, Asa, and Martin Junior traipsed along, toting their fishing gear. "Bud, how brave of you to try to stop your dad that night with your plane," said Ma. "How can we say thank you? I'm sorry it turned into a tragedy."

"If you need some work around here…?" Bud scanned the trees. "I could dust crops for you."

"I'll never believe that planes fly and spray weeds. I didn't even imagine the possibility," said Nell.

"It doesn't surprise me. Scientists in Russia have been talking about space travel in rockets for years," said Bud. *I don't imagine I'll live long enough to see rockets traveling to space.*

"We'd like you to visit. Be a part of this family. Don't just do a flyover," said Nell.

The big group by the creek surprised Nell. Sheriff Tiffany was there in his uniform. Ned McMinn was with him. He ran to his aunt and grandma. He threw his arms around them. "Thank you, Aunt. I love you, Grandma Sadie. I never wanted you to be ashamed of me."

Sheriff Tiffany put his hands in the air. "The missing log case is closed. The culprits are behind bars. I'm here to wish Mrs. Sadie Jane a happy birthday."

Maude and the girls couldn't wait to surprise Nell and Ma. Nell held tight to Arlie's hand. Ellen walked behind chatting with Sheriff Tiffany.

Mortimer strode from the burned cabin with another fellow, with his head down, hidden by thick brush.

Jack said, "Morty's been checking those charred rafters. They're good beams. He believes we could sand off that black. The cabin structure would still have its integrity."

"I keep thinking of Da's fiddle songs," said Jack. "Perhaps, I can play his fiddle, but I need another instrument to accompany me?" Jack scanned the brush.

Threading her arms through those of Ma and Nell, Maude beamed. "My family's finished bootlegging. Can we turn the picture of your granddaughter, Sister Mary, upright again? It's set face down on the organ. I know you didn't want her involved in underhandedness. What a funny way to keep her out of it."

Ma kissed Maude's cheeks. "But you're another one, Maude. You surprised everyone, helping plant Da's Tipperary walnut seeds."

"Morty thought this old metal plaque belonged here," said Jack. "Ma gave it to him after the Pea Ridge Church foundation was flattened. It was a lucky find. He saw the metal glistening in the sunlight. *'Even if the world was going to pieces, I'd still plant my apple tree.'*"

"Marie's got her work clothes on," said Maude. "She's like her grandpa, planting trees."

Marie's big grin said it all.

"Even Anna's wearing coveralls." Maude plopped her down on a blanket.

"As much as I want to go out to California and see the redwoods," confessed Willard McCoy, "I'll never forget how pretty this is. I'm glad all my leftover saplings found a home in the planting down here."

Shaking her hair out of her tight bun, Maude said, "Here's Da's old map I found in the cabin. He wanted a break between the varied species of trees in case disease spread."

"I'll be the first one to admit when I'm wrong," said Jack. He wrapped his arm around Maude and the girls. "All of my girls have taken an interest in planting the memorial

grove." He fluffed the top of Anna's head. "There are so many of the legacy nuts that are sprouting. Saplings are shooting up . . . oh my, the male bluebird is back."
"You and the girls did all of this?" asked Nell.

Maude covered her mouth with her apron "I'm, er. I'm … glad the girls and I changed our minds about fieldwork. Wren and Willard helped so much. But someone else knows these woods and started this …."
Who could that be?
Nell looked all around. The creek bottom didn't look the same.
I've been so busy. I haven't noticed.
"What's all this?" Small walnut trees sprouted up in neat rows? The trees were groomed and thinned? Several baby black walnuts and other saplings were growing in rows on both sides of the cart path along the creek bottom? Someone had been mowing or scything weeds and grass. Paths?
Who? Who did this? It's like what Da wanted.

Sheriff Tiffany took Ellen Webber's elbow before she tripped. "Someday, there'll be an avenue of awe-inspiring trees, with wide spaces …."
"Let me tell you what a little girl told me about spacing," offered Jack. "She…."
"I know a little girl whose hair rippled up as she leaped down the ridge."
A voice from long ago came from the brush and interrupted Jack. A cascade of sunlight made it hard to see.

"Nell, I think you've waited long enough for your Da's dream."

There. It's that voice I know again? I feel my legs going out from under me. It's been a long time. I didn't think Da's legacy, the gift of the world, could make me hear things? But can it be?

Then the man emerged from the bright sunlight, "Nell, you had the grace to keep a homeless man from being pushed aside."

Nell squinted. She shook her head.

It's the old, bearded man, but he looks different?

The hermit had washed and put on clean clothes. His eyes were much improved. "I can't ever repay you, Nell." He'd trimmed his beard neat and clean. He reached in his pocket. He played a few bars of an old Irish lullaby.

The music made Nell stammer. "B ...Bi ... Bill, Bill Drew? You were here all along? My childhood friend, Bill Drew?"

Then I knew that feeling again, stronger than ever. It was as if my knees were going to go out from under me. Bill Drew, the hermit has been here all along, talking to Ma. When I felt the most alone, Lord, I was never alone. Shy and hiding with his poor, terrible red eyes, he was the one in the woods when I lay under the trees. He accompanied Mike in the Klondike. He saved the burlap bags from Tom's burn pile, so we could plant the legacy. All I can do is try to keep the moisture behind my eyes. I can't, and I'm thankful for this, Lord.

Bill clasped the shaking Nell to his chest. They held each other. Bill stepped back, he said, "My dearest friend, we've both lost so much." He ducked his chin down on his chest. He peered in Nell's eyes. "We've gained the gift of the world when we understand that most legacies'll fit in a nutshell when family and friends, although apart, share undying faith, hope, and love for one another."

The End

True events have inspired *The Nutshell Legacy*. I want my siblings and others who may have given up on a dream, or become discouraged, or experienced rejection and feelings of abandonment to know the importance of family and perseverance.

Ma Sadie was one of the first pioneers in Schuyler County, Illinois. Sadie's mother crossed the Ohio River from Kentucky with a church group that was against slavery. Sadie was known as a midwife and for her sweetness. All the family said she was welcome anywhere. Sadie's children fought over which family she stayed with the longest. Sadie and Michael had forty-one grandchildren. My Grandma Anna Lois was the youngest. Sadie lived with Nell and Kathryne at the end of her life. Nell lived across the road from the homestead. Sadie lived a long life and raised all nine of her children to adulthood.

Michael did leave Tipperary, about 1848, with his three brothers. They were extremely poor. Michael Patrick's homestead has a tree-lined ridge. I also know they had at least one orchard. Michael's name and lineage have been shown to be related to royalty in Ireland. Michael P. did put the candy between the floorboards at Christmas time.

Michael Patrick bought land sight unseen, for his sons' inheritance in Kansas. He does have a tear in his eye in the family portrait. When the older kids went to Kansas, he said, "I don't think I'll ever see them again." The older children lived on the same road. Michael Patrick died when Nell was thirteen.

My great-great grandparents' desire was to not lose their ninth child, Nell, who was born Bridgett Ella. She was born prematurely and not expected to live. When Bridgett was young, she refused to be called by her given name. She witnessed all eight of her older siblings move away. She was known for her diminutive size. Everyone who knew Nell remembered her as a fireball and for working right alongside her brother, Jack. Nell's child died tragically of milk sickness. She outlived Joe by many years. My Grandma Anna Lois's memory of Nell was of her always sitting beside the potbellied stove praying. Nell lived to be ninety-eight years old.

My Grandma Anna Lois told me that Nell helped her with her lessons. Anna Lois listened to my writing as a child, which is how I gleaned the idea of the importance of school. Maude played the piano and organ at local Christian churches. Kathryne played for her Grandma Sadie. I met my great-grandfather Jack when I was little. I met Great-Aunt Nell only once when she was in a nursing home. I was instructed to stay on the swing set while my Grandma Anna Lois went inside to visit Aunt Nell. My grandma had told me stories about how much Nell missed living in the country. That day, when I was at the nursing home and attempted to stay outside, I found a bluebirds' egg. I took it inside. It made my Great-Aunt Nell cry. I had to be taken outside, so as not to further disturb her.

Edmond returned to live on the family homestead in Illinois for several years. When Mary-Jane died he returned to Kansas. He gave Katheryne, his daughter, to Nell, to raise.

Martin moved to Kansas, and his son, Martin Junior, returned to the homestead to fish. Morty lived in Missouri. Mike went to the Klondike. The Glissons mined coal on the homestead for years.

Jack was a semipro boxer in St. Louis in the early 1900s. It was said that townspeople gathered around to cheer for him, because he was so well thought of when he came home from St. Louis. Jack was known his entire life for his easy manner and cordiality. When the Depression came, a banker with a premonition of what might be coming helped Jack get all the money he had in the world out of the bank. When he was in his nineties, he was fit and healthy. When Maude died, Jack had a small picture of her in his breast pocket. He'd carried it there since they were married. He lived to be ninety-four.

A hermit lived for many years in the woods across the road from the homestead. He loved receiving books, magazines, and newspapers.

Ned McMinn arrived at the homestead, during Prohibition, needing help with the storage of alcohol about 1922.

Honora's life was filled with tragedies. Honora lost her husband and at least five of her nine children before she died. The event about a brother hiding in the cemetery is true. She died of tuberculosis in a sanitorium in St. Louis.

Mary-Jane died while giving birth to her fifth child. Her oldest daughter, Mary, was a nun. Grandma Sadie kept a picture of Sister Mary on top of the organ. Kate lived in St. Louis and for several months in Montana, where she died.

The Warings are fictional. A rich man was known to live in the township where the Glisson's lived in. The idea for a corrupt neighbor occurred because the county courthouse burned to the ground about this time. I incorporated the idea of a government leader involved in corruption. Elsie Powell was fictional too. My family did inherit heirloom rain lilies from England. Mose Johnson's cave is real to this area of Illinois. There were area sightings of Native Americans in the mid-1800s, but few in the 1870s.

One of Michael Patrick's brothers was rumored to have been involved in a fight after his arrival in the United States from Ireland, which eventually led to the death of his opponent.

The Forgotten Land in west-central Illinois is located in and around Adams County. The homestead was part of this forgotten land. Also, *David Copperfield* was a popular book at this time. Charles Dickens journeyed to St. Louis and parts of the Prairie State of Illinois. His books were quite revered in the country schools in central Illinois and many other parts of America.

Abe Lincoln was well-known as being a circuit rider in this part of Illinois.

 My Grandma Anna Lois, Jack's daughter, loved bluebirds and black walnuts all her life. Grandma said they would dart and swoop in a scalloping flight pattern low in the brush along the country roads. As more vehicles traveled the roads, their habitat was disturbed, and they were seen less and less in the area.

The homestead was my great-grandfather's dream and he believed in a God that would never abandon them. The homestead land of *The Nutshell Legacy* is inspired by true events. The land is now part of Illinois Wildlife for Acres. Part of the proceeds from this book will be donated to conservation in Illinois. I hope these true inspiring events help my readers to see past their rejections, losses, and sense of abandonment and find hope in family and perseverance.

Cast of Characters

Bill Drew: Son of William, neighbor, and friend
William Drew SR.: Travelled with Da from Tipperary
Mrs. Elizabeth Drew: Wife of William, Bill Drew's
mother, cousin of Joseph Powell in Putney, England,
Elsie's Aunt
Elsie Powell: Mrs. Drew's niece, Joseph Powell's
daughter
Doc Simpkins: Home from the goldfields
Sam Waring: Banker, county official
Bud Waring: Sam's son
Malcolm Waring: Sam's brother
Stephen: Waring's hired man
Sparks: Works for Waring
Miss MacClaren: Sam's secretary
Reverend Webber: Daughter, Bertha
Uncle Willie, Uncle Patrick, and Uncle James: Michael
Patrick Glisson's brothers
Charles McMinn: Marries Honora
Ned McMinn: Honora's son, brother Smoke
Asa Reynolds: Born to a slave mother, and returns
Joe Robertson
Lee Robertson: Infant son dies
Uncle Tom Robertson: Joe's uncle
Lana: Joe's cousin
Wren Glisson: Edmond and Lizzie's daughter
Dennis Dillon: Marries Mary Jane, mother of Sister Mary
Ellen Webber: Kate's daughter, brings Arlie
Arlie: Comes from MT
Pete Daniels: Ag Professor, his sister Esther, daughter
Honora

Gertrude Rein: Nell's friend
Robert Coffman: Neighbor
Luella Coffman: Neighbor's daughter
Mr. Skiles: Teacher
Helen Keith: Teacher
Judge Camean: Hears court case
Thomas Camean: Director of County home
Alice Orr: Resident of County home
Maude Glisson
Sheriff Rippon: Retires, replaced by Sheriff Tiffany from Wyoming
Marie Glisson: Jack and Maude's oldest daughter
Anna Lois Glisson: Jack and Maude's younger daughter
Willard McCoy: Wren's boyfriend

The Library of Congress has cataloged the hardcover
edition on as follows:

Grosfield, Lorrie P.
The Nutshell Legacy/Lorrie P. Grosfield—1st Edition

1. Family and Relationships—Fiction.
2. Christian Historical Fiction
3. Teachers—Fiction
4. Widowers—Fiction.
5. Illinois—Fiction.
Cover Illustrated: Kristen Nelson
Cover Formatted: Tara Cavosie

CIP Block
Title: The Nutshell Legacy
Subtitle: None
Author's Name: Lorrie P. Grosfield
Illustrator:
One other title: Hallie the Hero
No previous publishing, with the exception of three (less than 500 words) magazine articles with Cobblestone Publishing 2002-2005.
LCCN: 1-130114655311
ISBNS: The Nutshell Legacy: paperback: 979-8-9888362-3-0
The Nutshell Legacy: hardback: 979-8-9888362-4-7
The Nutshell Legacy: eBook: 979-8-9888362-5-4
Bibliographical References: none
Book has an index: NO
Name of Publisher: Lorrie P. Grosfield, self-publishing, 1017 3rd Ave. West, Kalispell, MT 59901
Year of Publishing: 2023
What edition: N/A
Categorize Work: Christian Historical Fiction
Historical Fiction General, Fiction Religious
Christian Historical Fiction
Ages or grades: 12 year olds and older

Category Codes:
Payment:

Publisher's Cataloging-in-Publication data

Names: Grosfield, Lorrie P., author.
Title: The nutshell legacy / Lorrie P. Grosfield.
Description: Kalispell, MT: Lorrie P. Grosfield, 2023.
Identifiers: LCCN: xxxxxxxxxx | ISBN: 979-8-9888362-4-7
(hardcover) | 979-8-9888362-3-0 (paperback) | 979-8-
9888362-5-4 (ebook)
Subjects: LCSH: Farmers--Illinois--History--Fiction. |
Family farms--Illinois--History-- Fiction. | Farm life--
Fiction. | Illinois--History--19th century-- Fiction. |
Christian fiction. | BISAC FICTION / Historical | FICTION /
Christian / Historical